Allan Quatermain

Allan Quatermain

H. Rider Haggard

MINT EDITIONS

Allan Quatermain was first published in 1887.

This edition published by Mint Editions 2021.

ISBN 9781513277615 | E-ISBN 9781513278025

Published by Mint Editions®

 MINT
EDITIONS

minteditionbooks.com

Publishing Director: Jennifer Newens
Design & Production: Rachel Lopez Metzger
Project Manager: Micaela Clark
Typesetting: Westchester Publishing Services

Contents

Introduction

December 23

I have just buried my boy, my poor handsome boy of whom I was so proud, and my heart is broken. It is very hard having only one son to lose him thus, but God's will be done. Who am I that I should complain? The great wheel of Fate rolls on like a Juggernaut, and crushes us all in turn, some soon, some late—it does not matter when, in the end, it crushes us all. We do not prostrate ourselves before it like the poor Indians; we fly hither and thither—we cry for mercy; but it is of no use, the black Fate thunders on and in its season reduces us to powder.

'Poor Harry to go so soon! just when his life was opening to him. He was doing so well at the hospital, he had passed his last examination with honours, and I was proud of them, much prouder than he was, I think. And then he must needs go to that smallpox hospital. He wrote to me that he was not afraid of smallpox and wanted to gain the experience; and now the disease has killed him, and I, old and grey and withered, am left to mourn over him, without a chick or child to comfort me. I might have saved him, too—I have money enough for both of us, and much more than enough—King Solomon's Mines provided me with that; but I said, "No, let the boy earn his living, let him labour that he may enjoy rest." But the rest has come to him before the labour. Oh, my boy, my boy!

'I am like the man in the Bible who laid up much goods and builded barns—goods for my boy and barns for him to store them in; and now his soul has been required of him, and I am left desolate. I would that it had been my soul and not my boy's!

'We buried him this afternoon under the shadow of the grey and ancient tower of the church of this village where my house is. It was a dreary December afternoon, and the sky was heavy with snow, but not much was falling. The coffin was put down by the grave, and a few big flakes lit upon it. They looked very white upon the black cloth! There was a little hitch about getting the coffin down into the grave—the necessary ropes had been forgotten: so we drew back from it, and waited in silence watching the big flakes fall gently one by one like heavenly benedictions, and melt in tears on Harry's pall. But that was not all. A robin redbreast came as bold as could be and lit upon the coffin and began to sing. And then I am afraid that I broke down, and so did Sir Henry Curtis, strong man though he is; and as for Captain Good, I saw him turn away too; even in my own distress I could not help noticing it.'

The above, signed 'Allan Quatermain', is an extract from my diary written two years and more ago. I copy it down here because it seems to me that it is the fittest beginning to the history that I am about to write, if it please God to spare me to finish it. If not, well it does not matter. That extract was penned seven thousand miles or so from the spot where I now lie painfully and slowly writing this, with a pretty girl standing by my side fanning the flies from my august countenance. Harry is there and I am here, and yet somehow I cannot help feeling that I am not far off Harry.

When I was in England I used to live in a very fine house—at least I call it a fine house, speaking comparatively, and judging from the standard of the houses I have been accustomed to all my life in Africa—not five hundred yards from the old church where Harry is asleep, and thither I went after the funeral and ate some food; for it is no good starving even if one has just buried all one's earthly hopes. But I could not eat much, and soon I took to walking, or rather limping—being permanently lame from the bite of a lion—up and down, up and down the oak-panelled vestibule; for there is a vestibule in my house in England. On all the four walls of this vestibule were placed pairs of horns—about a hundred pairs altogether, all of which I had shot myself. They are beautiful specimens, as I never keep any horns which are not in every way perfect, unless it may be now and again on account of the associations connected with them. In the centre of the room, however, over the wide fireplace, there was a clear space left on which I had fixed up all my rifles. Some of them I have had for forty years, old muzzle-loaders that nobody would look at nowadays. One was an elephant gun with strips of rimpi, or green hide, lashed round the stock and locks, such as used to be owned by the Dutchmen—a 'roer' they call it. That gun, the Boer I bought it from many years ago told me, had been used by his father at the battle of the Blood River, just after Dingaan swept into Natal and slaughtered six hundred men, women, and children, so that the Boers named the place where they died 'Weenen', or the 'Place of Weeping'; and so it is called to this day, and always will be called. And many an elephant have I shot with that old gun. She always took a handful of black powder and a three-ounce ball, and kicked like the very deuce.

Well, up and down I walked, staring at the guns and the horns which the guns had brought low; and as I did so there rose up in me a great craving:—I would go away from this place where I lived idly and at ease, back again to the wild land where I had spent my life, where I met my dear wife and poor Harry was born, and so many things, good, bad, and indifferent, had happened to me. The thirst for the wilderness was on me; I could tolerate this place no more; I would go and die as I had lived, among the wild game and the savages. Yes, as I walked, I began to long to see the moonlight gleaming silvery white over the wide veldt and mysterious sea of bush, and watch the lines of game travelling down the ridges to the water. The ruling passion is strong in death, they say, and my heart was dead that night. But, independently of my trouble, no man who has for forty years lived the life I have, can with impunity go coop himself in this prim English country, with its trim hedgerows and cultivated fields, its stiff formal manners, and its well-dressed crowds. He begins to long—ah, how he longs!—for the keen breath of the desert air; he dreams of the sight of Zulu impis breaking on their foes like surf upon the rocks, and his heart rises up in rebellion against the strict limits of the civilized life.

Ah! this civilization, what does it all come to? For forty years and more I lived among savages, and studied them and their ways; and now for several years I have lived here in England, and have in my own stupid manner done my best to learn the ways of the children of light; and what have I found? A great gulf fixed? No, only a very little one, that a plain man's thought may spring across. I say that as the savage is, so is the white man, only the latter is more inventive, and possesses the faculty of combination; save and except also that the savage, as I have known him, is to a large extent free from the greed of money, which eats like a cancer into the heart of the white man. It is a depressing conclusion, but in all essentials the savage and the child of civilization are identical. I dare say that the highly civilized lady reading this will smile at an old fool of a hunter's simplicity when she thinks of her black bead-bedecked sister; and so will the superfine cultured idler scientifically eating a dinner at his club, the cost of which would keep a starving family for a week. And yet, my dear young lady, what are those pretty things round your own neck?—they have a strong family resemblance, especially when you wear that *very* low dress, to the savage woman's beads. Your habit of turning round and round to the sound of horns and tom-toms, your fondness for pigments and powders, the way in which you love to subjugate yourself to the rich warrior who has captured you in marriage, and the quickness with which your taste in feathered head-dresses varies—all these things suggest touches of kinship; and you remember that in the fundamental principles of your nature you are quite identical. As for you, sir, who also laugh, let some man come and strike you in the face whilst you are enjoying that marvellous-looking dish, and we shall soon see how much of the savage there is in *you*.

There, I might go on for ever, but what is the good? Civilization is only savagery silver-gilt. A vainglory is it, and like a northern light, comes but to fade and leave the sky more dark. Out of the soil of barbarism it has grown like a tree, and, as I believe, into the soil like a tree it will once more, sooner or later, fall again, as the Egyptian civilization fell, as the Hellenic civilization fell, and as the Roman civilization and many others of which the world has now lost count, fell also. Do not let me, however, be understood as decrying our modern institutions, representing as they do the gathered experience of humanity applied for the good of all. Of course they have great advantages—hospitals for instance; but then, remember, we breed the sickly people who fill them. In a savage land they do not exist. Besides, the question will arise: How many of these blessings are due to Christianity as distinct from civilization? And so the balance sways and the story runs—here a gain, there a loss, and Nature's great average struck across the two, whereof the sum total forms one of the factors in that mighty equation in which the result will equal the unknown quantity of her purpose.

I make no apology for this digression, especially as this is an introduction which all young people and those who never like to think (and it is a bad habit) will naturally skip. It seems to me very desirable that we should sometimes try to understand the limitations of our nature, so that we may not be carried away by the pride of knowledge. Man's cleverness is almost indefinite, and stretches like an elastic band, but human nature is like an iron ring. You can go round and round it, you can polish it highly, you can even flatten it a little on one side, whereby you will make it bulge out the other, but you will *never*, while the world endures and man is man, increase its total circumference. It is the one fixed unchangeable thing—fixed as the stars, more enduring than the mountains, as unalterable as the way of the Eternal. Human nature is God's kaleidoscope, and the little bits of coloured glass which represent our passions, hopes, fears, joys, aspirations towards good and evil and what not, are turned in His mighty hand as surely and as certainly as it turns the stars, and continually fall into new patterns and combinations. But the composing elements remain the same, nor will there be one more bit of coloured glass nor one less for ever and ever.

This being so, supposing for the sake of argument we divide ourselves into twenty parts, nineteen savage and one civilized, we must look to the nineteen savage portions of our nature, if we would really understand ourselves, and not to the twentieth, which, though so insignificant in reality, is spread all over the other nineteen, making them appear quite different from what they really are, as the blacking does a boot, or the veneer a table. It is on the nineteen rough serviceable savage portions that we fall back on emergencies, not on the polished but unsubstantial twentieth. Civilization should wipe away our tears, and yet we weep and cannot be comforted. Warfare is abhorrent to her, and yet we strike out for hearth and home, for honour and fair fame, and can glory in the blow. And so on, through everything.

So, when the heart is stricken, and the head is humbled in the dust, civilization fails us utterly. Back, back, we creep, and lay us like little children on the great breast of Nature, she that perchance may soothe us and make us forget, or at least rid remembrance of its sting. Who has not in his great grief felt a longing to look upon the outward features of the universal Mother; to lie on the mountains and watch the clouds drive across the sky and hear the rollers break in thunder on the shore, to let his poor struggling life mingle for a while in her life; to feel the slow beat of her eternal heart, and to forget his woes, and let his identity be swallowed in the vast imperceptibly moving energy of her of whom we are, from whom we came, and with whom we shall again be mingled, who gave us birth, and will in a day to come give us our burial also.

And so in my trouble, as I walked up and down the oak-panelled vestibule of my house there in Yorkshire, I longed once more to throw myself into the arms of Nature. Not the Nature which you know, the Nature that waves in well-kept woods and smiles out in corn-fields, but Nature as she was in the age when creation was complete, undefiled as yet by any human sinks of sweltering humanity. I would go again where the wild game was, back to the land whereof none know the history, back to the savages, whom I love, although some of them are almost as merciless as Political Economy. There, perhaps, I should be able to learn to think of poor Harry lying in the churchyard, without feeling as though my heart would break in two.

And now there is an end of this egotistical talk, and there shall be no more of it. But if you whose eyes may perchance one day fall upon my written thoughts have got so far as this, I ask you to persevere, since what I have to tell you is not without its interest, and it has never been told before, nor will again.

I

THE CONSUL'S YARN

A week had passed since the funeral of my poor boy Harry, and one evening I was in my room walking up and down and thinking, when there was a ring at the outer door. Going down the steps I opened it myself, and in came my old friends Sir Henry Curtis and Captain John Good, RN. They entered the vestibule and sat themselves down before the wide hearth, where, I remember, a particularly good fire of logs was burning.

'It is very kind of you to come round,' I said by way of making a remark; 'it must have been heavy walking in the snow.'

They said nothing, but Sir Henry slowly filled his pipe and lit it with a burning ember. As he leant forward to do so the fire got hold of a gassy bit of pine and flared up brightly, throwing the whole scene into strong relief, and I thought, What a splendid-looking man he is! Calm, powerful face, clear-cut features, large grey eyes, yellow beard and hair—altogether a magnificent specimen of the higher type of humanity. Nor did his form belie his face. I have never seen wider shoulders or a deeper chest. Indeed, Sir Henry's girth is so great that, though he is six feet two high, he does not strike one as a tall man. As I looked at him I could not help thinking what a curious contrast my little dried-up self presented to his grand face and form. Imagine to yourself a small, withered, yellow-faced man of sixty-three, with thin hands, large brown eyes, a head of grizzled hair cut short and standing up like a half-worn scrubbing-brush—total weight in my clothes, nine stone six—and you will get a very fair idea of Allan Quatermain, commonly called Hunter Quatermain, or by the natives 'Macumazahn'—Anglicè, he who keeps a bright look-out at night, or, in vulgar English, a sharp fellow who is not to be taken in.

Then there was Good, who is not like either of us, being short, dark, stout—*very* stout—with twinkling black eyes, in one of which an eyeglass is everlastingly fixed. I say stout, but it is a mild term; I regret to state that of late years Good has been running to fat in a most disgraceful way. Sir Henry tells him that it comes from idleness and over-feeding, and Good does not like it at all, though he cannot deny it.

We sat for a while, and then I got a match and lit the lamp that stood ready on the table, for the half-light began to grow dreary, as it is apt to do when one has a short week ago buried the hope of one's life. Next, I opened a cupboard in the wainscoting and got a bottle of whisky and some tumblers and water. I always like to do these things for myself: it is irritating to me to have somebody continually at my elbow, as though I were an eighteen-month-old baby. All this while Curtis and Good had been silent, feeling, I suppose, that they had nothing to say that could do me any good, and content to give me the comfort of their presence and unspoken sympathy; for it was only their second visit since the funeral. And it is, by the way, from the *presence* of others that we really derive support in our dark hours of grief, and not from their talk, which often only serves to irritate us. Before a bad storm the game always herd together, but they cease their calling.

They sat and smoked and drank whisky and water, and I stood by the fire also smoking and looking at them.

At last I spoke. 'Old friends,' I said, 'how long is it since we got back from Kukuanaland?'

'Three years,' said Good. 'Why do you ask?'

'I ask because I think that I have had a long enough spell of civilization. I am going back to the veldt.'

Sir Henry laid his head back in his arm-chair and laughed one of his deep laughs. 'How very odd,' he said, 'eh, Good?'

Good beamed at me mysteriously through his eyeglass and murmured, 'Yes, odd—very odd.'

'I don't quite understand,' said I, looking from one to the other, for I dislike mysteries.

'Don't you, old fellow?' said Sir Henry; 'then I will explain. As Good and I were walking up here we had a talk.'

'If Good was there you probably did,' I put in sarcastically, for Good is a great hand at talking. 'And what may it have been about?'

'What do you think?' asked Sir Henry.

I shook my head. It was not likely that I should know what Good might be talking about. He talks about so many things.

'Well, it was about a little plan that I have formed—namely, that if you were willing we should pack up our traps and go off to Africa on another expedition.'

I fairly jumped at his words. 'You don't say so!' I said.

'Yes I do, though, and so does Good; don't you, Good?'

'Rather,' said that gentleman.

'Listen, old fellow,' went on Sir Henry, with considerable animation of manner. 'I'm tired of it too, dead-tired of doing nothing more except play the squire in a country that is sick of squires. For a year or more I have been getting as restless as an old elephant who scents danger. I am always dreaming of Kukuanaland and Gagool and King Solomon's Mines. I can assure you I have become the victim of an almost unaccountable craving. I am sick of shooting pheasants and partridges, and want to have a go at some large game again. There, you know the feeling—when one has once tasted brandy and water, milk becomes insipid to the palate. That year we spent together up in Kukuanaland seems to me worth all the other years of my life put together. I dare say that I am a fool for my pains, but I can't help it; I long to go, and, what is more, I mean to go.' He paused, and then went on again. 'And, after all, why should I not go? I have no wife or parent, no chick or child to keep me. If anything happens to me the baronetcy will go to my brother George and his boy, as it would ultimately do in any case. I am of no importance to any one.'

'Ah!' I said, 'I thought you would come to that sooner or later. And now, Good, what is your reason for wanting to trek; have you got one?'

'I have,' said Good, solemnly. 'I never do anything without a reason; and it isn't a lady—at least, if it is, it's several.'

I looked at him again. Good is so overpoweringly frivolous. 'What is it?' I said.

'Well, if you really want to know, though I'd rather not speak of a delicate and strictly personal matter, I'll tell you: I'm getting too fat.'

'Shut up, Good!' said Sir Henry. 'And now, Quatermain, tell us, where do you propose going to?'

I lit my pipe, which had gone out, before answering.

'Have you people ever heard of Mt Kenia?' I asked.

'Don't know the place,' said Good.

'Did you ever hear of the Island of Lamu?' I asked again.

'No. Stop, though—isn't it a place about 300 miles north of Zanzibar?'

'Yes. Now listen. What I have to propose is this. That we go to Lamu and thence make our way about 250 miles inland to Mt Kenia; from Mt Kenia on inland to Mt Lekakisera, another 200 miles, or thereabouts, beyond which no white man has to the best of my belief ever been; and then, if we get so far, right on into the unknown interior. What do you say to that, my hearties?'

'It's a big order,' said Sir Henry, reflectively.

'You are right,' I answered, 'it is; but I take it that we are all three of us in search of a big order. We want a change of scene, and we are likely to get one—a thorough change. All my life I have longed to visit those parts, and I mean to do it before I die. My poor boy's death has broken the last link between me and civilization, and I'm off to my native wilds. And now I'll tell you another thing, and that is, that for years and years I have heard rumours of a great white race which is supposed to have its home somewhere up in this direction, and I have a mind to see if there is any truth in them. If you fellows like to come, well and good; if not, I'll go alone.'

'I'm your man, though I don't believe in your white race,' said Sir Henry Curtis, rising and placing his arm upon my shoulder.

'Ditto,' remarked Good. 'I'll go into training at once. By all means let's go to Mt Kenia and the other place with an unpronounceable name, and look for a white race that does not exist. It's all one to me.'

'When do you propose to start?' asked Sir Henry.

'This day month,' I answered, 'by the British India steamboat; and don't you be so certain that things have no existence because you do not happen to have heard of them. Remember King Solomon's mines!'

Some fourteen weeks or so had passed since the date of this conversation, and this history goes on its way in very different surroundings.

After much deliberation and inquiry we came to the conclusion that our best starting-point for Mt Kenia would be from the neighbourhood of the mouth of the Tana River, and not from Mombassa, a place over 100 miles nearer Zanzibar. This conclusion we arrived at from information given to us by a German trader whom we met upon the steamer at Aden. I think that he was the dirtiest German I ever knew; but he was a good fellow, and gave us a great deal of valuable information. 'Lamu,' said he, 'you goes to Lamu—oh ze beautiful place!' and he turned up his fat face and beamed with mild rapture. 'One year and a half I live there and never change my shirt—never at all.'

And so it came to pass that on arriving at the island we disembarked with all our goods and chattels, and, not knowing where to go, marched boldly up to the house of Her Majesty's Consul, where we were most hospitably received.

Lamu is a very curious place, but the things which stand out most clearly in my memory in connection with it are its exceeding dirtiness

H. RIDER HAGGARD

and its smells. These last are simply awful. Just below the Consulate is the beach, or rather a mud bank that is called a beach. It is left quite bare at low tide, and serves as a repository for all the filth, offal, and refuse of the town. Here it is, too, that the women come to bury coconuts in the mud, leaving them there till the outer husk is quite rotten, when they dig them up again and use the fibres to make mats with, and for various other purposes. As this process has been going on for generations, the condition of the shore can be better imagined than described. I have smelt many evil odours in the course of my life, but the concentrated essence of stench which arose from that beach at Lamu as we sat in the moonlit night—not under, but *on* our friend the Consul's hospitable roof—and sniffed it, makes the remembrance of them very poor and faint. No wonder people get fever at Lamu. And yet the place was not without a certain quaintness and charm of its own, though possibly— indeed probably—it was one which would quickly pall.

'Well, where are you gentlemen steering for?' asked our friend the hospitable Consul, as we smoked our pipes after dinner.

'We propose to go to Mt Kenia and then on to Mt Lekakisera,' answered Sir Henry. 'Quatermain has got hold of some yarn about there being a white race up in the unknown territories beyond.'

The Consul looked interested, and answered that he had heard something of that, too.

'What have you heard?' I asked.

'Oh, not much. All I know about it is that a year or so ago I got a letter from Mackenzie, the Scotch missionary, whose station, "The Highlands", is placed at the highest navigable point of the Tana River, in which he said something about it.'

'Have you the letter?' I asked.

'No, I destroyed it; but I remember that he said that a man had arrived at his station who declared that two months' journey beyond Mt Lekakisera, which no white man has yet visited—at least, so far as I know—he found a lake called Laga, and that then he went off to the north-east, a month's journey, over desert and thorn veldt and great mountains, till he came to a country where the people are white and live in stone houses. Here he was hospitably entertained for a while, till at last the priests of the country set it about that he was a devil, and the people drove him away, and he journeyed for eight months and reached Mackenzie's place, as I heard, dying. That's all I know; and if you ask me, I believe that it is a lie; but if you want to find out more about it, you had better go up the Tana to Mackenzie's place and ask him for information.'

Sir Henry and I looked at each other. Here was something tangible.

'I think that we will go to Mr. Mackenzie's,' I said.

'Well,' answered the Consul, 'that is your best way, but I warn you that you are likely to have a rough journey, for I hear that the Masai are about, and, as you know, they are not pleasant customers. Your best plan will be to choose a few picked men for personal servants and hunters, and to hire bearers from village to village. It will give you an infinity of trouble, but perhaps on the whole it will prove a cheaper and more advantageous course than engaging a caravan, and you will be less liable to desertion.'

Fortunately there were at Lamu at this time a party of Wakwafi Askari (soldiers). The Wakwafi, who are a cross between the Masai and the Wataveta, are a fine manly race, possessing many of the good qualities of the Zulu, and a great capacity for civilization. They are also great hunters. As it happened, these particular men had recently been on a long trip with an Englishman named Jutson, who had started from Mombasa, a port about 150 miles below Lamu, and journeyed right round Kilimanjaro, one of the highest known mountains in Africa. Poor fellow, he had died of fever when on his return journey, and within a day's march of Mombasa. It does seem hard that he should have gone off thus when within a few hours of safety, and after having survived so many perils, but so it was. His hunters buried him, and then came on to Lamu in a dhow. Our friend the Consul suggested to us that we had better try and hire these men, and accordingly on the following morning we started to interview the party, accompanied by an interpreter.

In due course we found them in a mud hut on the outskirts of the town. Three of the men were sitting outside the hut, and fine frank-looking fellows they were, having a more or less civilized appearance. To them we cautiously opened the object of our visit, at first with very scant success. They declared that they could not entertain any such idea, that they were worn and weary with long travelling, and that their hearts were sore at the loss of their master. They meant to go back to their homes and rest awhile. This did not sound very promising, so by way of effecting a diversion I asked where the remainder of them were. I was told there were six, and I saw but three. One of the men said they slept in the hut, and were yet resting after their labours—'sleep weighed down their eyelids, and sorrow made their hearts as lead: it was

H. RIDER HAGGARD

best to sleep, for with sleep came forgetfulness. But the men should be awakened.'

Presently they came out of the hut, yawning—the first two men being evidently of the same race and style as those already before us; but the appearance of the third and last nearly made me jump out of my skin. He was a very tall, broad man, quite six foot three, I should say, but gaunt, with lean, wiry-looking limbs. My first glance at him told me that he was no Wakwafi: he was a pure bred Zulu. He came out with his thin aristocratic-looking hand placed before his face to hide a yawn, so I could only see that he was a 'Keshla' or ringed man, and that he had a great three-cornered hole in his forehead. In another second he removed his hand, revealing a powerful-looking Zulu face, with a humorous mouth, a short woolly beard, tinged with grey, and a pair of brown eyes keen as a hawk's. I knew my man at once, although I had not seen him for twelve years. 'How do you do, Umslopogaas?' I said quietly in Zulu.

The tall man (who among his own people was commonly known as the 'Woodpecker', and also as the 'Slaughterer') started, and almost let the long-handled battleaxe he held in his hand fall in his astonishment. Next second he had recognized me, and was saluting me in an outburst of sonorous language which made his companions the Wakwafi stare.

'Koos' (chief), he began, 'Koos-y-Pagete! Koos-y-umcool! (Chief from of old—mighty chief) Koos! Baba! (father) Macumazahn, old hunter, slayer of elephants, eater up of lions, clever one! watchful one! brave one! quick one! whose shot never misses, who strikes straight home, who grasps a hand and holds it to the death (i.e. is a true friend) Koos! Baba! Wise is the voice of our people that says, "Mountain never meets with mountain, but at daybreak or at even man shall meet again with man." Behold! a messenger came up from Natal, "Macumazahn is dead!" cried he. "The land knows Macumazahn no more." That is years ago. And now, behold, now in this strange place of stinks I find Macumazahn, my friend. There is no room for doubt. The brush of the old jackal has gone a little grey; but is not his eye as keen, and are not his teeth as sharp? Ha! ha! Macumazahn, mindest thou how thou didst plant the ball in the eye of the charging buffalo—mindest thou—'

I had let him run on thus because I saw that his enthusiasm was producing a marked effect upon the minds of the five Wakwafi, who appeared to understand something of his talk; but now I thought it time to put a stop to it, for there is nothing that I hate so much as this Zulu system of extravagant praising—'bongering' as they call it. 'Silence!' I said. 'Has all thy noisy talk been stopped up since last I saw thee that it breaks out thus, and sweeps us away? What doest thou here with these men—thou whom I left a chief in Zululand? How is it that thou art far from thine own place, and gathered together with strangers?'

Umslopogaas leant himself upon the head of his long battleaxe (which was nothing else but a pole-axe, with a beautiful handle of rhinoceros horn), and his grim face grew sad.

'My Father,' he answered, 'I have a word to tell thee, but I cannot speak it before these low people (umfagozana),' and he glanced at the Wakwafi Askari; 'it is for thine own ear. My Father, this will I say,' and here his face grew stern again, 'a woman betrayed me to the death, and covered my name with shame—ay, my own wife, a round-faced girl, betrayed me; but I escaped from death; ay, I broke from the very hands of those who came to slay me. I struck but three blows with this mine axe Inkosikaas—surely my Father will remember it—one to the right, one to the left, and one in front, and yet I left three men dead. And then I fled, and, as my Father knows, even now that I am old my feet are as the feet of the Sassaby, and there breathes not the man who, by running, can touch me again when once I have bounded from his side. On I sped, and after me came the messengers of death, and their voice was as the voice of dogs that hunt. From my own kraal I flew, and, as I passed, she who had betrayed me was drawing water from the spring. I fleeted by her like the shadow of Death, and as I went I smote with mine axe, and lo! her head fell: it fell into the water pan. Then I fled north. Day after day I journeyed on; for three moons I journeyed, resting not, stopping not, but running on towards forgetfulness, till I met the party of the white hunter who is now dead, and am come hither with his servants. And nought have I brought with me. I who was high-born, ay, of the blood of Chaka, the great king—a chief, and a captain of the regiment of the Nkomabakosi—am a wanderer in strange places, a man without a kraal. Nought have I brought save this mine axe; of all my belongings this remains alone. They have divided my cattle; they have taken my wives; and my children know my face no more. Yet with this axe'—and he swung the formidable weapon round his head, making the air hiss as he clove it—'will I cut another path to fortune. I have spoken.'

I shook my head at him. 'Umslopogaas,' I said, 'I know thee from of old. Ever ambitious, ever plotting to be great, I fear me that thou hast overreached thyself at last. Years ago, when thou wouldst have plotted against Cetywayo, son of Panda, I warned thee, and thou didst listen. But now, when I was not by thee to stay thy hand, thou hast dug a pit for thine own feet to fall in. Is it not so? But what is done is done. Who can make the dead tree green, or gaze again upon last year's light? Who can recall the spoken word, or bring back the spirit of the fallen? That which Time swallows comes not up again. Let it be forgotten!

'And now, behold, Umslopogaas, I know thee for a great warrior and a brave man, faithful to the death. Even in Zululand, where all the men are brave, they called thee the "Slaughterer", and at night told stories round the fire of thy strength and deeds. Hear me now. Thou seest this great man, my friend'—and I pointed to Sir Henry; 'he also is a warrior as great as thou, and, strong as thou art, he could throw thee over his shoulder. Incubu is his name. And thou seest this one also; him with the round stomach, the shining eye, and the pleasant face. Bougwan (glass eye) is his name, and a good man is he and a true, being of a curious tribe who pass their life upon the water, and live in floating kraals.

'Now, we three whom thou seest would travel inland, past Dongo Egere, the great white mountain (Mt Kenia), and far into the unknown beyond. We know not what we shall find there; we go to hunt and seek adventures, and new places, being tired of sitting still, with the same old things around us. Wilt thou come with us? To thee shall be given command of all our servants; but what shall befall thee, that I know not. Once before we three journeyed thus, in search of adventure, and we took with us a man such as thou—one Umbopa; and, behold, we left him the king of a great country, with twenty Impis (regiments), each of 3,000 plumed warriors, waiting on his word. How it shall go with thee, I know not; mayhap death awaits thee and us. Wilt thou throw thyself to Fortune and come, or fearest thou, Umslopogaas?'

The great man smiled. 'Thou art not altogether right, Macumazahn,' he said; 'I have plotted in my time, but it was not ambition that led me to my fall; but, shame on me that I should have to say it, a fair woman's face. Let it pass. So we are going to see something like the old times again, Macumazahn, when we fought and hunted in Zululand? Ay, I will come. Come life, come death, what care I, so that the blows fall fast and the blood runs red? I grow old, I grow old, and I have not fought enough! And yet am I a warrior among warriors; see my scars'—and he pointed to countless cicatrices, stabs and cuts, that marked the skin of his chest and legs and arms. 'See the hole in my head; the brains gushed out therefrom, yet did I slay him who smote, and live. Knowest thou how many men I have slain, in fair hand-to-hand combat, Macumazahn? See, here is the tale of them'—and he pointed to long rows of notches cut in the rhinoceros-horn handle of his axe. 'Number them, Macumazahn—one hundred and three—and I have never counted but those whom I have ripped open, nor have I reckoned those whom another man had struck.'

'Be silent,' I said, for I saw that he was getting the blood-fever on him; 'be silent; well art thou called the "Slaughterer". We would not hear of thy deeds of blood. Remember, if thou comest with us, we fight not save in self-defence. Listen, we need servants. These men,' and I pointed to the Wakwafi, who had retired a little way during our 'indaba' (talk), 'say they will not come.'

'Will not come!' shouted Umslopogaas; 'where is the dog who says he will not come when my Father orders? Here, thou'—and with a single bound he sprang upon the Wakwafi with whom I had first spoken, and, seizing him by the arm, dragged him towards us. 'Thou dog!' he said, giving the terrified man a shake, 'didst thou say that thou wouldst not go with my Father? Say it once more and I will choke thee'—and his long fingers closed round his throat as he said it—'thee, and those with thee. Hast thou forgotten how I served thy brother?'

'Nay, we will come with the white man,' gasped the man.

'White man!' went on Umslopogaas, in simulated fury, which a very little provocation would have made real enough; 'of whom speakest thou, insolent dog?'

'Nay, we will go with the great chief.'

'So!' said Umslopogaas, in a quiet voice, as he suddenly released his hold, so that the man fell backward. 'I thought you would.'

'That man Umslopogaas seems to have a curious moral ascendency over his companions,' Good afterwards remarked thoughtfully.

II

THE BLACK HAND

In due course we left Lamu, and ten days afterwards we found ourselves at a spot called Charra, on the Tana River, having gone through many adventures which need not be recorded here. Amongst other things we visited a ruined city, of which there are many on this coast, and which must once, to judge from their extent and the numerous remains of mosques and stone houses, have been very populous places. These ruined cities are immeasurably ancient, having, I believe, been places of wealth and importance as far back as the Old Testament times, when they were centres of trade with India and elsewhere. But their glory has departed now—the slave trade has finished them—and where wealthy merchants from all parts of the then civilized world stood and bargained in the crowded market-places, the lion holds his court at night, and instead of the chattering of slaves and the eager voices of the bidders, his awful note goes echoing down the ruined corridors. At this particular place we discovered on a mound, covered up with rank growth and rubbish, two of the most beautiful stone doorways that it is possible to conceive. The carving on them was simply exquisite, and I only regret that we had no means of getting them away. No doubt they had once been the entrances to a palace, of which, however, no traces were now to be seen, though probably its ruins lay under the rising mound.

Gone! quite gone! the way that everything must go. Like the nobles and the ladies who lived within their gates, these cities have had their day, and now they are as Babylon and Nineveh, and as London and Paris will one day be. Nothing may endure. That is the inexorable law. Men and women, empires and cities, thrones, principalities, and powers, mountains, rivers, and unfathomed seas, worlds, spaces, and universes, all have their day, and all must go. In this ruined and forgotten place the moralist may behold a symbol of the universal destiny. For this system of ours allows no room for standing still—nothing can loiter on the road and check the progress of things upwards towards Life, or the rush of things downwards towards Death. The stern policeman Fate moves us and them on, on, uphill and downhill and across the level;

there is no resting-place for the weary feet, till at last the abyss swallows us, and from the shores of the Transitory we are hurled into the sea of the Eternal.

At Charra we had a violent quarrel with the headman of the bearers we had hired to go as far as this, and who now wished to extort large extra payment from us. In the result he threatened to set the Masai—about whom more anon—on to us. That night he, with all our hired bearers, ran away, stealing most of the goods which had been entrusted to them to carry. Luckily, however, they had not happened to steal our rifles, ammunition, and personal effects; not because of any delicacy of feeling on their part, but owing to the fact that they chanced to be in the charge of the five Wakwafis. After that, it was clear to us that we had had enough of caravans and of bearers. Indeed, we had not much left for a caravan to carry. And yet, how were we to get on?

It was Good who solved the question. 'Here is water,' he said, pointing to the Tana River; 'and yesterday I saw a party of natives hunting hippopotami in canoes. I understand that Mr. Mackenzie's mission station is on the Tana River. Why not get into canoes and paddle up to it?'

This brilliant suggestion was, needless to say, received with acclamation; and I instantly set to work to buy suitable canoes from the surrounding natives. I succeeded after a delay of three days in obtaining two large ones, each hollowed out of a single log of some light wood, and capable of holding six people and baggage. For these two canoes we had to pay nearly all our remaining cloth, and also many other articles.

On the day following our purchase of the two canoes we effected a start. In the first canoe were Good, Sir Henry, and three of our Wakwafi followers; in the second myself, Umslopogaas, and the other two Wakwafis. As our course lay upstream, we had to keep four paddles at work in each canoe, which meant that the whole lot of us, except Good, had to row away like galley-slaves; and very exhausting work it was. I say, except Good, for, of course, the moment that Good got into a boat his foot was on his native heath, and he took command of the party. And certainly he worked us. On shore Good is a gentle, mild-mannered man, and given to jocosity; but, as we found to our cost, Good in a boat was a perfect demon. To begin with, he knew all about it, and we didn't. On all nautical subjects, from the torpedo fittings of a man-of-war down to the best way of handling the paddle of an African canoe, he was a perfect mine of information, which, to say the least of it, we were not. Also his ideas of discipline were of the sternest, and, in short, he came the royal naval officer over us pretty considerably, and paid us out amply for all the chaff we were wont to treat him to on land; but, on the other hand, I am bound to say that he managed the boats admirably.

After the first day Good succeeded, with the help of some cloth and a couple of poles, in rigging up a sail in each canoe, which lightened our labours not a little. But the current ran very strong against us, and at the best we were not able to make more than twenty miles a day. Our plan was to start at dawn, and paddle along till about half-past ten, by which time the sun got too hot to allow of further exertion. Then we moored our canoes to the bank, and ate our frugal meal; after which we ate or otherwise amused ourselves till about three o'clock, when we again started, and rowed till within an hour of sundown, when we called a halt for the night. On landing in the evening, Good would at once set to work, with the help of the Askari, to build a little 'scherm', or small enclosure, fenced with thorn bushes, and to light a fire. I, with Sir Henry and Umslopogaas, would go out to shoot something for the pot. Generally this was an easy task, for all sorts of game abounded on the banks of the Tana. One night Sir Henry shot a young cow-giraffe, of which the marrow-bones were excellent; on another I got a couple of waterbuck right and left; and once, to his own intense satisfaction, Umslopogaas (who, like most Zulus, was a vile shot with a rifle) managed to kill a fine fat eland with a Martini I had lent him. Sometimes we varied our food by shooting some guinea-fowl, or bush-bustard (paau)—both of which were numerous—with a shot-gun, or by catching a supply of beautiful yellow fish, with which the waters of the Tana swarmed, and which form, I believe, one of the chief food-supplies of the crocodiles.

Three days after our start an ominous incident occurred. We were just drawing in to the bank to make our camp as usual for the night, when we caught sight of a figure standing on a little knoll not forty yards away, and intensely watching our approach. One glance was sufficient—although I was personally unacquainted with the tribe—to tell me that he was a Masai Elmoran, or young warrior. Indeed, had I had any doubts, they would have quickly been dispelled by the terrified exclamation of *'Masai!'* that burst simultaneously from the lips of our Wakwafi followers, who are, as I think I have said, themselves bastard Masai.

And what a figure he presented as he stood there in his savage war-gear! Accustomed as I have been to savages all my life, I do not think that I have ever before seen anything quite so ferocious or awe-inspiring. To begin with, the man was enormously tall, quite as tall as Umslopogaas, I should say, and beautifully, though somewhat slightly, shaped; but with the face of a devil. In his right hand he held a spear about five and a half feet long, the blade being two and a half feet in length, by nearly three inches in width, and having an iron spike at the end of the handle that measured more than a foot. On his left arm was a large and well-made elliptical shield of buffalo hide, on which were painted strange heraldic-looking devices. On his shoulders was a huge cape of hawk's feathers, and round his neck was a 'naibere', or strip of cotton, about seventeen feet long, by one and a half broad, with a stripe of colour running down the middle of it. The tanned goatskin robe, which formed his ordinary attire in times of peace, was tied lightly round his waist, so as to serve the purposes of a belt, and through it were stuck, on the right and left sides respectively, his short pear-shaped sime, or sword, which is made of a single piece of steel, and carried in a wooden sheath, and an enormous knobkerrie. But perhaps the most remarkable feature of his attire consisted of a headdress of ostrich-feathers, which was fixed on the chin, and passed in front of the ears to the forehead, and, being shaped like an ellipse, completely framed the face, so that the diabolical countenance appeared to project from a sort of feather fire-screen. Round the ankles he wore black fringes of hair, and, projecting from the upper portion of the calves, to which they were attached, were long spurs like spikes, from which flowed down tufts of the beautiful black and waving hair of the Colobus monkey. Such was the elaborate array of the Masai Elmoran who stood watching the approach of our two canoes, but it is one which, to be appreciated, must be seen; only those who see it do not often live to describe it. Of course I could not make out all these details of his full dress on the occasion of this my first introduction, being, indeed, amply taken up with the consideration of the general effect, but I had plenty of subsequent opportunities of becoming acquainted with the items that went to make it up.

Whilst we were hesitating what to do, the Masai warrior drew himself up in a dignified fashion, shook his huge spear at us, and, turning, vanished on the further side of the slope.

'Hulloa!' holloaed Sir Henry from the other boat; 'our friend the caravan leader has been as good as his word, and set the Masai after us. Do you think it will be safe to go ashore?'

I did not think it would be at all safe; but, on the other hand, we had no means of cooking in the canoes, and nothing that we could eat raw, so it was difficult to know what to do. At last Umslopogaas simplified matters by volunteering to go and reconnoitre, which he did, creeping off into the bush like a snake, while we hung off in the stream waiting for him. In half an hour he returned, and told us that there was not a Masai to be seen anywhere about, but that he had discovered a spot where they had recently been encamped, and that from various indications he judged that they must have moved on an hour or so before; the man we saw having, no doubt, been left to report upon our movements.

Thereupon we landed; and, having posted a sentry, proceeded to cook and eat our evening meal. This done, we took the situation into our serious consideration. Of course, it was possible that the apparition of the Masai warrior had nothing to do with us, that he was merely one of a band bent upon some marauding and murdering expedition against another tribe. But when we recalled the threat of the caravan leader, and reflected on the ominous way in which the warrior had shaken his spear at us, this did not appear very probable. On the contrary, what did seem probable was that the party was after us and awaiting a favourable opportunity to attack us. This being so, there were two things that we could do—one of which was to go on, and the other to go back. The latter idea was, however, rejected at once, it being obvious that we should encounter as many dangers in retreat as in advance; and, besides, we had made up our minds to journey onwards at any price. Under these circumstances, however, we did not consider it safe to sleep ashore, so we got into our canoes, and, paddling out into the middle of the stream, which was not very wide here, managed to anchor them by means of big stones fastened to ropes made of coconut-fibre, of which there were several fathoms in each canoe.

Here the mosquitoes nearly ate us up alive, and this, combined with anxiety as to our position, effectually prevented me from sleeping as the others were doing, notwithstanding the attacks of the aforesaid Tana mosquitoes. And so I lay awake, smoking and reflecting on many things, but, being of a practical turn of mind, chiefly on how we were to give those Masai villains the slip. It was a beautiful moonlight night, and, notwithstanding the mosquitoes, and the great risk we were running from fever from sleeping in such a spot, and forgetting that I had the cramp very badly in my right leg from squatting in a constrained position in the canoe, and that the Wakwafi who was sleeping beside me smelt horribly, I really began to enjoy myself. The moonbeams played upon the surface of the running water that speeded unceasingly past us towards the sea, like men's lives towards the grave, till it glittered like a wide sheet of silver, that is in the open where the trees threw no shadows. Near the banks, however, it was very dark, and the night wind sighed sadly in the reeds. To our left, on the further side of the river, was a little sandy bay which was clear of trees, and here I could make out the forms of numerous antelopes advancing to the water, till suddenly there came an ominous roar, whereupon they all made off hurriedly. Then after a pause I caught sight of the massive form of His Majesty the Lion, coming down to drink his fill after meat. Presently he moved on, then came a crashing of the reeds about fifty yards above us, and a few minutes later a huge black mass rose out of the water, about twenty yards from me, and snorted. It was the head of a hippopotamus. Down it went without a sound, only to rise again within five yards of where I sat. This was decidedly too near to be comfortable, more especially as the hippopotamus was evidently animated by intense curiosity to know what on earth our canoes were. He opened his great mouth, to yawn, I suppose, and gave me an excellent view of his ivories; and I could not help reflecting how easily he could crunch up our frail canoe with a single bite. Indeed, I had half a mind to give him a ball from my eight-bore, but on reflection determined to let him alone unless he actually charged the boat. Presently he sank again as noiselessly as before, and I saw no more of him. Just then, on looking towards the bank on our right, I fancied that I caught sight of a dark figure flitting between the tree trunks. I have very keen sight, and I was almost sure that I saw something, but whether it was bird, beast, or man I could not say. At the moment, however, a dark cloud passed over the moon, and I saw no more of it. Just then, too, although all the other sounds of the forest had ceased, a species of horned owl with which I was well acquainted began to hoot with great persistency. After that, save for the rustling of trees and reeds when the wind caught them, there was complete silence.

But somehow, in the most unaccountable way, I had suddenly become nervous. There was no particular reason why I should be, beyond the ordinary reasons which surround the Central African traveller, and yet I undoubtedly was. If there is one thing more than another of which I have the most complete and entire scorn and disbelief, it is of presentiments, and yet here I was all of a sudden filled with and possessed by a most undoubted presentiment of approaching evil. I would not give way to it, however, although I felt the cold perspiration stand out upon my forehead. I would not arouse the others. Worse and worse I grew, my pulse fluttered like a dying man's, my nerves thrilled with the horrible sense of impotent terror which anybody who is subject to nightmare will be familiar with, but still my will triumphed over my fears, and I lay quiet (for I was half sitting, half lying, in the bow of the canoe), only turning my face so as to command a view of Umslopogaas and the two Wakwafi who were sleeping alongside of and beyond me.

In the distance I heard a hippopotamus splash faintly, then the owl hooted again in a kind of unnatural screaming note, and the wind began to moan plaintively through the trees, making a heart-chilling music. Above was the black bosom of the cloud, and beneath me swept the black flood of the water, and I felt as though I and Death were utterly alone between them. It was very desolate.

Suddenly my blood seemed to freeze in my veins, and my heart to stand still. Was it fancy, or were we moving? I turned my eyes to look for the other canoe which should be alongside of us. I could not see it, but instead I saw a lean and clutching black hand lifting itself above the gunwale of the little boat. Surely it was a nightmare! At the same instant a dim but devilish-looking face appeared to rise out of the water, and then came a lurch of the canoe, the quick flash of a knife, and an awful yell from the Wakwafi who was sleeping by my side (the same poor fellow whose odour had been annoying me), and something warm spurted into my face. In an instant the spell was broken; I knew that it was no nightmare, but that we were attacked by swimming Masai. Snatching at the first weapon that came to hand, which happened to be Umslopogaas' battleaxe, I struck with all my force in the direction in which I had seen the flash of the knife. The blow fell upon a man's arm, and, catching it against the thick wooden gunwale of the canoe, completely severed it from the body just above the wrist. As for its owner, he uttered no sound or cry. Like a ghost he came, and like a ghost he went, leaving behind him a bloody hand still gripping a great knife, or rather a short sword, that was buried in the heart of our poor servant.

Instantly there arose a hubbub and confusion, and I fancied, rightly or wrongly, that I made out several dark heads gliding away towards the right-hand bank, whither we were rapidly drifting, for the rope by which we were moored had been severed with a knife. As soon as I had realized this fact, I also realized that the scheme had been to cut the boat loose so that it should drift on to the right bank (as it would have done with the natural swing of the current), where no doubt a party of Masai were waiting to dig their shovel-headed spears into us. Seizing one paddle myself, I told Umslopogaas to take another (for the remaining Askari was too frightened and bewildered to be of any use), and together we rowed vigorously out towards the middle of the stream; and not an instant too soon, for in another minute we should have been aground, and then there would have been an end of us.

As soon as we were well out, we set to work to paddle the canoe upstream again to where the other was moored; and very hard and dangerous work it was in the dark, and with nothing but the notes of Good's stentorian shouts, which he kept firing off at intervals like a fog-horn, to guide us. But at last we fetched up, and were thankful to find that they had not been molested at all. No doubt the owner of the same hand that severed our rope should have severed theirs also, but was led away from his purpose by an irresistible inclination to murder when he got the chance, which, while it cost us a man and him his hand, undoubtedly saved all the rest of us from massacre. Had it not been for that ghastly apparition over the side of the boat—an apparition that I shall never forget till my dying hour—the canoe would undoubtedly have drifted ashore before I realized what had happened, and this history would never have been written by me.

III

THE MISSION STATION

We made the remains of our rope fast to the other canoe, and sat waiting for the dawn and congratulating ourselves upon our merciful escape, which really seemed to result more from the special favour of Providence than from our own care or prowess. At last it came, and I have not often been more grateful to see the light, though so far as my canoe was concerned it revealed a ghastly sight. There in the bottom of the little boat lay the unfortunate Askari, the sime, or sword, in his bosom, and the severed hand gripping the handle. I could not bear the sight, so hauling up the stone which had served as an anchor to the other canoe, we made it fast to the murdered man and dropped him overboard, and down he went to the bottom, leaving nothing but a train of bubbles behind him. Alas! when our time comes, most of us like him leave nothing but bubbles behind, to show that we have been, and the bubbles soon burst. The hand of his murderer we threw into the stream, where it slowly sank. The sword, of which the handle was ivory, inlaid with gold (evidently Arab work), I kept and used as a hunting-knife, and very useful it proved.

Then, a man having been transferred to my canoe, we once more started on in very low spirits and not feeling at all comfortable as to the future, but fondly hoping to arrive at the 'Highlands' station by night. To make matters worse, within an hour of sunrise it came on to rain in torrents, wetting us to the skin, and even necessitating the occasional baling of the canoes, and as the rain beat down the wind we could not use the sails, and had to get along as best as we could with our paddles.

At eleven o'clock we halted on an open piece of ground on the left bank of the river, and, the rain abating a little, managed to make a fire and catch and broil some fish. We did not dare to wander about to search for game. At two o'clock we got off again, taking a supply of broiled fish with us, and shortly afterwards the rain came on harder than ever. Also the river began to get exceedingly difficult to navigate on account of the numerous rocks, reaches of shallow water, and the increased force of the current; so that it soon became clear to us that we should not reach the Rev. Mackenzie's hospitable roof that night—a prospect that did not tend to enliven us. Toil as we would, we could not make more than an average of a mile an hour, and at five o'clock in the afternoon (by which time we were all utterly worn out) we reckoned that we were still quite ten miles below the station. This being so, we set to work to make the best arrangements we could for the night. After our recent experience, we simply did not dare to land, more especially as the banks of the Tana were clothed with dense bush that would have given cover to five thousand Masai, and at first I thought that we were going to have another night of it in the canoes. Fortunately, however, we espied a little rocky islet, not more than fifteen miles or so square, situated nearly in the middle of the river. For this we paddled, and, making fast the canoes, landed and made ourselves as comfortable as circumstances would permit, which was very uncomfortable indeed. As for the weather, it continued to be simply vile, the rain coming down in sheets till we were chilled to the marrow, and utterly preventing us from lighting a fire. There was, however, one consoling circumstance about this rain; our Askari declared that nothing would induce the Masai to make an attack in it, as they intensely disliked moving about in the wet, perhaps, as Good suggested, because they hate the idea of washing. We ate some insipid and sodden cold fish—that is, with the exception of Umslopogaas, who, like most Zulus, cannot bear fish—and took a pull of brandy, of which we fortunately had a few bottles left, and then began what, with one exception—when we same three white men nearly perished of cold on the snow of Sheba's Breast in the course of our journey to Kukuanaland—was, I think, the most trying night I ever experienced. It seemed absolutely endless, and once or twice I feared that two of the Askari would have died of the wet, cold, and exposure. Indeed, had it not been for timely doses of brandy I am sure that they would have died, for no African people can stand much exposure, which first paralyses and then kills them. I could see that even that iron old warrior Umslopogaas felt it keenly; though, in strange contrast to the Wakwafis, who groaned and bemoaned their fate unceasingly, he never uttered a single complaint. To make matters worse, about one in the morning we again heard the owl's ominous hooting, and had at once to prepare ourselves for another attack; though, if it had been attempted, I do not think that we could have offered a very effective resistance. But either the owl was a real one this time, or else the Masai were themselves too miserable to think of offensive operations, which, indeed, they rarely, if ever, undertake in bush veldt. At any rate, we saw nothing of them.

At last the dawn came gliding across the water, wrapped in wreaths of ghostly mist, and, with the daylight, the rain ceased; and then, out came the glorious sun, sucking up the mists and warming the chill air. Benumbed, and utterly exhausted, we dragged ourselves to our feet, and went and stood in the bright rays, and were thankful for them. I can quite understand how it is that primitive people become sun worshippers, especially if their conditions of life render them liable to exposure.

In half an hour more we were once again making fair progress with the help of a good wind. Our spirits had returned with the sunshine, and we were ready to laugh at difficulties and dangers that had been almost crushing on the previous day.

And so we went on cheerily till about eleven o'clock. Just as we were thinking of halting as usual, to rest and try to shoot something to eat, a sudden bend in the river brought us in sight of a substantial-looking European house with a veranda round it, splendidly situated upon a hill, and surrounded by a high stone wall with a ditch on the outer side. Right against and overshadowing the house was an enormous pine, the top of which we had seen through a glass for the last two days, but of course without knowing that it marked the site of the mission station. I was the first to see the house, and could not restrain myself from giving a hearty cheer, in which the others, including the natives, joined lustily. There was no thought of halting now. On we laboured, for, unfortunately, though the house seemed quite near, it was still a long way off by river, until at last, by one o'clock, we found ourselves at the bottom of the slope on which the building stood. Running the canoes to the bank, we disembarked, and were just hauling them up on to the shore, when we perceived three figures, dressed in ordinary English-looking clothes, hurrying down through a grove of trees to meet us.

'A gentleman, a lady, and a little girl,' exclaimed Good, after surveying the trio through his eyeglass, 'walking in a civilized fashion, through a civilized garden, to meet us in this place. Hang me, if this isn't the most curious thing we have seen yet!'

Good was right: it certainly did seem odd and out of place—more like a scene out of a dream or an Italian opera than a real tangible fact; and the sense of unreality was not lessened when we heard ourselves addressed in good broad Scotch, which, however, I cannot reproduce.

'How do you do, sirs,' said Mr. Mackenzie, a grey-haired, angular man, with a kindly face and red cheeks; 'I hope I see you very well. My natives told me an hour ago they spied two canoes with white men in them coming up the river; so we have just come down to meet you.'

'And it is very glad that we are to see a white face again, let me tell you,' put in the lady—a charming and refined-looking person.

We took off our hats in acknowledgment, and proceeded to introduce ourselves.

'And now,' said Mr. Mackenzie, 'you must all be hungry and weary; so come on, gentlemen, come on, and right glad we are to see you. The last white who visited us was Alphonse—you will see Alphonse presently—and that was a year ago.'

Meanwhile we had been walking up the slope of the hill, the lower portion of which was fenced off, sometimes with quince fences and sometimes with rough stone walls, into Kaffir gardens, just now full of crops of mealies, pumpkins, potatoes, etc. In the corners of these gardens were groups of neat mushroom-shaped huts, occupied by Mr. Mackenzie's mission natives, whose women and children came pouring out to meet us as we walked. Through the centre of the gardens ran the roadway up which we were walking. It was bordered on each side by a line of orange trees, which, although they had only been planted ten years, had in the lovely climate of the uplands below Mt Kenia, the base of which is about 5,000 feet above the coastline level, already grown to imposing proportions, and were positively laden with golden fruit. After a stiffish climb of a quarter of a mile or so—for the hillside was steep—we came to a splendid quince fence, also covered with fruit, which enclosed, Mr. Mackenzie told us, a space of about four acres of ground that contained his private garden, house, church, and outbuildings, and, indeed, the whole hilltop. And what a garden it was! I have always loved a good garden, and I could have thrown up my hands for joy when I saw Mr. Mackenzie's. First there were rows upon rows of standard European fruit-trees, all grafted; for on top of this hill the climate was so temperate that nearly all the English vegetables, trees, and flowers flourished luxuriantly, even including several varieties of the apple, which, generally, runs to wood in a warm climate and obstinately refuses to fruit. Then there were strawberries and tomatoes (such tomatoes!), and melons and cucumbers, and, indeed, every sort of vegetable and fruit.

'Well, you have something like a garden!' I said, overpowered with admiration not untouched by envy.

'Yes,' answered the missionary, 'it is a very good garden, and has well repaid my labour; but it is the climate that I have to thank. If you stick a peach-stone into the ground it will bear fruit the fourth year, and a rose-cutting will bloom in a year. It is a lovely clime.'

Just then we came to a ditch about ten feet wide, and full of water, on the other side of which was a loopholed stone wall eight feet high, and with sharp flints plentifully set in mortar on the coping.

'There,' said Mr. Mackenzie, pointing to the ditch and wall, 'this is my magnum opus; at least, this and the church, which is the other side of the house. It took me and twenty natives two years to dig the ditch and build the wall, but I never felt safe till it was done; and now I can defy all the savages in Africa, for the spring that fills the ditch is inside the wall, and bubbles out at the top of the hill winter and summer alike, and I always keep a store of four months' provision in the house.'

Crossing over a plank and through a very narrow opening in the wall, we entered into what Mrs. Mackenzie called *her* domain—namely, the flower garden, the beauty of which is really beyond my power to describe. I do not think I ever saw such roses, gardenias, or camellias (all reared from seeds or cuttings sent from England); and there was also a patch given up to a collection of bulbous roots mostly collected by Miss Flossie, Mr. Mackenzie's little daughter, from the surrounding country, some of which were surpassingly beautiful. In the middle of this garden, and exactly opposite the veranda, a beautiful fountain of clear water bubbled up from the ground, and fell into a stone-work basin which had been carefully built to receive it, whence the overflow found its way by means of a drain to the moat round the outer wall, this moat in its turn serving as a reservoir, whence an unfailing supply of water was available to irrigate all the gardens below. The house itself, a massively built single-storied building, was roofed with slabs of stone, and had a handsome veranda in front. It was built on three sides of a square, the fourth side being taken up by the kitchens, which stood separate from the house—a very good plan in a hot country. In the centre of this square thus formed was, perhaps, the most remarkable object that we had yet seen in this charming place, and that was a single tree of the conifer tribe, varieties of which grow freely on the highlands of this part of Africa. This splendid tree, which Mr. Mackenzie informed us was a landmark for fifty miles round, and which we had ourselves seen for the last forty miles of our journey, must have been nearly three hundred feet in height, the trunk measuring about sixteen feet in diameter at a yard from the ground. For some seventy feet it rose a beautiful tapering brown pillar without a single branch, but at that height splendid dark green boughs, which, looked at from below, had the appearance of gigantic fern-leaves, sprang out horizontally from the trunk, projecting right over the house and flower-garden, to both of which they furnished a grateful proportion of shade, without—being so high up—offering any impediment to the passage of light and air.

'What a beautiful tree!' exclaimed Sir Henry.

'Yes, you are right; it is a beautiful tree. There is not another like it in all the country round, that I know of,' answered Mr. Mackenzie. 'I call it my watch tower. As you see, I have a rope ladder fixed to the lowest bough; and if I want to see anything that is going on within fifteen miles or so, all I have to do is to run up it with a spyglass. But you must be hungry, and I am sure the dinner is cooked. Come in, my friends; it is but a rough place, but well enough for these savage parts; and I can tell you what, we have got—a French cook.' And he led the way on to the veranda.

As I was following him, and wondering what on earth he could mean by this, there suddenly appeared, through the door that opened on to the veranda from the house, a dapper little man, dressed in a neat blue cotton suit, with shoes made of tanned hide, and remarkable for a bustling air and most enormous black mustachios, shaped into an upward curve, and coming to a point for all the world like a pair of buffalo-horns.

'Madame bids me for to say that dinnar is sarved. Messieurs, my compliments;' then suddenly perceiving Umslopogaas, who was loitering along after us and playing with his battleaxe, he threw up his hands in astonishment. 'Ah, mais quel homme!' he exclaimed in French, 'quel sauvage affreux! Take but note of his huge choppare and the great pit in his head.'

'Ay,' said Mr. Mackenzie; 'what are you talking about, Alphonse?'

'Talking about!' replied the little Frenchman, his eyes still fixed upon Umslopogaas, whose general appearance seemed to fascinate him; 'why I talk of him'—and he rudely pointed—'of ce monsieur noir.'

At this everybody began to laugh, and Umslopogaas, perceiving that he was the object of remark, frowned ferociously, for he had a most lordly dislike of anything like a personal liberty.

'Parbleu!' said Alphonse, 'he is angered—he makes the grimace. I like not his air. I vanish.' And he did with considerable rapidity.

Mr. Mackenzie joined heartily in the shout of laughter which we indulged in. 'He is a queer character—Alphonse,' he said. 'By and by I will tell you his history; in the meanwhile let us try his cooking.'

'Might I ask,' said Sir Henry, after we had eaten a most excellent dinner, 'how you came to have a French cook in these wilds?'

'Oh,' answered Mrs. Mackenzie, 'he arrived here of his own accord about a year ago, and asked to be taken into our service. He had got into some trouble in France, and fled to Zanzibar, where he found an application had been made by the French Government for his extradition. Whereupon he rushed off up-country, and fell in, when nearly starved, with our caravan of men, who were bringing us our annual supply of goods, and was brought on here. You should get him to tell you the story.'

When dinner was over we lit our pipes, and Sir Henry proceeded to give our host a description of our journey up here, over which he looked very grave.

'It is evident to me,' he said, 'that those rascally Masai are following you, and I am very thankful that you have reached this house in safety. I do not think that they will dare to attack you here. It is unfortunate, though, that nearly all my men have gone down to the coast with ivory and goods. There are two hundred of them in the caravan, and the consequence is that I have not more than twenty men available for defensive purposes in case they should attack us. But, still, I will just give a few orders;' and, calling a black man who was loitering about outside in the garden, he went to the window, and addressed him in a Swahili dialect. The man listened, and then saluted and departed.

'I am sure I devoutly hope that we shall bring no such calamity upon you,' said I, anxiously, when he had taken his seat again. 'Rather than bring those bloodthirsty villains about your ears, we will move on and take our chance.'

'You will do nothing of the sort. If the Masai come, they come, and there is an end on it; and I think we can give them a pretty warm greeting. I would not show any man the door for all the Masai in the world.'

'That reminds me,' I said, 'the Consul at Lamu told me that he had had a letter from you, in which you said that a man had arrived here who reported that he had come across a white people in the interior. Do you think that there was any truth in his story? I ask, because I have once or twice in my life heard rumours from natives who have come down from the far north of the existence of such a race.'

Mr. Mackenzie, by way of answer, went out of the room and returned, bringing with him a most curious sword. It was long, and all the blade, which was very thick and heavy, was to within a quarter of an inch of the cutting edge worked into an ornamental pattern exactly as we work soft wood with a fret-saw, the steel, however, being invariably pierced in such a way as not to interfere with the strength of the sword. This in itself was sufficiently curious, but what was still more so was that all the edges of the hollow spaces cut through the substance of the blade were most beautifully inlaid with gold, which was in some way that I cannot understand welded on to the steel.

'There,' said Mr. Mackenzie, 'did you ever see a sword like that?'

We all examined it and shook our heads.

'Well, I have got it to show you, because this is what the man who said he had seen the white people brought with him, and because it does more or less give an air of truth to what I should otherwise have set down as a lie. Look here; I will tell you all that I know about the matter, which is not much. One afternoon, just before sunset, I was sitting on the veranda, when a poor, miserable, starved-looking man came limping up and squatted down before me. I asked him where he came from and what he wanted, and thereon he plunged into a long rambling narrative about how he belonged to a tribe far in the north, and how his tribe was destroyed by another tribe, and he with a few other survivors driven still further north past a lake named Laga. Thence, it appears, he made his way to another lake that lay up in the mountains, "a lake without a bottom" he called it, and here his wife and brother died of an infectious sickness—probably smallpox—whereon the people drove him out of their villages into the wilderness, where he wandered miserably over mountains for ten days, after which he got into dense thorn forest, and was one day found there by some *white men* who were hunting, and who took him to a place where all the people were white and lived in stone houses. Here he remained a week shut up in a house, till one night a man with a white beard, whom he understood to be a "medicine-man", came and inspected him, after which he was led off and taken through the thorn forest to the confines of the wilderness, and given food and this sword (at least so he said), and turned loose.'

'Well,' said Sir Henry, who had been listening with breathless interest, 'and what did he do then?'

'Oh! he seems, according to his account, to have gone through sufferings and hardships innumerable, and to have lived for weeks on roots and berries, and such things as he could catch and kill. But somehow he did live, and at last by slow degrees made his way south and reached this place. What the details of his journey were I never learnt, for I told him to return on the morrow, bidding one of my headmen look after him for the night. The headman took him away, but the poor man had the itch so badly that the headman's wife would not have him in the hut for fear of catching it, so he was given a blanket and told to sleep outside. As it happened, we had a lion hanging about here just then, and most unhappily he winded this unfortunate wanderer, and, springing on him, bit his head almost off without the people in the hut knowing anything about it, and there was an end of him and his story about the white people; and whether or no there is any truth in it is more than I can tell you. What do you think, Mr. Quatermain?'

I shook my head, and answered, 'I don't know. There are so many queer things hidden away in the heart of this great continent that I should be sorry to assert that there was no truth in it. Anyhow, we mean to try and find out. We intend to journey to Lekakisera, and thence, if we live to get so far, to this Lake Laga; and, if there are any white people beyond, we will do our best to find them.'

'You are very venturesome people,' said Mr. Mackenzie, with a smile, and the subject dropped.

IV

ALPHONSE AND HIS ANNETTE

After dinner we thoroughly inspected all the outbuildings and grounds of the station, which I consider the most successful as well as the most beautiful place of the sort that I have seen in Africa. We then returned to the veranda, where we found Umslopogaas taking advantage of this favourable opportunity to clean all the rifles thoroughly. This was the only *work* that he ever did or was asked to do, for as a Zulu chief it was beneath his dignity to work with his hands; but such as it was he did it very well. It was a curious sight to see the great Zulu sitting there upon the floor, his battleaxe resting against the wall behind him, whilst his long aristocratic-looking hands were busily employed, delicately and with the utmost care, cleaning the mechanism of the breech-loaders. He had a name for each gun. One—a double four-bore belonging to Sir Henry—was the Thunderer; another, my 500 Express, which had a peculiarly sharp report, was 'the little one who spoke like a whip'; the Winchester repeaters were 'the women, who talked so fast that you could not tell one word from another'; the six Martinis were 'the common people'; and so on with them all. It was very curious to hear him addressing each gun as he cleaned it, as though it were an individual, and in a vein of the quaintest humour. He did the same with his battle-axe, which he seemed to look upon as an intimate friend, and to which he would at times talk by the hour, going over all his old adventures with it—and dreadful enough some of them were. By a piece of grim humour, he had named this axe 'Inkosi-kaas', which is the Zulu word for chieftainess. For a long while I could not make out why he gave it such a name, and at last I asked him, when he informed me that the axe was very evidently feminine, because of her womanly habit of prying very deep into things, and that she was clearly a chieftainess because all men fell down before her, struck dumb at the sight of her beauty and power. In the same way he would consult 'Inkosi-kaas' if in any dilemma; and when I asked him why he did so, he informed me it was because she must needs be wise, having 'looked into so many people's brains'.

I took up the axe and closely examined this formidable weapon. It was, as I have said, of the nature of a pole-axe. The haft, made out of an enormous rhinoceros horn, was three feet three inches long, about an inch and a quarter thick, and with a knob at the end as large as a Maltese orange, left there to prevent the hand from slipping. This horn haft, though so massive, was as flexible as cane, and practically unbreakable; but, to make assurance doubly sure, it was whipped round at intervals of a few inches with copper wire—all the parts where the hands grip being thus treated. Just above where the haft entered the head were scored a number of little nicks, each nick representing a man killed in battle with the weapon. The axe itself was made of the most beautiful steel, and apparently of European manufacture, though Umslopogaas did not know where it came from, having taken it from the hand of a chief he had killed in battle many years before. It was not very heavy, the head weighing two and a half pounds, as nearly as I could judge. The cutting part was slightly concave in shape—not convex, as it generally the case with savage battleaxes—and sharp as a razor, measuring five and three-quarter inches across the widest part. From the back of the axe sprang a stout spike four inches long, for the last two of which it was hollow, and shaped like a leather punch, with an opening for anything forced into the hollow at the punch end to be pushed out above—in fact, in this respect it exactly resembled a butcher's pole-axe. It was with this punch end, as we afterwards discovered, that Umslopogaas usually struck when fighting, driving a neat round hole in his adversary's skull, and only using the broad cutting edge for a circular sweep, or sometimes in a melee. I think he considered the punch a neater and more sportsmanlike tool, and it was from his habit of pecking at his enemy with it that he got his name of 'Woodpecker'. Certainly in his hands it was a terribly efficient one.

Such was Umslopogaas' axe, Inkosi-kaas, the most remarkable and fatal hand-to-hand weapon that I ever saw, and one which he cherished as much as his own life. It scarcely ever left his hand except when he was eating, and then he always sat with it under his leg.

Just as I returned his axe to Umslopogaas, Miss Flossie came up and took me off to see her collection of flowers, African liliums, and blooming shrubs, some of which are very beautiful, many of the varieties being quite unknown to me and also, I believe, to botanical science. I asked her if she had ever seen or heard of the 'Goya' lily, which Central African explorers have told me they have occasionally met with and whose wonderful loveliness has filled them with astonishment. This lily, which the natives say blooms only once in ten years, flourishes in the most arid soil. Compared to the size of the bloom, the bulb is small, generally weighing about four pounds. As for the flower itself (which I afterwards saw under circumstances likely to impress its appearance fixedly in my mind), I know not how to describe its beauty and splendour, or the indescribable sweetness of its perfume. The flower—for it has only one bloom—rises from the crown of the bulb on a thick fleshy and flat-sided stem, the specimen that I saw measured fourteen inches in diameter, and is somewhat trumpet-shaped like the bloom of an ordinary 'longiflorum' set vertically. First there is the green sheath, which in its early stage is not unlike that of a water-lily, but which as the bloom opens splits into four portions and curls back gracefully towards the stem. Then comes the bloom itself, a single dazzling arch of white enclosing another cup of richest velvety crimson, from the heart of which rises a golden-coloured pistil. I have never seen anything to equal this bloom in beauty or fragrance, and as I believe it is but little known, I take the liberty to describe it at length. Looking at it for the first time I well remember that I realized how even in a flower there dwells something of the majesty of its Maker. To my great delight Miss Flossie told me that she knew the flower well and had tried to grow it in her garden, but without success, adding, however, that as it should be in bloom at this time of the year she thought that she could procure me a specimen.

After that I fell to asking her if she was not lonely up here among all these savage people and without any companions of her own age.

'Lonely?' she said. 'Oh, indeed no! I am as happy as the day is long, and besides I have my own companions. Why, I should hate to be buried in a crowd of white girls all just like myself so that nobody could tell the difference! Here,' she said, giving her head a little toss, 'I am I; and every native for miles around knows the "Water-lily",—for that is what they call me—and is ready to do what I want, but in the books that I have read about little girls in England it is not like that. Everybody thinks them a trouble, and they have to do what their schoolmistress likes. Oh! it would break my heart to be put in a cage like that and not to be free—free as the air.'

'Would you not like to learn?' I asked.

'So I do learn. Father teaches me Latin and French and arithmetic.'

'And are you never afraid among all these wild men?'

'Afraid? Oh no! they never interfere with me. I think they believe that I am "Ngai" (of the Divinity) because I am so white and have fair hair. And look here,' and diving her little hand into the bodice of her dress she produced a double-barrelled nickel-plated Derringer, 'I always carry that loaded, and if anybody tried to touch me I should shoot him. Once I shot a leopard that jumped upon my donkey as I was riding along. It frightened me very much, but I shot it in the ear and it fell dead, and I have its skin upon my bed. Look there!' she went on in an altered voice, touching me on the arm and pointing to some far-away object, 'I said just now that I had companions; there is one of them.'

I looked, and for the first time there burst upon my sight the glory of Mount Kenia. Hitherto the mountain had always been hidden in mist, but now its radiant beauty was unveiled for many thousand feet, although the base was still wrapped in vapour so that the lofty peak or pillar, towering nearly twenty thousand feet into the sky, appeared to be a fairy vision, hanging between earth and heaven, and based upon the clouds. The solemn majesty and beauty of this white peak are together beyond the power of my poor pen to describe. There it rose straight and sheer—a glittering white glory, its crest piercing the very blue of heaven. As I gazed at it with that little girl I felt my whole heart lifted up with an indescribable emotion, and for a moment great and wonderful thoughts seemed to break upon my mind, even as the arrows of the setting sun were breaking upon Kenia's snows. Mr. Mackenzie's natives call the mountain the 'Finger of God', and to me it did seem eloquent of immortal peace and of the pure high calm that surely lies above this fevered world. Somewhere I had heard a line of poetry,

A thing of beauty is a joy for ever,

and now it came into my mind, and for the first time I thoroughly understood what it meant. Base, indeed, would be the man who could look upon that mighty snow-wreathed pile—that white old tombstone of the years—and not feel his own utter insignificance, and, by whatever name he calls Him, worship God in his heart. Such sights are like visions of the spirit; they throw wide the windows of the chamber of our small selfishness and let in a breath of that air that rushes round the rolling spheres, and for a while illumine our darkness with a far-off gleam of the white light which beats upon the Throne.

Yes, such things of beauty are indeed a joy for ever, and I can well understand what little Flossie meant when she talked of Kenia as her companion. As Umslopogaas, savage old Zulu that he was, said when I pointed out to him the peak hanging in the glittering air: 'A man might look thereon for a thousand years and yet be hungry to see.' But he gave rather another colour to his poetical idea when he added in a sort of chant, and with a touch of that weird imagination for which the man was remarkable, that when he was dead he should like his spirit to sit upon that snow-clad peak for ever, and to rush down the steep white sides in the breath of the whirlwind, or on the flash of the lightning, and 'slay, and slay, and slay'.

'Slay what, you old bloodhound?' I asked.

This rather puzzled him, but at length he answered—

'The other shadows.'

'So thou wouldst continue thy murdering even after death?' I said.

'I murder not,' he answered hotly; 'I kill in fair fight. Man is born to kill. He who kills not when his blood is hot is a woman, and no man. The people who kill not are slaves. I say I kill in fair fight; and when I am "in the shadow", as you white men say, I hope to go on killing in fair fight. May my shadow be accursed and chilled to the bone for ever if it should fall to murdering like a bushman with his poisoned arrows!' And he stalked away with much dignity, and left me laughing.

Just then the spies whom our host had sent out in the morning to find out if there were any traces of our Masai friends about, returned, and reported that the country had been scoured for fifteen miles round without a single Elmoran being seen, and that they believed that those gentry had given up the pursuit and returned whence they came. Mr. Mackenzie gave a sigh of relief when he heard this, and so indeed did we, for we had had quite enough of the Masai to last us for some time. Indeed, the general opinion was that, finding we had reached the mission station in safety, they had, knowing its strength, given up the pursuit of us as a bad job. How ill-judged that view was the sequel will show.

After the spies had gone, and Mrs. Mackenzie and Flossie had retired for the night, Alphonse, the little Frenchman, came out, and Sir Henry, who is a very good French scholar, got him to tell us how he came to visit Central Africa, which he did in a most extraordinary lingo, that for the most part I shall not attempt to reproduce.

'My grandfather,' he began, 'was a soldier of the Guard, and served under Napoleon. He was in the retreat from Moscow, and lived for ten days on his own leggings and a pair he stole from a comrade. He used to get drunk—he died drunk, and I remember playing at drums on his coffin. My father—'

Here we suggested that he might skip his ancestry and come to the point.

'Bien, messieurs!' replied this comical little man, with a polite bow. 'I did only wish to demonstrate that the military principle is not hereditary. My grandfather was a splendid man, six feet two high, broad in proportion, a swallower of fire and gaiters. Also he was remarkable for his moustache. To me there remains the moustache and—nothing more.

'I am, messieurs, a cook, and I was born at Marseilles. In that dear town I spent my happy youth. For years and years I washed the dishes at the Hotel Continental. Ah, those were golden days!' and he sighed. 'I am a Frenchman. Need I say, messieurs, that I admire beauty? Nay, I adore the fair. Messieurs, we admire all the roses in a garden, but we pluck one. I plucked one, and alas, messieurs, it pricked my finger. She was a chambermaid, her name Annette, her figure ravishing, her face an angel's, her heart—alas, messieurs, that I should have to own it!—black and slippery as a patent leather boot. I loved to desperation, I adored her to despair. She transported me—in every sense; she inspired me. Never have I cooked as I cooked (for I had been promoted at the hotel) when Annette, my adored Annette, smiled on me. Never'—and here his manly voice broke into a sob—'never shall I cook so well again.' Here he melted into tears.

'Come, cheer up!' said Sir Henry in French, smacking him smartly on the back. 'There's no knowing what may happen, you know. To judge from your dinner today, I should say you were in a fair way to recovery.'

Alphonse stopped weeping, and began to rub his back. 'Monsieur,' he said, 'doubtless means to console, but his hand is heavy. To continue: we loved, and were happy in each other's love. The birds in their little nest could not be happier than Alphonse and his Annette. Then came the blow—sapristi!—when I think of it. Messieurs will forgive me if I wipe away a tear. Mine was an evil number; I was drawn for the conscription. Fortune would be avenged on me for having won the heart of Annette.

'The evil moment came; I had to go. I tried to run away, but I was caught by brutal soldiers, and they banged me with the butt-end of muskets till my mustachios curled with pain. I had a cousin a linen-draper, well-to-do, but very ugly. He had drawn a good number, and sympathized when they thumped me. "To thee, my cousin," I said, "to thee, in whose veins flows the blue blood of our heroic grandparent, to thee I consign Annette. Watch over her whilst I hunt for glory in the bloody field."

"'Make your mind easy,' said he; "I will." As the sequel shows, he did!

'I went. I lived in barracks on black soup. I am a refined man and a poet by nature, and I suffered tortures from the coarse horror of my surroundings. There was a drill sergeant, and he had a cane. Ah, that cane, how it curled! Alas, never can I forget it!

'One morning came the news; my battalion was ordered to Tonquin. The drill sergeant and the other coarse monsters rejoiced. I—I made enquiries about Tonquin. They were not satisfactory. In Tonquin are savage Chinese who rip you open. My artistic tastes—for I am also an artist—recoiled from the idea of being ripped open. The great man makes up his mind quickly. I made up my mind. I determined not to be ripped open. I deserted.

'I reached Marseilles disguised as an old man. I went to the house of my cousin—he in whom runs my grandfather's heroic blood—and there sat Annette. It was the season of cherries. They took a double stalk. At each end was a cherry. My cousin put one into his mouth, Annette put the other in hers. Then they drew the stalks in till their eyes met— and alas, alas that I should have to say it!—they kissed. The game was a pretty one, but it filled me with fury. The heroic blood of my grandfather boiled up in me. I rushed into the kitchen. I struck my cousin with the old man's crutch. He fell—I had slain him. Alas, I believe that I did slay him. Annette screamed. The gendarmes came. I fled. I reached the harbour. I hid aboard a vessel. The vessel put to sea. The captain found me and beat me. He took an opportunity. He posted a letter from a foreign port to the police. He did not put me ashore because I cooked so well. I cooked for him all the way to Zanzibar. When I asked for payment he kicked me. The blood of my heroic grandfather boiled within me, and I shook my fist in his face and vowed to have my revenge. He kicked me again. At Zanzibar there was a telegram. I cursed the man who invented telegraphs. Now I curse him again. I was to be arrested for desertion, for murder, and que sais-je? I escaped from the prison. I fled, I starved. I met the men of Monsieur le Cure. They brought me here. I am full of woe. But I return not to France. Better to risk my life in these horrible places than to know the Bagne.'

He paused, and we nearly choked with laughter, having to turn our faces away.

H. RIDER HAGGARD

'Ah! you weep, messieurs,' he said. 'No wonder—it is a sad story.'

'Perhaps,' said Sir Henry, 'the heroic blood of your grandparent will triumph after all; perhaps you will still be great. At any rate we shall see. And now I vote we go to bed. I am dead tired, and we had not much sleep on that confounded rock last night.'

And so we did, and very strange the tidy rooms and clean white sheets seemed to us after our recent experiences.

V

Umslopogaas Makes a Promise

N ext morning at breakfast I missed Flossie and asked where she
was.

'Well,' said her mother, 'when I got up this morning I found a
note put outside my door in which—But here it is, you can read it for
yourself,' and she gave me the slip of paper on which the following was
written:—

Dearest M—,
    It is just dawn, and I am off to the hills to get Mr. Q—a
bloom of the lily he wants, so don't expect me till you see
me. I have taken the white donkey; and nurse and a couple of
boys are coming with me—also something to eat, as I may be
away all day, for I am determined to get the lily if I have to
go twenty miles for it.

Flossie

'I hope she will be all right,' I said, a little anxiously; 'I never meant
her to trouble after the flower.'

'Ah, Flossie can look after herself,' said her mother; 'she often goes
off in this way like a true child of the wilderness.' But Mr. Mackenzie,
who came in just then and saw the note for the first time, looked rather
grave, though he said nothing.

After breakfast was over I took him aside and asked him whether it
would not be possible to send after the girl and get her back, having in
view the possibility of there still being some Masai hanging about, at
whose hands she might come to harm.

'I fear it would be of no use,' he answered. 'She may be fifteen miles off
by now, and it is impossible to say what path she has taken. There are the
hills;' and he pointed to a long range of rising ground stretching almost
parallel with the course followed by the river Tana, but gradually sloping
down to a dense bush-clad plain about five miles short of the house.

Here I suggested that we might get up the great tree over the
house and search the country round with a spyglass; and this, after

Mr. Mackenzie had given some orders to his people to try and follow Flossie's spoor, we did.

The ascent of the mighty tree was rather an alarming performance, even with a sound rope-ladder fixed at both ends to climb up, at least to a landsman; but Good came up like a lamplighter.

On reaching the height at which the first fern-shaped boughs sprang from the bole, we stepped without any difficulty upon a platform made of boards, nailed from one bough to another, and large enough to accommodate a dozen people. As for the view, it was simply glorious. In every direction the bush rolled away in great billows for miles and miles, as far as the glass would show, only here and there broken by the brighter green of patches of cultivation, or by the glittering surface of lakes. To the northwest, Kenia reared his mighty head, and we could trace the Tana river curling like a silver snake almost from his feet, and far away beyond us towards the ocean. It is a glorious country, and only wants the hand of civilized man to make it a most productive one.

But look as we would, we could see no signs of Flossie and her donkey, so at last we had to come down disappointed. On reaching the veranda I found Umslopogaas sitting there, slowly and lightly sharpening his axe with a small whetstone he always carried with him.

'What doest thou, Umslopogaas?' I asked.

'I smell blood,' was the answer; and I could get no more out of him.

After dinner we again went up the tree and searched the surrounding country with a spyglass, but without result. When we came down Umslopogaas was still sharpening Inkosi-kaas, although she already had an edge like a razor. Standing in front of him, and regarding him with a mixture of fear and fascination, was Alphonse. And certainly he did seem an alarming object—sitting there, Zulu fashion, on his haunches, a wild look upon his intensely savage and yet intellectual face, sharpening, sharpening, sharpening at the murderous-looking axe.

'Oh, the monster, the horrible man!' said the little French cook, lifting his hands in amazement. 'See but the hole in his head; the skin beats on it up and down like a baby's! Who would nurse such a baby?' and he burst out laughing at the idea.

For a moment Umslopogaas looked up from his sharpening, and a sort of evil light played in his dark eyes.

'What does the little "buffalo-heifer" (so named by Umslopogaas, on account of his mustachios and feminine characteristics) say? Let him be careful, or I will cut his horns. Beware, little man monkey, beware!'

Unfortunately Alphonse, who was getting over his fear of him, went on laughing at 'ce drole d'un monsieur noir'. I was about to warn him to desist, when suddenly the huge Zulu bounded off the veranda on to the open space where Alphonse was standing, his features alive with a sort of malicious enthusiasm, and began swinging the axe round and round over the Frenchman's head.

'Stand still,' I shouted; 'do not move as you value your life—he will not hurt you;' but I doubt if Alphonse heard me, being, fortunately for himself, almost petrified with horror.

Then followed the most extraordinary display of sword, or rather of axemanship, that I ever saw. First of all the axe went flying round and round over the top of Alphonse's head, with an angry whirl and such extraordinary swiftness that it looked like a continuous band of steel, ever getting nearer and yet nearer to that unhappy individual's skull, till at last it grazed it as it flew. Then suddenly the motion was changed, and it seemed to literally flow up and down his body and limbs, never more than an eighth of an inch from them, and yet never striking them. It was a wonderful sight to see the little man fixed there, having apparently realized that to move would be to run the risk of sudden death, while his black tormentor towered over him, and wrapped him round with the quick flashes of the axe. For a minute or more this went on, till suddenly I saw the moving brightness travel down the side of Alphonse's face, and then outwards and stop. As it did so a tuft of something black fell to the ground; it was the tip of one of the little Frenchman's curling mustachios.

Umslopogaas leant upon the handle of Inkosi-kaas, and broke into a long, low laugh; and Alphonse, overcome with fear, sank into a sitting posture on the ground, while we stood astonished at this exhibition of almost superhuman skill and mastery of a weapon. 'Inkosi-kaas is sharp enough,' he shouted; 'the blow that clipped the "buffalo-heifer's" horn would have split a man from the crown to the chin. Few could have struck it but I; none could have struck it and not taken off the shoulder too. Look, thou little heifer! Am I a good man to laugh at, thinkest thou? For a space hast thou stood within a hair's-breadth of death. Laugh not again, lest the hair's-breadth be wanting. I have spoken.'

'What meanest thou by such mad tricks?' I asked of Umslopogaas, indignantly. 'Surely thou art mad. Twenty times didst thou go near to slaying the man.'

'And yet, Macumazahn, I slew not. Thrice as Inkosi-kaas flew the spirit entered into me to end him, and send her crashing through his

H. RIDER HAGGARD

skull; but I did not. Nay, it was but a jest; but tell the "heifer" that it is not well to mock at such as I. Now I go to make a shield, for I smell blood, Macumazahn—of a truth I smell blood. Before the battle hast thou not seen the vulture grow of a sudden in the sky? They smell the blood, Macumazahn, and my scent is more keen than theirs. There is a dry ox-hide down yonder; I go to make a shield.'

'That is an uncomfortable retainer of yours,' said Mr. Mackenzie, who had witnessed this extraordinary scene. 'He has frightened Alphonse out of his wits; look!' and he pointed to the Frenchman, who, with a scared white face and trembling limbs, was making his way into the house. 'I don't think that he will ever laugh at "le monsieur noir" again.'

'Yes,' answered I, 'it is ill jesting with such as he. When he is roused he is like a fiend, and yet he has a kind heart in his own fierce way. I remember years ago seeing him nurse a sick child for a week. He is a strange character, but true as steel, and a strong stick to rest on in danger.'

'He says he smells blood,' said Mr. Mackenzie. 'I only trust he is not right. I am getting very fearful about my little girl. She must have gone far, or she would be home by now. It is half-past three o'clock.'

I pointed out that she had taken food with her, and very likely would not in the ordinary course of events return till nightfall; but I myself felt very anxious, and fear that my anxiety betrayed itself.

Shortly after this, the people whom Mr. Mackenzie had sent out to search for Flossie returned, stating that they had followed the spoor of the donkey for a couple of miles and had then lost it on some stony ground, nor could they discover it again. They had, however, scoured the country far and wide, but without success.

After this the afternoon wore drearily on, and towards evening, there still being no signs of Flossie, our anxiety grew very keen. As for the poor mother, she was quite prostrated by her fears, and no wonder, but the father kept his head wonderfully well. Everything that could be done was done: people were sent out in all directions, shots were fired, and a continuous outlook kept from the great tree, but without avail.

And then it grew dark, and still no sign of fair-haired little Flossie.

At eight o'clock we had supper. It was but a sorrowful meal, and Mrs. Mackenzie did not appear at it. We three also were very silent, for in addition to our natural anxiety as to the fate of the child, we were weighed down by the sense that we had brought this trouble on the head of our kind host. When supper was nearly at an end I made an excuse to leave the table. I wanted to get outside and think the situation over. I went on to the veranda and, having lit my pipe, sat down on a seat about a dozen feet from the right-hand end of the structure, which was, as the reader may remember, exactly opposite one of the narrow doors of the protecting wall that enclosed the house and flower garden. I had been sitting there perhaps six or seven minutes when I thought I heard the door move. I looked in that direction and I listened, but, being unable to make out anything, concluded that I must have been mistaken. It was a darkish night, the moon not having yet risen.

Another minute passed, when suddenly something round fell with a soft but heavy thud upon the stone flooring of the veranda, and came bounding and rolling along past me. For a moment I did not rise, but sat wondering what it could be. Finally, I concluded it must have been an animal. Just then, however, another idea struck me, and I got up quick enough. The thing lay quite still a few feet beyond me. I put down my hand towards it and it did not move: clearly it was not an animal. My hand touched it. It was soft and warm and heavy. Hurriedly I lifted it and held it up against the faint starlight.

It was a newly severed human head!

I am an old hand and not easily upset, but I own that that ghastly sight made me feel sick. How had the thing come there? Whose was it? I put it down and ran to the little doorway. I could see nothing, hear nobody. I was about to go out into the darkness beyond, but remembering that to do so was to expose myself to the risk of being stabbed, I drew back, shut the door, and bolted it. Then I returned to the veranda, and in as careless a voice as I could command called Curtis. I fear, however, that my tones must have betrayed me, for not only Sir Henry but also Good and Mackenzie rose from the table and came hurrying out.

'What is it?' said the clergyman, anxiously.

Then I had to tell them.

Mr. Mackenzie turned pale as death under his red skin. We were standing opposite the hall door, and there was a light in it so that I could see. He snatched the head up by the hair and held it against the light.

'It is the head of one of the men who accompanied Flossie,' he said with a gasp. 'Thank God it is not hers!'

We all stood and stared at each other aghast. What was to be done?

Just then there was a knocking at the door that I had bolted, and a voice cried, 'Open, my father, open!'

The door was unlocked, and in sped a terrified man. He was one of the spies who had been sent out.

'My father,' he cried, 'the Masai are on us! A great body of them have passed round the hill and are moving towards the old stone kraal down by the little stream. My father, make strong thy heart! In the midst of them I saw the white ass, and on it sat the Water-lily (Flossie). An Elmoran (young warrior) led the ass, and by its side walked the nurse weeping. The men who went with her in the morning I saw not.'

'Was the child alive?' asked Mr. Mackenzie, hoarsely.

'She was white as the snow, but well, my father. They passed quite close to me, and looking up from where I lay hid I saw her face against the sky.'

'God help her and us!' groaned the clergyman.

'How many are there of them?' I asked.

'More than two hundred—two hundred and half a hundred.'

Once more we looked one on the other. What was to be done? Just then there rose a loud insistent cry outside the wall.

'Open the door, white man; open the door! A herald—a herald to speak with thee.' Thus cried the voice.

Umslopogaas ran to the wall, and, reaching with his long arms to the coping, lifted his head above it and gazed over.

'I see but one man,' he said. 'He is armed, and carries a basket in his hand.'

'Open the door,' I said. 'Umslopogaas, take thine axe and stand thereby. Let one man pass. If another follows, slay.'

The door was unbarred. In the shadow of the wall stood Umslopogaas, his axe raised above his head to strike. Just then the moon came out. There was a moment's pause, and then in stalked a Masai Elmoran, clad in the full war panoply that I have already described, but bearing a large basket in his hand. The moonlight shone bright upon his great spear as he walked. He was physically a splendid man, apparently about thirty-five years of age. Indeed, none of the Masai that I saw were under six feet high, though mostly quite young. When he got opposite to us he halted, put down the basket, and stuck the spike of his spear into the ground, so that it stood upright.

'Let us talk,' he said. 'The first messenger we sent to you could not talk;' and he pointed to the head which lay upon the paving of the stoep—a ghastly sight in the moonlight; 'but I have words to speak if ye have ears to hear. Also I bring presents;' and he pointed to the basket and laughed with an air of swaggering insolence that is perfectly indescribable, and yet which one could not but admire, seeing that he was surrounded by enemies.

'Say on,' said Mr. Mackenzie.

'I am the "Lygonani" (war captain) of a party of the Masai of the Guasa Amboni. I and my men followed these three white men,' and he pointed to Sir Henry, Good, and myself, 'but they were too clever for us, and escaped hither. We have a quarrel with them, and are going to kill them.'

'Are you, my friend?' said I to myself.

'In following these men we this morning caught two black men, one black woman, a white donkey, and a white girl. One of the black men we killed—there is his head upon the pavement; the other ran away. The black woman, the little white girl, and the white ass we took and brought with us. In proof thereof have I brought this basket that she carried. Is it not thy daughter's basket?'

Mr. Mackenzie nodded, and the warrior went on.

'Good! With thee and thy daughter we have no quarrel, nor do we wish to harm thee, save as to thy cattle, which we have already gathered, two hundred and forty head—a beast for every man's father.'

Here Mr. Mackenzie gave a groan, as he greatly valued this herd of cattle, which he bred with much care and trouble.

'So, save for the cattle, thou mayst go free; more especially,' he added frankly, glancing at the wall, 'as this place would be a difficult one to take. But as to these men it is otherwise; we have followed them for nights and days, and must kill them. Were we to return to our kraal without having done so, all the girls would make a mock of us. So, however troublesome it may be, they must die.

'Now I have a proposition for thee. We would not harm the little girl; she is too fair to harm, and has besides a brave spirit. Give us one of these three men—a life for a life—and we will let her go, and throw in the black woman with her also. This is a fair offer, white man. We ask but for one, not for the three; we must take another opportunity to kill the other two. I do not even pick my man, though I should prefer the big one,' pointing to Sir Henry; 'he looks strong, and would die more slowly.'

'And if I say I will not yield the man?' said Mr. Mackenzie.

'Nay, say not so, white man,' answered the Masai, 'for then thy daughter dies at dawn, and the woman with her says thou hast no other child. Were she older I would take her for a servant; but as she is so young I will slay her with my own hand—ay, with this very spear. Thou canst come and see, an' thou wilt. I give thee a safe conduct;' and the fiend laughed aloud as his brutal jest.

Meanwhile I had been thinking rapidly, as one does in emergencies, and had come to the conclusion that I would exchange myself against Flossie. I scarcely like to mention the matter for fear it should be misunderstood. Pray do not let any one be misled into thinking that there was anything heroic about this, or any such nonsense. It was merely a matter of common sense and common justice. My life was an old and worthless one, hers was young and valuable. Her death would pretty well kill her father and mother also, whilst nobody would be much the worse for mine; indeed, several charitable institutions would have cause to rejoice thereat. It was indirectly through me that the dear little girl was in her present position. Lastly, a man was better fitted to meet death in such a peculiarly awful form than a sweet young girl. Not, however, that I meant to let these gentry torture me to death—I am far too much of a coward to allow that, being naturally a timid man; my plan was to see the girl safely exchanged and then to shoot myself, trusting that the Almighty would take the peculiar circumstances of the case into consideration and pardon the act. All this and more went through my mind in very few seconds.

'All right, Mackenzie,' I said, 'you can tell the man that I will exchange myself against Flossie, only I stipulate that she shall be safely in this house before they kill me.'

'Eh?' said Sir Henry and Good simultaneously. 'That you don't.'

'No, no,' said Mr. Mackenzie. 'I will have no man's blood upon my hands. If it please God that my daughter should die this awful death, His will be done. You are a brave man (which I am not by any means) and a noble man, Quatermain, but you shall not go.'

'If nothing else turns up I shall go,' I said decidedly.

'This is an important matter,' said Mackenzie, addressing the Lygonani, 'and we must think it over. You shall have our answer at dawn.'

'Very well, white man,' answered the savage indifferently; 'only remember if thy answer is late thy little white bud will never grow into a flower, that is all, for I shall cut it with this,' and he touched the spear. 'I should have thought that thou wouldst play a trick and attack us at night, but I know from the woman with the girl that your men are down at the coast, and that thou hast but twenty men here. It is not wise, white man,' he added with a laugh, 'to keep so small a garrison for your "boma" (kraal). Well, good night, and good night to you also, other white men, whose eyelids I shall soon close once and for all. At dawn thou wilt bring me word. If not, remember it shall be as I have said.' Then turning to Umslopogaas, who had all the while been standing behind him and shepherding him as it were, 'Open the door for me, fellow, quick now.'

This was too much for the old chief's patience. For the last ten minutes his lips had been, figuratively speaking, positively watering over the Masai Lygonani, and this he could not stand. Placing his long hand on the Elmoran's shoulder he gripped it and gave him such a twist as brought him face to face with himself. Then, thrusting his fierce countenance to within a few inches of the Masai's evil feather-framed features, he said in a low growling voice:—

'Seest thou me?'

'Ay, fellow, I see thee.'

'And seest thou this?' and he held Inkosi-kaas before his eyes.

'Ay, fellow, I see the toy; what of it?'

'Thou Masai dog, thou boasting windbag, thou capturer of little girls, with this "toy" will I hew thee limb from limb. Well for thee that thou art a herald, or even now would I strew thy members about the grass.'

The Masai shook his great spear and laughed loud and long as he answered, 'I would that thou stoodst against me man to man, and we would see,' and again he turned to go still laughing.

'Thou shalt stand against me man to man, be not afraid,' replied Umslopogaas, still in the same ominous voice. 'Thou shalt stand face to face with Umslopogaas, of the blood of Chaka, of the people of the Amazulu, a captain in the regiment of the Nkomabakosi, as many have done before, and bow thyself to Inkosi-kaas, as many have done before. Ay, laugh on, laugh on! tomorrow night shall the jackals laugh as they crunch thy ribs.'

When the Lygonani had gone, one of us thought of opening the basket he had brought as a proof that Flossie was really their prisoner. On lifting the lid it was found to contain a most lovely specimen of both bulb and flower of the Goya lily, which I have already described, in full bloom and quite uninjured, and what was more a note in Flossie's

H. RIDER HAGGARD

childish hand written in pencil upon a greasy piece of paper that had been used to wrap up some food in:—

> 'Dearest Father and Mother,' ran the note, 'The Masai caught us when we were coming home with the lily. I tried to escape but could not. They killed Tom: the other man ran away. They have not hurt nurse and me, but say that they mean to exchange us against one of Mr. Quatermain's party. *I will have nothing of the sort*. Do not let anybody give his life for me. Try and attack them at night; they are going to feast on three bullocks they have stolen and killed. I have my pistol, and if no help comes by dawn I will shoot myself. They shall not kill me. If so, remember me always, dearest father and mother. I am very frightened, but I trust in God. I dare not write any more as they are beginning to notice. Goodbye.
>
> Flossie

Scrawled across the outside of this was 'Love to Mr. Quatermain. They are going to take the basket, so he will get the lily.'

When I read those words, written by that brave little girl in an hour of danger sufficiently near and horrible to have turned the brain of a strong man, I own I wept, and once more in my heart I vowed that she should not die while my life could be given to save her.

Then eagerly, quickly, almost fiercely, we fell to discussing the situation. Again I said that I would go, and again Mackenzie negatived it, and Curtis and Good, like the true men that they are, vowed that, if I did, they would go with me, and die back to back with me.

'It is,' I said at last, 'absolutely necessary that an effort of some sort should be made before the morning.'

'Then let us attack them with what force we can muster, and take our chance,' said Sir Henry.

'Ay, ay,' growled Umslopogaas, in Zulu; 'spoken like a man, Incubu. What is there to be afraid of? Two hundred and fifty Masai, forsooth! How many are we? The chief there (Mr. Mackenzie) has twenty men, and thou, Macumazahn, hast five men, and there are also five white men—that is, thirty men in all—enough, enough. Listen now, Macumazahn, thou who art very clever and old in war. What says the maid? These men eat and make merry; let it be their funeral feast. What said the dog whom I hope to hew down at daybreak? That he feared no attack because we were so few. Knowest thou the old kraal where the men have camped? I saw it this morning; it is thus:' and he drew an oval on the floor; 'here is the big entrance, filled up with thorn bushes, and opening on to a steep rise. Why, Incubu, thou and I with axes will hold it against an hundred men striving to break out! Look, now; thus shall the battle go. Just as the light begins to glint upon the oxen's horns—not before, or it will be too dark, and not later, or they will be awakening and perceive us—let Bougwan creep round with ten men to the top end of the kraal, where the narrow entrance is. Let them silently slay the sentry there so that he makes no sound, and stand ready. Then, Incubu, let thee and me and one of the Askari—the one with the broad chest—he is a brave man—creep to the wide entrance that is filled with thorn bushes, and there also slay the sentry, and armed with battleaxes take our stand also one on each side of the pathway, and one a few paces beyond to deal with such as pass the twain at the gate. It is there that the rush will come. That will leave sixteen men. Let these men be divided into two parties, with one of which shalt thou go, Macumazahn, and with one the "praying man" (Mr. Mackenzie), and, all armed with rifles, let them make their way one to the right side of the kraal and one to the left; and when thou, Macumazahn, lowest like an ox, all shall open fire with the guns upon the sleeping men, being very careful not to hit the little maid. Then shall Bougwan at the far end and his ten men raise the war-cry, and, springing over the wall, put the Masai there to the sword. And it shall happen that, being yet heavy with food and sleep, and bewildered by the firing of the guns, the falling of men, and the spears of Bougwan, the soldiers shall rise and rush like wild game towards the thorn-stopped entrance, and there the bullets from either side shall plough through them, and there shall Incubu and the Askari and I wait for those who break across. Such is my plan, Macumazahn; if thou hast a better, name it.'

When he had done, I explained to the others such portions of his scheme as they had failed to understand, and they all joined with me in expressing the greatest admiration of the acute and skilful programme devised by the old Zulu, who was indeed, in his own savage fashion, the finest general I ever knew. After some discussion we determined to accept the scheme, as it stood, it being the only one possible under the circumstances, and giving the best chance of success that such a forlorn hope would admit of—which, however, considering the enormous odds and the character of our foe, was not very great.

'Ah, old lion!' I said to Umslopogaas, 'thou knowest how to lie in wait as well as how to bite, where to seize as well as where to hang on.'

'Ay, ay, Macumazahn,' he answered. 'For thirty years have I been a warrior, and have seen many things. It will be a good fight. I smell blood—I tell thee, I smell blood.'

VI

THE NIGHT WEARS ON

A s may be imagined, at the very first sign of a Masai the entire population of the Mission Station had sought refuge inside the stout stone wall, and were now to be seen—men, women, and countless children—huddled up together in little groups, and all talking at once in awed tones of the awfulness of Masai manners and customs, and of the fate that they had to expect if those bloodthirsty savages succeeded in getting over the stone wall.

Immediately after we had settled upon the outline of our plan of action as suggested by Umslopogaas, Mr. Mackenzie sent for four sharp boys of from twelve to fifteen years of age, and despatched them to various points where they could keep an outlook upon the Masai camp, with others to report from time to time what was going on. Other lads and even women were stationed at intervals along the wall in order to guard against the possibility of surprise.

After this the twenty men who formed his whole available fighting force were summoned by our host into the square formed by the house, and there, standing by the bole of the great conifer, he earnestly addressed them and our four Askari. Indeed, it formed a very impressive scene—one not likely to be forgotten by anybody who witnessed it. Immediately by the tree stood the angular form of Mr. Mackenzie, one arm outstretched as he talked, and the other resting against the giant bole, his hat off, and his plain but kindly face clearly betraying the anguish of his mind. Next to him was his poor wife, who, seated on a chair, had her face hidden in her hand. On the other side of her was Alphonse, looking exceedingly uncomfortable, and behind him stood the three of us, with Umslopogaas' grim and towering form in the background, resting, as usual, on his axe. In front stood and squatted the group of armed men—some with rifles in their hands, and others with spears and shields—following with eager attention every word that fell from the speaker's lips. The white light of the moon peering in beneath the lofty boughs threw a strange wild glamour over the scene, whilst the melancholy soughing of the night wind passing through the millions of pine needles overhead added a sadness of its own to what was already a sufficiently tragic occasion.

'Men,' said Mr. Mackenzie, after he had put all the circumstances of the case fully and clearly before them, and explained to them the proposed plan of our forlorn hope—'men, for years I have been a good friend to you, protecting you, teaching you, guarding you and yours from harm, and ye have prospered with me. Ye have seen my child—the Water-lily, as ye call her—grow year by year, from tenderest infancy to tender childhood, and from childhood on towards maidenhood. She has been your children's playmate, she has helped to tend you when sick, and ye have loved her.'

'We have,' said a deep voice, 'and we will die to save her.'

'I thank you from my heart—I thank you. Sure am I that now, in this hour of darkest trouble; now that her young life is like to be cut off by cruel and savage men—who of a truth "know not what they do"—ye will strive your best to save her, and to save me and her mother from broken hearts. Think, too, of your own wives and children. If she dies, her death will be followed by an attack upon us here, and at the best, even if we hold our own, your houses and gardens will be destroyed, and your goods and cattle swept away. I am, as ye well know, a man of peace. Never in all these years have I lifted my hand to shed man's blood; but now I say strike, strike, in the name of God, Who bade us protect our lives and homes. Swear to me,' he went on with added fervour—'swear to me that whilst a man of you remains alive ye will strive your uttermost with me and with these brave white men to save the child from a bloody and cruel death.'

'Say no more, my father,' said the same deep voice, that belonged to a stalwart elder of the Mission; 'we swear it. May we and ours die the death of dogs, and our bones be thrown to the jackals and the kites, if we break the oath! It is a fearful thing to do, my father, so few to strike at so many, yet will we do it or die in the doing. We swear!'

'Ay, thus say we all,' chimed in the others.

'Thus say we all,' said I.

'It is well,' went on Mr. Mackenzie. 'Ye are true men and not broken reeds to lean on. And now, friends—white and black together—let us kneel and offer up our humble supplication to the Throne of Power, praying that He in the hollow of Whose hand lie all our lives, Who giveth life and giveth death, may be pleased to make strong our arms that we may prevail in what awaits us at the morning's light.'

And he knelt down, an example that we all followed except Umslopogaas, who still stood in the background, grimly leaning on

Inkosi-kaas. The fierce old Zulu had no gods and worshipped nought, unless it were his battleaxe.

'Oh God of gods!' began the clergyman, his deep voice, tremulous with emotion, echoing up in the silence even to the leafy roof; 'Protector of the oppressed, Refuge of those in danger, Guardian of the helpless, hear Thou our prayer! Almighty Father, to Thee we come in supplication. Hear Thou our prayer! Behold, one child hast Thou given us—an innocent child, nurtured in Thy knowledge—and now she lies beneath the shadow of the sword, in danger of a fearful death at the hands of savage men. Be with her now, oh God, and comfort her! Save her, oh Heavenly Father! Oh God of battle, Who teacheth our hands to war and our fingers to fight, in Whose strength are hid the destinies of men, be Thou with us in the hour of strife. When we go forth into the shadow of death, make Thou us strong to conquer. Breathe Thou upon our foes and scatter them; turn Thou their strength to water, and bring their high-blown pride to nought; compass us about with Thy protection; throw over us the shield of Thy power; forget us not now in the hour of our sore distress; help us now that the cruel man would dash our little ones against the stones! Hear Thou our prayer! And for those of us who, kneeling now on earth in health before Thee, shall at the sunrise adore Thy Presence on the Throne, hear our prayer! Make them clean, oh God; wash away their offences in the blood of the Lamb; and when their spirits pass, oh receive Thou them into the haven of the just. Go forth, oh Father, go forth with us into the battle, as with the Israelites of old. Oh God of battle, hear Thou our prayer!'

He ceased, and after a moment's silence we all rose, and then began our preparations in good earnest. As Umslopogaas said, it was time to stop 'talking' and get to business. The men who were to form each little party were carefully selected, and still more carefully and minutely instructed as to what was to be done. After much consideration it was agreed that the ten men led by Good, whose duty it was to stampede the camp, were not to carry firearms; that is, with the exception of Good himself, who had a revolver as well as a short sword—the Masai 'sime' which I had taken from the body of our poor servant who was murdered in the canoe. We feared that if they had firearms the result of three cross-fires carried on at once would be that some of our own people would be shot; besides, it appeared to all of us that the work they had to do would best be carried out with cold steel—especially to Umslopogaas, who was, indeed, a great advocate of cold steel. We had with us four Winchester repeating rifles, besides half a dozen Martinis. I armed myself with one of the repeaters—my own; an excellent weapon for this kind of work, where great rapidity of fire is desirable, and fitted with ordinary flap-sights instead of the cumbersome sliding mechanism which they generally have. Mr. Mackenzie took another, and the two remaining ones were given to two of his men who understood the use of them and were noted shots. The Martinis and some rifles of Mr. Mackenzie's were served out, together with a plentiful supply of ammunition, to the other natives who were to form the two parties whose duty it was to be to open fire from separate sides of the kraal on the sleeping Masai, and who were fortunately all more or less accustomed to the use of a gun.

As for Umslopogaas, we know how he was armed—with an axe. It may be remembered that he, Sir Henry, and the strongest of the Askari were to hold the thorn-stopped entrance to the kraal against the anticipated rush of men striving to escape. Of course, for such a purpose as this guns were useless. Therefore Sir Henry and the Askari proceeded to arm themselves in like fashion. It so happened that Mr. Mackenzie had in his little store a selection of the very best and English-made hammer-backed axe-heads. Sir Henry selected one of these weighing about two and a half pounds and very broad in the blade, and the Askari took another a size smaller. After Umslopogaas had put an extra edge on these two axe-heads, we fixed them to three feet six helves, of which Mr. Mackenzie fortunately had some in stock, made of a light but exceedingly tough native wood, something like English ash, only more springy. When two suitable helves had been selected with great care and the ends of the hafts notched to prevent the hand from slipping, the axe-heads were fixed on them as firmly as possible, and the weapons immersed in a bucket of water for half an hour. The result of this was to swell the wood in the socket in such a fashion that nothing short of burning would get it out again. When this important matter had been attended to by Umslopogaas, I went into my room and proceeded to open a little tin-lined deal case, which contained—what do you think?—nothing more or less than four mail shirts.

It had happened to us three on a previous journey that we had made in another part of Africa to owe our lives to iron shirts of native make, and remembering this, I had suggested before we started on our present hazardous expedition that we should have some made to fit us. There was a little difficulty about this, as armour-making is pretty well an extinct art, but they can do most things in the way of steel work in

Birmingham if they are put to it and you will pay the price, and the end of it was that they turned us out the loveliest steel shirts it is possible to see. The workmanship was exceedingly fine, the web being composed of thousands upon thousands of stout but tiny rings of the best steel made. These shirts, or rather steel-sleeved and high-necked jerseys, were lined with ventilated wash leather, were not bright, but browned like the barrel of a gun; and mine weighed exactly seven pounds and fitted me so well that I found I could wear it for days next to my skin without being chafed. Sir Henry had two, one of the ordinary make, viz. a jersey with little dependent flaps meant to afford some protection to the upper part of the thighs, and another of his own design fashioned on the pattern of the garments advertised as 'combinations' and weighing twelve pounds. This combination shirt, of which the seat was made of wash-leather, protected the whole body down to the knees, but was rather more cumbersome, inasmuch as it had to be laced up at the back and, of course, involved some extra weight. With these shirts were what looked like four brown cloth travelling caps with ear pieces. Each of these caps was, however, quilted with steel links so as to afford a most valuable protection for the head.

It seems almost laughable to talk of steel shirts in these days of bullets, against which they are of course quite useless; but where one has to do with savages, armed with cutting weapons such as assegais or battleaxes, they afford the most valuable protection, being, if well made, quite invulnerable to them. I have often thought that if only the English Government had in our savage wars, and more especially in the Zulu war, thought fit to serve out light steel shirts, there would be many a man alive today who, as it is, is dead and forgotten.

To return: on the present occasion we blessed our foresight in bringing these shirts, and also our good luck, in that they had not been stolen by our rascally bearers when they ran away with our goods. As Curtis had two, and after considerable deliberation, had made up his mind to wear his combination one himself—the extra three or four pounds' weight being a matter of no account to so strong a man, and the protection afforded to the thighs being a very important matter to a fighting man not armed with a shield of any kind—I suggested that he should lend the other to Umslopogaas, who was to share the danger and the glory of his post. He readily consented, and called the Zulu, who came bearing Sir Henry's axe, which he had now fixed up to his satisfaction, with him. When we showed him the steel shirt, and explained to him that we wanted him to wear it, he at first declined, saying that he had fought in his own skin for thirty years, and that he was not going to begin now to fight in an iron one. Thereupon I took a heavy spear, and, spreading the shirt upon the floor, drove the spear down upon it with all my strength, the weapon rebounding without leaving a mark upon the tempered steel. This exhibition half converted him; and when I pointed out to him how necessary it was that he should not let any old-fashioned prejudices he might possess stand in the way of a precaution which might preserve a valuable life at a time when men were scarce, and also that if he wore this shirt he might dispense with a shield, and so have both hands free, he yielded at once, and proceeded to invest his frame with the 'iron skin'. And indeed, although made for Sir Henry, it fitted the great Zulu like a skin. The two men were almost of a height; and, though Curtis looked the bigger man, I am inclined to think that the difference was more imaginary than real, the fact being that, although he was plumper and rounder, he was not really bigger, except in the arm. Umslopogaas had, comparatively speaking, thin arms, but they were as strong as wire ropes. At any rate, when they both stood, axe in hand, invested in the brown mail, which clung to their mighty forms like a web garment, showing the swell of every muscle and the curve of every line, they formed a pair that any ten men might shrink from meeting.

It was now nearly one o'clock in the morning, and the spies reported that, after having drunk the blood of the oxen and eaten enormous quantities of meat, the Masai were going to sleep round their watchfires; but that sentries had been posted at each opening of the kraal. Flossie, they added, was sitting not far from the wall in the centre of the western side of the kraal, and by her were the nurse and the white donkey, which was tethered to a peg. Her feet were bound with a rope, and warriors were lying about all round her.

As there was absolutely nothing further that could be done then we all took some supper, and went to lie down for a couple of hours. I could not help admiring the way in which old Umslopogaas flung himself upon the floor, and, unmindful of what was hanging over him, instantly sank into a deep sleep. I do not know how it was with the others, but I could not do as much. Indeed, as is usual with me on these occasions, I am sorry to say that I felt rather frightened; and, now that some of the enthusiasm had gone out of me, and I began to calmly contemplate what we had undertaken to do, truth compels me to add that I did not like it. We were but thirty men all told, a good many of whom were no doubt quite unused to fighting, and we were going to engage two hundred and fifty of the fiercest, bravest, and most formidable savages in Africa, who, to make matters worse, were protected by a stone wall. It was, indeed, a mad undertaking, and what made it even madder was the exceeding improbability of our being able to take up our positions without attracting the notice of the sentries. Of course if we once did that—and any slight accident, such as the chance discharge of a gun, might do it—we were done for, for the whole camp would be up in a second, and our only hope lay in surprise.

The bed whereon I lay indulging in these uncomfortable reflections was near an open window that looked on to the veranda, through which came an extraordinary sound of groaning and weeping. For a time I could not make out what it was, but at last I got up and, putting my head out of the window, stared about. Presently I saw a dim figure kneeling on the end of the veranda and beating his breast—in which I recognized Alphonse. Not being able to understand his French talk or what on earth he was at, I called to him and asked him what he was doing.

'Ah, monsieur,' he sighed, 'I do make prayer for the souls of those whom I shall slay tonight.'

'Indeed,' I said, 'then I wish that you would do it a little more quietly.'

Alphonse retreated, and I heard no more of his groans. And so the time passed, till at length Mr. Mackenzie called me in a whisper through the window, for of course everything had now to be done in the most absolute silence. 'Three o'clock,' he said: 'we must begin to move at half-past.'

I told him to come in, and presently he entered, and I am bound to say that if it had not been that just then I had not got a laugh anywhere about me, I should have exploded at the sight he presented armed for battle. To begin with, he had on a clergyman's black swallow-tail and a kind of broad-rimmed black felt hat, both of which he had donned on account, he said, of their dark colour. In his hand was the Winchester repeating rifle we had lent him; and stuck in an elastic cricketing belt, like those worn by English boys, were, first, a huge buckhorn-handled carving knife with a guard to it, and next a long-barrelled Colt's revolver.

'Ah, my friend,' he said, seeing me staring at his belt, 'you are looking at my "carver". I thought it might come in handy if we came to close quarters; it is excellent steel, and many is the pig I have killed with it.'

By this time everybody was up and dressing. I put on a light Norfolk jacket over my mail shirt in order to have a pocket handy to hold my cartridges, and buckled on my revolver. Good did the same, but Sir Henry put on nothing except his mail shirt, steel-lined cap, and a pair of 'veldt-schoons' or soft hide shoes, his legs being bare from the knees down. His revolver he strapped on round his middle outside the armoured shirt.

Meanwhile Umslopogaas was mustering the men in the square under the big tree and going the rounds to see that each was properly armed, etc. At the last moment we made one change. Finding that two of the men who were to have gone with the firing parties knew little or nothing of guns, but were good spearsmen, we took away their rifles, supplied them with shields and long spears of the Masai pattern, and took them off to join Curtis, Umslopogaas, and the Askari in holding the wide opening; it having become clear to us that three men, however brave and strong, were too few for the work.

VII

A Slaughter Grim and Great

Then there was a pause, and we stood there in the chilly silent darkness waiting till the moment came to start. It was, perhaps, the most trying time of all—that slow, slow quarter of an hour. The minutes seemed to drag along with leaden feet, and the quiet, the solemn hush, that brooded over all—big, as it were, with a coming fate, was most oppressive to the spirits. I once remember having to get up before dawn to see a man hanged, and I then went through a very similar set of sensations, only in the present instance my feelings were animated by that more vivid and personal element which naturally appertains rather to the person to be operated on than to the most sympathetic spectator. The solemn faces of the men, well aware that the short passage of an hour would mean for some, and perhaps all of them, the last great passage to the unknown or oblivion; the bated whispers in which they spoke; even Sir Henry's continuous and thoughtful examination of his woodcutter's axe and the fidgety way in which Good kept polishing his eyeglass, all told the same tale of nerves stretched pretty nigh to breaking-point. Only Umslopogaas, leaning as usual upon Inkosi-kaas and taking an occasional pinch of snuff, was to all appearance perfectly and completely unmoved. Nothing could touch his iron nerves.

The moon went down. For a long while she had been getting nearer and nearer to the horizon. Now she finally sank and left the world in darkness save for a faint grey tinge in the eastern sky that palely heralded the dawn.

Mr. Mackenzie stood, watch in hand, his wife clinging to his arm and striving to stifle her sobs.

'Twenty minutes to four,' he said, 'it ought to be light enough to attack at twenty minutes past four. Captain Good had better be moving, he will want three or four minutes' start.'

Good gave one final polish to his eyeglass, nodded to us in a jocular sort of way—which I could not help feeling it must have cost him something to muster up—and, ever polite, took off his steel-lined cap to Mrs. Mackenzie and started for his position at the head of the kraal, to reach which he had to make a detour by some paths known to the natives.

Just then one of the boys came in and reported that everybody in the Masai camp, with the exception of the two sentries who were walking up and down in front of the respective entrances, appeared to be fast asleep. Then the rest of us took the road. First came the guide, then Sir Henry, Umslopogaas, the Wakwafi Askari, and Mr. Mackenzie's two mission natives armed with long spears and shields. I followed immediately after with Alphonse and five natives all armed with guns, and Mr. Mackenzie brought up the rear with the six remaining natives.

The cattle kraal where the Masai were camped lay at the foot of the hill on which the house stood, or, roughly speaking, about eight hundred yards from the Mission buildings. The first five hundred yards of this distance we traversed quietly indeed, but at a good pace; after that we crept forward as silently as a leopard on his prey, gliding like ghosts from bush to bush and stone to stone. When I had gone a little way I chanced to look behind me, and saw the redoubtable Alphonse staggering along with white face and trembling knees, and his rifle, which was at full cock, pointed directly at the small of my back. Having halted and carefully put the rifle at 'safety', we started again, and all went well till we were within one hundred yards or so of the kraal, when his teeth began to chatter in the most aggressive way.

'If you don't stop that I will kill you,' I whispered savagely; for the idea of having all our lives sacrificed to a tooth-chattering cook was too much for me. I began to fear that he would betray us, and heartily wished we had left him behind.

'But, monsieur, I cannot help it,' he answered, 'it is the cold.'

Here was a dilemma, but fortunately I devised a plan. In the pocket of the coat I had on was a small piece of dirty rag that I had used some time before to clean a gun with. 'Put this in your mouth,' I whispered again, giving him the rag; 'and if I hear another sound you are a dead man.' I knew that that would stifle the clatter of his teeth. I must have looked as if I meant what I said, for he instantly obeyed me, and continued his journey in silence.

Then we crept on again.

At last we were within fifty yards of the kraal. Between us and it was an open space of sloping grass with only one mimosa bush and a couple of tussocks of a sort of thistle for cover. We were still hidden in fairly thick bush. It was beginning to grow light. The stars had paled and a sickly gleam played about the east and was reflected on the earth. We could see the outline of the kraal clearly enough, and could also make out the faint glimmer of the dying embers of the Masai campfires. We halted and watched, for the sentry we knew was posted at the opening. Presently he appeared, a fine tall fellow, walking idly up and down within five paces of the thorn-stopped entrance. We had hoped to catch him napping, but it was not to be. He seemed particularly wide awake. If we could not kill that man, and kill him silently, we were lost. There we crouched and watched him. Presently Umslopogaas, who was a few paces ahead of me, turned and made a sign, and next second I saw him go down on his stomach like a snake, and, taking an opportunity when the sentry's head was turned, begin to work his way through the grass without a sound.

The unconscious sentry commenced to hum a little tune, and Umslopogaas crept on. He reached the shelter of the mimosa bush unperceived and there waited. Still the sentry walked up and down. Presently he turned and looked over the wall into the camp. Instantly the human snake who was stalking him glided on ten yards and got behind one of the tussocks of the thistle-like plant, reaching it as the Elmoran turned again. As he did so his eye fell upon this patch of thistles, and it seemed to strike him that it did not look quite right. He advanced a pace towards it—halted, yawned, stooped down, picked up a little pebble and threw it at it. It hit Umslopogaas upon the head, luckily not upon the armour shirt. Had it done so the clink would have betrayed us. Luckily, too, the shirt was browned and not bright steel, which would certainly have been detected. Apparently satisfied that there was nothing wrong, he then gave over his investigations and contented himself with leaning on his spear and standing gazing idly at the tuft. For at least three minutes did he stand thus, plunged apparently in a gentle reverie, and there we lay in the last extremity of anxiety, expecting every moment that we should be discovered or that some untoward accident would happen. I could hear Alphonse's teeth going like anything on the oiled rag, and turning my head round made an awful face at him. But I am bound to state that my own heart was at much the same game as the Frenchman's castanets, while the perspiration was pouring from my body, causing the wash-leather-lined shirt to stick to me unpleasantly, and altogether I was in the pitiable state known by schoolboys as a 'blue fright'.

At last the ordeal came to an end. The sentry glanced at the east, and appeared to note with satisfaction that his period of duty was coming to an end—as indeed it was, once and for all—for he rubbed his hands and began to walk again briskly to warm himself.

The moment his back was turned the long black snake glided on again, and reached the other thistle tuft, which was within a couple of paces of his return beat.

Back came the sentry and strolled right past the tuft, utterly unconscious of the presence that was crouching behind it. Had he looked down he could scarcely have failed to see, but he did not do so.

He passed, and then his hidden enemy erected himself, and with outstretched hand followed in his tracks.

A moment more, and, just as the Elmoran was about to turn, the great Zulu made a spring, and in the growing light we could see his long lean hands close round the Masai's throat. Then followed a convulsive twining of the two dark bodies, and in another second I saw the Masai's head bent back, and heard a sharp crack, something like that of a dry twig snapping, and he fell down upon the ground, his limbs moving spasmodically.

Umslopogaas had put out all his iron strength and broken the warrior's neck.

For a moment he knelt upon his victim, still gripping his throat till he was sure that there was nothing more to fear from him, and then he rose and beckoned to us to advance, which we did on all fours, like a colony of huge apes. On reaching the kraal we saw that the Masai had still further choked this entrance, which was about ten feet wide—no doubt in order to guard against attack—by dragging four or five tops of mimosa trees up to it. So much the better for us, I reflected; the more obstruction there was the slower would they be able to come through. Here we separated; Mackenzie and his party creeping up under the shadow of the wall to the left, while Sir Henry and Umslopogaas took their stations one on each side of the thorn fence, the two spearmen and the Askari lying down in front of it. I and my men crept on up the right side of the kraal, which was about fifty paces long.

When I was two-thirds up I halted, and placed my men at distances of four paces from one another, keeping Alphonse close to me, however. Then I peeped for the first time over the wall. It was getting fairly light now, and the first thing I saw was the white donkey, exactly opposite to me, and close by it I could make out the pale face of little Flossie, who was sitting as the lad had described, some ten paces from the wall. Round her lay many warriors, sleeping. At distances all over the surface of the kraal were the remains of fires, round each of which slept some five-and-twenty Masai, for the most part gorged with food. Now and then a man would raise himself, yawn, and look at the east, which was turning primrose; but none got up. I determined to wait another five minutes, both to allow the light to increase, so that we could make better shooting, and to give Good and his party—of whom we could see or hear nothing—every opportunity to make ready.

The quiet dawn began to throw her ever-widening mantle over plain and forest and river—mighty Kenia, wrapped in the silence of eternal snows, looked out across the earth—till presently a beam from the unrisen sun lit upon his heaven-kissing crest and purpled it with blood; the sky above grew blue, and tender as a mother's smile; a bird began to pipe his morning song, and a little breeze passing through the bush shook down the dewdrops in millions to refresh the waking world. Everywhere was peace and the happiness of arising strength, everywhere save in the heart of cruel man!

Suddenly, just as I was nerving myself for the signal, having already selected my man on whom I meant to open fire—a great fellow sprawling on the ground within three feet of little Flossie—Alphonse's teeth began to chatter again like the hoofs of a galloping giraffe, making a great noise in the silence. The rag had dropped out in the agitation of his mind. Instantly a Masai within three paces of us woke, and, sitting up, gazed about him, looking for the cause of the sound. Moved beyond myself, I brought the butt-end of my rifle down on to the pit of the Frenchman's stomach. This stopped his chattering; but, as he doubled up, he managed to let off his gun in such a manner that the bullet passed within an inch of my head.

There was no need for a signal now. From both sides of the kraal broke out a waving line of fire, in which I myself joined, managing with a snap shot to knock over my Masai by Flossie, just as he was jumping up. Then from the top end of the kraal there rang an awful yell, in which I rejoiced to recognize Good's piercing notes rising clear and shrill above the din, and in another second followed such a scene as I have never seen before nor shall again. With an universal howl of terror and fury the brawny crowd of savages within the kraal sprang to their feet, many of them to fall again beneath our well-directed hail of lead before they had moved a yard. For a moment they stood undecided, and then hearing the cries and curses that rose unceasingly from the top end of the kraal, and bewildered by the storm of bullets, they as by one impulse rushed down towards the thorn-stopped entrance. As they went we kept pouring our fire with terrible effect into the thickening mob as fast as we could load. I had emptied my repeater of the ten shots it contained and was just beginning to slip in some more when I bethought me of little Flossie. Looking up, I saw that the white donkey was lying kicking, having been knocked over either by one of our bullets or a Masai spear-thrust. There were no living Masai near, but the black nurse was on her feet and with a spear cutting the rope that bound Flossie's feet. Next second she ran to the wall of the kraal and began to climb over it, an example which the little girl followed. But Flossie was evidently very stiff and cramped, and could only go slowly, and as she went two Masai flying down the kraal caught sight of her and rushed towards her to kill her. The first fellow came up just as the poor little girl, after a desperate effort to climb the wall, fell back into the kraal. Up flashed the great spear, and as it did so a bullet from my rifle found its home in the holder's ribs, and over he went like a shot rabbit. But behind him was the other man, and, alas, I had only that one cartridge in the magazine! Flossie had scrambled to her feet and was facing the second man, who was advancing with raised spear. I turned my head aside and felt sick as death. I could not bear to see him stab her. Glancing up again, to my surprise I saw the Masai's spear lying on the ground, while the man himself was staggering about with both hands to his head. Suddenly I saw a puff of smoke proceeding apparently from Flossie, and the man fell down headlong. Then I remembered the Derringer pistol she carried, and saw that she had fired both barrels of it at him, thereby saving her life. In another instant she had made an effort, and assisted by the nurse, who was lying on the top, had scrambled over the wall, and I knew that she was, comparatively speaking, safe.

All this takes time to tell, but I do not suppose that it took more than fifteen seconds to enact. I soon got the magazine of the repeater filled again with cartridges, and once more opened fire, not on the seething black mass which was gathering at the end of the kraal, but on fugitives who bethought them to climb the wall. I picked off several of these men, moving down towards the end of the kraal as I did so, and arriving at the corner, or rather the bend of the oval, in time to see, and by means of my rifle to assist in, the mighty struggle that took place there.

By this time some two hundred Masai—allowing that we had up to the present accounted for fifty—had gathered together in front of the thorn-stopped entrance, driven thither by the spears of Good's men, whom they doubtless supposed were a large force instead of being but ten strong. For some reason it never occurred to them to try and rush the wall, which they could have scrambled over with comparative ease; they all made for the fence, which was really a strongly interwoven fortification. With a bound the first warrior went at it, and even before he touched the ground on the other side I saw Sir Henry's great axe swing up and fall with awful force upon his feather head-piece, and he sank into the middle of the thorns. Then with a yell and a crash they began to break through as they might, and ever as they came the great axe swung and Inkosi-kaas flashed and they fell dead one by one, each man thus helping to build up a barrier against his fellows. Those who escaped the axes of the pair fell at the hands of the Askari and the two Mission Kaffirs, and those who passed scatheless from them were brought low by my own and Mackenzie's fire.

Faster and more furious grew the fighting. Single Masai would spring upon the dead bodies of their comrades, and engage one or other of the axemen with their long spears; but, thanks chiefly to the mail shirts, the result was always the same. Presently there was a great swing of the axe, a crashing sound, and another dead Masai. That is, if the man was engaged with Sir Henry. If it was Umslopogaas that he fought with the result indeed would be the same, but it would be differently attained. It was but rarely that the Zulu used the crashing double-handed stroke; on the contrary, he did little more than tap continually at his adversary's head, pecking at it with the pole-axe end of the axe as a woodpecker pecks at rotten wood. Presently a peck would go home, and his enemy would drop down with a neat little circular hole in his forehead or skull, exactly similar to that which a cheese-scoop makes in a cheese. He never used the broad blade of the axe except when hard pressed, or when striking at a shield. He told me afterwards that he did not consider it sportsmanlike.

Good and his men were quite close by now, and our people had to cease firing into the mass for fear of killing some of them (as it was, one of them was slain in this way). Mad and desperate with fear, the Masai by a frantic effort burst through the thorn fence and piled-up dead, and, sweeping Curtis, Umslopogaas, and the other three before them, into the open. And now it was that we began to lose men fast.

Down went our poor Askari who was armed with the axe, a great spear standing out a foot behind his back; and before long the two spearsmen who had stood with him went down too, dying fighting like tigers; and others of our party shared their fate. For a moment I feared the fight was lost—certainly it trembled in the balance. I shouted to my men to cast down their rifles, and to take spears and throw themselves into the melee. They obeyed, their blood being now thoroughly up, and Mr. Mackenzie's people followed their example.

This move had a momentary good result, but still the fight hung in the balance.

Our people fought magnificently, hurling themselves upon the dark mass of Elmoran, hewing, thrusting, slaying, and being slain. And ever above the din rose Good's awful yell of encouragement as he plunged to wherever the fight was thickest; and ever, with an almost machine-like regularity, the two axes rose and fell, carrying death and disablement at every stroke. But I could see that the strain was beginning to tell upon Sir Henry, who was bleeding from several flesh wounds: his breath was coming in gasps, and the veins stood out on his forehead like blue and knotted cords. Even Umslopogaas, man of iron that he was, was hard pressed. I noticed that he had given up 'woodpecking', and was now using the broad blade of Inkosi-kaas, 'browning' his enemy wherever he could hit him, instead of drilling scientific holes in his head. I myself did not go into the melee, but hovered outside like the swift 'back' in a football scrimmage, putting a bullet through a Masai whenever I got a chance. I was more use so. I fired forty-nine cartridges that morning, and I did not miss many shots.

Presently, do as we would, the beam of the balance began to rise against us. We had not more than fifteen or sixteen effectives left now, and the Masai had at least fifty. Of course if they had kept their heads, and shaken themselves together, they could soon have made an end of the matter; but that is just what they did not do, not having yet recovered from their start, and some of them having actually fled from their sleeping-places without their weapons. Still by now many individuals were fighting with their normal courage and discretion, and this alone was sufficient to defeat us. To make matters worse just then, when Mackenzie's rifle was empty, a brawny savage armed with a 'sime', or sword, made a rush for him. The clergyman flung down his gun, and drawing his huge carver from his elastic belt (his revolver had dropped out in the fight), they closed in desperate struggle. Presently, locked in a close embrace, missionary and Masai rolled on the ground behind the wall, and for some time I, being amply occupied with my own affairs, and in keeping my skin from being pricked, remained in ignorance of his fate or how the duel had ended.

To and fro surged the fight, slowly turning round like the vortex of a human whirlpool, and the matter began to look very bad for us. Just then, however, a fortunate thing happened. Umslopogaas, either by accident or design, broke out of the ring and engaged a warrior at some few paces from it. As he did so, another man ran up and struck him with all his force between his shoulders with his great spear, which, falling on the tough steel shirt, failed to pierce it and rebounded. For a moment the man stared aghast—protective armour being unknown among these tribes—and then he yelled out at the top of his voice—

'*They are devils—bewitched, bewitched!*' And seized by a sudden panic, he threw down his spear, and began to fly. I cut short his career with a bullet, and Umslopogaas brained his man, and then the panic spread to the others.

'*Bewitched, bewitched!*' they cried, and tried to escape in every direction, utterly demoralized and broken-spirited, for the most part even throwing down their shields and spears.

On the last scene of that dreadful fight I need not dwell. It was a slaughter great and grim, in which no quarter was asked or given. One incident, however, is worth detailing. Just as I was hoping that it was all done with, suddenly from under a heap of slain where he had been hiding, an unwounded warrior sprang up, and, clearing the piles of dying dead like an antelope, sped like the wind up the kraal towards the spot where I was standing at the moment. But he was not alone, for Umslopogaas came gliding on his tracks with the peculiar swallow-like motion for which he was noted, and as they neared me I recognized in the Masai the herald of the previous night. Finding that, run as he would, his pursuer was gaining on him, the man halted and turned round to give battle. Umslopogaas also pulled up.

'Ah, ah,' he cried, in mockery, to the Elmoran, 'it is thou whom I talked with last night—the Lygonani! the Herald! the capturer of little girls—he who would kill a little girl! And thou didst hope to stand man to man and face to face with Umslopogaas, an Induna of the tribe of the Maquilisini, of the people of the Amazulu? Behold, thy prayer is granted! And I didst swear to hew thee limb from limb, thou insolent dog. Behold, I will do it even now!'

The Masai ground his teeth with fury, and charged at the Zulu with his spear. As he came, Umslopogaas deftly stepped aside, and swinging Inkosi-kaas high above his head with both hands, brought the broad blade down with such fearful force from behind upon the Masai's shoulder just where the neck is set into the frame, that its razor edge shore right through bone and flesh and muscle, almost severing the head and one arm from the body.

'*Ou!*' exclaimed Umslopogaas, contemplating the corpse of his foe; 'I have kept my word. It was a good stroke.'

VIII

Alphonse Explains

A nd so the fight was ended. On returning from the shocking scene it suddenly struck me that I had seen nothing of Alphonse since the moment, some twenty minutes before—for though this fight has taken a long while to describe, it did not take long in reality—when I had been forced to hit him in the wind with the result of nearly getting myself shot. Fearing that the poor little man had perished in the battle, I began to hunt among the dead for his body, but, not being able either to see or hear anything of it, I concluded that he must have survived, and walked down the side of the kraal where we had first taken our stand, calling him by name. Now some fifteen paces back from the kraal wall stood a very ancient tree of the banyan species. So ancient was it that all the inside had in the course of ages decayed away, leaving nothing but a shell of bark.

'Alphonse,' I called, as I walked down the wall. 'Alphonse!'

'Oui, monsieur,' answered a voice. 'Here am I.'

I looked round but could see nobody. 'Where?' I cried.

'Here am I, monsieur, in the tree.'

I looked, and there, peering out of a hole in the trunk of the banyan about five feet from the ground, I saw a pale face and a pair of large mustachios, one clipped short and the other as lamentably out of curl as the tail of a newly whipped pug. Then, for the first time, I realized what I had suspected before—namely, that Alphonse was an arrant coward. I walked up to him. 'Come out of that hole,' I said.

'Is it finished, monsieur?' he asked anxiously; 'quite finished? Ah, the horrors I have undergone, and the prayers I have uttered!'

'Come out, you little wretch,' I said, for I did not feel amiable; 'it is all over.'

'So, monsieur, then my prayers have prevailed? I emerge,' and he did.

As we were walking down together to join the others, who were gathered in a group by the wide entrance to the kraal, which now resembled a veritable charnel-house, a Masai, who had escaped so far and been hiding under a bush, suddenly sprang up and charged furiously at us. Off went Alphonse with a howl of terror, and after him flew the Masai, bent upon doing some execution before he died. He soon overtook the poor little Frenchman, and would have finished him then and there had I not, just as Alphonse made a last agonized double in the vain hope of avoiding the yard of steel that was flashing in his immediate rear, managed to plant a bullet between the Elmoran's broad shoulders, which brought matters to a satisfactory conclusion so far as the Frenchman was concerned. But just then he tripped and fell flat, and the body of the Masai fell right on the top of him, moving convulsively in the death struggle. Thereupon there arose such a series of piercing howls that I concluded that before he died the savage must have managed to stab poor Alphonse. I ran up in a hurry and pulled the Masai off, and there beneath him lay Alphonse covered with blood and jerking himself about like a galvanized frog. Poor fellow! thought I, he is done for, and kneeling down by him I began to search for his wound as well as his struggles would allow.

'Oh, the hole in my back!' he yelled. 'I am murdered. I am dead. Oh, Annette!'

I searched again, but could see no wound. Then the truth dawned on me—the man was frightened, not hurt.

'Get up!' I shouted, 'Get up. Aren't you ashamed of yourself? You are not touched.'

Thereupon he rose, not a penny the worse. 'But, monsieur, I thought I was,' he said apologetically; 'I did not know that I had conquered.' Then, giving the body of the Masai a kick, he exclaimed triumphantly, 'Ah, dog of a black savage, thou art dead; what victory!'

Thoroughly disgusted, I left Alphonse to look after himself, which he did by following me like a shadow, and proceeded to join the others by the large entrance. The first thing that I saw was Mackenzie, seated on a stone with a handkerchief twisted round his thigh, from which he was bleeding freely, having, indeed, received a spear-thrust that passed right through it, and still holding in his hand his favourite carving knife now bent nearly double, from which I gathered that he had been successful in his rough and tumble with the Elmoran.

'Ah, Quatermain!' he sang out in a trembling, excited voice, 'so we have conquered; but it is a sorry sight, a sorry sight;' and then breaking into broad Scotch and glancing at the bent knife in his hand, 'It fashes me sair to have bent my best carver on the breastbone of a savage,' and he laughed hysterically. Poor fellow, what between his wound and the killing excitement he had undergone his nerves were much shaken, and no wonder! It is hard upon a man of peace and kindly heart to be called upon to join in such a gruesome business. But there, fate puts us sometimes into very comical positions!

At the kraal entrance the scene was a strange one. The slaughter was over by now, and the wounded men had been put out of their pain, for no quarter had been given. The bush-closed entrance was trampled flat, and in place of bushes it was filled with the bodies of dead men. Dead men, everywhere dead men—they lay about in knots, they were flung by ones and twos in every position upon the open spaces, for all the world like the people on the grass in one of the London parks on a particularly hot Sunday in August. In front of this entrance, on a space which had been cleared of dead and of the shields and spears which were scattered in all directions as they had fallen or been thrown from the hands of their owners, stood and lay the survivors of the awful struggle, and at their feet were four wounded men. We had gone into the fight thirty strong, and of the thirty but fifteen remained alive, and five of them (including Mr. Mackenzie) were wounded, two mortally. Of those who held the entrance, Curtis and the Zulu alone remained. Good had lost five men killed, I had lost two killed, and Mackenzie no less than five out of the six with him. As for the survivors they were, with the exception of myself who had never come to close quarters, red from head to foot—Sir Henry's armour might have been painted that colour—and utterly exhausted, except Umslopogaas, who, as he grimly stood on a little mound above a heap of dead, leaning as usual upon his axe, did not seem particularly distressed, although the skin over the hole in his head palpitated violently.

'Ah, Macumazahn!' he said to me as I limped up, feeling very sick, 'I told thee that it would be a good fight, and it has. Never have I seen a better, or one more bravely fought. As for this iron shirt, surely it is "tagati" (bewitched); nothing could pierce it. Had it not been for the garment I should have been *there*,' and he nodded towards the great pile of dead men beneath him.

'I give it thee; thou art a brave man,' said Sir Henry, briefly.

'Koos!' answered the Zulu, deeply pleased both at the gift and the compliment. 'Thou, too, Incubu, didst bear thyself as a man, but I must give thee some lessons with the axe; thou dost waste thy strength.'

Just then Mackenzie asked about Flossie, and we were all greatly relieved when one of the men said he had seen her flying towards the house with the nurse. Then bearing such of the wounded as could be moved at the moment with us, we slowly made our way towards the Mission-house, spent with toil and bloodshed, but with the glorious sense of victory against overwhelming odds glowing in our hearts. We had saved the life of the little maid, and taught the Masai of those parts a lesson that they will not forget for ten years—but at what a cost!

Painfully we made our way up the hill which, just a little more than an hour before, we had descended under such different circumstances. At the gate of the wall stood Mrs. Mackenzie waiting for us. When her eyes fell upon us, however, she shrieked out, and covered her face with her hands, crying, 'Horrible, horrible!' Nor were her fears allayed when she discovered her worthy husband being borne upon an improvized stretcher; but her doubts as to the nature of his injury were soon set at rest. Then when in a few brief words I had told her the upshot of the struggle (of which Flossie, who had arrived in safety, had been able to explain something) she came up to me and solemnly kissed me on the forehead.

'God bless you all, Mr. Quatermain; you have saved my child's life,' she said simply.

Then we went in and got our clothes off and doctored our wounds; I am glad to say I had none, and Sir Henry's and Good's were, thanks to those invaluable chain shirts, of a comparatively harmless nature, and to be dealt with by means of a few stitches and sticking-plaster. Mackenzie's, however, were serious, though fortunately the spear had not severed any large artery. After that we had a bath, and what a luxury it was! And having clad ourselves in ordinary clothes, proceeded to the dining-room, where breakfast was set as usual. It was curious sitting down there, drinking tea and eating toast in an ordinary nineteenth-century sort of way just as though we had not employed the early hours in a regular primitive hand-to-hand Middle-Ages kind of struggle. As Good said, the whole thing seemed more as though one had had a bad nightmare just before being called, than as a deed done. When we were finishing our breakfast the door opened, and in came little Flossie, very pale and tottery, but quite unhurt. She kissed us all and thanked us. I congratulated her on the presence of mind she had shown in shooting the Masai with her Derringer pistol, and thereby saving her own life.

'Oh, don't talk of it!' she said, beginning to cry hysterically; 'I shall never forget his face as he went turning round and round, never—I can see it now.'

I advised her to go to bed and get some sleep, which she did, and awoke in the evening quite recovered, so far as her strength was concerned. It struck me as an odd thing that a girl who could find the nerve to shoot a huge black ruffian rushing to kill her with a spear should have been so affected at the thought of it afterwards; but it is, after all, characteristic of the sex. Poor Flossie! I fear that her nerves will not get over that night in the Masai camp for many a long year. She told me afterwards that it was the suspense that was so awful, having to sit there hour after hour through the livelong night utterly ignorant as to whether or not any attempt was to be made to rescue her. She said that on the whole she did not expect it, knowing how few of us, and how many of the Masai—who, by the way, came continually to stare at her, most of them never having seen a white person before, and handled her arms and hair with their filthy paws. She said also that she had made up her mind that if she saw no signs of succour by the time the first rays of the rising sun reached the kraal she would kill herself with the pistol, for the nurse had heard the Lygonani say that they were to be tortured to death as soon as the sun was up if one of the white men did not come in their place. It was an awful resolution to have to take, but she meant to act on it, and I have little doubt but what she would have done so. Although she was at an age when in England girls are in the schoolroom and come down to dessert, this 'child of the wilderness' had more courage, discretion, and power of mind than many a woman of mature age nurtured in idleness and luxury, with minds carefully drilled and educated out of any originality or self-resource that nature may have endowed them with.

When breakfast was over we all turned in and had a good sleep, only getting up in time for dinner; after which meal we once more adjourned, together with all the available population—men, women, youths, and girls—to the scene of the morning's slaughter, our object being to bury our own dead and get rid of the Masai by flinging them into the Tana River, which ran within fifty yards of the kraal. On reaching the spot we disturbed thousands upon thousands of vultures and a sort of brown bush eagle, which had been flocking to the feast from miles and miles away. Often have I watched these great and repulsive birds, and marvelled at the extraordinary speed with which they arrive on a scene of slaughter. A buck falls to your rifle, and within a minute high in the blue ether appears a speck that gradually grows into a vulture, then another, and another. I have heard many theories advanced to account for the wonderful power of perception nature has given these birds. My own, founded on a good deal of observation, is that the vultures, gifted as they are with powers of sight greater than those given by the most powerful glass, quarter out the heavens among themselves, and hanging in mid-air at a vast height—probably from two to three miles above the earth—keep watch, each of them, over an enormous stretch of country. Presently one of them spies food, and instantly begins to sink towards it. Thereon his next neighbour in the airy heights sailing leisurely through the blue gulf, at a distance perhaps of some miles, follows his example, knowing that food has been sighted. Down he goes, and all the vultures within sight of him follow after, and so do all those in sight of them. In this way the vultures for twenty miles round can be summoned to the feast in a few minutes.

We buried our dead in solemn silence, Good being selected to read the Burial Service over them (in the absence of Mr. Mackenzie, confined to bed), as he was generally allowed to possess the best voice and most impressive manner. It was melancholy in the extreme, but, as Good said, it might have been worse, for we might have had 'to bury ourselves'. I pointed out that this would have been a difficult feat, but I knew what he meant.

Next we set to work to load an ox-wagon which had been brought round from the Mission with the dead bodies of the Masai, having first collected the spears, shields, and other arms. We loaded the wagon five times, about fifty bodies to the load, and emptied it into the Tana. From this it was evident that very few of the Masai could have escaped. The crocodiles must have been well fed that night. One of the last bodies we picked up was that of the sentry at the upper end. I asked Good how he managed to kill him, and he told me that he had crept up much as Umslopogaas had done, and stabbed him with his sword. He groaned a good deal, but fortunately nobody heard him. As Good said, it was a horrible thing to have to do, and most unpleasantly like cold-blooded murder.

And so with the last body that floated away down the current of the Tana ended the incident of our attack on the Masai camp. The spears and shields and other arms we took up to the Mission, where they filled an outhouse. One incident, however, I must not forget to mention. As we were returning from performing the obsequies of our Masai friends we passed the hollow tree where Alphonse had secreted himself in the morning. It so happened that the little man himself was with us assisting in our unpleasant task with a far better will than he had shown where live Masai were concerned. Indeed, for each body that he handled he found an appropriate sarcasm. Alphonse throwing Masai into the Tana was a very different creature from Alphonse flying for dear life from the spear of a live Masai. He was quite merry and gay, he clapped his hands and warbled snatches of French songs as the grim dead warriors went 'splash' into the running waters to carry a message of death and defiance to their kindred a hundred miles below. In short, thinking that he wanted taking down a peg, I suggested holding a court-martial on him for his conduct in the morning.

Accordingly we brought him to the tree where he had hidden, and proceeded to sit in judgment on him, Sir Henry explaining to him in the very best French the unheard-of cowardice and enormity of his conduct, more especially in letting the oiled rag out of his mouth, whereby he nearly aroused the Masai camp with teeth-chattering and brought about the failure of our plans: ending up with a request for an explanation.

But if we expected to find Alphonse at a loss and put him to open shame we were destined to be disappointed. He bowed and scraped and smiled, and acknowledged that his conduct might at first blush appear strange, but really it was not, inasmuch as his teeth were not chattering from fear—oh, dear no! oh, certainly not! he marvelled how the 'messieurs' could think of such a thing—but from the chill air of the morning. As for the rag, if monsieur could have but tasted its evil flavour, being compounded indeed of a mixture of stale paraffin oil, grease, and gunpowder, monsieur himself would have spat it out. But he did nothing of the sort; he determined to keep it there till, alas! his stomach 'revolted', and the rag was ejected in an access of involuntary sickness.

'And what have you to say about getting into the hollow tree?' asked Sir Henry, keeping his countenance with difficulty.

'But, monsieur, the explanation is easy; oh, most easy! it was thus: I stood there by the kraal wall, and the little grey monsieur hit me in the stomach so that my rifle exploded, and the battle began. I watched whilst recovering myself from monsieur's cruel blow; then, messieurs, I felt the heroic blood of my grandfather boil up in my veins. The sight made me mad. I ground my teeth! Fire flashed from my eyes! I shouted "En avant!" and longed to slay. Before my eyes there rose a vision of my heroic grandfather! In short, I was mad! I was a warrior indeed!

But then in my heart I heard a small voice: "Alphonse," said the voice, "restrain thyself, Alphonse! Give not way to this evil passion! These men, though black, are brothers! And thou wouldst slay them? Cruel Alphonse!" The voice was right. I knew it; I was about to perpetrate the most horrible cruelties: to wound! to massacre! to tear limb from limb! And how restrain myself? I looked round; I saw the tree, I perceived the hole. "Entomb thyself," said the voice, "and hold on tight! Thou wilt thus overcome temptation by main force!" It was bitter, just when the blood of my heroic grandfather boiled most fiercely; but I obeyed! I dragged my unwilling feet along; I entombed myself! Through the hole I watched the battle! I shouted curses and defiance on the foe! I noted them fall with satisfaction! Why not? I had not robbed them of their lives. Their gore was not upon my head. The blood of my heroic—'

'Oh, get along with you, you little cur!' broke out Sir Henry, with a shout of laughter, and giving Alphonse a good kick which sent him flying off with a rueful face.

In the evening I had an interview with Mr. Mackenzie, who was suffering a good deal from his wounds, which Good, who was a skilful though unqualified doctor, was treating him for. He told me that this occurrence had taught him a lesson, and that, if he recovered safely, he meant to hand over the Mission to a younger man, who was already on his road to join him in his work, and return to England.

'You see, Quatermain,' he said, 'I made up my mind to it, this very morning, when we were creeping down those benighted savages. "If we live through this and rescue Flossie alive," I said to myself, "I will go home to England; I have had enough of savages." Well, I did not think that we should live through it at the time; but thanks be to God and you four, we have lived through it, and I mean to stick to my resolution, lest a worse thing befall us. Another such time would kill my poor wife. And besides, Quatermain, between you and me, I am well off; it is thirty thousand pounds I am worth today, and every farthing of it made by honest trade and savings in the bank at Zanzibar, for living here costs me next to nothing. So though it will be hard to leave this place, which I have made to blossom like a rose in the wilderness, and harder still to leave the people I have taught, I shall go.'

'I congratulate you on your decision,' answered I, 'for two reasons. The first is, that you owe a duty to your wife and daughter, and more especially to the latter, who should receive some education and mix with girls of her own race, otherwise she will grow up wild, shunning her kind. The other is, that as sure as I am standing here, sooner or later the Masai will try to avenge the slaughter inflicted on them today. Two or three men are sure to have escaped the confusion who will carry the story back to their people, and the result will be that a great expedition will one day be sent against you. It might be delayed for a year, but sooner or later it will come. Therefore, if only for that reason, I should go. When once they have learnt that you are no longer here they may perhaps leave the place alone.'

'You are quite right,' answered the clergyman. 'I will turn my back upon this place in a month. But it will be a wrench, it will be a wrench.'

IX

Into the Unknown

A week had passed, and we all sat at supper one night in the Mission dining-room, feeling very much depressed in spirits, for the reason that we were going to say goodbye to our kind friends, the Mackenzies, and depart upon our way at dawn on the morrow. Nothing more had been seen or heard of the Masai, and save for a spear or two which had been overlooked and was rusting in the grass, and a few empty cartridges where we had stood outside the wall, it would have been difficult to tell that the old cattle kraal at the foot of the slope had been the scene of so desperate a struggle. Mackenzie was, thanks chiefly to his being so temperate a man, rapidly recovering from his wound, and could get about on a pair of crutches; and as for the other wounded men, one had died of gangrene, and the rest were in a fair way to recovery. Mr. Mackenzie's caravan of men had also returned from the coast, so that the station was now amply garrisoned.

Under these circumstances we concluded, warm and pressing as were the invitations for us to stay, that it was time to move on, first to Mount Kenia, and thence into the unknown in search of the mysterious white race which we had set our hearts on discovering. This time we were going to progress by means of the humble but useful donkey, of which we had collected no less than a dozen, to carry our goods and chattels, and, if necessary, ourselves. We had now but two Wakwafis left for servants, and found it quite impossible to get other natives to venture with us into the unknown parts we proposed to explore—and small blame to them. After all, as Mr. Mackenzie said, it was odd that three men, each of whom possessed many of those things that are supposed to make life worth living—health, sufficient means, and position, etc.—should from their own pleasure start out upon a wild-goose chase, from which the chances were they never would return. But then that is what Englishmen are, adventurers to the backbone; and all our magnificent muster-roll of colonies, each of which will in time become a great nation, testify to the extraordinary value of the spirit of adventure which at first sight looks like a mild form of lunacy. 'Adventurer'—he that goes out to meet whatever may come. Well, that is what we all do in the world one way or another, and, speaking for myself, I am proud of the title, because it implies a brave heart and a trust in Providence. Besides, when many and many a noted Croesus, at whose feet the people worship, and many and many a time-serving and word-coining politician are forgotten, the names of those grand-hearted old adventurers who have made England what she is, will be remembered and taught with love and pride to little children whose unshaped spirits yet slumber in the womb of centuries to be. Not that we three can expect to be numbered with such as these, yet have we done something—enough, perhaps, to throw a garment over the nakedness of our folly.

That evening, whilst we were sitting on the veranda, smoking a pipe before turning in, who should come up to us but Alphonse, and, with a magnificent bow, announce his wish for an interview. Being requested to 'fire away', he explained at some length that he was anxious to attach himself to our party—a statement that astonished me not a little, knowing what a coward the little man was. The reason, however, soon appeared. Mr. Mackenzie was going down to the coast, and thence on to England. Now, if he went down country, Alphonse was persuaded that he would be seized, extradited, sent to France, and to penal servitude. This was the idea that haunted him, as King Charles's head haunted Mr. Dick, and he brooded over it till his imagination exaggerated the danger ten times. As a matter of fact, the probability is that his offence against the laws of his country had long ago been forgotten, and that he would have been allowed to pass unmolested anywhere except in France; but he could not be got to see this. Constitutional coward as the little man was, he infinitely preferred to face the certain hardships and great risks and dangers of such an expedition as ours, than to expose himself, notwithstanding his intense longing for his native land, to the possible scrutiny of a police officer—which is after all only another exemplification of the truth that, to the majority of men, a far-off foreseen danger, however shadowy, is much more terrible than the most serious present emergency. After listening to what he had to say, we consulted among ourselves, and finally agreed, with Mr. Mackenzie's knowledge and consent, to accept his offer. To begin with, we were very short-handed, and Alphonse was a quick, active fellow, who could turn his hand to anything, and cook—ah, he *could* cook! I believe that he would have made a palatable dish of those gaiters of his heroic grandfather which he was so fond of talking about. Then he was a good-tempered little man, and merry as a monkey, whilst his pompous, vainglorious talk was a source of infinite amusement to us; and what is more, he never bore malice. Of course, his being so pronounced a coward was a great drawback to him, but now that we knew his weakness we could more or less guard against it. So, after warning him of the undoubted risks he was exposing himself to, we told him that we would accept his offer on condition that he would promise implicit obedience to our orders. We also promised to give him wages at the rate of ten pounds a month should he ever return to a civilized country to receive them. To all of this he agreed with alacrity, and retired to write a letter to his Annette, which Mr. Mackenzie promised to post when he got down country. He read it to us afterwards, Sir Henry translating, and a wonderful composition it was. I am sure the depth of his devotion and the narration of his sufferings in a barbarous country, 'far, far from thee, Annette, for whose adored sake I endure such sorrow,' ought to have touched the feelings of the stoniest-hearted chambermaid.

Well, the morrow came, and by seven o'clock the donkeys were all loaded, and the time of parting was at hand. It was a melancholy business, especially saying goodbye to dear little Flossie. She and I were great friends, and often used to have talks together—but her nerves had never got over the shock of that awful night when she lay in the power of those bloodthirsty Masai. 'Oh, Mr. Quatermain,' she cried, throwing her arms round my neck and bursting into tears, 'I can't bear to say goodbye to you. I wonder when we shall meet again?'

'I don't know, my dear little girl,' I said, 'I am at one end of life and you are at the other. I have but a short time before me at best, and most things lie in the past, but I hope that for you there are many long and happy years, and everything lies in the future. By-and-by you will grow into a beautiful woman, Flossie, and all this wild life will be like a far-off dream to you; but I hope, even if we never do meet again, that you will think of your old friend and remember what I say to you now. Always try to be good, my dear, and to do what is right, rather than what happens to be pleasant, for in the end, whatever sneering people may say, what is good and what is happy are the same. Be unselfish, and whenever you can, give a helping hand to others—for the world is full of suffering, my dear, and to alleviate it is the noblest end that we can set before us. If you do that you will become a sweet and God-fearing woman, and make many people's lives a little brighter, and then you will not have lived, as so many of your sex do, in vain. And now I have given you a lot of old-fashioned advice, and so I am going to give you something to sweeten it with. You see this little piece of paper. It is what is called a cheque. When we are gone give it to your father with this note—not before, mind. You will marry one day, my dear little Flossie, and it is to buy you a wedding present which you are to wear, and your daughter after you, if you have one, in remembrance of Hunter Quatermain.'

Poor little Flossie cried very much, and gave me a lock of her bright hair in return, which I still have. The cheque I gave her was for a thousand pounds (which being now well off, and having no calls upon me except those of charity, I could well afford), and in the note I directed her father to invest it for her in Government security, and when she married or came of age to buy her the best diamond necklace he could get for the money and accumulated interest. I chose diamonds because I think that now that King Solomon's Mines are lost to the world, their price will never be much lower than it is at present, so that if in after-life she should ever be in pecuniary difficulties, she will be able to turn them into money.

Well, at last we got off, after much hand-shaking, hat-waving, and also farewell saluting from the natives, Alphonse weeping copiously (for he has a warm heart) at parting with his master and mistress; and I was not sorry for it at all, for I hate those goodbyes. Perhaps the most affecting thing of all was to witness Umslopogaas' distress at parting with Flossie, for whom the grim old warrior had conceived a strong affection. He used to say that she was as sweet to see as the only star on a dark night, and was never tired of loudly congratulating himself on having killed the Lygonani who had threatened to murder her. And that was the last we saw of the pleasant Mission-house—a true oasis in the desert—and of European civilization. But I often think of the Mackenzies, and wonder how they got down country, and if they are now safe and well in England, and will ever see these words. Dear little Flossie! I wonder how she fares there where there are no black folk to do her imperious bidding, and no sky-piercing snow-clad Kenia for her to look at when she gets up in the morning. And so goodbye to Flossie.

After leaving the Mission-house we made our way, comparatively unmolested, past the base of Mount Kenia, which the Masai call 'Donyo Egere', or the 'speckled mountain', on account of the black patches of rock that appear upon its mighty spire, where the sides are too precipitous to allow of the snow lying on them; then on past the lonely lake Baringo, where one of our two remaining Askari, having unfortunately trodden on a puff-adder, died of snake-bite, in spite of all our efforts to save him. Thence we proceeded a distance of about a hundred and fifty miles to another magnificent snow-clad mountain called Lekakisera, which has never, to the best of my belief, been visited before by a European, but which I cannot now stop to describe. There we rested a fortnight, and then started out into the trackless and uninhabited forest of a vast district called Elgumi. In this forest alone there are more elephants than I ever met with or heard of before. The mighty mammals literally swarm there entirely unmolested by man, and only kept down by the natural law that prevents any animals increasing beyond the capacity of the country they inhabit to support them. Needless to say, however, we did not shoot many of them, first because we could not afford to waste ammunition, of which our stock was getting perilously low, a donkey loaded with it having been swept away in fording a flooded river; and secondly, because we could not carry away the ivory, and did not wish to kill for the mere sake of slaughter. So we let the great beasts be, only shooting one or two in self-protection. In this district, the elephants, being unacquainted with the hunter and his tender mercies, would allow one to walk up to within twenty yards of them in the open, while they stood, with their great ears cocked for all the world like puzzled and gigantic puppy-dogs, and stared at that new and extraordinary phenomenon—man. Occasionally, when the inspection did not prove satisfactory, the staring ended in a trumpet and a charge, but this did not often happen. When it did we had to use our rifles. Nor were elephants the only wild beasts in the great Elgumi forest. All sorts of large game abounded, including lions—confound them! I have always hated the sight of a lion since one bit my leg and lamed me for life. As a consequence, another thing that abounded was the dreadful tsetse fly, whose bite is death to domestic animals. Donkeys have, together with men, hitherto been supposed to enjoy a peculiar immunity from its attacks; but all I have to say, whether it was on account of their poor condition, or because the tsetse in those parts is more poisonous than usual, I do not know, but ours succumbed to its onslaught. Fortunately, however, that was not till two months or so after the bites had been inflicted, when suddenly, after a two days' cold rain, they all died, and on removing the skins of several of them I found the long yellow streaks upon the flesh which are characteristic of death from bites from the tsetse, marking the spot where the insect had inserted his proboscis. On emerging from the great Elgumi forest, we, still steering northwards, in accordance with the information Mr. Mackenzie had collected from the unfortunate wanderer who reached him only to die so tragically, struck the base in due course of the large lake, called Laga by the natives, which is about fifty miles long by twenty broad, and of which, it may be remembered, he made mention. Thence we pushed on nearly a month's journey over great rolling uplands, something like those in the Transvaal, but diversified by patches of bush country.

All this time we were continually ascending at the rate of about one hundred feet every ten miles. Indeed the country was on a slope which appeared to terminate at a mass of snow-tipped mountains, for which we were steering, and where we learnt the second lake of which the wanderer had spoken as the lake without a bottom was situated. At length we arrived there, and, having ascertained that there *was* a large lake on top of the mountains, ascended three thousand feet more till we came to a precipitous cliff or edge, to find a great sheet of water some twenty miles square lying fifteen hundred feet below us, and evidently occupying an extinct volcanic crater or craters of vast extent. Perceiving villages on the border of this lake, we descended with great difficulty through forests of pine trees, which now clothed the precipitous sides of the crater, and were well received by the people, a simple, unwarlike folk, who had never seen or even heard of a white man before, and treated us with great reverence and kindness, supplying us with as much food and milk as we could eat and drink. This wonderful and beautiful lake lay, according to our aneroid, at a height of no less than 11,450 feet above sea-level, and its climate was quite cold, and not at all unlike that of England. Indeed, for the first three days of our stay there we saw little or nothing of the scenery on account of an unmistakable Scotch mist which prevailed. It was this rain that set the tsetse poison working in our remaining donkeys, so that they all died.

This disaster left us in a very awkward position, as we had now no means of transport whatever, though on the other hand we had not much to carry. Ammunition, too, was very short, amounting to but one hundred and fifty rounds of rifle cartridges and some fifty shot-gun cartridges. How to get on we did not know; indeed it seemed to us that we had about reached the end of our tether. Even if we had been inclined to abandon the object of our search, which, shadow as it was, was by no means the case, it was ridiculous to think of forcing our way back some seven hundred miles to the coast in our present plight; so we came to the conclusion that the only thing to be done was to stop where we were—the natives being so well disposed and food plentiful—for the present, and abide events, and try to collect information as to the countries beyond.

Accordingly, having purchased a capital log canoe, large enough to hold us all and our baggage, from the headman of the village we were staying in, presenting him with three empty cold-drawn brass cartridges by way of payment, with which he was perfectly delighted, we set out to make a tour of the lake in order to find the most favourable place to make a camp. As we did not know if we should return to this village, we put all our gear into the canoe, and also a quarter of cooked water-buck, which when young is delicious eating, and off we set, natives having already gone before us in light canoes to warn the inhabitants of the other villages of our approach.

As we were puddling leisurely along Good remarked upon the extraordinary deep blue colour of the water, and said that he understood from the natives, who were great fishermen—fish, indeed, being their principal food—that the lake was supposed to be wonderfully deep, and to have a hole at the bottom through which the water escaped and put out some great fire that was raging below.

I pointed out to him that what he had heard was probably a legend arising from a tradition among the people which dated back to the time when one of the extinct parasitic volcanic cones was in activity. We saw several round the borders of the lake which had no doubt been working at a period long subsequent to the volcanic death of the central crater which now formed the bed of the lake itself. When it finally became extinct the people would imagine that the water from the lake had run down and put out the big fire below, more especially as, though it was constantly fed by streams running from the snow-tipped peaks about, there was no visible exit to it.

The farther shore of the lake we found, on approaching it, to consist of a vast perpendicular wall of rock, which held the water without any intermediate sloping bank, as elsewhere. Accordingly we paddled parallel with this precipice, at a distance of about a hundred paces from it, shaping our course for the end of the lake, where we knew that there was a large village.

As we went we began to pass a considerable accumulation of floating rushes, weed, boughs of trees, and other rubbish, brought, Good supposed, to this spot by some current, which he was much puzzled to account for. Whilst we were speculating about this, Sir Henry pointed out a flock of large white swans, which were feeding on the drift some little way ahead of us. Now I had already noticed swans flying about this lake, and, having never come across them before in Africa, was exceedingly anxious to obtain a specimen. I had questioned the natives about them, and learnt that they came from over the mountain, always arriving at certain periods of the year in the early morning, when it was very easy to catch them, on account of their exhausted condition. I also asked them what country they came from, when they shrugged their shoulders, and said that on the top of the great black precipice was stony inhospitable land, and beyond that were mountains with snow, and full of wild beasts, where no people lived, and beyond the mountains were hundreds of miles of dense thorn forest, so thick that even the elephants could not get through it, much less men. Next I asked them if they had ever heard of white people like ourselves living on the farther side of the mountains and the thorn forest, whereat they laughed. But afterwards a very old woman came and told me that when she was a little girl her grandfather had told her that in his youth *his* grandfather had crossed the desert and the mountains, and pierced the thorn forest, and seen a white people who lived in stone kraals beyond. Of course, as this took the tale back some two hundred and fifty years, the information was very indefinite; but still there it was again, and on thinking it over I grew firmly convinced that there was some truth in all these rumours, and equally firmly determined to solve the mystery. Little did I guess in what an almost miraculous way my desire was to be gratified.

Well, we set to work to stalk the swans, which kept drawing, as they fed, nearer and nearer to the precipice, and at last we pushed the canoe under shelter of a patch of drift within forty yards of them. Sir Henry had the shot-gun, loaded with No. 1, and, waiting for a chance, got two in a line, and, firing at their necks, killed them both. Up rose the rest, thirty or more of them, with a mighty splashing; and, as they did so, he gave them the other barrel. Down came one fellow with a broken wing, and I saw the leg of another drop and a few feathers start out of his back; but he went on quite strong. Up went the swans, circling ever higher till at last they were mere specks level with the top of the frowning precipice, when I saw them form into a triangle and head off for the unknown north-east. Meanwhile we had picked up our two dead ones, and beautiful birds they were, weighing not less than about thirty pounds each, and were chasing the winged one, which had scrambled over a mass of driftweed into a pool of clear water beyond. Finding a difficulty in forcing the canoe through the rubbish, I told our only remaining Wakwafi servant, whom I knew to be an excellent swimmer, to jump over, dive under the drift, and catch him, knowing that as there were no crocodiles in this lake he could come to no harm. Entering into the fun of the thing, the man obeyed, and soon was dodging about after the winged swan in fine style, getting gradually nearer to the rock wall, against which the water washed as he did so.

Presently he gave up swimming after the swan, and began to cry out that he was being carried away; and, indeed, we saw that, though he was swimming with all his strength towards us, he was being drawn slowly to the precipice. With a few desperate strokes of our paddles we pushed the canoe through the crust of drift and rowed towards the man as hard as we could, but, fast as we went, he was drawn faster to the rock. Suddenly I saw that before us, just rising eighteen inches or so above the surface of the lake, was what looked like the top of the arch of a submerged cave or railway tunnel. Evidently, from the watermark on the rock several feet above it, it was generally entirely submerged; but there had been a dry season, and the cold had prevented the snow from melting as freely as usual; so the lake was low and the arch showed. Towards this arch our poor servant was being sucked with frightful rapidity. He was not more than ten fathoms from it, and we were about twenty when I saw it, and with little help from us the canoe flew along after him. He struggled bravely, and I thought that we should have saved him, when suddenly I perceived an expression of despair come upon his face, and there before our eyes he was sucked down into the cruel swirling blue depths, and vanished. At the same moment I felt our canoe seized as with a mighty hand, and propelled with resistless force towards the rock.

We realized our danger now and rowed, or rather paddled, furiously in our attempt to get out of the vortex. In vain; in another second we were flying straight for the arch like an arrow, and I thought that we were lost. Luckily I retained sufficient presence of mind to shout out, instantly setting the example by throwing myself into the bottom of the canoe, 'Down on your faces—down!' and the others had the sense to take the hint. In another instant there was a grinding noise, and the boat was pushed down till the water began to trickle over the sides, and I thought that we were gone. But no, suddenly the grinding ceased, and we could again feel the canoe flying along. I turned my head a little—I dared not lift it—and looked up. By the feeble light that yet reached the canoe, I could make out that a dense arch of rock hung just over our heads, and that was all. In another minute I could not even see as much as that, for the faint light had merged into shadow, and the shadows had been swallowed up in darkness, utter and complete.

For an hour or so we lay there, not daring to lift our heads for fear lest the brains should be dashed out of them, and scarcely able to speak even, on account of the noise of the rushing water which drowned our voices. Not, indeed, that we had much inclination to speak, seeing that we were overwhelmed by the awfulness of our position and the imminent fear of instant death, either by being dashed against the sides of the cavern, or on a rock, or being sucked down in the raging waters, or perhaps asphyxiated by want of air. All of these and many other modes of death presented themselves to my imagination as I lay at the bottom of the canoe, listening to the swirl of the hurrying waters which ran whither we knew not. One only other sound could I hear, and that was Alphonse's intermittent howl of terror coming from the centre of the canoe, and even that seemed faint and unnatural. Indeed, the whole thing overpowered my brain, and I began to believe that I was the victim of some ghastly spirit-shaking nightmare.

X

The Rose of Fire

On we flew, drawn by the mighty current, till at last I noticed that the sound of the water was not half so deafening as it had been, and concluded that this must be because there was more room for the echoes to disperse in. I could now hear Alphonse's howls much more distinctly; they were made up of the oddest mixture of invocations to the Supreme Power and the name of his beloved Annette that it is possible to conceive; and, in short, though their evident earnestness saved them from profanity, were, to say the least, very remarkable. Taking up a paddle I managed to drive it into his ribs, whereon he, thinking that the end had come, howled louder than ever. Then I slowly and cautiously raised myself on my knees and stretched my hand upwards, but could touch no roof. Next I took the paddle and lifted it above my head as high as I could, but with the same result. I also thrust it out laterally to the right and left, but could touch nothing except water. Then I bethought me that there was in the boat, amongst our other remaining possessions, a bull's-eye lantern and a tin of oil. I groped about and found it, and having a match on me carefully lit it, and as soon as the flame had got a hold of the wick I turned it on down the boat. As it happened, the first thing the light lit on was the white and scared face of Alphonse, who, thinking that it was all over at last, and that he was witnessing a preliminary celestial phenomenon, gave a terrific yell and was with difficulty reassured with the paddle. As for the other three, Good was lying on the flat of his back, his eyeglass still fixed in his eye, and gazing blankly into the upper darkness. Sir Henry had his head resting on the thwarts of the canoe, and with his hand was trying to test the speed of the water. But when the beam of light fell upon old Umslopogaas I could really have laughed. I think I have said that we had put a roast quarter of water-buck into the canoe. Well, it so happened that when we all prostrated ourselves to avoid being swept out of the boat and into the water by the rock roof, Umslopogaas's head had come down uncommonly near this roast buck, and so soon as he had recovered a little from the first shock of our position it occurred to him that he was hungry. Thereupon he coolly cut off a chop with

Inkosi-kaas, and was now employed in eating it with every appearance of satisfaction. As he afterwards explained, he thought that he was going 'on a long journey', and preferred to start on a full stomach. It reminded me of the people who are going to be hanged, and who are generally reported in the English daily papers to have made 'an excellent breakfast'.

As soon as the others saw that I had managed to light the lamp, we bundled Alphonse into the farther end of the canoe with a threat which calmed him down wonderfully, that if he would insist upon making the darkness hideous with his cries we would put him out of suspense by sending him to join the Wakwafi and wait for Annette in another sphere, and began to discuss the situation as well as we could. First, however, at Good's suggestion, we bound two paddles mast-fashion in the bows so that they might give us warning against any sudden lowering of the roof of the cave or waterway. It was clear to us that we were in an underground river or, as Alphonse defined it, 'main drain', which carried off the superfluous waters of the lake. Such rivers are well known to exist in many parts of the world, but it has not often been the evil fortune of explorers to travel by them. That the river was wide we could clearly see, for the light from the bull's-eye lantern failed to reach from shore to shore, although occasionally, when the current swept us either to one side or the other, we could distinguish the rock wall of the tunnel, which, as far as we could make out, appeared to arch about twenty-five feet above our heads. As for the current itself, it ran, Good estimated, at least eight knots, and, fortunately for us, was, as is usual, fiercest in the middle of the stream. Still, our first act was to arrange that one of us, with the lantern and a pole there was in the canoe, should always be in the bows ready, if possible, to prevent us from being stove in against the side of the cave or any projecting rock. Umslopogaas, having already dined, took the first turn. This was absolutely, with one exception, all that we could do towards preserving our safety. The exception was that another of us took up a position in the stern with a paddle by means of which it was possible to steer the canoe more or less and to keep her from the sides of the cave. These matters attended to, we made a somewhat sparing meal off the cold buck's meat (for we did not know how long it might have to last us), and then feeling in rather better spirits I gave my opinion that, serious as it undoubtedly was, I did not consider our position altogether without hope, unless, indeed, the natives were right, and the river plunged straight down into the

H. RIDER HAGGARD

bowels of the earth. If not, it was clear that it must emerge somewhere, probably on the other side of the mountains, and in that case all we had to think of was to keep ourselves alive till we got there, wherever 'there' might be. But, of course, as Good lugubriously pointed out, on the other hand we might fall victims to a hundred unsuspected horrors—or the river might go on winding away inside the earth till it dried up, in which case our fate would indeed be an awful one.

'Well, let us hope for the best and prepare ourselves for the worst,' said Sir Henry, who is always cheerful and even spirited—a very tower of strength in the time of trouble. 'We have come out of so many queer scrapes together, that somehow I almost fancy we shall come out of this,' he added.

This was excellent advice, and we proceeded to take it each in our separate way—that is, except Alphonse, who had by now sunk into a sort of terrified stupor. Good was at the helm and Umslopogaas in the bows, so there was nothing left for Sir Henry and myself to do except to lie down in the canoe and think. It certainly was a curious, and indeed almost a weird, position to be placed in—rushing along, as we were, through the bowels of the earth, borne on the bosom of a Stygian river, something after the fashion of souls being ferried by Charon, as Curtis said. And how dark it was! The feeble ray from our little lamp did but serve to show the darkness. There in the bows sat old Umslopogaas, like Pleasure in the poem, watchful and untiring, the pole ready to his hand, and behind in the shadow I could just make out the form of Good peering forward at the ray of light in order to make out how to steer with the paddle that he held and now and again dipped into the water.

'Well, well,' thought I, 'you have come in search of adventures, Allan my boy, and you have certainly got them. At your time of life, too! You ought to be ashamed of yourself; but somehow you are not, and, awful as it all is, perhaps you will pull through after all; and if you don't, why, you cannot help it, you see! And when all's said and done an underground river will make a very appropriate burying-place.'

At first, however, I am bound to say that the strain upon the nerves was very great. It is trying to the coolest and most experienced person not to know from one hour to another if he has five minutes more to live, but there is nothing in this world that one cannot get accustomed to, and in time we began to get accustomed even to that. And, after all, our anxiety, though no doubt natural, was, strictly speaking, illogical, seeing that we never know what is going to happen to us the next minute, even when we sit in a well-drained house with two policemen patrolling under the window—nor how long we have to live. It is all arranged for us, my sons, so what is the use of bothering?

It was nearly midday when we made our dive into darkness, and we had set our watch (Good and Umslopogaas) at two, having agreed that it should be of a duration of five hours. At seven o'clock, accordingly, Sir Henry and I went on, Sir Henry at the bow and I at the stern, and the other two lay down and went to sleep. For three hours all went well, Sir Henry only finding it necessary once to push us off from the side; and I that but little steering was required to keep us straight, as the violent current did all that was needed, though occasionally the canoe showed a tendency which had to be guarded against to veer and travel broadside on. What struck me as the most curious thing about this wonderful river was: how did the air keep fresh? It was muggy and thick, no doubt, but still not sufficiently so to render it bad or even remarkably unpleasant. The only explanation that I can suggest is that the water of the lake had sufficient air in it to keep the atmosphere of the tunnel from absolute stagnation, this air being given out as it proceeded on its headlong way. Of course I only give the solution of the mystery for what it is worth, which perhaps is not much.

When I had been for three hours or so at the helm, I began to notice a decided change in the temperature, which was getting warmer. At first I took no notice of it, but when, at the expiration of another half-hour, I found that it was getting hotter and hotter, I called to Sir Henry and asked him if he noticed it, or if it was only my imagination. 'Noticed it!' he answered; 'I should think so. I am in a sort of Turkish bath.' Just about then the others woke up gasping, and were obliged to begin to discard their clothes. Here Umslopogaas had the advantage, for he did not wear any to speak of, except a moocha.

Hotter it grew, and hotter yet, till at last we could scarcely breathe, and the perspiration poured out of us. Half an hour more, and though we were all now stark naked, we could hardly bear it. The place was like an antechamber of the infernal regions proper. I dipped my hand into the water and drew it out almost with a cry; it was nearly boiling. We consulted a little thermometer we had—the mercury stood at 123 degrees. From the surface of the water rose a dense cloud of steam. Alphonse groaned out that we were already in purgatory, which indeed we were, though not in the sense that he meant it. Sir Henry suggested that we must be passing near the seat of some underground volcanic fire, and I am inclined to think, especially in the light of what subsequently occurred, that he was right. Our sufferings for some time after this really pass my powers of description. We no longer perspired, for all the perspiration had been sweated out of us. We simply lay in the bottom of the boat, which we were now physically incapable of directing, feeling like hot embers, and I fancy undergoing very much the same sensations that the poor fish do when they are dying on land—namely, that of slow suffocation. Our skins began to crack, and the blood to throb in our heads like the beating of a steam-engine.

This had been going on for some time, when suddenly the river turned a little, and I heard Sir Henry call out from the bows in a hoarse, startled voice, and, looking up, saw a most wonderful and awful thing. About half a mile ahead of us, and a little to the left of the centre of the stream—which we could now see was about ninety feet broad—a huge pillar-like jet of almost white flame rose from the surface of the water and sprang fifty feet into the air, when it struck the roof and spread out some forty feet in diameter, falling back in curved sheets of fire shaped like the petals of a full-blown rose. Indeed this awful gas jet resembled nothing so much as a great flaming flower rising out of the black water. Below was the straight stalk, a foot or more thick, and above the dreadful bloom. And as for the fearfulness of it and its fierce and awesome beauty, who can describe it? Certainly I cannot. Although we were now some five hundred yards away, it, notwithstanding the steam, lit up the whole cavern as clear as day, and we could see that the roof was here about forty feet above us, and washed perfectly smooth with water. The rock was black, and here and there I could make out long shining lines of ore running through it like great veins, but of what metal they were I know not.

On we rushed towards this pillar of fire, which gleamed fiercer than any furnace ever lit by man.

'Keep the boat to the right, Quatermain—to the right,' shouted Sir Henry, and a minute afterwards I saw him fall forward senseless. Alphonse had already gone. Good was the next to go. There they lay as though dead; only Umslopogaas and I kept our senses. We were within fifty yards of it now, and I saw the Zulu's head fall forward on his hands. He had gone too, and I was alone. I could not breathe; the fierce heat dried me up. For yards and yards round the great rose of fire the rock-roof was red-hot. The wood of the boat was almost burning. I saw the feathers on one of the dead swans begin to twist and shrivel up; but I would not give in. I knew that if I did we should pass within three or four yards of the gas jet and perish miserably. I set the paddle so as to turn the canoe as far from it as possible, and held on grimly.

My eyes seemed to be bursting from my head, and through my closed lids I could see the fierce light. We were nearly opposite now; it roared like all the fires of hell, and the water boiled furiously around it. Five seconds more. We were past; I heard the roar behind me.

Then I too fell senseless. The next thing that I recollect is feeling a breath of air upon my face. My eyes opened with great difficulty. I looked up. Far, far above me there was light, though around me was great gloom. Then I remembered and looked. The canoe still floated down the river, and in the bottom of it lay the naked forms of my companions. 'Were they dead?' I wondered. 'Was I left alone in this awful place?' I knew not. Next I became conscious of a burning thirst. I put my hand over the edge of the boat into the water and drew it up again with a cry. No wonder: nearly all the skin was burnt off the back of it. The water, however, was cold, or nearly so, and I drank pints and splashed myself all over. My body seemed to suck up the fluid as one may see a brick wall suck up rain after a drought; but where I was burnt the touch of it caused intense pain. Then I bethought myself of the others, and, dragging myself towards them with difficulty, I sprinkled them with water, and to my joy they began to recover—Umslopogaas first, then the others. Next they drank, absorbing water like so many sponges. Then, feeling chilly—a queer contrast to our recent sensations—we began as best we could to get into our clothes. As we did so Good pointed to the port side of the canoe: it was all blistered with heat, and in places actually charred. Had it been built like our civilized boats, Good said that the planks would certainly have warped and let in enough water to sink us; but fortunately it was dug out of the soft, willowy wood of a single great tree, and had sides nearly three inches and a bottom four inches thick. What that awful flame was we never discovered, but I suppose that there was at this spot a crack or hole in the bed of the river through which a vast volume of gas forced its way from its volcanic home in the bowels of the earth towards the upper air. How it first became ignited is, of course, impossible to say—probably, I should think, from some spontaneous explosion of mephitic gases.

As soon as we had got some things together and shaken ourselves together a little, we set to work to make out where we were now. I have said that there was light above, and on examination we found that it came from the sky. Our river that was, Sir Henry said, a literal realization of the wild vision of the poet, was no longer underground, but was running on its darksome way, not now through 'caverns measureless to man', but between two frightful cliffs which cannot have been less than two thousand feet high. So high were they, indeed, that though the sky was above us, where we were was dense gloom—not darkness indeed, but the gloom of a room closely shuttered in the daytime. Up on either side rose the great straight cliffs, grim and forbidding, till the eye grew dizzy with trying to measure their sheer height. The little space of sky that marked where they ended lay like a thread of blue upon their soaring blackness, which was unrelieved by any tree or creeper. Here and there, however, grew ghostly patches of a long grey lichen, hanging motionless to the rock as the white beard to the chin of a dead man. It seemed as though only the dregs or heavier part of the light had sunk to the bottom of this awful place. No bright-winged sunbeam could fall so low: they died far, far above our heads.

By the river's edge was a little shore formed of round fragments of rock washed into this shape by the constant action of water, and giving the place the appearance of being strewn with thousands of fossil cannon balls. Evidently when the water of the underground river is high there is no beach at all, or very little, between the border of the stream and the precipitous cliffs; but now there was a space of seven or eight yards. And here, on this beach, we determined to land, in order to rest ourselves a little after all that we had gone through and to stretch our limbs. It was a dreadful place, but it would give an hour's respite from the terrors of the river, and also allow of our repacking and arranging the canoe. Accordingly we selected what looked like a favourable spot, and with some little difficulty managed to beach the canoe and scramble out on to the round, inhospitable pebbles.

'My word,' called out Good, who was on shore the first, 'what an awful place! It's enough to give one a fit.' And he laughed.

Instantly a thundering voice took up his words, magnifying them a hundred times. '*Give one a fit—Ho! ho! ho!*'—'*A fit, Ho! ho! ho!*' answered another voice in wild accents from far up the cliff—*a fit! a fit! a fit!* chimed in voice after voice—each flinging the words to and fro with shouts of awful laughter to the invisible lips of the other till the whole place echoed with the words and with shrieks of fiendish merriment, which at last ceased as suddenly as they had begun.

'Oh, mon Dieu!' yelled Alphonse, startled quite out of such self-command as he possessed.

'*Mon Dieu! Mon Dieu! Mon Dieu!*' the Titanic echoes thundered, shrieked, and wailed in every conceivable tone.

'Ah,' said Umslopogaas calmly, 'I clearly perceive that devils live here. Well, the place looks like it.'

I tried to explain to him that the cause of all the hubbub was a very remarkable and interesting echo, but he would not believe it.

'Ah,' he said, 'I know an echo when I hear one. There was one lived opposite my kraal in Zululand, and the Intombis (maidens) used to talk with it. But if what we hear is a full-grown echo, mine at home can only have been a baby. No, no—they are devils up there. But I don't think much of them, though,' he added, taking a pinch of snuff. 'They can copy what one says, but they don't seem to be able to talk on their own account, and they dare not show their faces,' and he relapsed into silence, and apparently paid no further attention to such contemptible fiends.

After this we found it necessary to keep our conversation down to a whisper—for it was really unbearable to have every word one uttered tossed to and fro like a tennis-ball, as precipice called to precipice.

But even our whispers ran up the rocks in mysterious murmurs till at last they died away in long-drawn sighs of sound. Echoes are delightful and romantic things, but we had more than enough of them in that dreadful gulf.

As soon as we had settled ourselves a little on the round stones, we went on to wash and dress our burns as well as we could. As we had but a little oil for the lantern, we could not spare any for this purpose, so we skinned one of the swans, and used the fat off its breast, which proved an excellent substitute. Then we repacked the canoe, and finally began to take some food, of which I need scarcely say we were in need, for our insensibility had endured for many hours, and it was, as our watches showed, midday. Accordingly we seated ourselves in a circle, and were soon engaged in discussing our cold meat with such appetite as we could muster, which, in my case at any rate, was not much, as I felt sick and faint after my sufferings of the previous night, and had besides a racking headache. It was a curious meal. The gloom was so intense that we could scarcely see the way to cut our food and convey it to our mouths. Still we got on pretty well, till I happened to look behind me—my attention being attracted by a noise of something crawling

H. RIDER HAGGARD

over the stones, and perceived sitting upon a rock in my immediate rear a huge species of black freshwater crab, only it was five times the size of any crab I ever saw. This hideous and loathsome-looking animal had projecting eyes that seemed to glare at one, very long and flexible antennae or feelers, and gigantic claws. Nor was I especially favoured with its company. From every quarter dozens of these horrid brutes were creeping up, drawn, I suppose, by the smell of the food, from between the round stones and out of holes in the precipice. Some were already quite close to us. I stared quite fascinated by the unusual sight, and as I did so I saw one of the beasts stretch out its huge claw and give the unsuspecting Good such a nip behind that he jumped up with a howl, and set the 'wild echoes flying' in sober earnest. Just then, too, another, a very large one, got hold of Alphonse's leg, and declined to part with it, and, as may be imagined, a considerable scene ensued. Umslopogaas took his axe and cracked the shell of one with the flat of it, whereon it set up a horrid screaming which the echoes multiplied a thousandfold, and began to foam at the mouth, a proceeding that drew hundreds more of its friends out of unsuspected holes and corners. Those on the spot perceiving that the animal was hurt fell upon it like creditors on a bankrupt, and literally rent it limb from limb with their huge pincers and devoured it, using their claws to convey the fragments to their mouths. Seizing whatever weapons were handy, such as stones or paddles, we commenced a war upon the monsters—whose numbers were increasing by leaps and bounds, and whose stench was overpowering. So fast as we cracked their armour others seized the injured ones and devoured them, foaming at the mouth, and screaming as they did so. Nor did the brutes stop at that. When they could they nipped hold of us—and awful nips they were—or tried to steal the meat. One enormous fellow got hold of the swan we had skinned and began to drag it off. Instantly a score of others flung themselves upon the prey, and then began a ghastly and disgusting scene. How the monsters foamed and screamed, and rent the flesh, and each other! It was a sickening and unnatural sight, and one that will haunt all who saw it till their dying day—enacted as it was in the deep, oppressive gloom, and set to the unceasing music of the many-toned nerve-shaking echoes. Strange as it may seem to say so, there was something so shockingly human about these fiendish creatures—it was as though all the most evil passions and desires of man had got into the shell of a magnified crab and gone mad. They were so dreadfully courageous and intelligent, and they looked as if they *understood*. The whole scene might have furnished material for another canto of Dante's 'Inferno', as Curtis said.

'I say, you fellows, let's get out of this or we shall all go off our heads,' sung out Good; and we were not slow to take the hint. Pushing the canoe, around which the animals were now crawling by hundreds and making vain attempts to climb, off the rocks, we bundled into it and got out into mid-stream, leaving behind us the fragments of our meal and the screaming, foaming, stinking mass of monsters in full possession of the ground.

'Those are the devils of the place,' said Umslopogaas with the air of one who has solved a problem, and upon my word I felt almost inclined to agree with him.

Umslopogaas' remarks were like his axe—very much to the point.

'What's to be done next?' said Sir Henry blankly.

'Drift, I suppose,' I answered, and we drifted accordingly. All the afternoon and well into the evening we floated on in the gloom beneath the far-off line of blue sky, scarcely knowing when day ended and night began, for down in that vast gulf the difference was not marked, till at length Good pointed out a star hanging right above us, which, having nothing better to do, we observed with great interest. Suddenly it vanished, the darkness became intense, and a familiar murmuring sound filled the air. 'Underground again,' I said with a groan, holding up the lamp. Yes, there was no doubt about it. I could just make out the roof. The chasm had come to an end and the tunnel had recommenced. And then there began another long, long night of danger and horror. To describe all its incidents would be too wearisome, so I will simply say that about midnight we struck on a flat projecting rock in mid-stream and were as nearly as possible overturned and drowned. However, at last we got off, and went upon the uneven tenor of our way. And so the hours passed till it was nearly three o'clock. Sir Henry, Good, and Alphonse were asleep, utterly worn out; Umslopogaas was at the bow with the pole, and I was steering, when I perceived that the rate at which we were travelling had perceptibly increased. Then, suddenly, I heard Umslopogaas make an exclamation, and next second came a sound as of parting branches, and I became aware that the canoe was being forced through hanging bushes or creepers. Another minute, and the breath of sweet open air fanned my face, and I felt that we had emerged from the tunnel and were floating upon clear water. I say felt, for I could see nothing, the darkness being absolutely pitchy, as it often is just before the dawn. But even this could scarcely damp my joy. We were out of that dreadful river, and wherever we might have got to this at least was something to be thankful for. And so I sat down and inhaled the sweet night air and waited for the dawn with such patience as I could command.

XI

THE FROWNING CITY

For an hour or more I sat waiting (Umslopogaas having meanwhile gone to sleep also) till at length the east turned grey, and huge misty shapes moved over the surface of the water like ghosts of long-forgotten dawns. They were the vapours rising from their watery bed to greet the sun. Then the grey turned to primrose, and the primrose grew to red. Next, glorious bars of light sprang up across the eastern sky, and through them the radiant messengers of the dawn came speeding upon their arrowy way, scattering the ghostly vapours and awaking the mountains with a kiss, as they flew from range to range and longitude to longitude. Another moment, and the golden gates were open and the sun himself came forth as a bridegroom from his chamber, with pomp and glory and a flashing as of ten million spears, and embraced the night and covered her with brightness, and it was day.

But as yet I could see nothing save the beautiful blue sky above, for over the water was a thick layer of mist exactly as though the whole surface had been covered with billows of cotton wool. By degrees, however, the sun sucked up the mists, and then I saw that we were afloat upon a glorious sheet of blue water of which I could not make out the shore. Some eight or ten miles behind us, however, there stretched as far as the eye could reach a range of precipitous hills that formed a retaining wall of the lake, and I have no doubt but that it was through some entrance in these hills that the subterranean river found its way into the open water. Indeed, I afterwards ascertained this to be the fact, and it will be some indication of the extraordinary strength and directness of the current of the mysterious river that the canoe, even at this distance, was still answering to it. Presently, too, I, or rather Umslopogaas, who woke up just then, discovered another indication, and a very unpleasant one it was. Perceiving some whitish object upon the water, Umslopogaas called my attention to it, and with a few strokes of the paddle brought the canoe to the spot, whereupon we discovered that the object was the body of a man floating face downwards. This was bad enough, but imagine my horror when Umslopogaas having turned him on to his back with the paddle, we recognized in the sunken features the lineaments of—whom do you suppose? None other than our poor servant who had been sucked down two days before in the waters of the subterranean river. It quite frightened me. I thought that we had left him behind for ever, and behold! borne by the current, he had made the awful journey with us, and with us had reached the end. His appearance also was dreadful, for he bore traces of having touched the pillar of fire—one arm being completely shrivelled up and all his hair being burnt off. The features were, as I have said, sunken, and yet they preserved upon them that awful look of despair that I had seen upon his living face as the poor fellow was sucked down. Really the sight unnerved me, weary and shaken as I felt with all that we had gone through, and I was heartily glad when suddenly and without any warning the body began to sink just as though it had had a mission, which having been accomplished, it retired; the real reason no doubt being that turning it on its back allowed a free passage to the gas. Down it went to the transparent depths—fathom after fathom we could trace its course till at last a long line of bright air-bubbles, swiftly chasing each other to the surface, alone remained where it had passed. At length these, too, were gone, and that was an end of our poor servant. Umslopogaas thoughtfully watched the body vanish.

'What did he follow us for?' he asked. ''Tis an ill omen for thee and me, Macumazahn.' And he laughed.

I turned on him angrily, for I dislike these unpleasant suggestions. If people have such ideas, they ought in common decency to keep them to themselves. I detest individuals who make on the subject of their disagreeable presentiments, or who, when they dream that they saw one hanged as a common felon, or some such horror, will insist upon telling one all about it at breakfast, even if they have to get up early to do it.

Just then, however, the others woke up and began to rejoice exceedingly at finding that we were out of that dreadful river and once more beneath the blue sky. Then followed a babel of talk and suggestions as to what we were to do next, the upshot of all of which was that, as we were excessively hungry, and had nothing whatsoever left to eat except a few scraps of biltong (dried game-flesh), having abandoned all that remained of our provisions to those horrible freshwater crabs, we determined to make for the shore. But a new difficulty arose. We did not know where the shore was, and, with the exception of the cliffs through which the subterranean river made its entry, could see nothing but a wide expanse of sparkling blue water. Observing, however, that the long flights of aquatic birds kept flying from our left, we concluded that they were advancing from their feeding-grounds on shore to pass the day in the lake, and accordingly headed the boat towards the quarter whence they came, and began to paddle. Before long, however, a stiffish breeze sprang up, blowing directly in the direction we wanted, so we improvized a sail with a blanket and the pole, which took us along merrily. This done, we devoured the remnants of our biltong, washed down with the sweet lake water, and then lit our pipes and awaited whatever might turn up.

When we had been sailing for an hour, Good, who was searching the horizon with the spy-glass, suddenly announced joyfully that he saw land, and pointed out that, from the change in the colour of the water, he thought we must be approaching the mouth of a river. In another minute we perceived a great golden dome, not unlike that of St Paul's, piercing the morning mists, and while we were wondering what in the world it could be, Good reported another and still more important discovery, namely, that a small sailing-boat was advancing towards us. This bit of news, which we were very shortly able to verify with our own eyes, threw us into a considerable flutter. That the natives of this unknown lake should understand the art of sailing seemed to suggest that they possessed some degree of civilization. In a few more minutes it became evident that the occupant or occupants of the advancing boat had made us out. For a moment or two she hung in the wind as though in doubt, and then came tacking towards us with great swiftness. In ten more minutes she was within a hundred yards, and we saw that she was a neat little boat—not a canoe 'dug out', but built more or less in the European fashion with planks, and carrying a singularly large sail for her size. But our attention was soon diverted from the boat to her crew, which consisted of a man and a woman, *nearly as white as ourselves*.

We stared at each other in amazement, thinking that we must be mistaken; but no, there was no doubt about it. They were not fair, but the two people in the boat were decidedly of a white as distinguished from a black race, as white, for instance, as Spaniards or Italians. It was a patent fact. So it was true, after all; and, mysteriously led by a Power beyond our own, we had discovered this wonderful people. I could have shouted for joy when I thought of the glory and the wonder of the thing; and as it was, we all shook hands and congratulated each other on the unexpected success of our wild search. All my life had I heard rumours of a white race that existed in the highlands of this vast continent, and longed to put them to the proof, and now here I saw it with my own eyes, and was dumbfounded. Truly, as Sir Henry said, the old Roman was right when he wrote 'Ex Africa semper aliquid novi', which he tells me means that out of Africa there always comes some new thing.

The man in the boat was of a good but not particularly fine physique, and possessed straight black hair, regular aquiline features, and an intelligent face. He was dressed in a brown cloth garment, something like a flannel shirt without the sleeves, and in an unmistakable kilt of the same material. The legs and feet were bare. Round the right arm and left leg he wore thick rings of yellow metal that I judged to be gold. The woman had a sweet face, wild and shy, with large eyes and curling brown hair. Her dress was made of the same material as the man's, and consisted, as we afterwards discovered, first of a linen under-garment that hung down to her knee, and then of a single long strip of cloth, about four feet wide by fifteen long, which was wound round the body in graceful folds and finally flung over the left shoulder so that the end, which was dyed blue or purple or some other colour, according to the social standing of the wearer, hung down in front, the right arm and breast being, however, left quite bare. A more becoming dress, especially when, as in the present case, the wearer was young and pretty, it is quite impossible to conceive. Good (who has an eye for such things) was greatly struck with it, and so indeed was I. It was so simple and yet so effective.

Meanwhile, if we had been astonished at the appearance of the man and woman, it was clear that they were far more astonished at us. As for the man, he appeared to be overcome with fear and wonder, and for a while hovered round our canoe, but would not approach. At last, however, he came within hailing distance, and called to us in a language that sounded soft and pleasing enough, but of which we could not understand one word. So we hailed back in English, French, Latin, Greek, German, Zulu, Dutch, Sisutu, Kukuana, and a few other native dialects that I am acquainted with, but our visitor did not understand any of these tongues; indeed, they appeared to bewilder him. As for the lady, she was busily employed in taking stock of us, and Good was returning the compliment by staring at her hard through his eyeglass, a proceeding that she seemed rather to enjoy than otherwise. At length, the man, being unable to make anything of us, suddenly turned his boat round and began to head off for the shore, his little boat skimming away before the wind like a swallow. As she passed across our bows the man turned to attend to the large sail, and Good promptly took the opportunity to kiss his hand to the young lady. I was horrified at this proceeding, both on general grounds and because I feared that she might take offence, but to my delight she did not, for, first glancing round and seeing that her husband, or brother, or whoever he was, was engaged, she promptly kissed hers back.

'Ah!' said I. 'It seems that we have at last found a language that the people of this country understand.'

'In which case,' said Sir Henry, 'Good will prove an invaluable interpreter.'

I frowned, for I do not approve of Good's frivolities, and he knows it, and I turned the conversation to more serious subjects. 'It is very clear to me,' I said, 'that the man will be back before long with a host of his fellows, so we had best make up our minds as to how we are going to receive them.'

'The question is how will they receive us?' said Sir Henry.

As for Good he made no remark, but began to extract a small square tin case that had accompanied us in all our wanderings from under a pile of baggage. Now we had often remonstrated with Good about this tin case, inasmuch as it had been an awkward thing to carry, and he had never given any very explicit account as to its contents; but he had insisted on keeping it, saying mysteriously that it might come in very useful one day.

'What on earth are you going to do, Good?' asked Sir Henry.

'Do—why dress, of course! You don't expect me to appear in a new country in these things, do you?' and he pointed to his soiled and worn garments, which were however, like all Good's things, very tidy, and with every tear neatly mended.

We said no more, but watched his proceedings with breathless interest. His first step was to get Alphonse, who was thoroughly competent in such matters, to trim his hair and beard in the most approved fashion. I think that if he had had some hot water and a cake of soap at hand he would have shaved off the latter; but he had not. This done, he suggested that we should lower the sail of the canoe and all take a bath, which we did, greatly to the horror and astonishment of Alphonse, who lifted his hands and exclaimed that these English were indeed a wonderful people. Umslopogaas, who, though he was, like most high-bred Zulus, scrupulously cleanly in his person, did not see the fun of swimming about in a lake, also regarded the proceeding with mild amusement. We got back into the canoe much refreshed by the cold water, and sat to dry in the sun, whilst Good undid his tin box, and produced first a beautiful clean white shirt, just as it had left a London steam laundry, and then some garments wrapped first in brown, then in white, and finally in silver paper. We watched this undoing with the tenderest interest and much speculation. One by one Good removed the dull husks that hid their splendours, carefully folding and replacing each piece of paper as he did so; and there at last lay, in all the majesty of its golden epaulettes, lace, and buttons, a Commander of the Royal Navy's full-dress uniform—dress sword, cocked hat, shiny patent leather boots and all. We literally gasped.

'*What!*' we said, '*what!* Are you going to put those things on?'

'Certainly,' he answered composedly; 'you see so much depends upon a first impression, especially,' he added, 'as I observe that there are ladies about. One at least of us ought to be decently dressed.'

We said no more; we were simply dumbfounded, especially when we considered the artful way in which Good had concealed the contents of that box for all these months. Only one suggestion did we make— namely, that he should wear his mail shirt next his skin. He replied that he feared it would spoil the set of his coat, now carefully spread in the sun to take the creases out, but finally consented to this precautionary measure. The most amusing part of the affair, however, was to see old Umslopogaas's astonishment and Alphonse's delight at Good's transformation. When at last he stood up in all his glory, even down to the medals on his breast, and contemplated himself in the still waters of the lake, after the fashion of the young gentleman in ancient history, whose name I cannot remember, but who fell in love with his own shadow, the old Zulu could no longer restrain his feelings.

'Oh, Bougwan!' he said. 'Oh, Bougwan! I always thought thee an ugly little man, and fat—fat as the cows at calving time; and now thou art like a blue jay when he spreads his tail out. Surely, Bougwan, it hurts my eyes to look at thee.'

Good did not much like this allusion to his fat, which, to tell the truth, was not very well deserved, for hard exercise had brought him down three inches; but on the whole he was pleased at Umslopogaas's admiration. As for Alphonse, he was quite delighted.

'Ah! but Monsieur has the beautiful air—the air of the warrior. It is the ladies who will say so when we come to get ashore. Monsieur is complete; he puts me in mind of my heroic grand—'

Here we stopped Alphonse.

As we gazed upon the beauties thus revealed by Good, a spirit of emulation filled our breasts, and we set to work to get ourselves up as well as we could. The most, however, that we were able to do was to array ourselves in our spare suits of shooting clothes, of which we each had several, all the fine clothes in the world could never make it otherwise than scrubby and insignificant; but Sir Henry looked what he is, a magnificent man in his nearly new tweed suit, gaiters, and boots. Alphonse also got himself up to kill, giving an extra turn to his enormous moustaches. Even old Umslopogaas, who was not in a general way given to the vain adorning of his body, took some oil out of the lantern and a bit of tow, and polished up his head-ring with it till it shone like Good's patent leather boots. Then he put on the mail shirt Sir Henry had given him and his 'moocha', and, having cleaned up Inkosi-kaas a little, stood forth complete.

All this while, having hoisted the sail again as soon as we had finished bathing, we had been progressing steadily for the land, or, rather, for the mouth of a great river. Presently—in all about an hour and a half after the little boat had left us—we saw emerging from the river or harbour a large number of boats, ranging up to ten or twelve tons burden. One of these was propelled by twenty-four oars, and most of the rest sailed. Looking through the glass we soon made out that the row-boat was an official vessel, her crew being all dressed in a sort of uniform, whilst on the half-deck forward stood an old man of venerable appearance, and with a flowing white beard, and a sword strapped to his side, who was evidently the commander of the craft. The other boats were apparently occupied by people brought out by curiosity, and were rowing or sailing towards us as quickly as they could.

'Now for it,' said I. 'What is the betting? Are they going to be friendly or to put an end to us?'

Nobody could answer this question, and, not liking the warlike appearance of the old gentleman and his sword, we felt a little anxious.

Just then Good spied a school of hippopotami on the water about two hundred yards off us, and suggested that it would not be a bad plan to impress the natives with a sense of our power by shooting some of them if possible. This, unluckily enough, struck us as a good idea, and accordingly we at once got out our eight-bore rifles, for which we still had a few cartridges left, and prepared for action. There were four of the animals, a big bull, a cow, and two young ones, one three parts grown.

We got up to them without difficulty, the great animals contenting themselves with sinking down into the water and rising again a few yards farther on; indeed, their excessive tameness struck me as being peculiar. When the advancing boats were about five hundred yards away, Sir Henry opened the ball by firing at the three parts grown young one. The heavy bullet struck it fair between the eyes, and, crashing through the skull, killed it, and it sank, leaving a long train of blood behind it. At the same moment I fired at the cow, and Good at the old bull. My shot took effect, but not fatally, and down went the hippopotamus with a prodigious splashing, only to rise again presently blowing and grunting furiously, dyeing all the water round her crimson, when I killed her with the left barrel. Good, who is an execrable shot, missed the head of the bull altogether, the bullet merely cutting the side of his face as it passed. On glancing up, after I had fired my second shot, I perceived that the people we had fallen among were evidently ignorant of the nature of firearms, for the consternation caused by our shots and their effect upon the animals was prodigious. Some of the parties in the boats began to cry out in fear; others turned and made off as hard as they could; and even the old gentleman with the sword looked greatly puzzled and alarmed, and halted his big row-boat. We had, however, but little time for observation, for just then the old bull, rendered furious by the wound he had received, rose fair within forty yards of us, glaring savagely. We all fired, and hit him in various places, and down he went, badly wounded. Curiosity now began to overcome the fear of the onlookers, and some of them sailed on up close to us, amongst these being the man and woman whom we had first seen a couple of hours or so before, who drew up almost alongside. Just then the great brute rose again within ten yards of their base, and instantly with a roar of fury made at it open-mouthed. The woman shrieked, and the man tried to give the boat way, but without success. In another second I saw the huge red jaws and gleaming ivories close with a crunch on the frail craft, taking an enormous mouthful out of its side and capsizing it. Down went the boat, leaving its occupants struggling in the water. Next moment, before we could do anything towards saving them, the huge and furious creature was up again and making open-mouthed at the poor girl, who was struggling in the water. Lifting my rifle just as the grinding jaws were about to close on her, I fired over her head right down the hippopotamus's throat. Over he went, and commenced turning round and round, snorting, and blowing red streams of blood through his nostrils. Before he could recover himself, however, I let him have the other barrel in the side of the throat, and that finished him. He never moved or struggled again, but instantly sank. Our next effort was directed towards saving the girl, the man having swum off towards another boat; and in this we were fortunately successful, pulling her into the canoe (amidst the shouts of the spectators) considerably exhausted and frightened, but otherwise unhurt.

Meanwhile the boats had gathered together at a distance, and we could see that the occupants, who were evidently much frightened, were consulting what to do. Without giving them time for further consideration, which we thought might result unfavourably to ourselves, we instantly took our paddles and advanced towards them, Good standing in the bow and taking off his cocked hat politely in every direction, his amiable features suffused by a bland but intelligent smile. Most of the craft retreated as we advanced, but a few held their ground, while the big row-boat came on to meet us. Presently we were alongside, and I could see that our appearance—and especially Good's and Umslopogaas's—filled the venerable-looking commander with astonishment, not unmixed with awe. He was dressed after the same fashion as the man we first met, except that his shirt was not made of brown cloth, but of pure white linen hemmed with purple. The kilt, however, was identical, and so were the thick rings of gold around the arm and beneath the left knee. The rowers wore only a kilt, their bodies being naked to the waist. Good took off his hat to the old gentleman with an extra flourish, and inquired after his health in the purest English, to which he replied by laying the first two fingers of his right hand horizontally across his lips and holding them there for a moment, which we took as his method of salutation. Then he also addressed some remarks to us in the same soft accents that had distinguished our first interviewer, which we were forced to indicate we did not understand by shaking our heads and shrugging our shoulders. This last Alphonse, being to the manner born, did to perfection, and in so polite a way that nobody could take any offence. Then we came a standstill, till I, being exceedingly hungry, thought I might as well call attention to the fact, and did so first by opening my mouth and pointing down it, and then rubbing my stomach. These signals the old gentleman clearly understood, for he nodded his head vigorously, and pointed towards the harbour; and at the same time one of the men on his boat threw us a line and motioned to us to make it fast, which we did. The row-boat then took us in tow, and went with great rapidity towards the mouth of the river, accompanied by all the other boats. In about twenty minutes more we reached the entrance to the harbour, which was crowded with boats full of people who had come out to see us. We observed that all the occupants were more or less of the same type, though some were fairer than others. Indeed, we noticed certain ladies whose skin was of a most dazzling whiteness; and the darkest shade of colour which we saw was about that of a rather swarthy Spaniard. Presently the wide river gave a sweep, and when it did so an exclamation of astonishment and delight burst from our lips as we caught our first view of the place that we afterwards knew as Milosis, or the Frowning City (from mi, which means city, and losis, a frown).

At a distance of some five hundred yards from the river's bank rose a sheer precipice of granite, two hundred feet or so in height, which had no doubt once formed the bank itself—the intermediate space of land now utilized as docks and roadways having been gained by draining, and deepening and embanking the stream.

On the brow of this precipice stood a great building of the same granite that formed the cliff, built on three sides of a square, the fourth side being open, save for a kind of battlement pierced at its base by a little door. This imposing place we afterwards discovered was the palace of the queen, or rather of the queens. At the back of the palace the town sloped gently upwards to a flashing building of white marble, crowned by the golden dome which we had already observed. The city was, with the exception of this one building, entirely built of red granite, and laid out in regular blocks with splendid roadways between. So far as we could see also the houses were all one-storied and detached, with gardens round them, which gave some relief to the eye wearied with the vista of red granite. At the back of the palace a road of extraordinary width stretched away up the hill for a distance of a mile and a half or so, and appeared to terminate at an open space surrounding the gleaming building that crowned the hill. But right in front of us was the wonder and glory of Milosis—the great staircase of the palace, the magnificence of which took our breath away. Let the reader imagine, if he can, a splendid stairway, sixty-five feet from balustrade to balustrade, consisting of two vast flights, each of one hundred and twenty-five steps of eight inches in height by three feet broad, connected by a flat resting-place sixty feet in length, and running from the palace wall on the edge of the precipice down to meet a waterway or canal cut to its foot from the river. This marvellous staircase was supported upon a single enormous granite arch, of which the resting-place between the two flights formed the crown; that is, the connecting open space lay upon it. From this archway sprang a subsidiary flying arch, or rather something that resembled a flying arch in shape, such as none of us had seen in any other country, and of which the beauty and wonder surpassed all that we had ever imagined. Three hundred feet from point to point, and no less than five hundred and fifty round the curve, that half-arc soared touching the bridge it supported for a space of fifty feet only, one end resting on and built into the parent archway, and the other embedded in the solid granite of the side of the precipice.

This staircase with its supports was, indeed, a work of which any living man might have been proud, both on account of its magnitude and its surpassing beauty. Four times, as we afterwards learnt, did the work, which was commenced in remote antiquity, fail, and was then abandoned for three centuries when half-finished, till at last there rose a youthful engineer named Rademas, who said that he would complete it successfully, and staked his life upon it. If he failed he was to be hurled from the precipice he had undertaken to scale; if he succeeded, he was to be rewarded by the hand of the king's daughter. Five years was given to him to complete the work, and an unlimited supply of labour and material. Three times did his arch fall, till at last, seeing failure to be inevitable, he determined to commit suicide on the morrow of the third collapse. That night, however, a beautiful woman came to him in a dream and touched his forehead, and of a sudden he saw a vision of the completed work, and saw too through the masonry and how the difficulties connected with the flying arch that had hitherto baffled his genius were to be overcome. Then he awoke and once more commenced the work, but on a different plan, and behold! he achieved it, and on the last day of the five years he led the princess his bride up the stair and into the palace. And in due course he became king by right of his wife, and founded the present Zu-Vendi dynasty, which is to this day called the 'House of the Stairway', thus proving once more how energy and talent are the natural stepping-stones to grandeur. And to commemorate his triumph he fashioned a statue of himself dreaming, and of the fair woman who touched him on the forehead, and placed it in the great hall of the palace, and there it stands to this day.

Such was the great stair of Milosis, and such the city beyond. No wonder they named it the 'Frowning City', for certainly those mighty works in solid granite did seem to frown down upon our littleness in their sombre splendour. This was so even in the sunshine, but when the storm-clouds gathered on her imperial brow Milosis looked more like a supernatural dwelling-place, or some imagining of a poet's brain, than what she is—a mortal city, carven by the patient genius of generations out of the red silence of the mountain side.

XII

The Sister Queens

The big rowing-boat glided on up the cutting that ran almost to the foot of the vast stairway, and then halted at a flight of steps leading to the landing-place. Here the old gentleman disembarked, and invited us to do so likewise, which, having no alternative, and being nearly starved, we did without hesitation—taking our rifles with us, however. As each of us landed, our guide again laid his fingers on his lips and bowed deeply, at the same time ordering back the crowds which had assembled to gaze on us. The last to leave the canoe was the girl we had picked out of the water, for whom her companion was waiting. Before she went away she kissed my hand, I suppose as a token of gratitude for having saved her from the fury of the hippopotamus; and it seemed to me that she had by this time quite got over any fear she might have had of us, and was by no means anxious to return in such a hurry to her lawful owners. At any rate, she was going to kiss Good's hand as well as mine, when the young man interfered and led her off. As soon as we were on shore, a number of the men who had rowed the big boat took possession of our few goods and chattels, and started with them up the splendid staircase, our guide indicating to us by means of motions that the things were perfectly safe. This done, he turned to the right and led the way to a small house, which was, as I afterwards discovered, an inn. Entering into a good-sized room, we saw that a wooden table was already furnished with food, presumably in preparation for us. Here our guide motioned us to be seated on a bench that ran the length of the table. We did not require a second invitation, but at once fell to ravenously on the viands before us, which were served on wooden platters, and consisted of cold goat's-flesh, wrapped up in some kind of leaf that gave it a delicious flavour, green vegetables resembling lettuces, brown bread, and red wine poured from a skin into horn mugs. This wine was peculiarly soft and good, having something of the flavour of Burgundy. Twenty minutes after we sat down at that hospitable board we rose from it, feeling like new men. After all that we had gone through we needed two things, food and rest, and the food of itself was a great blessing to us. Two girls of the same charming cast of face as the first whom we had seen waited on us while we ate, and very nicely they did it. They were also dressed in the same fashion namely, in a white linen petticoat coming to the knee, and with the toga-like garment of brown cloth, leaving bare the right arm and breast. I afterwards found out that this was the national dress, and regulated by an iron custom, though of course subject to variations. Thus, if the petticoat was pure white, it signified that the wearer was unmarried; if white, with a straight purple stripe round the edge, that she was married and a first or legal wife; if with a black stripe, that she was a widow. In the same way the toga, or 'kaf', as they call it, was of different shades of colour, from pure white to the deepest brown, according to the rank of the wearer, and embroidered at the end in various ways. This also applies to the 'shirts' or tunics worn by the men, which varied in material and colour; but the kilts were always the same except as regards quality. One thing, however, every man and woman in the country wore as the national insignia, and that was the thick band of gold round the right arm above the elbow, and the left leg beneath the knee. People of high rank also wore a torque of gold round the neck, and I observed that our guide had one on.

So soon as we had finished our meal our venerable conductor, who had been standing all the while, regarding us with inquiring eyes, and our guns with something as like fear as his pride would allow him to show, bowed towards Good, whom he evidently took for the leader of the party on account of the splendour of his apparel, and once more led the way through the door and to the foot of the great staircase. Here we paused for a moment to admire two colossal lions, each hewn from a single block of pure black marble, and standing rampant on the terminations of the wide balustrades of the staircase. These lions are magnificently executed, and it is said were sculptured by Rademas, the great prince who designed the staircase, and who was without doubt, to judge from the many beautiful examples of his art that we saw afterwards, one of the finest sculptors who ever lived, either in this or any other country. Then we climbed almost with a feeling of awe up that splendid stair, a work executed for all time and that will, I do not doubt, be admired thousands of years hence by generations unborn unless an earthquake should throw it down. Even Umslopogaas, who as a general rule made it a point of honour not to show astonishment, which he considered undignified, was fairly startled out of himself, and asked if the 'bridge had been built by men or devils', which was his vague way of alluding to any supernatural power. But Alphonse did not care about it. Its solid grandeur jarred upon the frivolous little Frenchman, who said that it was all 'tres magnifique, mais triste—ah, triste!' and went on to suggest that it would be improved if the balustrades were *gilt*.

On we went up the first flight of one hundred and twenty steps, across the broad platform joining it to the second flight, where we paused to admire the glorious view of one of the most beautiful stretches of country that the world can show, edged by the blue waters of the lake. Then we passed on up the stair till at last we reached the top, where we found a large standing space to which there were three entrances, all of small size. Two of these opened on to rather narrow galleries or roadways cut in the face of the precipice that ran round the palace walls and led to the principal thoroughfares of the city, and were used by the inhabitants passing up and down from the docks. These were defended by gates of bronze, and also, as we afterwards learnt, it was possible to let down a portion of the roadways themselves by withdrawing certain bolts, and thus render it quite impracticable for an enemy to pass. The third entrance consisted of a flight of ten curved black marble steps leading to a doorway cut in the palace wall. This wall was in itself a work of art, being built of huge blocks of granite to the height of forty feet, and so fashioned that its face was concave, whereby it was rendered practically impossible for it to be scaled. To this doorway our guide led us. The door, which was massive, and made of wood protected by an outer gate of bronze, was closed; but on our approach it was thrown wide, and we were met by the challenge of a sentry, who was armed with a heavy triangular-bladed spear, not unlike a bayonet in shape, and a cutting sword, and protected by breast and back plates of skilfully prepared hippopotamus hide, and a small round shield fashioned of the same tough material. The sword instantly attracted our attention; it was practically identical with the one in the possession of Mr. Mackenzie which he had obtained from the ill-starred wanderer. There was no mistaking the gold-lined fretwork cut in the thickness of the blade. So the man had told the truth after all. Our guide instantly gave a password, which the soldier acknowledged by letting the iron shaft of his spear fall with a ringing sound upon the pavement, and we passed on through the massive wall into the courtyard of the palace. This was about forty yards square, and laid out in flower-beds full of lovely shrubs and plants, many of which were quite new to me. Through the centre of this garden ran a broad walk formed of powdered shells brought from the lake in the place of gravel. Following this we came to another doorway with a round heavy arch, which is hung with thick curtains, for there are no doors in the palace itself. Then came another short passage, and we were in the great hall of the palace, and once more stood astonished at the simple and yet overpowering grandeur of the place.

The hall is, as we afterwards learnt, one hundred and fifty feet long by eighty wide, and has a magnificent arched roof of carved wood. Down the entire length of the building there are on either side, and at a distance of twenty feet from the wall, slender shafts of black marble springing sheer to the roof, beautifully fluted, and with carved capitals. At one end of this great place which these pillars support is the group of which I have already spoken as executed by the King Rademas to commemorate his building of the staircase; and really, when we had time to admire it, its loveliness almost struck us dumb. The group, of which the figures are in white, and the rest is black marble, is about half as large again as life, and represents a young man of noble countenance and form sleeping heavily upon a couch. One arm is carelessly thrown over the side of this couch, and his head reposes upon the other, its curling locks partially hiding it. Bending over him, her hand resting on his forehead, is a draped female form of such white loveliness as to make the beholder's breath stand still. And as for the calm glory that shines upon her perfect face—well, I can never hope to describe it. But there it rests like the shadow of an angel's smile; and power, love, and divinity all have their part in it. Her eyes are fixed upon the sleeping youth, and perhaps the most extraordinary thing about this beautiful work is the success with which the artist has succeeded in depicting on the sleeper's worn and weary face the sudden rising of a new and spiritual thought as the spell begins to work within his mind. You can see that an inspiration is breaking in upon the darkness of the man's soul as the dawn breaks in upon the darkness of night. It is a glorious piece of statuary, and none but a genius could have conceived it. Between each of the black marble columns is some such group of figures, some allegorical, and some representing the persons and wives of deceased monarchs or great men; but none of them, in our opinion, comes up to the one I have described, although several are from the hand of the sculptor and engineer, King Rademas.

In the exact centre of the hall was a solid mass of black marble about the size of a baby's arm-chair, which it rather resembled in appearance. This, as we afterwards learnt, was the sacred stone of this remarkable people, and on it their monarchs laid their hand after the ceremony of coronation, and swore by the sun to safeguard the interests of the empire, and to maintain its customs, traditions, and laws. This stone was evidently exceedingly ancient (as indeed all stones are), and was scored down its sides with long marks or lines, which Sir Henry said proved it to have been a fragment that at some remote period in its history had been ground in the iron jaws of glaciers. There was a curious prophecy about this block of marble, which was reported among the people to have fallen from the sun, to the effect that when it was shattered into fragments a king of alien race should rule over the land. As the stone, however, looked remarkably solid, the native princes seemed to have a fair chance of keeping their own for many a long year.

At the end of the hall is a dais spread with rich carpets, on which two thrones are set side by side. These thrones are shaped like great chairs, and made of solid gold. The seats are richly cushioned, but the backs are left bare, and on each is carved the emblem of the sun, shooting out his fiery rays in all directions. The footstools are golden lions couchant, with yellow topazes set in them for eyes. There are no other gems about them.

The place is lighted by numerous but narrow windows, placed high up, cut on the principle of the loopholes to be seen in ancient castles, but innocent of glass, which was evidently unknown here.

Such is a brief description of this splendid hall in which we now found ourselves, compiled of course from our subsequent knowledge of it. On this occasion we had but little time for observation, for when we entered we perceived that a large number of men were gathered together in front of the two thrones, which were unoccupied. The principal among them were seated on carved wooden chairs ranged to the right and the left of the thrones, but not in front of them, and were dressed in white tunics, with various embroideries and different coloured edgings, and armed with the usual pierced and gold-inlaid swords. To judge from the dignity of their appearance, they seemed one and all to be individuals of very great importance. Behind each of these great men stood a small knot of followers and attendants.

Seated by themselves, in a little group to the left of the throne, were six men of a different stamp. Instead of wearing the ordinary kilt, they were clothed in long robes of pure white linen, with the same symbol of the sun that is to be seen on the back of the chairs, emblazoned in gold thread upon the breast. This garment was girt up at the waist with a simple golden curb-like chain, from which hung long elliptic plates of the same metal, fashioned in shiny scales like those of a fish, that, as their wearers moved, jingled and reflected the light. They were all men of mature age and of a severe and impressive cast of features, which was rendered still more imposing by the long beards they wore.

The personality of one individual among them, however, impressed us at once. He seemed to stand out among his fellows and refuse to be overlooked. He was very old—eighty at least—and extremely tall, with a long snow-white beard that hung nearly to his waist. His features were aquiline and deeply cut, and his eyes were grey and cold-looking. The heads of the others were bare, but this man wore a round cap entirely covered with gold embroidery, from which we judged that he was a person of great importance; and indeed we afterwards discovered that he was Agon, the High Priest of the country. As we approached, all these men, including the priests, rose and bowed to us with the greatest courtesy, at the same time placing the two fingers across the lips in salutation. Then soft-footed attendants advanced from between the pillars, bearing seats, which were placed in a line in front of the thrones. We three sat down, Alphonse and Umslopogaas standing behind us. Scarcely had we done so when there came a blare of trumpets from some passage to the right, and a similar blare from the left. Next a man with a long white wand of ivory appeared just in front of the right-hand throne, and cried out something in a loud voice, ending with the word *Nyleptha*, repeated three times; and another man, similarly attired, called out a similar sentence before the other throne, but ending with the word *Sorais*, also repeated thrice. Then came the tramp of armed men from each side entrance, and in filed about a score of picked and magnificently accoutred guards, who formed up on each side of the thrones, and let their heavy iron-handled spears fall simultaneously with a clash upon the black marble flooring. Another double blare of trumpets, and in from either side, each attended by six maidens, swept the two Queens of Zu-Vendis, everybody in the hall rising to greet them as they came.

I have seen beautiful women in my day, and am no longer thrown into transports at the sight of a pretty face; but language fails me when I try to give some idea of the blaze of loveliness that then broke upon us in the persons of these sister Queens. Both were young—perhaps five-and-twenty years of age—both were tall and exquisitely formed; but there the likeness stopped. One, Nyleptha, was a woman of dazzling fairness; her right arm and breast bare, after the custom of her people, showed like snow even against her white and gold-embroidered 'kaf', or toga. And as for her sweet face, all I can say is, that it was one that few men could look on and forget. Her hair, a veritable crown of gold, clustered in short ringlets over her shapely head, half hiding the ivory brow, beneath which eyes of deep and glorious grey flashed out in tender majesty. I cannot attempt to describe her other features, only the mouth was most sweet, and curved like Cupid's bow, and over the whole countenance there shone an indescribable look of loving-kindness, lit up by a shadow of delicate humour that lay upon her face like a touch of silver on a rosy cloud.

She wore no jewels, but on her neck, arm, and knee were the usual torques of gold, in this instance fashioned like a snake; and her dress was of pure white linen of excessive fineness, plentifully embroidered with gold and with the familiar symbols of the sun.

Her twin sister, Sorais, was of a different and darker type of beauty. Her hair was wavy like Nyleptha's but coal-black, and fell in masses on her shoulders; her complexion was olive, her eyes large, dark, and lustrous; the lips were full, and I thought rather cruel. Somehow her face, quiet and even cold as it is, gave an idea of passion in repose, and caused one to wonder involuntarily what its aspect would be if anything occurred to break the calm. It reminded me of the deep sea, that even on the bluest days never loses its visible stamp of power, and in its murmuring sleep is yet instinct with the spirit of the storm. Her figure, like her sister's, was almost perfect in its curves and outlines, but a trifle more rounded, and her dress was absolutely the same.

As this lovely pair swept onwards to their respective thrones, amid the deep attentive silence of the Court, I was bound to confess to myself that they did indeed fulfil my idea of royalty. Royal they were in every way—in form, in grace, and queenly dignity, and in the barbaric splendour of their attendant pomp. But methought that they needed no guards or gold to proclaim their power and bind the loyalty of wayward men. A glance from those bright eyes or a smile from those sweet lips, and while the red blood runs in the veins of youth women such as these will never lack subjects ready to do their biddings to the death.

But after all they were women first and queens afterwards, and therefore not devoid of curiosity. As they passed to their seats I saw both of them glance swiftly in our direction. I saw, too, that their eyes passed by me, seeing nothing to charm them in the person of an insignificant and grizzled old man. Then they looked with evident astonishment on the grim form of old Umslopogaas, who raised his axe in salutation. Attracted next by the splendour of Good's apparel, for a second their glance rested on him like a humming moth upon a flower, then off it darted to where Sir Henry Curtis stood, the sunlight from a window playing upon his yellow hair and peaked beard, and marking the outlines of his massive frame against the twilight of the somewhat gloomy hall. He raised his eyes, and they met the fair Nyleptha's full, and thus for the first time the goodliest man and woman that it has ever been my lot to see looked one upon another. And why it was I know not, but I saw the swift blood run up Nyleptha's skin as the pink lights run up the morning sky. Red grew her fair bosom and shapely arm, red the swanlike neck; the rounded cheeks blushed red as the petals of a rose, and then the crimson flood sank back to whence it came and left her pale and trembling.

I glanced at Sir Henry. He, too, had coloured up to the eyes.

'Oh, my word!' thought I to myself, 'the ladies have come on the stage, and now we may look to the plot to develop itself.' And I sighed and shook my head, knowing that the beauty of a woman is like the beauty of the lightning—a destructive thing and a cause of desolation. By the time that I had finished my reflections both the Queens were on the thrones, for all this had happened in about six seconds. Once more the unseen trumpets blared out, and then the Court seated itself, and Queen Sorais motioned to us to do likewise.

Next from among the crowd whither he had withdrawn stepped forward our guide, the old gentleman who had towed us ashore, holding by the hand the girl whom we had seen first and afterwards rescued from the hippopotamus. Having made obeisance he proceeded to address the Queens, evidently describing to them the way and place where we had been found. It was most amusing to watch the astonishment, not unmixed with fear, reflected upon their faces as they listened to his tale. Clearly they could not understand how we had reached the lake and been found floating on it, and were inclined to attribute our presence to supernatural causes. Then the narrative proceeded, as I judged from the frequent appeals that our guide made to the girl, to the point where we had shot the hippopotami, and we at once perceived that there was something very wrong about those hippopotami, for the history was frequently interrupted by indignant exclamations from the little group of white-robed priests and even from the courtiers, while the two Queens listened with an amazed expression, especially when our guide pointed to the rifles in our hands as being the means of destruction. And here, to make matters clear, I may as well explain at once that the inhabitants of Zu-Vendis are sun-worshippers, and that for some reason or another the hippopotamus is sacred among them. Not that they do not kill it, because at a certain season of the year they slaughter thousands—which are specially preserved in large lakes up the country—and use their hides for armour for soldiers; but this does not prevent them from considering these animals as sacred to the sun. Now, as ill luck would have it, the particular hippopotami we had shot were a family of tame animals that were kept in the mouth of the port and daily fed by priests whose special duty it was to attend to them. When we shot them I thought that the brutes were suspiciously tame, and this was, as we afterwards ascertained, the cause of it. Thus it came about that in attempting to show off we had committed sacrilege of a most aggravated nature.

When our guide had finished his tale, the old man with the long beard and round cap, whose appearance I have already described, and who was, as I have said, the High Priest of the country, and known by the name of Agon, rose and commenced an impassioned harangue. I did not like the look of his cold grey eye as he fixed it on us. I should have liked it still less had I known that in the name of the outraged majesty of his god he was demanding that the whole lot of us should be offered up as a sacrifice by means of being burnt alive.

After he had finished speaking the Queen Sorais addressed him in a soft and musical voice, and appeared, to judge from his gestures of dissent, to be putting the other side of the question before him. Then Nyleptha spoke in liquid accents. Little did we know that she was pleading for our lives. Finally, she turned and addressed a tall, soldierlike man of middle age with a black beard and a long plain sword, whose name, as we afterwards learnt, was Nasta, and who was the greatest lord in the country; apparently appealing to him for support. Now when Sir Henry had caught her eye and she had blushed so rosy red, I had seen that the incident had not escaped this man's notice, and, what is more, that it was eminently disagreeable to him, for he bit his lip and his hand tightened on his sword-hilt. Afterwards we learnt that he was an aspirant for the hand of this Queen in marriage, which accounted for it. This being so, Nyleptha could not have appealed to a worse person, for, speaking in slow, heavy tones, he appeared to confirm all that the High Priest Agon had said. As he spoke, Sorais put her elbow on her knee, and, resting her chin on her hand, looked at him with a suppressed smile upon her lips, as though she saw through the man, and was determined to be his match; but Nyleptha grew very angry, her cheek flushed, her eyes flashed, and she did indeed look lovely. Finally she turned to Agon and seemed to give some sort of qualified assent, for he bowed at her words; and as she spoke she moved her hands as though to emphasize what she said; while all the time Sorais kept her chin on her hand and smiled. Then suddenly Nyleptha made a sign, the trumpets blew again, and everybody rose to leave the hall save ourselves and the guards, whom she motioned to stay.

When they were all gone she bent forward and, smiling sweetly, partially by signs and partially by exclamations made it clear to us that she was very anxious to know where we came from. The difficulty was how to explain, but at last an idea struck me. I had my large pocket-book in my pocket and a pencil. Taking it out, I made a little sketch of a lake, and then as best I could I drew the underground river and the lake at the other end. When I had done this I advanced to the steps of the throne and gave it to her. She understood it at once and clapped her hands with delight, and then descending from the throne took it to her sister Sorais, who also evidently understood. Next she took the pencil from me, and after examining it with curiosity proceeded to make a series of delightful little sketches, the first representing herself holding out both hands in welcome, and a man uncommonly like Sir Henry taking them. Next she drew a lovely little picture of a hippopotamus rolling about dying in the water, and of an individual, in whom we had no difficulty in recognizing Agon the High Priest, holding up his hands in horror on the bank. Then followed a most alarming picture of a dreadful fiery furnace and of the same figure, Agon, poking us into it with a forked stick. This picture perfectly horrified me, but I was a little reassured when she nodded sweetly and proceeded to make a fourth drawing—a man again uncommonly like Sir Henry, and of two women, in whom I recognized Sorais and herself, each with one arm around him, and holding a sword in protection over him. To all of these Sorais, who I saw was employed in carefully taking us all in—especially Curtis—signified her approval by nodding.

At last Nyleptha drew a final sketch of a rising sun, indicating that she must go, and that we should meet on the following morning; whereat Sir Henry looked so disappointed that she saw it, and, I suppose by way of consolation, extended her hand to him to kiss, which he did with pious fervour. At the same time Sorais, off whom Good had never taken his eyeglass during the whole indaba (interview), rewarded him by giving him her hand to kiss, though, while she did so, her eyes were fixed upon Sir Henry. I am glad to say that I was not implicated in these proceedings; neither of them gave *me* her hand to kiss.

Then Nyleptha turned and addressed the man who appeared to be in command of the bodyguard, apparently from her manner and his frequent obeisances, giving him very stringent and careful orders; after which, with a somewhat coquettish nod and smile, she left the hall, followed by Sorais and most of the guards.

When the Queens had gone, the officer whom Nyleptha had addressed came forward and with many tokens of deep respect led us from the hall through various passages to a sumptuous set of apartments opening out of a large central room lighted with brazen swinging lamps (for it was now dusk) and richly carpeted and strewn with couches. On a table in the centre of the room was set a profusion of food and fruit, and, what is more, flowers. There was a delicious wine also in ancient-looking sealed earthenware flagons, and beautifully chased golden and ivory cups to drink it from. Servants, male and female, also were there to minister to us, and whilst we ate, from some recess outside the apartment

'The silver lute did speak between
The trumpet's lordly blowing;'

and altogether we found ourselves in a sort of earthly paradise which was only disturbed by the vision of that disgusting High Priest who intended to commit us to the flames. But so very weary were we with our labours that we could scarcely keep ourselves awake through the sumptuous meal, and as soon as it was over we indicated that we desired to sleep. As a further precaution against surprise we left Umslopogaas with his axe to sleep in the main chamber near the curtained doorways leading to the apartments which we occupied respectively, Good and I in the one, and Sir Henry and Alphonse in the other. Then throwing off our clothes, with the exception of the mail shirts, which we considered it safer to keep on, we flung ourselves down upon the low and luxurious couches, and drew the silk-embroidered coverlids over us.

In two minutes I was just dropping off when I was aroused by Good's voice.

'I say, Quatermain,' he said, 'did you ever see such eyes?'

'Eyes!' I said, crossly; 'what eyes?'

'Why, the Queen's, of course! Sorais, I mean—at least I think that is her name.'

'Oh, I don't know,' I yawned; 'I didn't notice them much: I suppose they are good eyes,' and again I dropped off.

Five minutes or so elapsed, and I was once more awakened.

'I say, Quatermain,' said the voice.

'Well,' I answered testily, 'what is it now?'

'Did you notice her ankle? The shape—'

This was more than I could stand. By my bed stood the veldtschoons I had been wearing. Moved quite beyond myself, I took them up and threw them straight at Good's head—and hit it.

Afterwards I slept the sleep of the just, and a very heavy sleep it must be. As for Good, I don't know if he went to sleep or if he continued to pass Sorais' beauties in mental review, and, what is more, I don't care.

XIII

About the Zu-Vendi People

A nd now the curtain is down for a few hours, and the actors in this novel drama are plunged in dewy sleep. Perhaps we should except Nyleptha, whom the reader may, if poetically inclined, imagine lying in her bed of state encompassed by her maidens, tiring women, guards, and all the other people and appurtenances that surround a throne, and yet not able to slumber for thinking of the strangers who had visited a country where no such strangers had ever come before, and wondering, as she lay awake, who they were and what their past has been, and if she was ugly compared to the women of their native place. I, however, not being poetically inclined, will take advantage of the lull to give some account of the people among whom we found ourselves, compiled, needless to state, from information which we subsequently collected.

The name of this country, to begin at the beginning, is Zu-Vendis, from Zu, 'yellow', and Vendis, 'place or country'. Why it is called the Yellow Country I have never been able to ascertain accurately, nor do the inhabitants themselves know. Three reasons are, however, given, each of which would suffice to account for it. The first is that the name owes its origin to the great quantity of gold that is found in the land. Indeed, in this respect Zu-Vendis is a veritable Eldorado, the precious metal being extraordinarily plentiful. At present it is collected from purely alluvial diggings, which we subsequently inspected, and which are situated within a day's journey from Milosis, being mostly found in pockets and in nuggets weighing from an ounce up to six or seven pounds in weight. But other diggings of a similar nature are known to exist, and I have besides seen great veins of gold-bearing quartz. In Zu-Vendis gold is a much commoner metal than silver, and thus it has curiously enough come to pass that silver is the legal tender of the country.

The second reason given is, that at certain times of the year the native grasses of the country, which are very sweet and good, turn as yellow as ripe corn; and the third arises from a tradition that the people were originally yellow skinned, but grew white after living for many generations upon these high lands. Zu-Vendis is a country about the size of France, is, roughly speaking, oval in shape; and on every side cut off from the surrounding territory by illimitable forests of impenetrable thorn, beyond which are said to be hundreds of miles of morasses, deserts, and great mountains. It is, in short, a huge, high tableland rising up in the centre of the dark continent, much as in southern Africa flat-topped mountains rise from the level of the surrounding veldt. Milosis itself lies, according to my aneroid, at a level of about nine thousand feet above the sea, but most of the land is even higher, the greatest elevation of the open country being, I believe, about eleven thousand feet. As a consequence the climate is, comparatively speaking, a cold one, being very similar to that of southern England, only brighter and not so rainy. The land is, however, exceedingly fertile, and grows all cereals and temperate fruits and timber to perfection; and in the lower-lying parts even produces a hardy variety of sugar-cane. Coal is found in great abundance, and in many places crops out from the surface; and so is pure marble, both black and white. The same may be said of almost every metal except silver, which is scarce, and only to be obtained from a range of mountains in the north.

Zu-Vendis comprises in her boundaries a great variety of scenery, including two ranges of snow-clad mountains, one on the western boundary beyond the impenetrable belt of thorn forest, and the other piercing the country from north to south, and passing at a distance of about eighty miles from Milosis, from which town its higher peaks are distinctly visible. This range forms the chief watershed of the land. There are also three large lakes—the biggest, namely that whereon we emerged, and which is named Milosis after the city, covering some two hundred square miles of country—and numerous small ones, some of them salt.

The population of this favoured land is, comparatively speaking, dense, numbering at a rough estimate from ten to twelve millions. It is almost purely agricultural in its habits, and divided into great classes as in civilized countries. There is a territorial nobility, a considerable middle class, formed principally of merchants, officers of the army, etc.; but the great bulk of the people are well-to-do peasants who live upon the lands of the lords, from whom they hold under a species of feudal tenure. The best bred people in the country are, as I think I have said, pure whites with a somewhat southern cast of countenance; but the common herd are much darker, though they do not show any negro or other African characteristics. As to their descent I can give no certain information. Their written records, which extend back for about a thousand years, give no hint of it. One very ancient chronicler does indeed, in alluding to some old tradition that existed in his day, talk of it as having probably originally 'come down with the people from the coast', but that may mean little or nothing. In short, the origin of the Zu-Vendi is lost in the mists of time. Whence they came or of what race they are no man knows. Their architecture and some of their sculptures suggest an Egyptian or possibly an Assyrian origin; but it is well known that their present remarkable style of building has only sprung up within the last eight hundred years, and they certainly retain no traces of Egyptian theology or customs. Again, their appearance and some of their habits are rather Jewish; but here again it seems hardly conceivable that they should have utterly lost all traces of the Jewish religion. Still, for aught I know, they may be one of the lost ten tribes whom people are so fond of discovering all over the world, or they may not. I do not know, and so can only describe them as I find them, and leave wiser heads than mine to make what they can out of it, if indeed this account should ever be read at all, which is exceedingly doubtful.

And now after I have said all this, I am, after all, going to hazard a theory of my own, though it is only a very little one, as the young lady said in mitigation of her baby. This theory is founded on a legend which I have heard among the Arabs on the east coast, which is to the effect that 'more than two thousand years ago' there were troubles in the country which was known as Babylonia, and that thereon a vast horde of Persians came down to Bushire, where they took ship and were driven by the north-east monsoon to the east coast of Africa, where, according to the legend, 'the sun and fire worshippers' fell into conflict with the belt of Arab settlers who even then were settled on the east coast, and finally broke their way through them, and, vanishing into the interior, were no more seen. Now, I ask, is it not at least possible that the Zu-Vendi people are the descendants of these 'sun and fire worshippers' who broke through the Arabs and vanished? As a matter of fact, there is a good deal in their characters and customs that tallies with the somewhat vague ideas that I have of Persians. Of course we have no books of reference here, but Sir Henry says that if his memory does not fail him, there was a tremendous revolt in Babylon about 500 BC, whereon a vast multitude were expelled from the city. Anyhow, it is a well-established fact that there have been many separate emigrations of Persians from the Persian Gulf to the east coast of Africa up to as lately as seven hundred years ago. There are Persian tombs at Kilwa, on the east coast, still in good repair, which bear dates showing them to be just seven hundred years old.

In addition to being an agricultural people, the Zu-Vendi are, oddly enough, excessively warlike, and as they cannot from the exigencies of their position make war upon other nations, they fight among each other like the famed Kilkenny cats, with the happy result that the population never outgrows the power of the country to support it. This habit of theirs is largely fostered by the political condition of the country. The monarchy is nominally an absolute one, save in so far as it is tempered by the power of the priests and the informal council of the great lords; but, as in many other institutions, the king's writ does not run unquestioned throughout the length and breadth of the land. In short, the whole system is a purely feudal one (though absolute serfdom or slavery is unknown), all the great lords holding nominally from the throne, but a number of them being practically independent, having the power of life and death, waging war against and making peace with their neighbours as the whim or their interests lead them, and even on occasion rising in open rebellion against their royal master or mistress, and, safely shut up in their castles and fenced cities, as far from the seat of government, successfully defying them for years.

Zu-Vendis has had its king-makers as well as England, a fact that will be well appreciated when I state that eight different dynasties have sat upon the throne in the last one thousand years, every one of which took its rise from some noble family that succeeded in grasping the purple after a sanguinary struggle. At the date of our arrival in the country things were a little better than they had been for some centuries, the last king, the father of Nyleptha and Sorais, having been an exceptionally able and vigorous ruler, and, as a consequence, he kept down the power of the priests and nobles. On his death, two years before we reached Zu-Vendis, the twin sisters, his children, were, following an ancient precedent, called to the throne, since an attempt to exclude either would instantly have provoked a sanguinary civil war; but it was generally felt in the country that this measure was a most unsatisfactory one, and could hardly be expected to be permanent. Indeed, as it was, the various intrigues that were set on foot by ambitious nobles to obtain the hand of one or other of the queens in marriage had disquieted the country, and the general opinion was that there would be bloodshed before long.

I will now pass on to the question of the Zu-Vendi religion, which is nothing more or less than sun-worship of a pronounced and highly developed character. Around this sun-worship is grouped the entire social system of the Zu-Vendi. It sends its roots through every institution and custom of the land. From the cradle to the grave the Zu-Vendi follows the sun in every sense of the saying. As an infant he is solemnly held up in its light and dedicated to 'the symbol of good, the expression of power, and the hope of Eternity', the ceremony answering to our baptism. Whilst still a tiny child, his parents point out the glorious orb as the presence of a visible and beneficent god, and he worships it at its up-rising and down-setting. Then when still quite small, he goes, holding fast to the pendent end of his mother's 'kaf' (toga), up to the temple of the Sun of the nearest city, and there, when at midday the bright beams strike down upon the golden central altar and beat back the fire that burns thereon, he hears the white-robed priests raise their solemn chant of praise and sees the people fall down to adore, and then, amidst the blowing of the golden trumpets, watches the sacrifice thrown into the fiery furnace beneath the altar. Here he comes again to be declared 'a man' by the priests, and consecrated to war and to good works; here before the solemn altar he leads his bride; and here too, if differences shall unhappily arise, he divorces her.

And so on, down life's long pathway till the last mile is travelled, and he comes again armed indeed, and with dignity, but no longer a man. Here they bear him dead and lay his bier upon the falling brazen doors before the eastern altar, and when the last ray from the setting sun falls upon his white face the bolts are drawn and he vanishes into the raging furnace beneath and is ended.

The priests of the Sun do not marry, but are recruited as young men specially devoted to the work by their parents and supported by the State. The nomination to the higher offices of the priesthood lies with the Crown, but once appointed the nominees cannot be dispossessed, and it is scarcely too much to say that they really rule the land. To begin with, they are a united body sworn to obedience and secrecy, so that an order issued by the High Priest at Milosis will be instantly and unhesitatingly acted upon by the resident priest of a little country town three or four hundred miles off. They are the judges of the land, criminal and civil, an appeal lying only to the lord paramount of the district, and from him to the king; and they have, of course, practically unlimited jurisdiction over religious and moral offences, together with a right of excommunication, which, as in the faiths of more highly civilized lands, is a very effective weapon. Indeed, their rights and powers are almost unlimited, but I may as well state here that the priests of the Sun are wise in their generation, and do not push things too far. It is but very seldom that they go to extremes against anybody, being more inclined to exercise the prerogative of mercy than run the risk of exasperating the powerful and vigorous-minded people on whose neck they have set their yoke, lest it should rise and break it off altogether.

Another source of the power of the priests is their practical monopoly of learning, and their very considerable astronomical knowledge, which enables them to keep a hold on the popular mind by predicting eclipses and even comets. In Zu-Vendis only a few of the upper classes can read and write, but nearly all the priests have this knowledge, and are therefore looked upon as learned men.

The law of the country is, on the whole, mild and just, but differs in several respects from our civilized law. For instance, the law of England is much more severe upon offences against property than against the person, as becomes a people whose ruling passion is money. A man may half kick his wife to death or inflict horrible sufferings upon his children at a much cheaper rate of punishment than he can compound for the theft of a pair of old boots. In Zu-Vendis this is not so, for there they rightly or wrongly look upon the person as of more consequence than goods and chattels, and not, as in England, as a sort of necessary appendage to the latter. For murder the punishment is death, for treason death, for defrauding the orphan and the widow, for sacrilege, and for attempting to quit the country (which is looked on as a sacrilege) death. In each case the method of execution is the same, and a rather awful one. The culprit is thrown alive into the fiery furnace beneath one of the altars to the Sun. For all other offences, including the offence of idleness, the punishment is forced labour upon the vast national buildings which are always going on in some part of the country, with or without periodical floggings, according to the crime.

The social system of the Zu-Vendi allows considerable liberty to the individual, provided he does not offend against the laws and customs of the country. They are polygamous in theory, though most of them have only one wife on account of the expense. By law a man is bound to provide a separate establishment for each wife. The first wife also is the legal wife, and her children are said to be 'of the house of the Father'. The children of the other wives are of the houses of their respective mothers. This does not, however, imply any slur upon either mother or children. Again, a first wife can, on entering into the married state, make a bargain that her husband shall marry no other wife. This, however, is very rarely done, as the women are the great upholders of polygamy, which not only provides for their surplus numbers but gives greater importance to the first wife, who is thus practically the head of several households. Marriage is looked upon as primarily a civil contract, and, subject to certain conditions and to a proper provision for children, is dissoluble at the will of both contracting parties, the divorce, or 'unloosing', being formally and ceremoniously accomplished by going through certain portions of the marriage ceremony backwards.

The Zu-Vendi are on the whole a very kindly, pleasant, and light-hearted people. They are not great traders and care little about money, only working to earn enough to support themselves in that class of life in which they were born. They are exceedingly conservative, and look with disfavour upon changes. Their legal tender is silver, cut into little squares of different weights; gold is the baser coin, and is about of the same value as our silver. It is, however, much prized for its beauty, and largely used for ornaments and decorative purposes. Most of the trade, however, is carried on by means of sale and barter, payment being made in kind. Agriculture is the great business of the country, and is really well understood and carried out, most of the available acreage being under cultivation. Great attention is also given to the breeding of cattle and horses, the latter being unsurpassed by any I have ever seen either in Europe or Africa.

The land belongs theoretically to the Crown, and under the Crown to the great lords, who again divide it among smaller lords, and so on down to the little peasant farmer who works his forty 'reestu' (acres) on a system of half-profits with his immediate lord. In fact the whole system is, as I have said, distinctly feudal, and it interested us much to meet with such an old friend far in the unknown heart of Africa.

The taxes are very heavy. The State takes a third of a man's total earnings, and the priesthood about five per cent on the remainder. But on the other hand, if a man through any cause falls into bona fide misfortune the State supports him in the position of life to which he belongs. If he is idle, however, he is sent to work on the Government undertakings, and the State looks after his wives and children. The State also makes all the roads and builds all town houses, about which

H. RIDER HAGGARD

great care is shown, letting them out to families at a small rent. It also keeps up a standing army of about twenty thousand men, and provides watchmen, etc. In return for their five per cent the priests attend to the service of the temples, carry out all religious ceremonies, and keep schools, where they teach whatever they think desirable, which is not very much. Some of the temples also possess private property, but priests as individuals cannot hold property.

And now comes a question which I find some difficulty in answering. Are the Zu-Vendi a civilized or barbarous people? Sometimes I think the one, sometimes the other. In some branches of art they have attained the very highest proficiency. Take for instance their buildings and their statuary. I do not think that the latter can be equalled either in beauty or imaginative power anywhere in the world, and as for the former it may have been rivalled in ancient Egypt, but I am sure that it has never been since. But, on the other hand, they are totally ignorant of many other arts. Till Sir Henry, who happened to know something about it, showed them how to do it by mixing silica and lime, they could not make a piece of glass, and their crockery is rather primitive. A water-clock is their nearest approach to a watch; indeed, ours delighted them exceedingly. They know nothing about steam, electricity, or gunpowder, and mercifully for themselves nothing about printing or the penny post. Thus they are spared many evils, for of a truth our age has learnt the wisdom of the old-world saying, 'He who increaseth knowledge, increaseth sorrow.'

As regards their religion, it is a natural one for imaginative people who know no better, and might therefore be expected to turn to the sun and worship him as the all-Father, but it cannot justly be called elevating or spiritual. It is true that they do sometimes speak of the sun as the 'garment of the Spirit', but it is a vague term, and what they really adore is the fiery orb himself. They also call him the 'hope of eternity', but here again the meaning is vague, and I doubt if the phrase conveys any very clear impression to their minds. Some of them do indeed believe in a future life for the good—I know Nyleptha does firmly—but it is a private faith arising from the promptings of the spirit, not an essential of their creed. So on the whole I cannot say that I consider this sun-worship as a religion indicative of a civilized people, however magnificent and imposing its ritual, or however moral and high-sounding the maxims of its priests, many of whom, I am sure, have their own opinions on the whole subject; though of course they have nothing but praise for a system which provides them with so many of the good things of this world.

There are now only two more matters to which I need allude—namely, the language and the system of calligraphy. As for the former, it is soft-sounding, and very rich and flexible. Sir Henry says that it sounds something like modern Greek, but of course it has no connection with it. It is easy to acquire, being simple in its construction, and a peculiar quality about it is its euphony, and the way in which the sound of the words adapts itself to the meaning to be expressed. Long before we mastered the language, we could frequently make out what was meant by the ring of the sentence. It is on this account that the language lends itself so well to poetical declamation, of which these remarkable people are very fond. The Zu-Vendi alphabet seems, Sir Henry says, to be derived, like every other known system of letters, from a Phoenician source, and therefore more remotely still from the ancient Egyptian hieratic writing. Whether this is a fact I cannot say, not being learned in such matters. All I know about it is that their alphabet consists of twenty-two characters, of which a few, notably B, E, and O, are not very unlike our own. The whole affair is, however, clumsy and puzzling. But as the people of Zu-Vendi are not given to the writing of novels, or of anything except business documents and records of the briefest character, it answers their purpose well enough.

XIV

THE FLOWER TEMPLE

It was half-past eight by my watch when I woke on the morning following our arrival at Milosis, having slept almost exactly twelve hours, and I must say that I did indeed feel better. Ah, what a blessed thing is sleep! and what a difference twelve hours of it or so makes to us after days and nights of toil and danger. It is like going to bed one man and getting up another.

I sat up upon my silken couch—never had I slept upon such a bed before—and the first thing that I saw was Good's eyeglass fixed on me from the recesses of his silken couch. There was nothing else of him to be seen except his eyeglass, but I knew from the look of it that he was awake, and waiting till I woke up to begin.

'I say, Quatermain,' he commenced sure enough, 'did you observe her skin? It is as smooth as the back of an ivory hairbrush.'

'Now look here, Good,' I remonstrated, when there came a sound at the curtain, which, on being drawn, admitted a functionary, who signified by signs that he was there to lead us to the bath. We gladly consented, and were conducted to a delightful marble chamber, with a pool of running crystal water in the centre of it, into which we gaily plunged. When we had bathed, we returned to our apartment and dressed, and then went into the central room where we had supped on the previous evening, to find a morning meal already prepared for us, and a capital meal it was, though I should be puzzled to describe the dishes. After breakfast we lounged round and admired the tapestries and carpets and some pieces of statuary that were placed about, wondering the while what was going to happen next. Indeed, by this time our minds were in such a state of complete bewilderment that we were, as a matter of fact, ready for anything that might arrive. As for our sense of astonishment, it was pretty well obliterated. Whilst we were still thus engaged, our friend the captain of the guard presented himself, and with many obeisances signified that we were to follow him, which we did, not without doubts and heart-searchings—for we guessed that the time had come when we should have to settle the bill for those confounded hippopotami with our cold-eyed friend Agon, the High

Priest. However, there was no help for it, and personally I took great comfort in the promise of the protection of the sister Queens, knowing that if ladies have a will they can generally find a way; so off we started as though we liked it. A minute's walk through a passage and an outer court brought us to the great double gates of the palace that open on to the wide highway which runs uphill through the heart of Milosis to the Temple of the Sun a mile away, and thence down the slope on the farther side of the temple to the outer wall of the city.

These gates are very large and massive, and an extraordinarily beautiful work in metal. Between them—for one set is placed at the entrance to an interior, and one at that of the exterior wall—is a fosse, forty-five feet in width. This fosse is filled with water and spanned by a drawbridge, which when lifted makes the palace nearly impregnable to anything except siege guns. As we came, one half of the wide gates were flung open, and we passed over the drawbridge and presently stood gazing up one of the most imposing, if not the most imposing, roadways in the world. It is a hundred feet from curb to curb, and on either side, not cramped and crowded together, as is our European fashion, but each standing in its own grounds, and built equidistant from and in similar style to the rest, are a series of splendid, single-storied mansions, all of red granite. These are the town houses of the nobles of the Court, and stretch away in unbroken lines for a mile or more till the eye is arrested by the glorious vision of the Temple of the Sun that crowns the hill and heads the roadway.

As we stood gazing at this splendid sight, of which more anon, there suddenly dashed up to the gateway four chariots, each drawn by two white horses. These chariots are two-wheeled, and made of wood. They are fitted with a stout pole, the weight of which is supported by leathern girths that form a portion of the harness. The wheels are made with four spokes only, are tired with iron, and quite innocent of springs. In the front of the chariot, and immediately over the pole, is a small seat for the driver, railed round to prevent him from being jolted off. Inside the machine itself are three low seats, one at each side, and one with the back to the horses, opposite to which is the door. The whole vehicle is lightly and yet strongly made, and, owing to the grace of the curves, though primitive, not half so ugly as might be expected.

But if the chariots left something to be desired, the horses did not. They were simply splendid, not very large but strongly built, and well ribbed up, with small heads, remarkably large and round hoofs, and a great look of speed and blood. I have often wondered whence this breed, which presents many distinct characteristics, came, but like that of its owners, it history is obscure. Like the people the horses have always been there. The first and last of these chariots were occupied by guards, but the centre two were empty, except for the driver, and to these we were conducted. Alphonse and I got into the first, and Sir Henry, Good, and Umslopogaas into the one behind, and then suddenly off we went. And we did go! Among the Zu-Vendi it is not usual to trot horses either riding or driving, especially when the journey to be made is a short one—they go at full gallop. As soon as we were seated the driver called out, the horses sprang forward, and we were whirled away at a speed sufficient to take one's breath, and which, till I got accustomed to it, kept me in momentary fear of an upset. As for the wretched Alphonse, he clung with a despairing face to the side of what he called this 'devil of a fiacre', thinking that every moment was his last. Presently it occurred to him to ask where we were going, and I told him that, as far as I could ascertain, we were going to be sacrificed by burning. You should have seen his face as he grasped the side of the vehicle and cried out in his terror.

But the wild-looking charioteer only leant forward over his flying steeds and shouted; and the air, as it went singing past, bore away the sound of Alphonse's lamentations.

And now before us, in all its marvellous splendour and dazzling loveliness, shone out the Temple of the Sun—the peculiar pride of the Zu-Vendi, to whom it was what Solomon's, or rather Herod's, Temple was to the Jews. The wealth, and skill, and labour of generations had been given to the building of this wonderful place, which had been only finally completed within the last fifty years. Nothing was spared that the country could produce, and the result was indeed worthy of the effort, not so much on account of its size—for there are larger fanes in the world—as because of its perfect proportions, the richness and beauty of its materials, and the wonderful workmanship. The building (that stands by itself on a space of some eight acres of garden ground on the hilltop, around which are the dwelling-places of the priests) is built in the shape of a sunflower, with a dome-covered central hall, from which radiate twelve petal-shaped courts, each dedicated to one of the twelve months, and serving as the repositories of statues reared in memory of the illustrious dead. The width of the circle beneath the dome is three hundred feet, the height of the dome is four hundred feet, and the length of the rays is one hundred and fifty feet, and the height of their roofs three hundred feet, so that they run into the central dome exactly as the petals of the sunflower run into the great raised heart. Thus the exact measurement from the centre of the central altar to the extreme point of any one of the rounded rays would be three hundred feet (the width of the circle itself), or a total of six hundred feet from the rounded extremity of one ray or petal to the extremity of the opposite one.

The building itself is of pure and polished white marble, which shows out in marvellous contrast to the red granite of the frowning city, on whose brow it glistens indeed like an imperial diadem upon the forehead of a dusky queen. The outer surface of the dome and of the twelve petal courts is covered entirely with thin sheets of beaten gold; and from the extreme point of the roof of each of these petals a glorious golden form with a trumpet in its hand and widespread wings is figured in the very act of soaring into space. I really must leave whoever reads this to imagine the surpassing beauty of these golden roofs flashing when the sun strikes—flashing like a thousand fires aflame on a mountain of polished marble—so fiercely that the reflection can be clearly seen from the great peaks of the range a hundred miles away.

It is a marvellous sight—this golden flower upborne upon the cool white marble walls, and I doubt if the world can show such another. What makes the whole effect even more gorgeous is that a belt of a hundred and fifty feet around the marble wall of the temple is planted with an indigenous species of sunflower, which were at the time when we first saw them a sheet of golden bloom.

The main entrance to this wonderful place is between the two northernmost of the rays or petal courts, and is protected first by the usual bronze gates, and then by doors made of solid marble, beautifully carved with allegorical subjects and overlaid with gold. When these are passed there is only the thickness of the wall, which is, however, twenty-five feet (for the Zu-Vendi build for all time), and another slight wall also of white marble, introduced in order to avoid causing a visible gap in the inner skin of the wall, and you stand in the circular hall under the great dome. Advancing to the central altar you look upon as beautiful a sight as the imagination of man can conceive. You are in the middle of the holy place, and above you the great white marble dome (for the inner skin, like the outer, is of polished marble throughout) arches away in graceful curves something like that of St Paul's in London, only at a slighter angle, and from the funnel-like opening at the exact apex a bright beam of light pours down upon the golden altar. At the east and the west are other altars, and other beams of light stab the sacred twilight to the heart. In every direction, 'white, mystic, wonderful', open out the ray-like courts, each pierced through by a single arrow of light that serves to illumine its lofty silence and dimly to reveal the monuments of the dead.

Overcome at so awe-inspiring a sight, the vast loveliness of which thrills the nerves like a glance from beauty's eyes, you turn to the central golden altar, in the midst of which, though you cannot see it now, there burns a pale but steady flame crowned with curls of faint blue smoke. It is of marble overlaid with pure gold, in shape round like the sun, four feet in height, and thirty-six in circumference. Here also, hinged to the foundations of the altar, are twelve petals of beaten gold. All night and, except at one hour, all day also, these petals are closed over the altar itself exactly as the petals of a water-lily close over the yellow crown in stormy weather; but when the sun at midday pierces through the funnel in the dome and lights upon the golden flower, the petals open and reveal the hidden mystery, only to close again when the ray has passed.

Nor is this all. Standing in semicircles at equal distances from each other on the north and south of the sacred place are ten golden angels, or female winged forms, exquisitely shaped and draped. These figures, which are slightly larger than life-size, stand with bent heads in an attitude of adoration, their faces shadowed by their wings, and are most imposing and of exceeding beauty.

There is but one thing further which calls for description in this altar, which is, that to the east the flooring in front of it is not of pure white marble, as elsewhere throughout the building, but of solid brass, and this is also the case in front of the other two altars.

The eastern and western altars, which are semicircular in shape, and placed against the wall of the building, are much less imposing, and are not enfolded in golden petals. They are, however, also of gold, the sacred fire burns on each, and a golden-winged figure stands on either side of them. Two great golden rays run up the wall behind them, but where the third or middle one should be is an opening in the wall, wide on the outside, but narrow within, like a loophole turned inwards. Through the eastern loophole stream the first beams of the rising sun, and strike right across the circle, touching the folded petals of the great gold flower as they pass till they impinge upon the western altar. In the same way at night the last rays of the sinking sun rest for a while on the eastern altar before they die away into darkness. It is the promise of the dawn to the evening and the evening to the dawn.

With the exception of those three altars and the winged figures about them, the whole space beneath the vast white dome is utterly empty and devoid of ornamentation—a circumstance that to my fancy adds greatly to its splendour.

Such is a brief description of this wonderful and lovely building, to the glories of which, to my mind so much enhanced by their complete simplicity, I only wish I had the power to do justice. But I cannot, so it is useless talking more about it. But when I compare this great work of genius to some of the tawdry buildings and tinsel ornamentation produced in these latter days by European ecclesiastical architects, I feel that even highly civilized art might learn something from the Zu-Vendi masterpieces. I can only say that the exclamation which sprang to my lips as soon as my eyes first became accustomed to the dim light of that glorious building, and its white and curving beauties, perfect and thrilling as those of a naked goddess, grew upon me one by one, was, 'Well! a dog would feel religious here.' It is vulgarly put, but perhaps it conveys my meaning more clearly than any polished utterance.

At the temple gates our party was received by a guard of soldiers, who appeared to be under the orders of a priest; and by them we were conducted into one of the ray or 'petal' courts, as the priests call them, and there left for at least half-an-hour. Here we conferred together, and realizing that we stood in great danger of our lives, determined, if any attempt should be made upon us, to sell them as dearly as we could— Umslopogaas announcing his fixed intention of committing sacrilege on the person of Agon, the High Priest, by splitting his head with Inkosi-kaas. From where we stood we could perceive that an immense multitude were pouring into the temple, evidently in expectation of some unusual event, and I could not help fearing that we had to do with it. And here I may explain that every day, when the sunlight falls upon the central altar, and the trumpets sound, a burnt sacrifice is offered to the Sun, consisting generally of the carcase of a sheep or ox, or sometimes of fruit or corn. This event comes off about midday; of course, not always exactly at that hour, but as Zu-Vendis is situated not far from the Line, although—being so high above the sea it is very temperate—midday and the falling of the sunlight on the altar were generally simultaneous. Today the sacrifice was to take place at about eight minutes past twelve.

Just at twelve o'clock a priest appeared, and made a sign, and the officer of the guard signified to us that we were expected to advance, which we did with the best grace that we could muster, all except Alphonse, whose irrepressible teeth instantly began to chatter. In a few seconds we were out of the court and looking at a vast sea of human faces stretching away to the farthest limits of the great circle, all straining to catch a glimpse of the mysterious strangers who had committed sacrilege; the first strangers, mind you, who, to the knowledge of the multitude, had ever set foot in Zu-Vendis since such time that the memory of man runneth not to the contrary.

As we appeared there was a murmur through the vast crowd that went echoing away up the great dome, and we saw a visible blush of excitement grow on the thousands of faces, like a pink light on a stretch of pale cloud, and a very curious effect it was. On we passed down a lane cut through the heart of the human mass, till presently we stood upon the brazen patch of flooring to the east of the central altar, and immediately facing it. For some thirty feet around the golden-winged figures the space was roped off, and the multitudes stood outside the ropes. Within were a circle of white-robed gold-cinctured priests holding long golden trumpets in their hands, and immediately in front of us was our friend Agon, the High Priest, with his curious cap upon his head. His was the only covered head in that vast assemblage. We took our stand upon the brazen space, little knowing what was prepared for us beneath, but I noticed a curious hissing sound proceeding apparently from the floor for which I could not account. Then came a pause, and I looked around to see if there was any sign of the two Queens, Nyleptha and Sorais, but they were not there. To the right of us, however, was a bare space that I guessed was reserved for them.

We waited, and presently a far-off trumpet blew, apparently high up in the dome. Then came another murmur from the multitude, and up a long lane, leading to the open space to our right, we saw the two Queens walking side by side. Behind them were some nobles of the Court, among whom I recognized the great lord Nasta, and behind them again a body of about fifty guards. These last I was very glad to see. Presently they had all arrived and taken their stand, the two Queens in the front, the nobles to the right and left, and the guards in a double semicircle behind them.

Then came another silence, and Nyleptha looked up and caught my eye; it seemed to me that there was meaning in her glance, and I watched it narrowly. From my eye it travelled down to the brazen flooring, on the outer edge of which we stood. Then followed a slight and almost imperceptible sidelong movement of the head. I did not understand it, and it was repeated. Then I guessed that she meant us to move back off the brazen floor. One more glance and I was sure of it—there was danger in standing on the floor. Sir Henry was placed on one side of me, Umslopogaas on the other. Keeping my eyes fixed straight before me, I whispered to them, first in Zulu and then in English, to draw slowly back inch by inch till half their feet were resting on the marble flooring where the brass ceased. Sir Henry whispered on to Good and Alphonse, and slowly, very very slowly, we shifted backwards; so slowly that nobody, except Nyleptha and Sorais, who saw everything seemed to notice the movement. Then I glanced again at Nyleptha, and saw that, by an almost imperceptible nod, she indicated approval. All the while Agon's eyes were fixed upon the altar before him apparently in an ecstasy of contemplation, and mine were fixed upon the small of his back in another sort of ecstasy. Suddenly he flung up his long arm, and in a solemn and resounding voice commenced a chant, of which for convenience' sake I append a rough, a *very* rough, translation here, though, of course, I did not then comprehend its meaning. It was an invocation to the Sun, and ran somewhat as follows:—

There is silence upon the face of the Earth and the waters thereof!
Yea, the silence doth brood on the waters like a nesting bird;
The silence sleepeth also upon the bosom of the profound darkness,
Only high up in the great spaces star doth speak unto star,
The Earth is faint with longing and wet with the tears of her desire;
The star-girdled night doth embrace her, but she is not comforted.
She lies enshrouded in mists like a corpse in the grave-clothes,
And stretches her pale hands to the East.

Lo! away in the farthest East there is the shadow of a light;
The Earth seeth and lifts herself. She looks out from beneath the
hollow of her hand.

Then thy great angels fly forth from the Holy Place, oh Sun,
They shoot their fiery swords into the darkness and shrivel it up.
They climb the heavens and cast down the pale stars
from their thrones;
Yea, they hurl the changeful stars back into the womb of the night;
They cause the moon to become wan as the face of a dying man,
And behold! Thy glory comes, oh Sun!

Oh, Thou beautiful one, Thou drapest thyself in fire.
The wide heavens are thy pathway: thou rollest o'er them as a chariot.
The Earth is thy bride. Thou dost embrace her and she
brings forth children;
Yea, Thou favourest her, and she yields her increase.
Thou art the All Father and the giver of life, oh Sun.
The young children stretch out their hands and grow
in thy brightness;
The old men creep forth and seeing remember their strength.
Only the dead forget Thee, oh Sun!

When Thou art wroth then Thou dost hide Thy face;
Thou drawest around Thee a thick curtain of shadows.
Then the Earth grows cold and the Heavens are dismayed;
They tremble, and the sound thereof is the sound of thunder:
They weep, and their tears are outpoured in the rain;
They sigh, and the wild winds are the voice of their sighing.
The flowers die, the fruitful fields languish and turn pale;
The old men and the little children go unto their appointed place
When Thou withdrawest thy light, oh Sun!

Say, what art Thou, oh Thou matchless Splendour—
Who set Thee on high, oh Thou flaming Terror?
When didst Thou begin, and when is the day of Thy ending?
Thou art the raiment of the living Spirit.
None did place Thee on high, for Thou was the Beginning.
Thou shalt not be ended when thy children are forgotten;
Nay, Thou shalt never end, for thy hours are eternal.
Thou sittest on high within thy golden house and measurest
out the centuries.
Oh Father of Life! oh dark-dispelling Sun!

He ceased this solemn chant, which, though it seems a poor enough thing after going through my mill, is really beautiful and impressive in the original; and then, after a moment's pause, he glanced up towards the funnel-sloped opening in the dome and added—

Oh Sun, descend upon thine Altar!

As he spoke a wonderful and a beautiful thing happened. Down from on high flashed a splendid living ray of light, cleaving the twilight like a sword of fire. Full upon the closed petals it fell and ran shimmering down their golden sides, and then the glorious flower opened as though beneath the bright influence. Slowly it opened, and as the great petals fell wide and revealed the golden altar on which the fire ever burns, the priests blew a blast upon the trumpets, and from all the people there rose a shout of praise that beat against the domed roof and came echoing down the marble walls. And now the flower altar was open, and the sunlight fell full upon the tongue of sacred flame and beat it down, so that it wavered, sank, and vanished into the hollow recesses whence it rose. As it vanished, the mellow notes of the trumpets rolled out once more. Again the old priest flung up his hands and called aloud—

We sacrifice to thee, oh Sun!

Once more I caught Nylepetha's eye; it was fixed upon the brazen flooring.

'Look out,' I said, aloud; and as I said it, I saw Agon bend forward and touch something on the altar. As he did so, the great white sea of faces around us turned red and then white again, and a deep breath went up like a universal sigh. Nyleptha leant forward, and with an involuntary movement covered her eyes with her hand. Sorais turned and whispered to the officer of the royal bodyguard, and then with a rending sound the whole of the brazen flooring slid from before our feet, and there in its place was suddenly revealed a smooth marble shaft terminating in a most awful raging furnace beneath the altar, big enough and hot enough to heat the iron stern-post of a man-of-war.

With a cry of terror we sprang backwards, all except the wretched Alphonse, who was paralysed with fear, and would have fallen into the fiery furnace which had been prepared for us, had not Sir Henry caught him in his strong hand as he was vanishing and dragged him back.

Instantly there arose the most fearful hubbub, and we four got back to back, Alphonse dodging frantically round our little circle in his attempts to take shelter under our legs. We all had our revolvers on—for though we had been politely disarmed of our guns on leaving the palace, of course these people did not know what a revolver was. Umslopogaas, too, had his axe, of which no effort had been made to deprive him, and now he whirled it round his head and sent his piercing Zulu war-shout echoing up the marble walls in fine defiant fashion. Next second, the priests, baffled of their prey, had drawn swords from beneath their white robes and were leaping on us like hounds upon a stag at bay. I saw that, dangerous as action might be, we must act or be lost, so as the first man came bounding along—and a great tall fellow he was—I sent a heavy revolver ball through him, and down he fell at the mouth of the shaft, and slid, shrieking frantically, into the fiery gulf that had been prepared for us.

Whether it was his cries, or the, to them, awful sound and effect of the pistol shot, or what, I know not, but the other priests halted, paralysed and dismayed, and before they could come on again Sorais had called out something, and we, together with the two Queens and most of the courtiers, were being surrounded with a wall of armed men. In a moment it was done, and still the priests hesitated, and the people hung in the balance like a herd of startled buck as it were, making no sign one way or the other.

The last yell of the burning priest had died away, the fire had finished him, and a great silence fell upon the place.

Then the High Priest Agon turned, and his face was as the face of a devil. 'Let the sacrifice be sacrificed,' he cried to the Queens. 'Has not sacrilege enough been done by these strangers, and would ye, as Queens, throw the cloak of your majesty over evildoers? Are not the creatures sacred to the Sun dead? And is not a priest of the Sun also dead, but now slain by the magic of these strangers, who come as the winds out of heaven, whence we know not, and who are what we know not? Beware, oh Queens, how ye tamper with the great majesty of the God, even before His high altar! There is a Power that is more than your power; there is a Justice that is higher than your justice. Beware how ye lift an impious hand against it! Let the sacrifice be sacrificed, oh Queens.'

Then Sorais made answer in her deep quiet tones, that always seemed to me to have a suspicion of mockery about them, however serious the theme: 'Oh, Agon, thou hast spoken according to thy desire, and thou hast spoken truth. But it is thou who wouldst lift an impious hand against the justice of thy God. Bethink thee the midday sacrifice is accomplished; the Sun hath claimed his priest as a sacrifice.'

This was a novel idea, and the people applauded it.

'Bethink thee what are these men? They are strangers found floating on the bosom of a lake. Who brought them here? How came they here? How know you that they also are not servants of the Sun? Is this the hospitality that ye would have our nation show to those whom chance brings to them, to throw them to the flames? Shame on you! Shame on you! What is hospitality? To receive the stranger and show him favour. To bind up his wounds, and find a pillow for his head, and food for him to eat. But thy pillow is the fiery furnace, and thy food the hot savour of the flame. Shame on thee, I say!'

She paused a little to watch the effect of her speech upon the multitude, and seeing that it was favourable, changed her tone from one of remonstrance to one of command.

'Ho! place there,' she cried; 'place, I say; make way for the Queens, and those whom the Queens cover with their "kaf" (mantle).'

'And if I refuse, oh Queen?' said Agon between his teeth.

'Then will I cut a path with my guards,' was the proud answer; 'ay, even in the presence of thy sanctuary, and through the bodies of thy priests.'

Agon turned livid with baffled fury. He glanced at the people as though meditating an appeal to them, but saw clearly that their sympathies were all the other way. The Zu-Vendi are a very curious and sociable people, and great as was their sense of the enormity that we had committed in shooting the sacred hippopotami, they did not like the idea of the only real live strangers they had seen or heard of being consigned to a fiery furnace, thereby putting an end for ever to their chance of extracting knowledge and information from, and gossiping about us. Agon saw this and hesitated, and then for the first time Nyleptha spoke in her soft sweet voice.

'Bethink thee, Agon,' she said, 'as my sister Queen has said, these men may also be servants of the Sun. For themselves they cannot speak, for their tongues are tied. Let the matter be adjourned till such time as they have learnt our language. Who can be condemned without a hearing? When these men can plead for themselves, then it will be time to put them to the proof.'

Here was a clever loophole of escape, and the vindictive old priest took it, little as he liked it.

'So be it, oh Queens,' he said. 'Let the men go in peace, and when they have learnt our tongue then let them speak. And I, even I, will make humble supplication at the altar lest pestilence fall on the land by cause of the sacrilege.'

These words were received with a murmur of applause, and in another minute we were marching out of the temple surrounded by the royal guards.

But it was not till long afterwards that we learnt the exact substance of what had passed, and how hardly our lives had been wrung out of the cruel grip of the Zu-Vendi priesthood, in the face of which even the Queens were practically powerless. Had it not been for their strenuous efforts to protect us we should have been slain even before we set foot in the Temple of the Sun. The attempt to drop us bodily into the fiery pit as an offering was a last artifice to attain this end when several others quite unsuspected by us had already failed.

XV

SORAIS' SONG

After our escape from Agon and his pious crew we returned to our quarters in the palace and had a very good time. The two Queens, the nobles and the people vied with each other in doing us honour and showering gifts upon us. As for that painful little incident of the hippopotami it sank into oblivion, where we were quite content to leave it. Every day deputations and individuals waited on us to examine our guns and clothing, our chain shirts, and our instruments, especially our watches, with which they were much delighted. In short, we became quite the rage, so much so that some of the fashionable young swells among the Zu-Vendi began to copy the cut of some of our clothes, notably Sir Henry's shooting jacket. One day, indeed, a deputation waited on us and, as usual, Good donned his full-dress uniform for the occasion. This deputation seemed somehow to be a different class to those who generally came to visit us. They were little insignificant men of an excessively polite, not to say servile, demeanour; and their attention appeared to be chiefly taken up with observing the details of Good's full-dress uniform, of which they took copious notes and measurements. Good was much flattered at the time, not suspecting that he had to deal with the six leading tailors of Milosis. A fortnight afterwards, however, when on attending court as usual he had the pleasure of seeing some seven or eight Zu-Vendi 'mashers' arrayed in all the glory of a very fair imitation of his full-dress uniform, he changed his mind. I shall never forget his face of astonishment and disgust. It was after this, chiefly to avoid remark, and also because our clothes were wearing out and had to be saved up, that we resolved to adopt the native dress; and a very comfortable one we found it, though I am bound to say that I looked sufficiently ridiculous in it, and as for Alphonse! Only Umslopogaas would have none of these things; when his moocha was worn out the fierce old Zulu made him a new one, and went about unconcerned, as grim and naked as his own battleaxe.

Meanwhile we pursued our study of the language steadily and made very good progress. On the morning following our adventure in the temple, three grave and reverend signiors presented themselves

H. RIDER HAGGARD

armed with manuscript books, ink-horns and feather pens, and indicated that they had been sent to teach us. So, with the exception of Umslopogaas, we all buckled to with a will, doing four hours a day. As for Umslopogaas, he would have none of that either. He did not wish to learn that 'woman's talk', not he; and when one of the teachers advanced on him with a book and an ink-horn and waved them before him in a mild persuasive way, much as a churchwarden invitingly shakes the offertory bag under the nose of a rich but niggardly parishioner, he sprang up with a fierce oath and flashed Inkosi-kaas before the eyes of our learned friend, and there was an end of the attempt to teach *him* Zu-Vendi.

Thus we spent our mornings in useful occupation which grew more and more interesting as we proceeded, and the afternoons were given up to recreation. Sometimes we made trips, notably one to the gold mines and another to the marble quarries both of which I wish I had space and time to describe; and sometimes we went out hunting buck with dogs trained for that purpose, and a very exciting sport it is, as the country is full of agricultural enclosures and our horses were magnificent. This is not to be wondered at, seeing that the royal stables were at our command, in addition to which we had four splendid saddle horses given to us by Nyleptha.

Sometimes, again, we went hawking, a pastime that is in great favour among the Zu-Vendi, who generally fly their birds at a species of partridge which is remarkable for the swiftness and strength of its flight. When attacked by the hawk this bird appears to lose its head, and, instead of seeking cover, flies high into the sky, thus offering wonderful sport. I have seen one of these partridges soar up almost out of sight when followed by the hawk. Still better sport is offered by a variety of solitary snipe as big as a small woodcock, which is plentiful in this country, and which is flown at with a very small, agile, and highly-trained hawk with an almost red tail. The zigzagging of the great snipe and the lightning rapidity of the flight and movements of the red-tailed hawk make the pastime a delightful one. Another variety of the same amusement is the hunting of a very small species of antelope with trained eagles; and it certainly is a marvellous sight to see the great bird soar and soar till he is nothing but a black speck in the sunlight, and then suddenly come dashing down like a cannon-ball upon some cowering buck that is hidden in a patch of grass from everything but that piercing eye. Still finer is the spectacle when the eagle takes the buck running.

On other days we would pay visits to the country seats at some of the great lords' beautiful fortified places, and the villages clustering beneath their walls. Here we saw vineyards and corn-fields and well-kept park-like grounds, with such timber in them as filled me with delight, for I do love a good tree. There it stands so strong and sturdy, and yet so beautiful, a very type of the best sort of man. How proudly it lifts its bare head to the winter storms, and with what a full heart it rejoices when the spring has come again! How grand its voice is, too, when it talks with the wind: a thousand aeolian harps cannot equal the beauty of the sighing of a great tree in leaf. All day it points to the sunshine and all night to the stars, and thus passionless, and yet full of life, it endures through the centuries, come storm, come shine, drawing its sustenance from the cool bosom of its mother earth, and as the slow years roll by, learning the great mysteries of growth and of decay. And so on and on through generations, outliving individuals, customs, dynasties—all save the landscape it adorns and human nature—till the appointed day when the wind wins the long battle and rejoices over a reclaimed space, or decay puts the last stroke to his fungus-fingered work.

Ah, one should always think twice before one cuts down a tree!

In the evenings it was customary for Sir Henry, Good, and myself to dine, or rather sup, with their Majesties—not every night, indeed, but about three or four times a week, whenever they had not much company, or the affairs of state would allow of it. And I am bound to say that those little suppers were quite the most charming things of their sort that I ever had to do with. How true is the saying that the very highest in rank are always the most simple and kindly. It is from your half-and-half sort of people that you get pomposity and vulgarity, the difference between the two being very much what one sees every day in England between the old, out-at-elbows, broken-down county family, and the overbearing, purse-proud people who come and 'take the place'. I really think that Nyleptha's greatest charm is her sweet simplicity, and her kindly genuine interest even in little things. She is the simplest woman I ever knew, and where her passions are not involved, one of the sweetest; but she can look queenly enough when she likes, and be as fierce as any savage too.

For instance, never shall I forget that scene when I for the first time was sure that she was really in love with Curtis. It came about in this way—all through Good's weakness for ladies' society. When we had been employed for some three months in learning Zu-Vendi, it struck

Master Good that he was getting rather tired of the old gentlemen who did us the honour to lead us in the way that we should go, so he proceeded, without saying a word to anybody else, to inform them that it was a peculiar fact, but that we could not make any real progress in the deeper intricacies of a foreign language unless we were taught by ladies—young ladies, he was careful to explain. In his own country, he pointed out, it was habitual to choose the very best-looking and most charming girls who could be found to instruct any strangers who happened to come that way, etc.

All of this the old gentlemen swallowed open-mouthed. There was, they admitted, reason in what he said, since the contemplation of the beautiful, as their philosophy taught, induced a certain porosity of mind similar to that produced upon the physical body by the healthful influences of sun and air. Consequently it was probable that we might absorb the Zu-Vendi tongue a little faster if suitable teachers could be found. Another thing was that, as the female sex was naturally loquacious, good practice would be gained in the viva voce department of our studies.

To all of this Good gravely assented, and the learned gentlemen departed, assuring him that their orders were to fall in with our wishes in every way, and that, if possible, our views should be met.

Imagine, therefore the surprise and disgust of myself, and I trust and believe Sir Henry, when, on entering the room where we were accustomed to carry on our studies the following morning, we found, instead of our usual venerable tutors, three of the best-looking young women whom Milosis could produce—and that is saying a good deal— who blushed and smiled and curtseyed, and gave us to understand that they were there to carry on our instruction. Then Good, as we gazed at one another in bewilderment, thought fit to explain, saying that it had slipped his memory before—but the old gentlemen had told him, on the previous evening, that it was absolutely necessary that our further education should be carried on by the other sex. I was overwhelmed, and appealed to Sir Henry for advice in such a crisis.

'Well,' he said, 'you see the ladies are here, ain't they? If we sent them away, don't you think it might hurt their feelings, eh? One doesn't like to be rough, you see; and they look regular *blues*, don't they, eh?'

By this time Good had already begun his lessons with the handsomest of the three, and so with a sigh I yielded. That day everything went very well: the young ladies were certainly very clever, and they only smiled when we blundered. I never saw Good so attentive to his books before, and even Sir Henry appeared to tackle Zu-Vendi with a renewed zest. 'Ah,' thought I, 'will it always be thus?'

Next day we were much more lively, our work was pleasingly interspersed with questions about our native country, what the ladies were like there, etc., all of which we answered as best as we could in Zu-Vendi, and I heard Good assuring his teacher that her loveliness was to the beauties of Europe as the sun to the moon, to which she replied with a little toss of the head, that she was a plain teaching woman and nothing else, and that it was not kind 'to deceive a poor girl so'. Then we had a little singing that was really charming, so natural and unaffected. The Zu-Vendi love-songs are most touching. On the third day we were all quite intimate. Good narrated some of his previous love affairs to his fair teacher, and so moved was she that her sighs mingled with his own. I discoursed with mine, a merry blue-eyed girl, upon Zu-Vendian art, and never saw that she was waiting for an opportunity to drop a specimen of the cockroach tribe down my back, whilst in the corner Sir Henry and his governess appeared, so far as I could judge, to be going through a lesson framed on the great educational principles laid down by Wackford Squeers Esq., though in a very modified or rather spiritualized form. The lady softly repeated the Zu-Vendi word for 'hand', and he took hers; 'eyes', and he gazed deep into her brown orbs; 'lips', and—but just at that moment *my* young lady dropped the cockroach down my back and ran away laughing. Now if there is one thing I loathe more than another it is cockroaches, and moved quite beyond myself, and yet laughing at her impudence, I took up the cushion she had been sitting on and threw it after her. Imagine then my shame—my horror, and my distress—when the door opened, and, attended by two guards only, in walked *Nylepthra*. The cushion could not be recalled (it missed the girl and hit one of the guards on the head), but I instantly and ineffectually tried to look as though I had not thrown it. Good ceased his sighing, and began to murder Zu-Vendi at the top of his voice, and Sir Henry whistled and looked silly. As for the poor girls, they were utterly dumbfounded.

And Nylepthra! she drew herself up till her frame seemed to tower even above that of the tall guards, and her face went first red, and then pale as death.

'Guards,' she said in a quiet choked voice, and pointing at the fair but unconscious disciple of Wackford Squeers, 'slay me that woman.'

The men hesitated, as well they might.

'Will ye do my bidding,' she said again in the same voice, 'or will ye not?'

Then they advanced upon the girl with uplifted spears. By this time Sir Henry had recovered himself, and saw that the comedy was likely to turn into a tragedy.

'Stand back,' he said in a voice of thunder, at the same time getting in front of the terrified girl. 'Shame on thee, Nyleptha—shame! Thou shalt not kill her.'

'Doubtless thou hast good reason to try to protect her. Thou couldst hardly do less in honour,' answered the infuriated Queen; 'but she shall die—she shall die,' and she stamped her little foot.

'It is well,' he answered; 'then will I die with her. I am thy servant, oh Queen; do with me even as thou wilt.' And he bowed towards her, and fixed his clear eyes contemptuously on her face.

'I could wish to slay thee too,' she answered; 'for thou dost make a mock of me;' and then feeling that she was mastered, and I suppose not knowing what else to do, she burst into such a storm of tears and looked so royally lovely in her passionate distress, that, old as I am, I must say I envied Curtis his task of supporting her. It was rather odd to see him holding her in his arms considering what had just passed—a thought that seemed to occur to herself, for presently she wrenched herself free and went, leaving us all much disturbed.

Presently, however, one of the guards returned with a message to the girls that they were, on pain of death, to leave the city and return to their homes in the country, and that no further harm would come to them; and accordingly they went, one of them remarking philosophically that it could not be helped, and that it was a satisfaction to know that they had taught us a little serviceable Zu-Vendi. Mine was an exceedingly nice girl, and, overlooking the cockroach, I made her a present of my favourite lucky sixpence with a hole in it when she went away. After that our former masters resumed their course of instruction, needless to say to my great relief.

That night, when in fear and trembling we attended the royal supper table, we found that Nyleptha was laid up with a bad headache. That headache lasted for three whole days; but on the fourth she was present at supper as usual, and with the most gracious and sweet smile gave Sir Henry her hand to lead her to the table. No allusion was made to the little affair described above beyond her saying, with a charming air of innocence, that when she came to see us at our studies the other day she had been seized with a giddiness from which she had only now recovered. She supposed, she added with a touch of the humour that was common to her, that it was the sight of people working so hard which had affected her.

In reply Sir Henry said, dryly, that he had thought she did not look quite herself on that day, whereat she flashed one of those quick glances of hers at him, which if he had the feelings of a man must have gone through him like a knife, and the subject dropped entirely. Indeed, after supper was over Nyleptha condescended to put us through an examination to see what we had learnt, and to express herself well satisfied with the results. Indeed, she proceeded to give us, especially Sir Henry, a lesson on her own account, and very interesting we found it.

And all the while that we talked, or rather tried to talk, and laughed, Sorais would sit there in her carven ivory chair, and look at us and read us all like a book, only from time to time saying a few words, and smiling that quick ominous smile of hers which was more like a flash of summer lightning on a dark cloud than anything else. And as near to her as he dared would sit Good, worshipping through his eyeglass, for he really was getting seriously devoted to this sombre beauty, of whom, speaking personally, I felt terribly afraid. I watched her keenly, and soon I found out that for all her apparent impassibility she was at heart bitterly jealous of Nyleptha. Another thing I found out, and the discovery filled me with dismay, and that was, that she *also* was growing devoted to Sir Henry Curtis. Of course I could not be sure; it is not easy to read so cold and haughty a woman; but I noticed one or two little things, and, as elephant hunters know, dried grass shows which way the wind has set.

And so another three months passed over us, by which time we had all attained to a very considerable mastery of the Zu-Vendi language, which is an easy one to learn. And as the time went on we became great favourites with the people, and even with the courtiers, gaining an enormous reputation for cleverness, because, as I think I have said, Sir Henry was able to show them how to make glass, which was a national want, and also, by the help of a twenty-year almanac that we had with us, to predict various heavenly combinations which were quite unsuspected by the native astronomers. We even succeeded in demonstrating the principle of the steam-engine to a gathering of the learned men, who were filled with amazement; and several other things of the same sort we did. And so it came about that the people made up their minds that we must on no account be allowed to go out of the country (which indeed was an apparent impossibility even if we had wished it), and we were advanced to great honour and made officers to the bodyguards of the sister Queens while permanent quarters were assigned to us in the palace, and our opinion was asked upon questions of national policy.

But blue as the sky seemed, there was a cloud, and a big one, on the horizon. We had indeed heard no more of those confounded hippopotami, but it is not on that account to be supposed that our sacrilege was forgotten, or the enmity of the great and powerful priesthood headed by Agon appeased. On the contrary, it was burning the more fiercely because it was necessarily suppressed, and what had perhaps begun in bigotry was ending in downright direct hatred born of jealousy. Hitherto, the priests had been the wise men of the land, and were on this account, as well as from superstitious causes, looked on with peculiar veneration. But our arrival, with our outlandish wisdom and our strange inventions and hints of unimagined things, dealt a serious blow to this state of affairs, and, among the educated Zu-Vendi, went far towards destroying the priestly prestige. A still worse affront to them, however, was the favour with which we were regarded, and the trust that was reposed in us. All these things tended to make us excessively obnoxious to the great sacerdotal clan, the most powerful because the most united faction in the kingdom.

Another source of imminent danger to us was the rising envy of some of the great lords headed by Nasta, whose antagonism to us had at best been but thinly veiled, and which now threatened to break out into open flame. Nasta had for some years been a candidate for Nyleptha's hand in marriage, and when we appeared on the scene I fancy, from all I could gather, that though there were still many obstacles in his path, success was by no means out of his reach. But now all this had changed; the coy Nyleptha smiled no more in his direction, and he was not slow to guess the cause. Infuriated and alarmed, he turned his attention to Sorais, only to find that he might as well try to woo a mountain side. With a bitter jest or two about his fickleness, that door was closed on him for ever. So Nasta bethought himself of the thirty thousand wild swordsmen who would pour down at his bidding through the northern mountain passes, and no doubt vowed to adorn the gates of Milosis with our heads.

But first he determined, as I learned, to make one more attempt and to demand the hand of Nyleptha in the open Court after the formal annual ceremony of the signing of the laws that had been proclaimed by the Queens during the year.

Of this astounding fact Nyleptha heard with simulated nonchalance, and with a little trembling of the voice herself informed us of it as we sat at supper on the night preceding the great ceremony of the law-giving.

Sir Henry bit his lip, and do what he could to prevent it plainly showed his agitation.

'And what answer will the Queen be pleased to give to the great Lord?' asked I, in a jesting manner.

'Answer, Macumazahn' (for we had elected to pass by our Zulu names in Zu-Vendis), she said, with a pretty shrug of her ivory shoulder. 'Nay, I know not; what is a poor woman to do, when the wooer has thirty thousand swords wherewith to urge his love?' And from under her long lashes she glanced at Curtis.

Just then we rose from the table to adjourn into another room. 'Quatermain, a word, quick,' said Sir Henry to me. 'Listen. I have never spoken about it, but surely you have guessed: I love Nyleptha. What am I to do?'

Fortunately, I had more or less already taken the question into consideration, and was therefore able to give such answer as seemed the wisest to me.

'You must speak to Nyleptha tonight,' I said. 'Now is your time, now or never. Listen. In the sitting-chamber get near to her, and whisper to her to meet you at midnight by the Rademas statue at the end of the great hall. I will keep watch for you there. Now or never, Curtis.'

We passed on into the other room. Nyleptha was sitting, her hands before her, and a sad anxious look upon her lovely face. A little way off was Sorais talking to Good in her slow measured tones.

The time went on; in another quarter of an hour I knew that, according to their habit, the Queens would retire. As yet, Sir Henry had had no chance of saying a word in private: indeed, though we saw much of the royal sisters, it was by no means easy to see them alone. I racked my brains, and at last an idea came to me.

'Will the Queen be pleased,' I said, bowing low before Sorais, 'to sing to her servants? Our hearts are heavy this night; sing to us, oh Lady of the Night' (Sorais' favourite name among the people).

'My songs, Macumazahn, are not such as to lighten the heavy heart, yet will I sing if it pleases thee,' she answered; and she rose and went a few paces to a table whereon lay an instrument not unlike a zither, and struck a few wandering chords.

Then suddenly, like the notes of some deep-throated bird, her rounded voice rang out in song so wildly sweet, and yet with so eerie and sad a refrain, that it made the very blood stand still. Up, up soared the golden notes, that seemed to melt far away, and then to grow again and travel on, laden with all the sorrow of the world and all the despair of the lost. It was a marvellous song, but I had not time to listen to it properly. However, I got the words of it afterwards, and here is a translation of its burden, so far as it admits of being translated at all.

Sorais' Song

As a desolate bird that through darkness its lost way is winging,
As a hand that is helplessly raised when Death's sickle is swinging,
So is life! ay, the life that lends passion and breath to my singing.

As the nightingale's song that is full of a sweetness unspoken,
As a spirit unbarring the gates of the skies for a token,
So is love! ay, the love that shall fall when his pinion is broken.

As the tramp of the legions when trumpets their
challenge are sending,
As the shout of the Storm-god when lightnings the black
sky are rending,
So is power! ay, the power that shall lie in the dust at its ending.

So short is our life; yet with space for all things to forsake us,
A bitter delusion, a dream from which nought can awake us,
Till Death's dogging footsteps at morn or at eve shall o'ertake us.

Refrain

Oh, the world is fair at the dawning—dawning—dawning,
But the red sun sinks in blood—the red sun sinks in blood.

I only wish that I could write down the music too.

'Now, Curtis, now,' I whispered, when she began the second verse, and turned my back.

'Nyleptha,' he said—for my nerves were so much on the stretch that I could hear every word, low as it was spoken, even through Sorais' divine notes—'Nyleptha, I must speak with thee this night, upon my life I must. Say me not nay; oh, say me not nay!'

'How can I speak with thee?' she answered, looking fixedly before her; 'Queens are not like other people. I am surrounded and watched.'

'Listen, Nyleptha, thus. I will be before the statue of Rademas in the great hall at midnight. I have the countersign and can pass in. Macumazahn will be there to keep guard, and with him the Zulu. Oh come, my Queen, deny me not.'

'It is not seemly,' she murmured, 'and tomorrow—'

Just then the music began to die in the last wail of the refrain, and Sorais slowly turned her round.

'I will be there,' said Nyleptha, hurriedly; 'on thy life see that thou fail me not.'

XVI

BEFORE THE STATUE

It was night—dead night—and the silence lay on the Frowning City like a cloud.

Secretly, as evildoers, Sir Henry Curtis, Umslopogaas, and myself threaded our way through the passages towards a by-entrance to the great Throne Chamber. Once we were met by the fierce rattling challenge of the sentry. I gave the countersign, and the man grounded his spear and let us pass. Also we were officers of the Queens' bodyguard, and in that capacity had a right to come and go unquestioned.

We gained the hall in safety. So empty and so still was it, that even when we had passed the sound of our footsteps yet echoed up the lofty walls, vibrating faintly and still more faintly against the carven roof, like ghosts of the footsteps of dead men haunting the place that once they trod.

It was an eerie spot, and it oppressed me. The moon was full, and threw great pencils and patches of light through the high windowless openings in the walls, that lay pure and beautiful upon the blackness of the marble floor, like white flowers on a coffin. One of these silver arrows fell upon the statue of the sleeping Rademas, and of the angel form bent over him, illumining it, and a small circle round it, with a soft clear light, reminding me of that with which Catholics illumine the altars of their cathedrals.

Here by the statue we took our stand, and waited. Sir Henry and I close together, Umslopogaas some paces off in the darkness, so that I could only just make out his towering outline leaning on the outline of an axe.

So long did we wait that I almost fell asleep resting against the cold marble, but was suddenly aroused by hearing Curtis give a quick catching breath. Then from far away there came a little sound as though the statues that lined the walls were whispering to each other some message of the ages.

It was the faint sweep of a lady's dress. Nearer it grew, and nearer yet. We could see a figure steal from patch to patch of moonlight, and even hear the soft fall of sandalled feet. Another second and I saw the black silhouette of the old Zulu raise its arm in mute salute, and Nyleptha was before us.

Oh, how beautiful she looked as she paused a moment just within the circle of the moonlight! Her hand was pressed upon her heart, and her white bosom heaved beneath it. Round her head a broidered scarf was loosely thrown, partially shadowing the perfect face, and thus rendering it even more lovely; for beauty, dependent as it is to a certain extent upon the imagination, is never so beautiful as when it is half hid. There she stood radiant but half doubting, stately and yet so sweet. It was but a moment, but I then and there fell in love with her myself, and have remained so to this hour; for, indeed, she looked more like an angel out of heaven than a loving, passionate, mortal woman. Low we bowed before her, and then she spoke.

'I have come,' she whispered, 'but it was at great risk. Ye know not how I am watched. The priests watch me. Sorais watches me with those great eyes of hers. My very guards are spies upon me. Nasta watches me too. Oh, let him be careful!' and she stamped her foot. 'Let him be careful; I am a woman, and therefore hard to drive. Ay, and I am a Queen, too, and can still avenge. Let him be careful, I say, lest in place of giving him my hand I take his head,' and she ended the outburst with a little sob, and then smiled up at us bewitchingly and laughed.

'Thou didst bid me come hither, my Lord Incubu' (Curtis had taught her to call him so). 'Doubtless it is about business of the State, for I know that thou art ever full of great ideas and plans for my welfare and my people's. So even as a Queen should I have come, though I greatly fear the dark alone,' and again she laughed and gave him a glance from her grey eyes.

At this point I thought it wise to move a little, since secrets 'of the State' should not be made public property; but she would not let me go far, peremptorily stopping me within five yards or so, saying that she feared surprise. So it came to pass that, however unwillingly, I heard all that passed.

'Thou knowest, Nyleptha,' said Sir Henry, 'that it was for none of these things that I asked thee to meet me at this lonely place. Nyleptha, waste not the time in pleasantry, but listen to me, for—I love thee.'

As he said the words I saw her face break up, as it were, and change. The coquetry went out of it, and in its place there shone a great light of love which seemed to glorify it, and make it like that of the marble angel overhead. I could not help thinking that it must have been a touch of prophetic instinct which made the long dead Rademas limn, in the features of the angel of his inspiring vision, so strange a likeness of his own descendant. Sir Henry, also, must have observed and been struck by the likeness, for, catching the look upon Nyleptha's face, he glanced quickly from it to the moonlit statue, and then back again at his beloved.

'Thou sayest thou dost love me,' she said in a low voice, 'and thy voice rings true, but how am I to know that thou dost speak the truth?'

'Though,' she went on with proud humility, and in the stately third person which is so largely used by the Zu-Vendi, 'I be as nothing in the eyes of my lord,' and she curtseyed towards him, 'who comes from among a wonderful people, to whom my people are but children, yet here am I a queen and a leader of men, and if I would go to battle a hundred thousand spears shall sparkle in my train like stars glimmering down the path of the bent moon. And although my beauty be a little thing in the eyes of my lord,' and she lifted her broidered skirt and curtseyed again, 'yet here among my own people am I held right fair, and ever since I was a woman the great lords of my kingdom have made quarrel concerning me, as though forsooth,' she added with a flash of passion, 'I were a deer to be pulled down by the hungriest wolf, or a horse to be sold to the highest bidder. Let my lord pardon me if I weary my lord, but it hath pleased my lord to say that he loves me, Nyleptha, a Queen of the Zu-Vendi, and therefore would I say that though my love and my hand be not much to my lord, yet to me are they all.'

'Oh!' she cried, with a sudden and thrilling change of voice, and modifying her dignified mode of address. 'Oh, how can I know that thou lovest but me? How can I know that thou wilt not weary of me and seek thine own place again, leaving me desolate? Who is there to tell me but that thou lovest some other woman, some fair woman unknown to me, but who yet draws breath beneath this same moon that shines on me tonight? Tell me *how* am I to know?' And she clasped her hands and stretched them out towards him and looked appealingly into his face.

'Nyleptha,' answered Sir Henry, adopting the Zu-Vendi way of speech; 'I have told thee that I love thee; how am I to tell thee how much I love thee? Is there then a measure for love? Yet will I try. I say not that I have never looked upon another woman with favour, but this I say that I love thee with all my life and with all my strength; that I love thee now and shall love thee till I grow cold in death, ay, and as I believe beyond my death, and on and on for ever: I say that thy voice is music to my ear, and thy touch as water to a thirsty land, that when thou art there the world is beautiful, and when I see thee not it is as though the light was dead. Oh, Nyleptha, I will never leave thee; here and now for thy dear sake I will forget my people and my father's house, yea, I renounce them all. By thy side will I live, Nyleptha, and at thy side will I die.'

He paused and gazed at her earnestly, but she hung her head like a lily, and said never a word.

'Look!' he went on, pointing to the statue on which the moonlight played so brightly. 'Thou seest that angel woman who rests her hand upon the forehead of the sleeping man, and thou seest how at her touch his soul flames up and shines out through his flesh, even as a lamp at the touch of the fire, so is it with me and thee, Nyleptha. Thou hast awakened my soul and called it forth, and now, Nyleptha, it is not mine, not mine, but *thine* and thine only. There is no more for me to say; in thy hands is my life.' And he leaned back against the pedestal of the statue, looking very pale, and his eyes shining, but proud and handsome as a god.

Slowly, slowly she raised her head, and fixed her wonderful eyes, all alight with the greatness of her passion, full upon his face, as though to read his very soul. Then at last she spoke, low indeed, but clearly as a silver bell.

'Of a truth, weak woman that I am, I do believe thee. Ill will be the day for thee and for me also if it be my fate to learn that I have believed a lie. And now hearken to me, oh man, who hath wandered here from far to steal my heart and make me all thine own. I put my hand upon thy hand thus, and thus I, whose lips have never kissed before, do kiss thee on the brow; and now by my hand and by that first and holy kiss, ay, by my people's weal and by my throne that like enough I shall lose for thee—by the name of my high House, by the sacred Stone and by the eternal majesty of the Sun, I swear that for thee will I live and die. And I swear that I will love thee and thee only till death, ay, and beyond, if as thou sayest there be a beyond, and that thy will shall be my will, and thy ways my ways.

'Oh see, see, my lord! thou knowest not how humble is she who loves; I, who am a Queen, I kneel before thee, even at thy feet I do my homage;' and the lovely impassioned creature flung herself down on her knees on the cold marble before him. And after that I really do not know, for I could stand it no longer, and cleared off to refresh myself with a little of old Umslopogaas' society, leaving them to settle it their own way, and a very long time they were about it.

I found the old warrior leaning on Inkosi-kaas as usual, and surveying the scene in the patch of moonlight with a grim smile of amusement.

'Ah, Macumazahn,' he said, 'I suppose it is because I am getting old, but I don't think that I shall ever learn to understand the ways of you white people. Look there now, I pray thee, they are a pretty pair of doves, but what is all the fuss about, Macumazahn? He wants a wife, and she wants a husband, then why does he not pay his cows down like a man and have done with it? It would save a deal of trouble, and we should have had our night's sleep. But there they go, talk, talk, talk, and kiss, kiss, kiss, like mad things. Eugh!'

Some three-quarters of an hour afterwards the 'pair of doves' came strolling towards us, Curtis looking slightly silly, and Nyleptha remarking calmly that the moonlight made very pretty effects on the marble. Then, for she was in a most gracious mood, she took my hand and said that I was 'her Lord's' dear friend, and therefore most dear to her—not a word for my own sake, you see. Next she lifted Umslopogaas' axe, and examined it curiously, saying significantly as she did so that he might soon have cause to use it in defence of her.

After that she nodded prettily to us all, and casting a tender glance at her lover, glided off into the darkness like a beautiful vision.

When we got back to our quarters, which we did without accident, Curtis asked me jocularly what I was thinking about.

'I am wondering,' I answered, 'on what principle it is arranged that some people should find beautiful queens to fall in love with them, while others find nobody at all, or worse than nobody; and I am also wondering how many brave men's lives this night's work will cost.' It was rather nasty of me, perhaps, but somehow all the feelings do not evaporate with age, and I could not help being a little jealous of my old friend's luck. Vanity, my sons; vanity of vanities!

On the following morning, Good was informed of the happy occurrence, and positively rippled with smiles that, originating somewhere about the mouth, slowly travelled up his face like the rings in a duckpond, till they flowed over the brim of his eyeglass and went where sweet smiles go. The fact of the matter, however, was that not only was Good rejoiced about the thing on its own merits but also for personal reasons. He adored Sorais quite as earnestly as Sir Henry adored Nyleptha, and his adoration had not altogether prospered.

Indeed, it had seemed to him and to me also that the dark Cleopatra-like queen favoured Curtis in her own curious inscrutable way much more than Good. Therefore it was a relief to him to learn that his unconscious rival was permanently and satisfactorily attached in another direction. His face fell a little, however, when he was told that the whole thing was to be kept as secret as the dead, above all from Sorais for the present, inasmuch as the political convulsion which would follow such an announcement at the moment would be altogether too great to face and would very possibly, if prematurely made, shake Nyleptha from her throne.

That morning we again attended in the Throne Hall, and I could not help smiling to myself when I compared the visit to our last, and reflecting that, if walls could speak, they would have strange tales to tell.

What actresses women are! There, high upon her golden throne, draped in her blazoned 'kaf' or robe of state, sat the fair Nyleptha, and when Sir Henry came in a little late, dressed in the full uniform of an officer of her guard and humbly bent himself before her, she merely acknowledged his salute with a careless nod and turned her head coldly aside. It was a very large Court, for not only did the signing of the laws attract many outside of those whose duty it was to attend, but also the rumour that Nasta was going to publicly ask the hand of Nyleptha in marriage had gone abroad, with the result that the great hall was crowded to its utmost capacity. There were our friends the priests in force, headed by Agon, who regarded us with a vindictive eye; and a most imposing band they were, with their long white embroidered robes girt with a golden chain from which hung the fish-like scales. There, too, were a number of the lords, each with a band of brilliantly attired attendants, and prominent among them was Nasta, stroking his black beard meditatively and looking unusually pleasant. It was a splendid and impressive sight, especially when the officer after having read out each law handed them to the Queens to sign, whereon the trumpets blared out and the Queens' guard grounded their spears with a crash in salute. This reading and signing of the laws took a long time, but at length it came to an end, the last one reciting that 'whereas distinguished strangers, etc.', and proceeding to confer on the three of us the rank of 'lords', together with certain military commands and large estates bestowed by the Queen. When it was read the trumpets blared and the spears clashed down as usual, but I saw some of the lords turn and whisper to each other, while Nasta ground his teeth.

They did not like the favour that was shown to us, which under all the circumstances was not perhaps unnatural.

Then there came a pause, and Nasta stepped forward and bowing humbly, though with no humility in his eye, craved a boon at the hands of the Queen Nyleptha.

Nyleptha turned a little pale, but bowed graciously, and prayed the 'well-beloved lord' to speak on, whereon in a few straightforward soldier-like words he asked her hand in marriage.

Then, before she could find words to answer, the High Priest Agon took up the tale, and in a speech of real eloquence and power pointed out the many advantages of the proposed alliance; how it would consolidate the kingdom, for Nasta's dominions, of which he was virtually king, were to Zu-Vendis much what Scotland used to be to England; how it would gratify the wild mountaineers and be popular among the soldiery, for Nasta was a famous general; how it would set her dynasty firmly on the throne, and would gain the blessing and approval of the 'Sun', i.e. of the office of the High Priest, and so on. Many of his arguments were undoubtedly valid, and there was, looking at it from a political point of view, everything to be said for the marriage. But unfortunately it is difficult to play the game of politics with the persons of young and lovely queens as though they were ivory effigies of themselves on a chessboard. Nyleptha's face, while Agon spouted away, was a perfect study; she smiled indeed, but beneath the smile it set like a stone, and her eyes began to flash ominously.

At last he stopped, and she prepared herself to answer. Before she did so, however, Sorais leant towards her and said in a voice sufficiently loud for me to catch what she said, 'Bethink thee well, my sister, ere thou dost speak, for methinks that our thrones may hang upon thy words.'

Nyleptha made no answer, and with a shrug and a smile Sorais leant back again and listened.

'Of a truth a great honour has been done to me,' she said, 'that my poor hand should not only have been asked in marriage, but that Agon here should be so swift to pronounce the blessing of the Sun upon my union. Methinks that in another minute he would have wed us fast ere the bride had said her say. Nasta, I thank thee, and I will bethink me of thy words, but now as yet I have no mind for marriage, that is a cup of which none know the taste until they begin to drink it. Again I thank thee, Nasta,' and she made as though she would rise.

The great lord's face turned almost as black as his beard with fury, for he knew that the words amounted to a final refusal of his suit.

'Thanks be to the Queen for her gracious words,' he said, restraining himself with difficulty and looking anything but grateful, 'my heart shall surely treasure them. And now I crave another boon, namely, the royal leave to withdraw myself to my own poor cities in the north till such time as the Queen shall say my suit nay or yea. Mayhap,' he added, with a sneer, 'the Queen will be pleased to visit me there, and to bring with her these stranger lords,' and he scowled darkly towards us. 'It is but a poor country and a rough, but we are a hardy race of mountaineers, and there shall be gathered thirty thousand swordsmen to shout a welcome to her.'

This speech, which was almost a declaration of rebellion, was received in complete silence, but Nyleptha flushed up and answered it with spirit.

'Oh, surely, Nasta, I will come, and the strange lords in my train, and for every man of thy mountaineers who calls thee Prince, will I bring two from the lowlands who call me Queen, and we will see which is the staunchest breed. Till then farewell.'

The trumpets blared out, the Queens rose, and the great assembly broke up in murmuring confusion, and for myself I went home with a heavy heart foreseeing civil war.

After this there was quiet for a few weeks. Curtis and the Queen did not often meet, and exercised the utmost caution not to allow the true relation in which they stood to each other to leak out; but do what they would, rumours as hard to trace as a buzzing fly in a dark room, and yet quite as audible, began to hum round and round, and at last to settle on her throne.

XVII

THE STORM BREAKS

And now it was that the trouble which at first had been but a cloud as large as a man's hand began to loom very black and big upon our horizon, namely, Sorais' preference for Sir Henry. I saw the storm drawing nearer and nearer; and so, poor fellow, did he. The affection of so lovely and highly-placed a woman was not a thing that could in a general way be considered a calamity by any man, but, situated as Curtis was, it was a grievous burden to bear.

To begin with, Nyleptha, though altogether charming, was, it must be admitted, of a rather jealous disposition, and was sometimes apt to visit on her lover's head her indignation at the marks of what Alphonse would have called the 'distinguished consideration' with which her royal sister favoured him. Then the enforced secrecy of his relation to Nyleptha prevented Curtis from taking some opportunity of putting a stop, or trying to put a stop, to this false condition of affairs, by telling Sorais, in a casual but confidential way, that he was going to marry her sister. A third sting in Sir Henry's honey was that he knew that Good was honestly and sincerely attached to the ominous-looking but most attractive Lady of the Night. Indeed, poor Bougwan was wasting himself to a shadow of his fat and jolly self about her, his face getting so thin that his eyeglass would scarcely stick in it; while she, with a sort of careless coquetry, just gave him encouragement enough to keep him going, thinking, no doubt, that he might be useful as a stalking-horse. I tried to give him a hint, in as delicate a way as I could, but he flew into a huff and would not listen to me, so I was determined to let ill along, for fear of making it worse. Poor Good, he really was very ludicrous in his distress, and went in for all sorts of absurdities, under the belief that he was advancing his suit. One of them was the writing—with the assistance of one of the grave and revered signiors who instructed us, and who, whatever may have been the measure of his erudition, did not understand how to scan a line—of a most interminable Zu-Vendi love-song, of which the continually recurring refrain was something about 'I will kiss thee; oh yes, I will kiss thee!' Now among the Zu-Vendi it is a common and most harmless thing for young men to serenade ladies at night, as I believe they do in the southern countries of Europe, and sing all sorts of nonsensical songs to them. The young men may or may not be serious; but no offence is meant and none is taken, even by ladies of the highest rank, who accept the whole thing as an English girl would a gracefully-turned compliment.

Availing himself of this custom, Good bethought him that would serenade Sorais, whose private apartments, together with those of her maidens, were exactly opposite our own, on the further side of a narrow courtyard which divided one section of the great palace from another. Accordingly, having armed himself with a native zither, on which, being an adept with the light guitar, he had easily learned to strum, he proceeded at midnight—the fashionable hour for this sort of caterwauling—to make night hideous with his amorous yells. I was fast asleep when they began, but they soon woke me up—for Good possesses a tremendous voice and has no notion of time—and I ran to my window-place to see what was the matter. And there, standing in the full moonlight in the courtyard, I perceived Good, adorned with an enormous ostrich feather head-dress and a flowing silken cloak, which it is the right thing to wear upon these occasions, and shouting out the abominable song which he and the old gentleman had evolved, to a jerky, jingling accompaniment. From the direction of the quarters of the maids of honour came a succession of faint sniggerings; but the apartments of Sorais herself—whom I devoutly pitied if she happened to be there—were silent as the grave. There was absolutely no end to that awful song, with its eternal 'I will kiss thee!' and at last neither I nor Sir Henry, whom I had summoned to enjoy the sight, could stand it any longer; so, remembering the dear old story, I put my head to the window opening, and shouted, 'For Heaven's sake, Good, don't go on talking about it, but *kiss* her and let's all go to sleep!' That choked him off, and we had no more serenading.

The whole thing formed a laughable incident in a tragic business. How deeply thankful we ought to be that even the most serious matters have generally a silver lining about them in the shape of a joke, if only people could see it. The sense of humour is a very valuable possession in life, and ought to be cultivated in the Board schools—especially in Scotland.

Well, the more Sir Henry held off the more Sorais came on, as is not uncommon in such cases, till at last things got very queer indeed. Evidently she was, by some strange perversity of mind, quite blinded to the true state of the case; and I, for one, greatly dreaded the moment of her awakening. Sorais was a dangerous woman to be mixed up with, either with or without one's consent. At last the evil moment came, as I saw it must come. One fine day, Good having gone out hawking, Sir Henry and I were sitting quietly talking over the situation, especially with reference to Sorais, when a Court messenger arrived with a written note, which we with some difficulty deciphered, and which was to the effect that 'the Queen Sorais commanded the attendance of the Lord Incubu in her private apartments, whither he would be conducted by the bearer'.

'Oh my word!' groaned Sir Henry. 'Can't you go instead, old fellow?'

'Not if I know it,' I said with vigour. 'I had rather face a wounded elephant with a shot-gun. Take care of your own business, my boy. If you will be so fascinating you must take the consequences. I would not be in your place for an empire.'

'You remind me of when I was going to be flogged at school and the other boys came to console me,' he said gloomily. 'What right has this Queen to command my attendance, I should like to know? I won't go.'

'But you must; you are one of her officers and bound to obey her, and she knows it. And after all it will soon be over.'

'That's just what they used to say,' he said again. 'I only hope she won't put a knife into me. I believe that she is quite capable of it.' And off he started very faintheartedly, and no wonder.

I sat and waited, and at the end of about forty-five minutes he returned, looking a good deal worse than when he went.

'Give me something to drink,' he said hoarsely.

I got him a cup of wine, and asked what was the matter.

'What is the matter? Why if ever there was trouble there's trouble now. You know when I left you? Well, I was shown straight into Sorais' private chamber, and a wonderful place it is; and there she sat, quite alone, upon a silken couch at the end of the room, playing gently upon that zither of hers. I stood before her, and for a while she took no notice of me, but kept on playing and singing a little, and very sweet music it was. At last she looked up and smiled.

'"So thou art come," she said. "I thought perchance thou hadst gone about the Queen Nyleptha's business. Thou art ever on her business, and I doubt not a good servant and a true."

'To this I merely bowed, and said I was there to receive the Queen's word.

"'Ah yes, I would talk with thee, but be thou seated. It wearies me to look so high," and she made room for me beside her on the couch, placing herself with her back against the end, so as to have a view of my face.

"'It is not meet," I said, "that I should make myself equal with the Queen."

"'I said be seated," was her answer, so I sat down, and she began to look at me with those dark eyes of hers. There she sat like an incarnate spirit of beauty, hardly talking at all, and when she did, very low, but all the while looking at me. There was a white flower in her black hair, and I tried to keep my eyes on it and count the petals, but it was of no use. At last, whether it was her gaze, or the perfume in her hair, or what I do not know, but I almost felt as though I was being mesmerized. At last she roused herself.

"'Incubu," she said, "lovest thou power?"

'I replied that I supposed all men loved power of one sort or another.

"'Thou shalt have it," she said. "Lovest thou wealth?"

'I said I liked wealth for what it brought.

"'Thou shalt have it," she said. "And lovest thou beauty?"

'To this I replied that I was very fond of statuary and architecture, or something silly of that sort, at which she frowned, and there was a pause. By this time my nerves were on such a stretch that I was shaking like a leaf. I knew that something awful was going to happen, but she held me under a kind of spell, and I could not help myself.

"'Incubu," she said at length, "wouldst thou be a king? Listen, wouldst thou be a king? Behold, stranger, I am minded to make thee king of all Zu-Vendis, ay and husband of Sorais of the Night. Nay, peace and hear me. To no man among my people had I thus opened out my secret heart, but thou art an outlander and therefore I speak without shame, knowing all I have to offer and how hard it had been thee to ask. See, a crown lies at thy feet, my lord Incubu, and with that fortune a woman whom some have wished to woo. Now mayst thou answer, oh my chosen, and soft shall thy words fall upon mine ears."

"'Oh Sorais," I said, "I pray thee speak not thus"—you see I had not time to pick and choose my words—"for this thing cannot be. I am betrothed to thy sister Nyleptha, oh Sorais, and I love her and her alone."

'Next moment it struck me that I had said an awful thing, and I looked up to see the results. When I spoke, Sorais' face was hidden in her hands, and as my words reached her she slowly raised it, and I shrank back dismayed. It was ashy white, and her eyes were flaming. She rose to her feet and seemed to be choking, but the awful thing was that she was so quiet about it all. Once she looked at a side table, on which lay a dagger, and from it to me, as though she thought of killing me; but she did not take it up. At last she spoke one word, and one only—

'"*Go!*"

'And I went, and glad enough I was to get out of it, and here I am. Give me another cup of wine, there's a good fellow, and tell me, what is to be done?'

I shook my head, for the affair was indeed serious. As one of the poets says,

'Hell hath no fury like a woman scorned',

more especially if the woman is a queen and a Sorais, and indeed I feared the very worst, including imminent danger to ourselves.

'Nyleptha had better be told of this at once,' I said, 'and perhaps I had better tell her; she might receive your account with suspicion.'

'Who is captain of her guard tonight?' I went on.

'Good.'

'Very well then, there will be no chance of her being got at. Don't look surprised. I don't think that her sister would stick at that. I suppose one must tell Good of what has happened.'

'Oh, I don't know,' said Sir Henry. 'It would hurt his feelings, poor fellow! You see, he takes a lively personal interest in Sorais.'

'That's true; and after all, perhaps there is no need to tell him. He will find out the truth soon enough. Now, you mark my words, Sorais will throw in her lot with Nasta, who is sulking up in the North there, and there will be such a war as has not been known in Zu-Vendis for centuries. Look there!' and I pointed to two Court messengers, who were speeding away from the door of Sorais' private apartments. 'Now follow me,' and I ran up a stairway into an outlook tower that rose from the roof of our quarters, taking the spyglass with me, and looked out over the palace wall. The first thing we saw was one of the messengers speeding towards the Temple, bearing, without any doubt, the Queen's word to the High Priest Agon, but for the other I searched in vain. Presently, however, I spied a horseman riding furiously through the northern gate of the city, and in him I recognized the other messenger.

'Ah!' I said, 'Sorais is a woman of spirit. She is acting at once, and will strike quick and hard. You have insulted her, my boy, and the blood will flow in rivers before the stain is washed away, and yours with it, if she can get hold of you. Well, I'm off to Nyleptha. Just you stop where you are, old fellow, and try to get your nerves straight again. You'll need them all, I can tell you, unless I have observed human nature in the rough for fifty years for nothing.' And off I went accordingly.

I gained audience of the Queen without trouble. She was expecting Curtis, and was not best pleased to see my mahogany-coloured face instead.

'Is there aught wrong with my Lord, Macumazahn, that he waits not upon me? Say, is he sick?'

I said that he was well enough, and then, without further ado, I plunged into my story and told it from beginning to end. Oh, what a rage she flew into! It was a sight to see her, she looked so lovely.

'How darest thou come to me with such a tale?' she cried. 'It is a lie to say that my Lord was making love to Sorais, my sister.'

'Pardon me, oh Queen,' I answered, 'I said that Sorais was making love to thy lord.'

'Spin me no spiders' webs of words. Is not the thing the same thing? The one giveth, the other taketh; but the gift passes, and what matters it which is the most guilty? Sorais! oh, I hate her—Sorais is a queen and my sister. She had not stooped so low had he not shown the way. Oh, truly hath the poet said that man is like a snake, whom to touch is poison, and whom none can hold.'

'The remark, oh Queen, is excellent, but methinks thou hast misread the poet. Nyleptha,' I went on, 'thou knowest well that thy words are empty foolishness, and that this is no time for folly.'

'How darest thou?' she broke in, stamping her foot. 'Hast my false lord sent thee to me to insult me also? Who art thou, stranger, that thou shouldst speak to me, the Queen, after this sort? How darest thou?'

'Yea, I dare. Listen. The moments which thou dost waste in idle anger may well cost thee thy crown and all of us our lives. Already Sorais' horsemen go forth and call to arms. In three days' time Nasta will rouse himself in his fastnesses like a lion in the evening, and his growling will be heard throughout the North. The "Lady of the Night" (Sorais) hath a sweet voice, and she will not sing in vain. Her banner will be borne from range to range and valley to valley, and warriors will spring up in its track like dust beneath a whirlwind; half the army will echo her

H. RIDER HAGGARD

war-cry; and in every town and hamlet of this wide land the priests will call out against the foreigner and will preach her cause as holy. I have spoken, oh Queen!'

Nyleptha was quite calm now; her jealous anger had passed; and putting off the character of a lovely headstrong lady, with a rapidity and completeness that distinguished her, she put on that of a queen and a woman of business. The transformation was sudden but entire.

'Thy words are very wise, Macumazahn. Forgive me my folly. Ah, what a Queen I should be if only I had no heart! To be heartless—that is to conquer all. Passion is like the lightning, it is beautiful, and it links the earth to heaven, but alas it blinds!

'And thou thinkest that my sister Sorais would levy war upon me. So be it. She shall not prevail against me. I, too, have my friends and my retainers. There are many, I say, who will shout "Nyleptha!" when my pennon runs up on peak and pinnacle, and the light of my beacon fires leaps tonight from crag to crag, bearing the message of my war. I will break her strength and scatter her armies. Eternal night shall be the portion of Sorais of the Night. Give me that parchment and the ink. So. Now summon the officer in the ante-room. He is a trusty man.'

I did as I was bid! and the man, a veteran and quiet-looking gentleman of the guard, named Kara, entered, bowing low.

'Take this parchment,' said Nyleptha; 'it is thy warrant; and guard every place of in and outgoing in the apartments of my sister Sorais, the "Lady of the Night", and a Queen of the Zu-Vendi. Let none come in and none go out, or thy life shall pay the cost.'

The man looked startled, but he merely said, 'The Queen's word be done,' and departed. Then Nyleptha sent a messenger to Sir Henry, and presently he arrived looking uncommonly uncomfortable. I thought that another outburst was about to follow, but wonderful are the ways of woman; she said not a word about Sorais and his supposed inconstancy, greeting him with a friendly nod, and stating simply that she required his advice upon high matters. All the same there was a look in her eye, and a sort of suppressed energy in her manner towards him, that makes me think that she had not forgotten the affair, but was keeping it for a private occasion.

Just after Curtis arrived the officer returned, and reported that Sorais was *gone*. The bird had flown to the Temple, stating that she was going, as was sometimes the custom among Zu-Vendi ladies of rank, to spend the night in meditation before the altar. We looked at each other significantly. The blow had fallen very soon.

Then we set to work.

Generals who could be trusted were summoned from their quarters, and as much of the State affairs as was thought desirable was told to each, strict injunctions being given to them to get all their available force together. The same was done with such of the more powerful lords as Nyleptha knew she could rely on, several of whom left that very day for distant parts of the country to gather up their tribesmen and retainers. Sealed orders were dispatched to the rulers of far-off cities, and some twenty messengers were sent off before nightfall with instructions to ride early and late till they reached the distant chiefs to whom their letters were addressed: also many spies were set to work. All the afternoon and evening we laboured, assisted by some confidential scribes, Nyleptha showing an energy and resource of mind that astonished me, and it was eight o'clock before we got back to our quarters. Here we heard from Alphonse, who was deeply aggrieved because our non-return had spoilt his dinner (for he had turned cook again now), that Good had come back from his hawking and gone on duty. As instructions had already been given to the officer of the outer guard to double the sentries at the gate, and as we had no reason to fear any immediate danger, we did not think it worth while to hunt him up and tell him anything of what had passed, which at best was, under the peculiar circumstances of the case, one of those tasks that one prefers to postpone, so after swallowing our food we turned in to get some much-needed rest. Before we did so, however, it occurred to Curtis to tell old Umslopogaas to keep a look-out in the neighbourhood of Nyleptha's private apartments. Umslopogaas was now well known about the place, and by the Queen's order allowed to pass whither he would by the guards, a permission of which he often availed himself by roaming about the palace during the still hours in a nocturnal fashion that he favoured, and which is by no means uncommon amongst black men generally. His presence in the corridors would not, therefore, be likely to excite remark. Without any comment the Zulu took up his axe and departed, and we also departed to bed.

I seemed to have been asleep but a few minutes when I was awakened by a peculiar sensation of uneasiness. I felt that somebody was in the room and looking at me, and instantly sat up, to see to my surprise that it was already dawn, and that there, standing at the foot of my couch and looking peculiarly grim and gaunt in the grey light, was Umslopogaas himself.

'How long hast thou been there?' I asked testily, for it is not pleasant to be aroused in such a fashion.

'Mayhap the half of an hour, Macumazahn. I have a word for thee.'

'Speak on,' I said, now wide enough awake.

'As I was bid I went last night to the place of the White Queen and hid myself behind a pillar in the second anteroom, beyond which is the sleeping-place of the Queen. Bougwan (Good) was in the first anteroom alone, and outside the curtain of that room was a sentry, but I had a mind to see if I could pass in unseen, and I did, gliding behind them both. There I waited for many hours, when suddenly I perceived a dark figure coming secretly towards me. It was the figure of a woman, and in her hand she held a dagger. Behind that figure crept another unseen by the woman. It was Bougwan following in her tracks. His shoes were off, and for so fat a man he followed very well. The woman passed me, and the starlight shone upon her face.'

'Who was it?' I asked impatiently.

'The face was the face of the "Lady of the Night", and of a truth she is well named.

'I waited, and Bougwan passed me also. Then I followed. So we went slowly and without a sound up the long chamber. First the woman, then Bougwan, and then I; and the woman saw not Bougwan, and Bougwan saw not me. At last the "Lady of the Night" came to the curtains that shut off the sleeping place of the White Queen, and put out her left hand to part them. She passed through, and so did Bougwan, and so did I. At the far end of the room is the bed of the Queen, and on it she lay very fast asleep. I could hear her breathe, and see one white arm lying on the coverlid like a streak of snow on the dry grass. The "Lady of the Night" doubled herself thus, and with the long knife lifted crept towards the bed. So straight did she gaze thereat that she never thought to look behind her. When she was quite close Bougwan touched her on the arm, and she caught her breath and turned, and I saw the knife flash, and heard it strike. Well was it for Bougwan that he had the skin of iron on him, or he had been pierced. Then for the first time he saw who the woman was, and without a word he fell back astonished, and unable to speak. She, too, was astonished, and spoke not, but suddenly she laid her finger on her lip, thus, and walked towards and through the curtain, and with her went Bougwan. So close did she pass to me that her dress touched me, and I was nigh to slaying her as she went. In the first outer room she spoke to Bougwan in a whisper and, clasping her hands thus, she pleaded with him, but what she said I know not. And so they passed on to the second outer room, she pleading and he shaking his head, and saying, "Nay, nay, nay". And it seemed to me that he was about to call the guard, when she stopped talking and looked at him with great eyes, and I saw that he was bewitched by her beauty. Then she stretched out her hand and he kissed it, whereon I gathered myself together to advance and take her, seeing that now had Bougwan become a woman, and no longer knew the good from the evil, when behold! she was gone.'

'Gone!' I exclaimed.

'Ay, gone, and there stood Bougwan staring at the wall like one asleep, and presently he went too, and I waited a while and came away also.'

'Art thou sure, Umslopogaas,' said I, 'that thou hast not been a dreamer this night?'

In reply he opened his left hand, and produced about three inches of a blade of a dagger of the finest steel. 'If I be, Macumazahn, behold what the dream left with me. The knife broke upon Bougwan's bosom and as I passed I picked this up in the sleeping-place of the White Queen.'

XVIII

WAR! RED WAR!

Telling Umslopogaas to wait, I tumbled into my clothes and went off with him to Sir Henry's room, where the Zulu repeated his story word for word. It was a sight to watch Curtis' face as he heard it.

'Great Heavens!' he said: 'here have I been sleeping away while Nyleptha was nearly murdered—and all through me, too. What a fiend that Sorais must be! It would have served her well if Umslopogaas had cut her down in the act.'

'Ay,' said the Zulu. 'Fear not; I should have slain her ere she struck. I was but waiting the moment.'

I said nothing, but I could not help thinking that many a thousand doomed lives would have been saved if he had meted out to Sorais the fate she meant for her sister. And, as the issue proved, I was right.

After he had told his tale Umslopogaas went off unconcernedly to get his morning meal, and Sir Henry and I fell to talking.

At first he was very bitter against Good, who, he said, was no longer to be trusted, having designedly allowed Sorais to escape by some secret stair when it was his duty to have handed her over to justice. Indeed, he spoke in the most unmeasured terms on the matter. I let him run on awhile, reflecting to myself how easy we find it to be hard on the weaknesses of others, and how tender we are to our own.

'Really, my dear fellow,' I said at length, 'one would never think, to hear you talk, that you were the man who had an interview with this same lady yesterday, and found it rather difficult to resist her fascinations, notwithstanding your ties to one of the loveliest and most loving women in the world. Now suppose it was Nyleptha who had tried to murder Sorais, and *you* had caught her, and she had pleaded with you, would you have been so very eager to hand her over to an open shame, and to death by fire? Just look at the matter through Good's eyeglass for a minute before you denounce an old friend as a scoundrel.'

He listened to this jobation submissively, and then frankly acknowledged that he had spoken hardly. It is one of the best points in Sir Henry's character that he is always ready to admit it when he is in the wrong.

But, though I spoke up thus for Good, I was not blind to the fact that, however natural his behaviour might be, it was obvious that he was being involved in a very awkward and disgraceful complication. A foul and wicked murder had been attempted, and he had let the murderess escape, and thereby, among other things, allowed her to gain a complete ascendency over himself. In fact, he was in a fair way to become her tool—and no more dreadful fate can befall a man than to become the tool of an unscrupulous woman, or indeed of any woman. There is but one end to it: when he is broken, or has served her purpose, he is thrown away—turned out on the world to hunt for his lost self-respect. Whilst I was pondering thus, and wondering what was to be done—for the whole subject was a thorny one—I suddenly heard a great clamour in the courtyard outside, and distinguished the voice of Umslopogaas and Alphonse, the former cursing furiously, and the latter yelling in terror.

Hurrying out to see what was the matter, I was met by a ludicrous sight. The little Frenchman was running up the courtyard at an extraordinary speed, and after him sped Umslopogaas like a great greyhound. Just as I came out he caught him, and, lifting him right off his legs, carried him some paces to a beautiful but very dense flowering shrub which bore a flower not unlike the gardenia, but was covered with short thorns. Next, despite his howls and struggles, he with one mighty thrust plunged poor Alphonse head first into the bush, so that nothing but the calves of his legs and heels remained in evidence. Then, satisfied with what he had done, the Zulu folded his arms and stood grimly contemplating the Frenchman's kicks, and listening to his yells, which were awful.

'What art thou doing?' I said, running up. 'Wouldst thou kill the man? Pull him out of the bush!'

With a savage grunt he obeyed, seizing the wretched Alphonse by the ankle, and with a jerk that must have nearly dislocated it, tearing him out of the heart of the shrub. Never did I see such a sight as he presented, his clothes half torn off his back, and bleeding as he was in every direction from the sharp thorns. There he lay and yelled and rolled, and there was no getting anything out of him.

At last, however, he got up and, ensconcing himself behind me, cursed old Umslopogaas by every saint in the calendar, vowing by the blood of his heroic grandfather that he would poison him, and 'have his revenge'.

At last I got to the truth of the matter. It appeared that Alphonse habitually cooked Umslopogaas's porridge, which the latter ate for breakfast in the corner of the courtyard, just as he would have done at home in Zululand, from a gourd, and with a wooden spoon. Now Umslopogaas had, like many Zulus, a great horror of fish, which he considered a species of water-snake; so Alphonse, who was as fond of playing tricks as a monkey, and who was also a consummate cook, determined to make him eat some. Accordingly he grated up a quantity of white fish very finely, and mixed it with the Zulu's porridge, who swallowed it nearly all down in ignorance of what he was eating. But, unfortunately for Alphonse, he could not restrain his joy at this sight, and came capering and peering round, till at last Umslopogaas, who was very clever in his way, suspected something, and, after a careful examination of the remains of his porridge, discovered 'the buffalo heifer's trick', and, in revenge, served him as I have said. Indeed, the little man was fortunate not to get a broken neck for his pains; for, as one would have thought, he might have learnt from the episode of his display of axemanship that 'le Monsieur noir' was an ill person to play practical jokes upon.

This incident was unimportant enough in itself, but I narrate it because it led to serious consequences. As soon as he had stanched the bleeding from his scratches and washed himself, Alphonse went off still cursing, to recover his temper, a process which I knew from experience would take a very long time. When he had gone I gave Umslopogaas a jobation and told him that I was ashamed of his behaviour.

'Ah, well, Macumazahn,' he said, 'you must be gentle with me, for here is not my place. I am weary of it, weary to death of eating and drinking, of sleeping and giving in marriage. I love not this soft life in stone houses that takes the heart out of a man, and turns his strength to water and his flesh to fat. I love not the white robes and the delicate women, the blowing of trumpets and the flying of hawks. When we fought the Masai at the kraal yonder, ah, then life was worth the living, but here is never a blow struck in anger, and I begin to think I shall go the way of my fathers and lift Inkosi-kaas no more,' and he held up the axe and gazed at it in sorrow.

'Ah,' I said, 'that is thy complaint, is it? Thou hast the blood-sickness, hast thou? And the Woodpecker wants a tree. And at thy age, too. Shame on thee! Umslopogaas.'

'Ay, Macumazahn, mine is a red trade, yet is it better and more honest than some. Better is it to slay a man in fair fight than to suck out his heart's blood in buying and selling and usury after your white fashion. Many a man have I slain, yet is there never a one that I should fear to look in the face again, ay, many are there who once were friends, and whom I should be right glad to snuff with. But there! there! thou hast thy ways, and I mine: each to his own people and his own place. The high-veldt ox will die in the fat bush country, and so is it with me, Macumazahn. I am rough, I know it, and when my blood is warm I know not what to do, but yet wilt thou be sorry when the night swallows me and I am utterly lost in blackness, for in thy heart thou lovest me, my father, Macumazahn the fox, though I be nought but a broken-down Zulu war-dog—a chief for whom there is no room in his own kraal, an outcast and a wanderer in strange places: ay, I love thee, Macumazahn, for we have grown grey together, and there is that between us that cannot be seen, and yet is too strong for breaking;' and he took his snuff-box, which was made of an old brass cartridge, from the slit in his ear where he always carried it, and handed it to me for me to help myself.

I took the pinch of snuff with some emotion. It was quite true, I was much attached to the bloodthirsty old ruffian. I do not know what was the charm of his character, but it had a charm; perhaps it was its fierce honesty and directness; perhaps one admired his almost superhuman skill and strength, or it may have been simply that he was so absolutely unique. Frankly, with all my experience of savages, I never knew a man quite like him, he was so wise and yet such a child with it all; and though it seems laughable to say so, like the hero of the Yankee parody, he 'had a tender heart'. Anyway, I was very fond of him, though I should never have thought of telling him so.

'Ay, old wolf,' I said, 'thine is a strange love. Thou wouldst split me to the chin if I stood in thy path tomorrow.'

'Thou speakest truth, Macumazahn, that would I if it came in the way of duty, but I should love thee all the same when the blow had gone fairly home. Is there any chance of some fighting here, Macumazahn?' he went on in an insinuating voice. 'Methought that what I saw last night did show that the two great Queens were vexed one with another. Else had the "Lady of the Night" not brought that dagger with her.'

I agreed with him that it showed that more or less pique and irritation existed between the ladies, and told him how things stood, and that they were quarrelling over Incubu.

H. RIDER HAGGARD

'Ah, is it so?' he exclaimed, springing up in delight; 'then will there be war as surely as the rivers rise in the rains—war to the end. Women love the last blow as well as the last word, and when they fight for love they are pitiless as a wounded buffalo. See thou, Macumazahn, a woman will swim through blood to her desire, and think nought of it. With these eyes have I seen it once, and twice also. Ah, Macumazahn, we shall see this fine place of houses burning yet, and hear the battle cries come ringing up the street. After all, I have not wandered for nothing. Can this folk fight, think ye?'

Just then Sir Henry joined us, and Good arrived, too, from another direction, looking very pale and hollow-eyed. The moment Umslopogaas saw the latter he stopped his bloodthirsty talk and greeted him.

'Ah, Bougwan,' he cried, 'greeting to thee, Inkoos! Thou art surely weary. Didst thou hunt too much yesterday?' Then, without waiting for an answer, he went on—

'Listen, Bougwan, and I will tell thee a story; it is about a woman, therefore wilt thou hear it, is it not so?

'There was a man and he had a brother, and there was a woman who loved the man's brother and was beloved of the man. But the man's brother had a favourite wife and loved not the woman, and he made a mock of her. Then the woman, being very cunning and fierce-hearted for revenge, took counsel with herself and said to the man, "I love thee, and if thou wilt make war upon thy brother I will marry thee." And he knew it was a lie, yet because of his great love of the woman, who was very fair, did he listen to her words and made war. And when many people had been killed his brother sent to him, saying, "Why slayest thou me? What hurt have I done unto thee? From my youth up have I not loved thee? When thou wast little did I not nurture thee, and have we not gone down to war together and divided the cattle, girl by girl, ox by ox, and cow by cow? Why slayest thou me, my brother, son of my own mother?"

'Then the man's heart was heavy, and he knew that his path was evil, and he put aside the tempting of the woman and ceased to make war on his brother, and lived at peace in the same kraal with him. And after a time the woman came to him and said, "I have lost the past, I will be thy wife." And in his heart he knew that it was a lie and that she thought the evil thing, yet because of his love did he take her to wife.

'And the very night that they were wed, when the man was plunged into a deep sleep, did the woman arise and take his axe from his hand

and creep into the hut of his brother and slay him in his rest. Then did she slink back like a gorged lioness and place the thong of the red axe back upon his wrist and go her ways.

'And at the dawning the people came shouting, "Lousta is slain in the night," and they came unto the hut of the man, and there he lay asleep and by him was the red axe. Then did they remember the war and say, "Lo! he hath of a surety slain his brother," and they would have taken and killed him, but he rose and fled swiftly, and as he fleeted by he slew the woman.

'But death could not wipe out the evil she had done, and on him rested the weight of all her sin. Therefore is he an outcast and his name a scorn among his own people; for on him, and him only, resteth the burden of her who betrayed. And, therefore, does he wander afar, without a kraal and without an ox or a wife, and therefore will he die afar like a stricken buck and his name be accursed from generation to generation, in that the people say that he slew his brother, Lousta, by treachery in the night-time.'

The old Zulu paused, and I saw that he was deeply agitated by his own story. Presently he lifted his head, which he had bowed to his breast, and went on:

'I was the man, Bougwan. Ou! I was that man, and now hark thou! Even as I am so wilt thou be—a tool, a plaything, an ox of burden to carry the evil deeds of another. Listen! When thou didst creep after the "Lady of the Night" I was hard upon thy track. When she struck thee with the knife in the sleeping place of the White Queen I was there also; when thou didst let her slip away like a snake in the stones I saw thee, and I knew that she had bewitched thee and that a true man had abandoned the truth, and he who aforetime loved a straight path had taken a crooked way. Forgive me, my father, if my words are sharp, but out of a full heart are they spoken. See her no more, so shalt thou go down with honour to the grave. Else because of the beauty of a woman that weareth as a garment of fur shalt thou be even as I am, and perchance with more cause. I have said.'

Throughout this long and eloquent address Good had been perfectly silent, but when the tale began to shape itself so aptly to his own case, he coloured up, and when he learnt that what had passed between him and Sorais had been overseen he was evidently much distressed. And now, when at last he spoke, it was in a tone of humility quite foreign to him.

'I must say,' he said, with a bitter little laugh, 'that I scarcely thought that I should live to be taught my duty by a Zulu; but it just shows what we can come to. I wonder if you fellows can understand how humiliated I feel, and the bitterest part of it is that I deserve it all. Of course I should have handed Sorais over to the guard, but I could not, and that is a fact. I let her go and I promised to say nothing, more is the shame to me. She told me that if I would side with her she would marry me and make me king of this country, but thank goodness I did find the heart to say that even to marry her I could not desert my friends. And now you can do what you like, I deserve it all. All I have to say is that I hope that you may never love a woman with all your heart and then be so sorely tempted of her,' and he turned to go.

'Look here, old fellow,' said Sir Henry, 'just stop a minute. I have a little tale to tell you too.' And he went on to narrate what had taken place on the previous day between Sorais and himself.

This was a finishing stroke to poor Good. It is not pleasant to any man to learn that he has been made a tool of, but when the circumstances are as peculiarly atrocious as in the present case, it is about as bitter a pill as anybody can be called on to swallow.

'Do you know,' he said, 'I think that between you, you fellows have about worked a cure,' and he turned and walked away, and I for one felt very sorry for him. Ah, if the moths would always carefully avoid the candle, how few burnt wings there would be!

That day was a Court day, when the Queens sat in the great hall and received petitions, discussed laws, money grants, and so forth, and thither we adjourned shortly afterwards. On our way we were joined by Good, who was looking exceedingly depressed.

When we got into the hall Nyleptha was already on her throne and proceeding with business as usual, surrounded by councillors, courtiers, lawyers, priests, and an unusually strong guard. It was, however, easy to see from the air of excitement and expectation on the faces of everybody present that nobody was paying much attention to ordinary affairs, the fact being that the knowledge that civil war was imminent had now got abroad. We saluted Nyleptha and took our accustomed places, and for a little while things went on as usual, when suddenly the trumpets began to call outside the palace, and from the great crowd that was gathered there in anticipation of some unusual event there rose a roar of 'Sorais! Sorais!'

Then came the roll of many chariot wheels, and presently the great curtains at the end of the hall were drawn wide and through them entered the 'Lady of the Night' herself. Nor did she come alone. Preceding her was Agon, the High Priest, arrayed in his most gorgeous vestments, and on either side were other priests. The reason for their presence was obvious—coming with them it would have been sacrilege to attempt to detain her. Behind her were a number of the great lords, and behind them a small body of picked guards. A glance at Sorais herself was enough to show that her mission was of no peaceful kind, for in place of her gold embroidered 'kaf' she wore a shining tunic formed of golden scales, and on her head a little golden helmet. In her hand, too, she bore a toy spear, beautifully made and fashioned of solid silver. Up the hall she came, looking like a lioness in her conscious pride and beauty, and as she came the spectators fell back bowing and made a path for her. By the sacred stone she halted, and laying her hand on it, she cried out with a loud voice to Nyleptha on the throne, 'Hail, oh Queen!'

'All hail, my royal sister!' answered Nyleptha. 'Draw thou near. Fear not, I give thee safe conduct.'

Sorais answered with a haughty look, and swept on up the hall till she stood right before the thrones.

'A boon, oh Queen!' she cried again.

'Speak on, my sister; what is there that I can give thee who hath half our kingdom?'

'Thou canst tell me a true word—me and the people of Zu-Vendis. Art thou, or art thou not, about to take this foreign wolf,' and she pointed to Sir Henry with her toy spear, 'to be a husband to thee, and share thy bed and throne?'

Curtis winced at this, and turning towards Sorais, said to her in a low voice, 'Methinks that yesterday thou hadst other names than wolf to call me by, oh Queen!' and I saw her bite her lips as, like a danger flag, the blood flamed red upon her face. As for Nyleptha, who is nothing if not original, she, seeing that the thing was out, and that there was nothing further to be gained by concealment, answered the question in a novel and effectual manner, inspired thereto, as I firmly believe, by coquetry and a desire to triumph over her rival.

Up she rose and, descending from the throne, swept in all the glory of her royal grace on to where her lover stood. There she stopped and untwined the golden snake that was wound around her arm. Then she bade him kneel, and he dropped on one knee on the marble before her, and next, taking the golden snake with both her hands, she bent the pure soft metal round his neck, and when it was fast, deliberately kissed him on the brow and called him her 'dear lord'.

'Thou seest,' she said, when the excited murmur of the spectators had died away, addressing her sister as Sir Henry rose to his feet, 'I have put my collar round the "wolf's" neck, and behold! he shall be my watchdog, and that is my answer to thee, Queen Sorais, my sister, and to those with thee. Fear not,' she went on, smiling sweetly on her lover, and pointing to the golden snake she had twined round his massive throat, 'if my yoke be heavy, yet is it of pure gold, and it shall not gall thee.'

Then, turning to the audience, she continued in a clear proud tone, 'Ay, Lady of the Night, Lords, Priests, and People here gathered together, by this sign do I take the foreigner to husband, even here in the face of you all. What, am I a Queen, and yet not free to choose the man whom I will love? Then should I be lower than the meanest girl in all my provinces. Nay, he hath won my heart, and with it goes my hand, and throne, and all I have—ay, had he been a beggar instead of a great lord fairer and stronger than any here, and having more wisdom and knowledge of strange things, I had given him all, how much more so being what he is!' And she took his hand and gazed proudly on him, and holding it, stood there boldly facing the people. And such was her sweetness and the power and dignity of her person, and so beautiful she looked standing hand in hand there at her lover's side, so sure of him and of herself, and so ready to risk all things and endure all things for him, that most of those who saw the sight, which I am sure no one of them will ever forget, caught the fire from her eyes and the happy colour from her blushing face, and cheered her like wild things. It was a bold stroke for her to make, and it appealed to the imagination; but human nature in Zu-Vendis, as elsewhere, loves that which is bold and not afraid to break a rule, and is moreover peculiarly susceptible to appeals to its poetical side.

And so the people cheered till the roof rang; but Sorais of the Night stood there with downcast eyes, for she could not bear to see her sister's triumph, which robbed her of the man whom she had hoped to win, and in the awfulness of her jealous anger she trembled and turned white like an aspen in the wind. I think I have said somewhere of her that she reminded me of the sea on a calm day, having the same aspect of sleeping power about her. Well, it was all awake now, and like the face of the furious ocean it awed and yet fascinated me. A really handsome woman in a royal rage is always a beautiful sight, but such beauty and such a rage I never saw combined before, and I can only say that the effect produced was well worthy of the two.

She lifted her white face, the teeth set, and there were purple rings beneath her glowing eyes. Thrice she tried to speak and thrice she failed, but at last her voice came. Raising her silver spear, she shook it, and the light gleamed from it and from the golden scales of her cuirass.

'And thinkest thou, Nyleptha,' she said in notes which pealed through the great hall like a clarion, 'thinkest thou that I, Sorais, a Queen of the Zu-Vendi, will brook that this base outlander shall sit upon my father's throne and rear up half-breeds to fill the place of the great House of the Stairway? Never! never! while there is life in my bosom and a man to follow me and a spear to strike with. Who is on my side? Who?

'Now hand thou over this foreign wolf and those who came hither to prey with him to the doom of fire, for have they not committed the deadly sin against the sun? or, Nyleptha, I give thee War—red War! Ay, I say to thee that the path of thy passion shall be marked out by the blazing of thy towns and watered with the blood of those who cleave to thee. On thy head rest the burden of the deed, and in thy ears ring the groans of the dying and the cries of the widows and those who are left fatherless for ever and for ever.

'I tell thee I will tear thee, Nyleptha, the White Queen, from thy throne, and that thou shalt be hurled—ay, hurled even from the topmost stair of the great way to the foot thereof, in that thou hast covered the name of the House of him who built it with black shame. And I tell ye strangers—all save Bougwan, whom because thou didst do me a service I will save alive if thou wilt leave these men and follow me' (here poor Good shook his head vigorously and exclaimed 'Can't be done' in English)—'that I will wrap you in sheets of gold and hang you yet alive in chains from the four golden trumpets of the four angels that fly east and west and north and south from the giddiest pinnacles of the Temple, so that ye may be a token and a warning to the land. And as for thee, Incubu, thou shalt die in yet another fashion that I will not tell thee now.'

She ceased, panting for breath, for her passion shook her like a storm, and a murmur, partly of horror and partly of admiration, ran through the hall. Then Nyleptha answered calmly and with dignity:

'Ill would it become my place and dignity, oh sister, so to speak as thou hast spoken and so to threat as thou hast threatened. Yet if thou wilt make war, then will I strive to bear up against thee, for if my hand seem soft, yet shalt thou find it of iron when it grips thine armies by the throat. Sorais, I fear thee not. I weep for that which thou wilt bring upon our people and on thyself, but for myself I say—I fear thee not. Yet thou, who but yesterday didst strive to win my lover and my lord from me, whom today thou dost call a "foreign wolf", to be *thy* lover and *thy* lord' (here there was an immense sensation in the hall), 'thou who but last night, as I have learnt but since thou didst enter here, didst creep like a snake into my sleeping-place—ay, even by a secret way, and wouldst have foully murdered me, thy sister, as I lay asleep—'

'It is false, it is false!' rang out Agon's and a score of other voices.

'It is *not* false,' said I, producing the broken point of the dagger and holding it up. 'Where is the haft from which this flew, oh Sorais?'

'It is not false,' cried Good, determined at last to act like a loyal man. 'I took the Lady of the Night by the White Queen's bed, and on my breast the dagger broke.'

'Who is on my side?' cried Sorais, shaking her silver spear, for she saw that public sympathy was turning against her. 'What, Bougwan, thou comest not?' she said, addressing Good, who was standing close to her, in a low, concentrated voice. 'Thou pale-souled fool, for a reward thou shalt eat out thy heart with love of me and not be satisfied, and thou mightest have been my husband and a king! At least I hold *thee* in chains that cannot be broken.

'*War! War! War!*' she cried. 'Here, with my hand upon the sacred stone that shall endure, so runs the prophecy, till the Zu-Vendi set their necks beneath an alien yoke, I declare war to the end. Who follows Sorais of the Night to victory and honour?'

Instantly the whole concourse began to break up in indescribable confusion. Many present hastened to throw in their lot with the 'Lady of the Night', but some came from her following to us. Amongst the former was an under officer of Nyleptha's own guard, who suddenly turned and made a run for the doorway through which Sorais' people were already passing. Umslopogaas, who was present and had taken the whole scene in, seeing with admirable presence of mind that if this soldier got away others would follow his example, seized the man, who drew his sword and struck at him. Thereon the Zulu sprang back with a wild shout, and, avoiding the sword cuts, began to peck at his foe with his terrible axe, till in a few seconds the man's fate overtook him and he fell with a clash heavily and quite dead upon the marble floor.

This was the first blood spilt in the war.

'Shut the gates,' I shouted, thinking that we might perhaps catch Sorais so, and not being troubled with the idea of committing sacrilege. But the order came too late, her guards were already passing through them, and in another minute the streets echoed with the furious galloping of horses and the rolling of her chariots.

So, drawing half the people after her, Sorais was soon passing like a whirlwind through the Frowning City on her road to her headquarters at M'Arstuna, a fortress situated a hundred and thirty miles to the north of Milosis.

And after that the city was alive with the endless tramp of regiments and preparations for the gathering war, and old Umslopogaas once more began to sit in the sunshine and go through a show of sharpening Inkosi-kaas's razor edge.

XIX

A Strange Wedding

O ne person, however, did not succeed in getting out in time before the gates were shut, and that was the High Priest Agon, who, as we had every reason to believe, was Sorais' great ally, and the heart and soul of her party. This cunning and ferocious old man had not forgiven us for those hippopotami, or rather that was what he said. What he meant was that he would never brook the introduction of our wider ways of thought and foreign learning and influence while there was a possibility of stamping us out. Also he knew that we possessed a different system of religion, and no doubt was in daily terror of our attempting to introduce it into Zu-Vendis. One day he asked me if we had any religion in our country, and I told him that so far as I could remember we had ninety-five different ones. You might have knocked him down with a feather, and really it is difficult not to pity a high priest of a well-established cult who is haunted by the possible approach of one or all of ninety-five new religions.

When we knew that Agon was caught, Nyleptha, Sir Henry, and I discussed what was to be done with him. I was for closely incarcerating him, but Nyleptha shook her head, saying that it would produce a disastrous effect throughout the country. 'Ah!' she added, with a stamp of her foot, 'if I win and am once really Queen, I will break the power of those priests, with their rites and revels and dark secret ways.' I only wished that old Agon could have heard her, it would have frightened him.

'Well,' said Sir Henry, 'if we are not to imprison him, I suppose that we may as well let him go. He is of no use here.'

Nyleptha looked at him in a curious sort of way, and said in a dry little voice, 'Thinkest thou so, my lord?'

'Eh?' said Curtis. 'No, I do not see what is the use of keeping him.'

She said nothing, but continued looking at him in a way that was as shy as it was sweet.

Then at last he understood.

'Forgive me, Nyleptha,' he said, rather tremulously. 'Dost thou mean that thou wilt marry me, even now?'

'Nay, I know not; let my lord say,' was her rapid answer; 'but if my lord wills, the priest is there and the altar is there'—pointing to the entrance to a private chapel—'and am I not ready to do the will of my lord? Listen, oh my lord! In eight days or less thou must leave me and go down to war, for thou shalt lead my armies, and in war—men sometimes fall, and so I would for a little space have had thee all my own, if only for memory's sake;' and the tears overflowed her lovely eyes and rolled down her face like heavy drops of dew down the red heart of a rose.

'Mayhap, too,' she went on, 'I shall lose my crown, and with my crown my life and thine also. Sorais is very strong and very bitter, and if she prevails she will not spare. Who can read the future? Happiness is the world's White Bird, that alights seldom, and flies fast and far till one day he is lost in the clouds. Therefore should we hold him fast if by any chance he rests for a little space upon our hand. It is not wise to neglect the present for the future, for who knows what the future will be, Incubu? Let us pluck our flowers while the dew is on them, for when the sun is up they wither and on the morrow will others bloom that we shall never see.' And she lifted her sweet face to him and smiled into his eyes, and once more I felt a curious pang of jealousy and turned and went away. They never took much notice of whether I was there or not, thinking, I suppose, that I was an old fool, and that it did not matter one way or the other, and really I believe that they were right.

So I went back to our quarters and ruminated over things in general, and watched old Umslopogaas whetting his axe outside the window as a vulture whets his beak beside a dying ox.

And in about an hour's time Sir Henry came tearing over, looking very radiant and wildly excited, and found Good and myself and even Umslopogaas, and asked us if we should like to assist at a real wedding. Of course we said yes, and off we went to the chapel, where we found Agon looking as sulky as any High Priest possibly could, and no wonder. It appeared that he and Nyleptha had a slight difference of opinion about the coming ceremony. He had flatly refused to celebrate it, or to allow any of his priests to do so, whereupon Nyleptha became very angry and told him that she, as Queen, was head of the Church, and meant to be obeyed. Indeed, she played the part of a Zu-Vendi Henry the Eighth to perfection, and insisted that, if she wanted to be married, she would be married, and that he should marry her.

He still refused to go through the ceremony, so she clinched her argument thus—

'Well, I cannot execute a High Priest, because there is an absurd prejudice against it, and I cannot imprison him because all his subordinates would raise a crying that would bring the stars down on Zu-Vendis and crush it; but I *can* leave him to contemplate the altar of the Sun without anything to eat, because that is his natural vocation, and if thou wilt not marry me, O Agon! thou shalt be placed before the altar yonder with nought but a little water till such time as thou hast reconsidered the matter.'

Now, as it happened, Agon had been hurried away that morning without his breakfast, and was already exceedingly hungry, so he presently modified his views and consented to marry them, saying at the same time that he washed his hands of all responsibility in the matter.

So it chanced that presently, attended only by two of her favourite maidens, came the Queen Nyleptha, with happy blushing face and downcast eyes, dressed in pure white, without embroidery of any sort, as seems to be the fashion on these occasions in most countries of the world. She did not wear a single ornament, even her gold circlets were removed, and I thought that if possible she looked more lovely than ever without them, as really superbly beautiful women do.

She came, curtseyed low to Sir Henry, and then took his hand and led him up before the altar, and after a little pause, in a slow, clear voice uttered the following words, which are customary in Zu-Vendis if the bride desires and the man consents:—

'Thou dost swear by the Sun that thou wilt take no other woman to wife unless I lay my hand upon her and bid her come?'

'I swear it,' answered Sir Henry; adding in English, 'One is quite enough for me.'

Then Agon, who had been sulking in a corner near the altar, came forward and gabbled off something into his beard at such a rate that I could not follow it, but it appeared to be an invocation to the Sun to bless the union and make it fruitful. I observed that Nyleptha listened very closely to every word, and afterwards discovered that she was afraid lest Agon should play her a trick, and by going through the invocations backwards divorce them instead of marry them. At the end of the invocations they were asked, as in our service, if they took each other for husband and wife, and on their assenting they kissed each other before the altar, and the service was over, so far as their rites were concerned. But it seemed to me that there was yet something wanting, and so I produced a Prayer-Book, which has, together with the 'Ingoldsby Legends', that I often read when I lie awake at night, accompanied me in all my later wanderings. I gave it to my poor boy Harry years ago, and after his death I found it among his things and took it back again.

'Curtis,' I said, 'I am not a clergyman, and I do not know if what I am going to propose is allowable—I know it is not legal—but if you and the Queen have no objection I should like to read the English marriage service over you. It is a solemn step which you are taking, and I think that you ought, so far as circumstances will allow, to give it the sanction of your own religion.'

'I have thought of that,' he said, 'and I wish you would. I do not feel half married yet.'

Nyleptha raised no objection, fully understanding that her husband wished to celebrate the marriage according to the rites prevailing in his own country, and so I set to work and read the service, from 'Dearly beloved' to 'amazement', as well as I could; and when I came to 'I, Henry, take thee, Nyleptha,' I translated, and also 'I, Nyleptha, take thee, Henry,' which she repeated after me very well. Then Sir Henry took a plain gold ring from his little finger and placed it on hers, and so on to the end. The ring had been Curtis' mother's wedding-ring, and I could not help thinking how astonished the dear old Yorkshire lady would have been if she could have foreseen that her wedding-ring was to serve a similar purpose for Nyleptha, a Queen of the Zu-Vendi.

As for Agon, he was with difficulty kept calm while this second ceremony was going on, for he at once understood that it was religious in its nature, and doubtless bethought him of the ninety-five new faiths which loomed so ominously in his eyes. Indeed, he at once set me down as a rival High Priest, and hated me accordingly. However, in the end off he went, positively bristling with indignation, and I knew that we might look out for danger from his direction.

And off went Good and I, and old Umslopogaas also, leaving the happy pair to themselves, and very low we all felt. Marriages are supposed to be cheerful things, but my experience is that they are very much the reverse to everybody, except perhaps the two people chiefly interested. They mean the breaking-up of so many old ties as well as the undertaking of so many new ones, and there is always something sad about the passing away of the old order. Now to take this case for instance: Sir Henry Curtis is the best and kindest fellow and friend in the world, but he has never been quite the same since that little scene in the chapel. It is always Nyleptha this and Nyleptha that—Nyleptha, in short, from morning till night in one way or another, either expressed or understood. And as for the old friends—well, of course they have taken the place that old friends ought to take, and which ladies are as a rule very careful to see they do take when a man marries, and that is, the second place. Yes, he would be angry if anybody said so, but it is a fact for all that. He is not quite the same, and Nyleptha is very sweet and very charming, but I think that she likes him to understand that she has married *him*, and not Quatermain, Good, and Co. But there! what is the use of grumbling? It is all very right and proper, as any married lady would have no difficulty in explaining, and I am a selfish, jealous old man, though I hope I never show it.

So Good and I went and ate in silence and then indulged in an extra fine flagon of old Zu-Vendian to keep our spirits up, and presently one of our attendants came and told a story that gave us something to think about.

It may, perhaps, be remembered that, after his quarrel with Umslopogaas, Alphonse had gone off in an exceedingly ill temper to sulk over his scratches. Well, it appears that he walked right past the Temple to the Sun, down the wide road on the further side of the slope it crowns, and thence on into the beautiful park, or pleasure gardens, which are laid out just beyond the outer wall. After wandering about there for a little he started to return, but was met near the outer gate by Sorais' train of chariots, which were galloping furiously along the great northern road. When she caught sight of Alphonse, Sorais halted her train and called to him. On approaching he was instantly seized and dragged into one of the chariots and carried off, 'crying out loudly', as our informant said, and as from my general knowledge of him I can well believe.

At first I was much puzzled to know what object Sorais could have had in carrying off the poor little Frenchman. She could hardly stoop so low as to try to wreak her fury on one whom she knew was only a servant. At last, however, an idea occurred to me. We three were, as I think I have said, much revered by the people of Zu-Vendis at large, both because we were the first strangers they had ever seen, and because we were supposed to be the possessors of almost supernatural wisdom.

Indeed, though Sorais' cry against the 'foreign wolves'—or, to translate it more accurately, 'foreign hyenas'—was sure to go down very well with the nobles and the priests, it was not as we learnt, likely to be particularly effectual amongst the bulk of the population. The Zu-Vendi people, like the Athenians of old, are ever seeking for some new thing, and just because we were so new our presence was on the whole acceptable to them. Again, Sir Henry's magnificent personal appearance made a deep impression upon a race who possess a greater love of beauty than any other I have ever been acquainted with. Beauty may be prized in other countries, but in Zu-Vendis it is almost worshipped, as indeed the national love of statuary shows. The people said openly in the market-places that there was not a man in the country to touch Curtis in personal appearance, as with the exception of Sorais there was no woman who could compete with Nyleptha, and that therefore it was meet that they should marry; and that he had been sent by the Sun as a husband for their Queen. Now, from all this it will be seen that the outcry against us was to a considerable extent fictitious, and nobody knew it better than Sorais herself. Consequently it struck me that it might have occurred to her that down in the country and among the country people, it would be better to place the reason of her conflict with her sister upon other and more general grounds than Nyleptha's marriage with the stranger. It would be easy in a land where there had been so many civil wars to rake out some old cry that would stir up the recollection of buried feuds, and, indeed, she soon found an effectual one. This being so, it was of great importance to her to have one of the strangers with her whom she could show to the common people as a great Outlander, who had been so struck by the justice of her cause that he had elected to leave his companions and follow her standard.

This, no doubt, was the cause of her anxiety to get a hold of Good, whom she would have used till he ceased to be of service and then cast off. But Good having drawn back she grasped at the opportunity of securing Alphonse, who was not unlike him in personal appearance though smaller, no doubt with the object of showing him off in the cities and country as the great Bougwan himself. I told Good that I thought that that was her plan, and his face was a sight to see—he was so horrified at the idea.

'What,' he said, 'dress up that little wretch to represent me? Why, I shall have to get out of the country! My reputation will be ruined for ever.'

I consoled him as well as I could, but it is not pleasant to be personated all over a strange country by an arrant little coward, and I can quite sympathize with his vexation.

Well, that night Good and I messed as I have said in solitary grandeur, feeling very much as though we had just returned from burying a friend instead of marrying one, and next morning the work began in good earnest. The messages and orders which had been despatched by Nyleptha two days before now began to take effect, and multitudes of armed men came pouring into the city. We saw, as may be imagined, but very little of Nyleptha and not too much of Curtis during those next few days, but Good and I sat daily with the council of generals and loyal lords, drawing up plans of action, arranging commissariat matters, the distribution of commands, and a hundred and one other things. Men came in freely, and all the day long the great roads leading to Milosis were spotted with the banners of lords arriving from their distant places to rally round Nyleptha.

After the first few days it became clear that we should be able to take the field with about forty thousand infantry and twenty thousand cavalry, a very respectable force considering how short was the time we had to collect it, and that about half the regular army had elected to follow Sorais.

But if our force was large, Sorais' was, according to the reports brought in day by day by our spies, much larger. She had taken up her headquarters at a very strong town called M'Arstuna, situated, as I have said, to the north of Milosis, and all the countryside was flocking to her standard. Nasta had poured down from his highlands and was on his way to join her with no less than twenty-five thousand of his mountaineers, the most terrible soldiers to face in all Zu-Vendis. Another mighty lord, named Belusha, who lived in the great horse-breeding district, had come in with twelve thousand cavalry, and so on. Indeed, what between one thing and another, it seemed certain that she would gather a fully armed host of nearly one hundred thousand men.

And then came news that Sorais was proposing to break up her camp and march on the Frowning City itself, desolating the country as she came. Thereon arose the question whether it would be best to meet her at Milosis or to go out and give her battle. When our opinion was asked upon the subject, Good and I unhesitatingly gave it in favour of an advance. If we were to shut ourselves up in the city and wait to be attacked, it seemed to us that our inaction would be set down to fear. It is so important, especially on an occasion of this sort, when a very little will suffice to turn men's opinions one way or the other, to be up and doing something. Ardour for a cause will soon evaporate if the cause does not move but sits down to conquer. Therefore we cast our vote for moving out and giving battle in the open, instead of waiting till we were drawn from our walls like a badger from a hole.

Sir Henry's opinion coincided with ours, and so, needless to say, did that of Nyleptha, who, like a flint, was always ready to flash out fire. A great map of the country was brought and spread out before her. About thirty miles this side of M'Arstuna, where Sorais lay, and ninety odd miles from Milosis, the road ran over a neck of land some two and a half miles in width, and flanked on either side by forest-clad hills which, without being lofty, would, if the road were blocked, be quite impracticable for a great baggage-laden army to cross. She looked earnestly at the map, and then, with a quickness of perception that in some women amounts almost to an instinct, she laid her finger upon this neck of rising ground, and turning to her husband, said, with a proud air of confidence and a toss of the golden head—

'Here shalt thou meet Sorais' armies. I know the spot, here shalt thou meet them, and drive them before thee like dust before the storm.'

But Curtis looked grave and said nothing.

XX

The Battle of the Pass

It was on the third morning after this incident of the map that Sir Henry and I started. With the exception of a small guard, all the great host had moved on the night before, leaving the Frowning City very silent and empty. Indeed, it was found impossible to leave any garrison with the exception of a personal guard for Nyleptha, and about a thousand men who from sickness or one cause or another were unable to proceed with the army; but as Milosis was practically impregnable, and as our enemy was in front of and not behind us, this did not so much matter.

Good and Umslopogaas had gone on with the army, but Nyleptha accompanied Sir Henry and myself to the city gates, riding a magnificent white horse called Daylight, which was supposed to be the fleetest and most enduring animal in Zu-Vendis. Her face bore traces of recent weeping, but there were no tears in her eyes now, indeed she was bearing up bravely against what must have been a bitter trial to her. At the gate she reined in her horse and bade us farewell. On the previous day she had reviewed and addressed the officers of the great army, speaking to them such high, eloquent words, and expressing so complete a confidence in their valour and in their ultimate victory, that she quite carried their hearts away, and as she rode from rank to rank they cheered her till the ground shook. And now today the same mood seemed to be on her.

'Fare thee well, Macumazahn!' she said. 'Remember, I trust to thy wits, which are as a needle to a spear-handle compared to those of my people, to save us from Sorais. I know that thou wilt do thy duty.'

I bowed and explained to her my horror of fighting, and my fear lest I should lose my head, at which she laughed gently and turned to Curtis.

'Fare thee well, my lord!' she said. 'Come back with victory, and as a king, or on thy soldiers' spears.'

Sir Henry said nothing, but turned his horse to go; perhaps he had a bit of a lump in his throat. One gets over it afterwards, but these sort of partings are trying when one has only been married a week.

'Here,' added Nyleptha, 'will I greet thee when ye return in triumph. And now, my lords, once more, farewell!'

Then we rode on, but when we had gone a hundred and fifty yards or so, we turned and perceived her still sitting on her horse at the same spot, and looking out after us beneath her hand, and that was the last we saw of her. About a mile farther on, however, we heard galloping behind us, and looking round, saw a mounted soldier coming towards us, leading Nyleptha's matchless steed—Daylight.

'The Queen sends the white stallion as a farewell gift to her Lord Incubu, and bids me tell my lord that he is the fleetest and most enduring horse in all the land,' said the soldier, bending to his saddle-bow before us.

At first Sir Henry did not want to take the horse, saying that he was too good for such rough work, but I persuaded him to do so, thinking that Nyleptha would be hurt if he did not. Little did I guess at the time what service that noble horse would render in our sorest need. It is curious to look back and realize upon what trivial and apparently coincidental circumstances great events frequently turn as easily and naturally as a door on its hinges.

Well, we took the horse, and a beauty he was, it was a perfect pleasure to see him move, and Curtis having sent back his greetings and thanks, we proceeded on our journey.

By midday we overtook the rear-guard of the great army of which Sir Henry then formally took over the command. It was a heavy responsibility, and it oppressed him very much, but the Queen's injunctions on the point were such as did not admit of being trifled with. He was beginning to find out that greatness has its responsibilities as well as its glories.

Then we marched on without meeting with any opposition, almost indeed without seeing anybody, for the populations of the towns and villages along our route had for the most part fled, fearing lest they should be caught between the two rival armies and ground to powder like grain between the upper and the nether stones.

On the evening of the fourth day, for the progress of so great a multitude was necessarily slow, we camped two miles this side of the neck or ridge I have spoken of, and our outposts brought us word that Sorais with all her power was rolling down upon us, and had pitched her camp that night ten miles the farther side of the neck.

Accordingly before dawn we sent forward fifteen hundred cavalry to seize the position. Scarcely had they occupied it, however, before they were attacked by about as many of Sorais' horsemen, and a very smart little cavalry fight ensued, with a loss to us of about thirty men killed. On the advance of our supports, however, Sorais' force drew off, carrying their dead and wounded with them.

The main body of the army reached the neck about dinner-time, and I must say that Nyleptha's judgment had not failed her, it was an admirable place to give battle in, especially to a superior force.

The road ran down a mile or more, through ground too broken to admit of the handling of any considerable force, till it reached the crest of a great green wave of land, that rolled down a gentle slope to the banks of a little stream, and then rolled away again up a still gentler slope to the plain beyond, the distance from the crest of the land-wave down to the stream being a little over half a mile, and from the stream up to the plain beyond a trifle less. The length of this wave of land at its highest point, which corresponded exactly with the width of the neck of the land between the wooded hills, was about two miles and a quarter, and it was protected on either side by dense, rocky, bush-clad ground, that afforded a most valuable cover to the flanks of the army and rendered it almost impossible for them to be turned.

It was on the hither slope of this neck of land that Curtis encamped his army in the same formation that he had, after consultation with the various generals, Good, and myself, determined that they should occupy in the great pitched battle which now appeared to be imminent.

Our force of sixty thousand men was, roughly speaking, divided as follows. In the centre was a dense body of twenty thousand foot-soldiers, armed with spears, swords, and hippopotamus-hide shields, breast and back plates. These formed the chest of the army, and were supported by five thousand foot, and three thousand horse in reserve. On either side of this chest were stationed seven thousand horse arranged in deep, majestic squadrons; and beyond and on either side but slightly in front of them again were two bodies, each numbering about seven thousand five hundred spearmen, forming the right and left wings of the army, and each supported by a contingent of some fifteen hundred cavalry. This makes in all sixty thousand men.

Curtis commanded in chief, I was in command of the seven thousand horse between the chest and right wing, which was commanded by Good, and the other battalions and squadrons were entrusted to Zu-Vendis generals.

Scarcely had we taken up our positions before Sorais' vast army began to swarm on the opposite slope about a mile in front of us, till the whole place seemed alive with the multitude of her spearpoints, and the ground shook with the tramp of her battalions. It was evident that the spies had not exaggerated; we were outnumbered by at least a third. At first we expected that Sorais was going to attack us at once, as the clouds of cavalry which hung upon her flanks executed some threatening demonstrations, but she thought better of it, and there was no fight that day. As for the formation of her great forces I cannot now describe it with accuracy, and it would only serve to bewilder if I did, but I may say, generally, that in its leading features it resembled our own, only her reserve was much greater.

Opposite our right wing, and forming Sorais' left wing, was a great army of dark, wild-looking men, armed with sword and shield only, which, I was informed, was composed of Nasta's twenty-five thousand savage hillsmen.

'My word, Good,' said I, when I saw them, 'you will catch it tomorrow when those gentlemen charge!' whereat Good not unnaturally looked rather anxious.

All day we watched and waited, but nothing happened, and at last night fell, and a thousand watch-fires twinkled brightly on the slopes, to wane and die one by one like the stars they resembled. As the hours wore on, the silence gradually gathered more deeply over the opposing hosts.

It was a very wearying night, for in addition to the endless things that had to be attended to, there was our gnawing suspense to reckon with. The fray which tomorrow would witness would be so vast, and the slaughter so awful, that stout indeed must the heart have been that was not overwhelmed at the prospect. And when I thought of all that hung upon it, I own I felt ill, and it made me very sad to reflect that these mighty forces were gathered for destruction, simply to gratify the jealous anger of a woman. This was the hidden power which was to send those dense masses of cavalry, flashing like human thunderbolts across the plain, and to roll together the fierce battalions as clouds when hurricane meets hurricane. It was a dreadful thought, and set one wondering about the responsibilities of the great ones of the earth. Deep into the night we sat, with pale faces and heavy hearts, and took counsel, whilst the sentries tramped up and down, down and up, and the armed and plumed generals came and went, grim and shadow-like.

And so the time wore away, till everything was ready for the coming slaughter; and I lay down and thought, and tried to get a little rest, but could not sleep for fear of the morrow—for who could say what the morrow would bring forth? Misery and death, this was certain; beyond that we knew not, and I confess I was very much afraid. But as I realized then, it is useless to question that eternal Sphinx, the future. From day to day she reads aloud the riddles of the yesterday, of which the puzzled wordlings of all ages have not answered one, nor ever will, guess they never so wildly or cry they never so loud.

And so at length I gave up wondering, being forced humbly to leave the issue in the balancing hands of Providence and the morrow.

And at last up came the red sun, and the huge camps awoke with a clash, and a roar, and gathered themselves together for battle. It was a beautiful and awe-inspiring scene, and old Umslopogaas, leaning on his axe, contemplated it with grim delight.

'Never have I seen the like, Macumazahn, never,' he said. 'The battles of my people are as the play of children to what this will be. Thinkest thou that they will fight it out?'

'Ay,' I answered sadly, 'to the death. Content thyself, "Woodpecker", for once shalt thou peck thy fill.'

Time went on, and still there was no sign of an attack. A force of cavalry crossed the brook, indeed, and rode slowly along our front, evidently taking stock of our position and numbers. With this we did not attempt to interfere, as our decision was to stand strictly on the defensive, and not to waste a single man. The men breakfasted and stood to their arms, and the hours wore on. About midday, when the men were eating their dinner, for we thought they would fight better on full stomachs, a shout of '*Sorais, Sorais*' arose like thunder from the enemy's extreme right, and taking the glass, I was able to clearly distinguish the 'Lady of the Night' herself, surrounded by a glittering staff, and riding slowly down the lines of her battalions. And as she went, that mighty, thundering shout rolled along before her like the rolling of ten thousand chariots, or the roaring of the ocean when the gale turns suddenly and carries the noise of it to the listener's ears, till the earth shook, and the air was full of the majesty of sound.

Guessing that this was a prelude to the beginning of the battle, we remained still and made ready.

We had not long to wait. Suddenly, like flame from a cannon's mouth, out shot two great tongue-like forces of cavalry, and came charging down the slope towards the little stream, slowly at first, but gathering speed as they came. Before they got to the stream, orders reached me from Sir Henry, who evidently feared that the shock of such a charge, if allowed to fall unbroken upon our infantry, would be too much for them, to send five thousand sabres to meet the force opposite to me, at the moment when it began to mount the stiffest of the rise about four hundred yards from our lines. This I did, remaining behind myself with the rest of my men.

Off went the five thousand horsemen, drawn up in a wedge-like form, and I must say that the general in command handled them very ably. Starting at a hand gallop, for the first three hundred yards he rode straight at the tip of the tongue-shaped mass of cavalry which, numbering, so far as I could judge, about eight thousand sabres, was advancing to charge us. Then he suddenly swerved to the right and put on the pace, and I saw the great wedge curl round, and before the foe could check himself and turn to meet it, strike him about halfway down his length, with a crashing rending sound, like that of the breaking-up of vast sheets of ice. In sank the great wedge, into his heart, and as it cut its way hundreds of horsemen were thrown up on either side of it, just as the earth is thrown up by a ploughshare, or more like still, as the foaming water curls over beneath the bows of a rushing ship. In, yet in, vainly does the tongue twist its ends round in agony, like an injured snake, and strive to protect its centre; still farther in, by Heaven! right through, and so, amid cheer after cheer from our watching thousands, back again upon the severed ends, beating them down, driving them as a gale drives spray, till at last, amidst the rushing of hundreds of riderless horses, the flashing of swords, and the victorious clamour of their pursuers, the great force crumples up like an empty glove, then turns and gallops pell-mell for safety back to its own lines.

I do not think it reached them more than two-thirds as strong as it went out ten minutes before. The lines which were now advancing to the attack, opened and swallowed them up, and my force returned, having only suffered a loss of about five hundred men—not much, I thought, considering the fierceness of the struggle. I could also see that the opposing bodies of cavalry on our left wing were drawing back, but how the fight went with them I do not quite know. It is as much as I can do to describe what took place immediately around me.

By this time the dense masses of the enemy's left, composed almost entirely of Nasta's swordsmen, were across the little stream, and with alternate yells of 'Nasta' and 'Sorais', with dancing banners and gleaming swords, were swarming up towards us like ants.

Again I received orders to try and check this movement, and also the main advance against the chest of our army, by means of cavalry charges, and this I did to the best of my ability, by continually sending squadrons of about a thousand sabres out against them. These squadrons did the enemy much damage, and it was a glorious sight to see them flash down the hillside, and bury themselves like a living knife in the heart of the foe. But, also, we lost many men, for after the experience of a couple of these charges, which had drawn a sort of bloody St Andrew's cross of dead and dying through the centre of Nasta's host, our foes no longer attempted to offer an unyielding front to their irresistible weight, but opened out to let the rush go through, throwing themselves on the ground and hamstringing hundreds of horses as they passed.

And so, notwithstanding all that we could do, the enemy drew nearer, till at last he hurled himself upon Good's force of seven thousand five hundred regulars, who were drawn up to receive them in three strong squares. About the same time, too, an awful and heartshaking roar told me that the main battle had closed in on the centre and extreme left. I raised myself in my stirrups and looked down to my left; so far as the eye could see there was a long dazzling shimmer of steel as the sun glanced upon falling sword and thrusting spear.

To and fro swung the contending lines in that dread struggle, now giving way, now gaining a little in the mad yet ordered confusion of attack and defence. But it was as much as I could do to keep count of what was happening to our own wing; and, as for the moment the cavalry had fallen back under cover of Good's three squares, I had a fair view of this.

Nasta's wild swordsmen were now breaking in red waves against the sullen rock-like squares. Time after time did they yell out their war-cries, and hurl themselves furiously against the long triple ridges of spear points, only to be rolled back as billows are when they meet the cliff.

And so for four long hours the battle raged almost without a pause, and at the end of that time, if we had gained nothing we had lost nothing. Two attempts to turn our left flank by forcing a way through the wood by which it was protected had been defeated; and as yet Nasta's swordsmen had, notwithstanding their desperate efforts, entirely failed to break Good's three squares, though they had thinned their numbers by quite a third.

As for the chest of the army where Sir Henry was with his staff and Umslopogaas, it had suffered dreadfully, but it had held its own with honour, and the same may be said of our left battle.

At last the attacks slackened, and Sorais' army drew back, having, I began to think, had enough of it. On this point, however, I was soon undeceived, for splitting up her cavalry into comparatively small squadrons, she charged us furiously with them, all along the line, and then once more sullenly rolled her tens of thousands of sword and spearmen down upon our weakened squares and squadrons; Sorais herself directing the movement, as fearless as a lioness heading the main attack. On they came like an avalanche—I saw her golden helm gleaming in the van—our counter charges of cavalry entirely failing to check their forward sweep. Now they had struck us, and our centre bent in like a bow beneath the weight of their rush—it parted, and had not the ten thousand men in reserve charged down to its support it must have been utterly destroyed. As for Good's three squares, they were swept backwards like boats upon an incoming tide, and the foremost one was burst into and lost half its remaining men. But the effort was too fierce and terrible to last. Suddenly the battle came, as it were, to a turning-point, and for a minute or two stood still.

Then it began to move towards Sorais' camp. Just then, too, Nasta's fierce and almost invincible highlanders, either because they were disheartened by their losses or by way of a ruse, fell back, and the remains of Good's gallant squares, leaving the positions they had held for so many hours, cheered wildly, and rashly followed them down the slope, whereon the swarms of swordsmen turned to envelop them, and once more flung themselves upon them with a yell. Taken thus on every side, what remained of the first square was quickly destroyed, and I perceived that the second, in which I could see Good himself mounted on a large horse, was on the point of annihilation. A few more minutes and it was broken, its streaming colours sank, and I lost sight of Good in the confused and hideous slaughter that ensued.

Presently, however, a cream-coloured horse with a snow-white mane and tail burst from the ruins of the square and came rushing past me riderless and with wide streaming reins, and in it I recognized the charger that Good had been riding. Then I hesitated no longer, but taking with me half my effective cavalry force, which now amounted to between four and five thousand men, I commended myself to God, and, without waiting for orders, I charged straight down upon Nasta's swordsmen. Seeing me coming, and being warned by the thunder of my horses' hoofs, the majority of them faced round, and gave us a right warm welcome. Not an inch would they yield; in vain did we hack and trample them down as we ploughed a broad red furrow through their thousands; they seemed to re-arise by hundreds, driving their terrible sharp swords into our horses, or severing their hamstrings, and then hacking the troopers who came to the ground with them almost into pieces. My horse was speedily killed under me, but luckily I had a fresh one, my own favourite, a coal-black mare Nyleptha had given me, being held in reserve behind, and on this I afterwards mounted. Meanwhile I had to get along as best I could, for I was pretty well lost sight of by my men in the mad confusion of the moment. My voice, of course, could not be heard in the midst of the clanging of steel and the shrieks of rage and agony. Presently I found myself mixed up with the remnants of the square, which had formed round its leader Good, and was fighting desperately for existence. I stumbled against somebody, and glancing down, caught sight of Good's eyeglass. He had been beaten to his knee. Over him was a great fellow swinging a heavy sword. Somehow I managed to run the man through with the sime I had taken from the Masai whose hand I had cut off; but as I did so, he dealt me a frightful blow on the left side and breast with the sword, and though my chain shirt saved my life, I felt that I was badly hurt. For a minute I fell on to my hands and knees among the dead and dying, and turned sick and faint. When I came to again I saw that Nasta's spearmen, or rather those of them who remained, were retreating back across the stream, and that Good was there by me smiling sweetly.

'Near go that,' he shouted; 'but all's well that ends well.'

I assented, but I could not help feeling that it had not ended well for me. I was sorely hurt.

Just then we saw the smaller bodies of cavalry stationed on our extreme right and left, and which were now reinforced by the three thousand sabres which we had held in reserve, flash out like arrows from their posts and fall upon the disordered flanks of Sorais' forces, and that charge decided the issue of the battle. In another minute or two the enemy was in slow and sullen retreat across the little stream, where they once more re-formed. Then came another lull, during which I managed to get a second horse, and received my orders to advance from Sir Henry, and then with one fierce deep-throated roar, with a waving of banners and a wide flashing of steel, the remains of our army took the offensive and began to sweep down, slowly indeed, but irresistibly from the positions they had so gallantly held all day.

At last it was our turn to attack.

On we moved, over the piled-up masses of dead and dying, and were approaching the stream, when suddenly I perceived an extraordinary sight. Galloping wildly towards us, his arms tightly clasped around his horse's neck, against which his blanched cheek was tightly pressed, was a man arrayed in the full costume of a Zu-Vendi general, but in whom, as he came nearer, I recognized none other than our lost Alphonse. It was impossible even then to mistake those curling mustachios. In a minute he was tearing through our ranks and narrowly escaped being cut down, till at last somebody caught his horse's bridle, and he was brought to me just as a momentary halt occurred in our advance to allow what remained of our shattered squares to form into line.

'Ah, monsieur,' he gasped out in a voice that was nearly inarticulate with fright, 'grace to the sky, it is you! Ah, what I have endured! But you win, monsieur, you win; they fly, the laches. But listen, monsieur—I forget, it is no good; the Queen is to be murdered tomorrow at the first light in the palace of Milosis; her guards will leave their posts, and the priests are going to kill her. Ah yes! they little thought it, but I was ensconced beneath a banner, and I heard it all.'

'What?' I said, horror-struck; 'what do you mean?'

'What I say, monsieur; that devil of a Nasta he went last night to settle the affair with the Archbishop (Agon). The guard will leave open the little gate leading from the great stair and go away, and Nasta and Agon's priests will come in and kill her. Themselves they would not kill her.'

'Come with me,' I said, and, shouting to the staff-officer next to me to take over the command, I snatched his bridle and galloped as hard as I could for the spot, between a quarter and half a mile off, where I saw the royal pennon flying, and where I knew that I should find Curtis if he were still alive. On we tore, our horses clearing heaps of dead and dying men, and splashing through pools of blood, on past the long broken lines of spearmen to where, mounted on the white stallion Nyleptha had sent to him as a parting gift, I saw Sir Henry's form towering above the generals who surrounded him.

Just as we reached him the advance began again. A bloody cloth was bound around his head, but I saw that his eye was as bright and keen as ever. Beside him was old Umslopogaas, his axe red with blood, but looking quite fresh and uninjured.

'What's wrong, Quatermain?' he shouted.

'Everything. There is a plot to murder the Queen tomorrow at dawn. Alphonse here, who has just escaped from Sorais, has overheard it all,' and I rapidly repeated to him what the Frenchman had told me.

Curtis' face turned deadly pale and his jaw dropped.

'At dawn,' he gasped, 'and it is now sunset; it dawns before four and we are nearly a hundred miles off—nine hours at the outside. What is to be done?'

An idea entered into my head. 'Is that horse of yours fresh?' I said.

'Yes, I have only just got on to him—when my last was killed, and he has been fed.'

'So is mine. Get off him, and let Umslopogaas mount; he can ride well. We will be at Milosis before dawn, or if we are not—well, we cannot help it. No, no; it is impossible for you to leave now. You would be seen, and it would turn the fate of the battle. It is not half won yet. The soldiers would think you were making a bolt of it. Quick now.'

In a moment he was down, and at my bidding Umslopogaas sprang into the empty saddle.

'Now farewell,' I said. 'Send a thousand horsemen with remounts after us in an hour if possible. Stay, despatch a general to the left wing to take over the command and explain my absence.'

'You will do your best to save her, Quatermain?' he said in a broken voice.

'Ay, that I will. Go on; you are being left behind.'

He cast one glance at us, and accompanied by his staff galloped off to join the advance, which by this time was fording the little brook that now ran red with the blood of the fallen.

As for Umslopogaas and myself, we left that dreadful field as arrows leave a bow, and in a few minutes had passed right out of the sight of slaughter, the smell of blood, and the turmoil and shouting, which only came to our ears as a faint, far-off roaring like the sound of distant breakers.

XXI

Away! Away!

At the top of the rise we halted for a second to breathe our horses; and, turning, glanced at the battle beneath us, which, illumined as it was by the fierce rays of the sinking sun staining the whole scene red, looked from where we were more like some wild titanic picture than an actual hand-to-hand combat. The distinguishing scenic effect from that distance was the countless distinct flashes of light reflected from the swords and spears, otherwise the panorama was not so grand as might have been expected. The great green lap of sward in which the struggle was being fought out, the bold round outline of the hills behind, and the wide sweep of the plain beyond, seemed to dwarf it; and what was tremendous enough when one was in it, grew insignificant when viewed from the distance. But is it not thus with all the affairs and doings of our race about which we blow the loud trumpet and make such a fuss and worry? How utterly antlike, and morally and physically insignificant, must they seem to the calm eyes that watch them from the arching depths above!

'We win the day, Macumazahn,' said old Umslopogaas, taking in the whole situation with a glance of his practised eye. 'Look, the Lady of the Night's forces give on every side, there is no stiffness left in them, they bend like hot iron, they are fighting with but half a heart. But alas! the battle will in a manner be drawn, for the darkness gathers, and the regiments will not be able to follow and slay!'—and he shook his head sadly. 'But,' he added, 'I do not think that they will fight again. We have fed them with too strong a meat. Ah! it is well to have lived! At last I have seen a fight worth seeing.'

By this time we were on our way again, and as we went side by side I told him what our mission was, and how that, if it failed, all the lives that had been lost that day would have been lost in vain.

'Ah!' he said, 'nigh on a hundred miles and no horses but these, and to be there before the dawn! Well—away! away! man can but try, Macumazahn; and mayhap we shall be there in time to split that old "witch-finder's" (Agon's) skull for him. Once he wanted to burn us, the old "rain-maker", did he? And now he would set a snare for my mother

(Nyleptha), would he? Good! So sure as my name is the name of the Woodpecker, so surely, be my mother alive or dead, will I split him to the beard. Ay, by T'Chaka's head I swear it!' and he shook Inkosi-kaas as he galloped. By now the darkness was closing in, but fortunately there would be a moon later, and the road was good.

On we sped through the twilight, the two splendid horses we bestrode had got their wind by this, and were sweeping along with a wide steady stride that neither failed nor varied for mile upon mile. Down the side of slopes we galloped, across wide vales that stretched to the foot of far-off hills. Nearer and nearer grew the blue hills; now we were travelling up their steeps, and now we were over and passing towards others that sprang up like visions in the far, faint distance beyond.

On, never pausing or drawing rein, through the perfect quiet of the night, that was set like a song to the falling music of our horses' hoofs; on, past deserted villages, where only some forgotten starving dog howled a melancholy welcome; on, past lonely moated dwellings; on, through the white patchy moonlight, that lay coldly upon the wide bosom of the earth, as though there was no warmth in it; on, knee to knee, for hour after hour!

We spake not, but bent us forward on the necks of those two glorious horses, and listened to their deep, long-drawn breaths as they filled their great lungs, and to the regular unfaltering ring of their round hoofs. Grim and black indeed did old Umslopogaas look beside me, mounted upon the great white horse, like Death in the Revelation of St John, as now and again lifting his fierce set face he gazed out along the road, and pointed with his axe towards some distant rise or house.

And so on, still on, without break or pause for hour after hour.

At last I felt that even the splendid animal that I rode was beginning to give out. I looked at my watch; it was nearly midnight, and we were considerably more than half way. On the top of a rise was a little spring, which I remembered because I had slept by it a few nights before, and here I motioned to Umslopogaas to pull up, having determined to give the horses and ourselves ten minutes to breathe in. He did so, and we dismounted—that is to say, Umslopogaas did, and then helped me off, for what with fatigue, stiffness, and the pain of my wound, I could not do so for myself; and then the gallant horses stood panting there, resting first one leg and then another, while the sweat fell drip, drip, from them, and the steam rose and hung in pale clouds in the still night air.

Leaving Umslopogaas to hold the horses, I hobbled to the spring and drank deep of its sweet waters. I had had nothing but a single mouthful of wine since midday, when the battle began, and I was parched up, though my fatigue was too great to allow me to feel hungry. Then, having laved my fevered head and hands, I returned, and the Zulu went and drank. Next we allowed the horses to take a couple of mouthfuls each—no more; and oh, what a struggle we had to get the poor beasts away from the water! There were yet two minutes, and I employed it in hobbling up and down to try and relieve my stiffness, and in inspecting the condition of the horses. My mare, gallant animal though she was, was evidently much distressed; she hung her head, and her eye looked sick and dull; but Daylight, Nylepthas glorious horse—who, if he is served aright, should, like the steeds who saved great Rameses in his need, feed for the rest of his days out of a golden manger—was still comparatively speaking fresh, notwithstanding the fact that he had had by far the heavier weight to carry. He was 'tucked up', indeed, and his legs were weary, but his eye was bright and clear, and he held his shapely head up and gazed out into the darkness round him in a way that seemed to say that whoever failed *he* was good for those five-and-forty miles that yet lay between us and Milosis. Then Umslopogaas helped me into the saddle and—vigorous old savage that he was!—vaulted into his own without touching a stirrup, and we were off once more, slowly at first, till the horses got into their stride, and then more swiftly. So we passed over another ten miles, and then came a long, weary rise of some six or seven miles, and three times did my poor black mare nearly come to the ground with me. But on the top she seemed to gather herself together, and rattled down the slope with long, convulsive strides, breathing in gasps. We did that three or four miles more swiftly than any since we had started on our wild ride, but I felt it to be a last effort, and I was right. Suddenly my poor horse took the bit between her teeth and bolted furiously along a stretch of level ground for some three or four hundred yards, and then, with two or three jerky strides, pulled herself up and fell with a crash right on to her head, I rolling myself free as she did so. As I struggled to my feet the brave beast raised her head and looked at me with piteous bloodshot eyes, and then her head dropped with a groan and she was dead. Her heart was broken.

Umslopogaas pulled up beside the carcase, and I looked at him in dismay. There were still more than twenty miles to do by dawn, and how were we to do it with one horse? It seemed hopeless, but I had forgotten the old Zulu's extraordinary running powers.

Without a single word he sprang from the saddle and began to hoist me into it.

'What wilt thou do?' I asked.

'Run,' he answered, seizing my stirrup-leather.

Then off we went again, almost as fast as before; and oh, the relief it was to me to get that change of horses! Anybody who has ever ridden against time will know what it meant.

Daylight sped along at a long stretching hand-gallop, giving the gaunt Zulu a lift at every stride. It was a wonderful thing to see old Umslopogaas run mile after mile, his lips slightly parted and his nostrils agape like the horse's. Every five miles or so we stopped for a few minutes to let him get his breath, and then flew on again.

'Canst thou go farther,' I said at the third of these stoppages, 'or shall I leave thee to follow me?'

He pointed with his axe to a dim mass before us. It was the Temple of the Sun, now not more than five miles away.

'I reach it or I die,' he gasped.

Oh, that last five miles! The skin was rubbed from the inside of my legs, and every movement of my horse gave me anguish. Nor was that all. I was exhausted with toil, want of food and sleep, and also suffering very much from the blow I had received on my left side; it seemed as though a piece of bone or something was slowly piercing into my lung. Poor Daylight, too, was pretty nearly finished, and no wonder. But there was a smell of dawn in the air, and we might not stay; better that all three of us should die upon the road than that we should linger while there was life in us. The air was thick and heavy, as it sometimes is before the dawn breaks, and—another infallible sign in certain parts of Zu-Vendis that sunrise is at hand—hundreds of little spiders pendant on the end of long tough webs were floating about in it. These early-rising creatures, or rather their webs, caught upon the horse's and our own forms by scores, and, as we had neither the time nor the energy to brush them off, we rushed along covered with hundreds of long grey threads that streamed out a yard or more behind us—and a very strange appearance they must have given us.

And now before us are the huge brazen gates of the outer wall of the Frowning City, and a new and horrible doubt strikes me: What if they will not let us in?

'*Open! open!*' I shout imperiously, at the same time giving the royal password. '*Open! open!* a messenger, a messenger with tidings of the war!'

'What news?' cried the guard. 'And who art thou that ridest so madly, and who is that whose tongue lolls out'—and it actually did—'and who runs by thee like a dog by a chariot?'

'It is the Lord Macumazahn, and with him is his dog, his black dog. *Open! open!* I bring tidings.'

The great gates ran back on their rollers, and the drawbridge fell with a rattling crash, and we dashed on through the one and over the other.

'What news, my lord, what news?' cried the guard.

'Incubu rolls Sorais back, as the wind a cloud,' I answered, and was gone.

One more effort, gallant horse, and yet more gallant man!

So, fall not now, Daylight, and hold thy life in thee for fifteen short minutes more, old Zulu war-dog, and ye shall both live for ever in the annals of the land.

On, clattering through the sleeping streets. We are passing the Flower Temple now—one mile more, only one little mile—hold on, keep your life in thee, see the houses run past of themselves. Up, good horse, up, there—but fifty yards now. Ah! you see your stables and stagger on gallantly.

'Thank God, the palace at last!' and see, the first arrows of the dawn are striking on the Temple's golden dome. But shall I get in here, or is the deed done and the way barred?

Once more I give the password and shout '*Open! open!*'

No answer, and my heart grows very faint.

Again I call, and this time a single voice replies, and to my joy I recognize it as belonging to Kara, a fellow-officer of Nyleptha's guards, a man I know to be as honest as the light—indeed, the same whom Nyleptha had sent to arrest Sorais on the day she fled to the temple.

'Is it thou, Kara?' I cry; 'I am Macumazahn. Bid the guard let down the bridge and throw wide the gate. Quick, quick!'

Then followed a space that seemed to me endless, but at length the bridge fell and one half of the gate opened and we got into the courtyard, where at last poor Daylight fell down beneath me, as I thought, dead. Except Kara, there was nobody to be seen, and his look was wild, and his garments were all torn. He had opened the gate and let down the bridge alone, and was now getting them up and shut again (as, owing to a very ingenious arrangement of cranks and levers, one man could easily do, and indeed generally did do).

'Where are the guard?' I gasped, fearing his answer as I never feared anything before.

'I know not,' he answered; 'two hours ago, as I slept, was I seized and bound by the watch under me, and but now, this very moment, have I freed myself with my teeth. I fear, I greatly fear, that we are betrayed.'

His words gave me fresh energy. Catching him by the arm, I staggered, followed by Umslopogaas, who reeled after us like a drunken man, through the courtyards, up the great hall, which was silent as the grave, towards the Queen's sleeping-place.

We reached the first ante-room—no guards; the second, still no guards. Oh, surely the thing was done! we were too late after all, too late! The silence and solitude of those great chambers was dreadful, and weighed me down like an evil dream. On, right into Nyleptha's chamber we rushed and staggered, sick at heart, fearing the very worst; we saw there was a light in it, ay, and a figure bearing the light. Oh, thank God, it is the White Queen herself, the Queen unharmed! There she stands in her night gear, roused, by the clatter of our coming, from her bed, the heaviness of sleep yet in her eyes, and a red blush of fear and shame mantling her lovely breast and cheek.

'Who is it?' she cries. 'What means this? Oh, Macumazahn, is it thou? Why lookest thou so wildly? Thou comest as one bearing evil tidings—and my lord—oh, tell me not my lord is dead—not dead!' she wailed, wringing her white hands.

'I left Incubu wounded, but leading the advance against Sorais last night at sundown; therefore let thy heart have rest. Sorais is beaten back all along her lines, and thy arms prevail.'

'I knew it,' she cried in triumph. 'I knew that he would win; and they called him Outlander, and shook their wise heads when I gave him the command! Last night at sundown, sayest thou, and it is not yet dawn? Surely—'

'Throw a cloak around thee, Nyleptha,' I broke in, 'and give us wine to drink; ay, and call thy maidens quick if thou wouldst save thyself alive. Nay, stay not.'

Thus adjured she ran and called through the curtains towards some room beyond, and then hastily put on her sandals and a thick cloak, by which time a dozen or so of half-dressed women were pouring into the room.

'Follow us and be silent,' I said to them as they gazed with wondering eyes, clinging one to another. So we went into the first ante-room.

'Now,' I said, 'give us wine to drink and food, if ye have it, for we are near to death.'

The room was used as a mess-room for the officers of the guards, and from a cupboard some flagons of wine and some cold flesh were brought forth, and Umslopogaas and I drank, and felt life flow back into our veins as the good red wine went down.

'Hark to me, Nyleptha,' I said, as I put down the empty tankard. 'Hast thou here among these thy waiting-ladies any two of discretion?'

'Ay,' she said, 'surely.'

'Then bid them go out by the side entrance to any citizens whom thou canst bethink thee of as men loyal to thee, and pray them come armed, with all honest folk that they can gather, to rescue thee from death. Nay, question not; do as I say, and quickly. Kara here will let out the maids.'

She turned, and selecting two of the crowd of damsels, repeated the words I had uttered, giving them besides a list of the names of the men to whom each should run.

'Go swiftly and secretly; go for your very lives,' I added.

In another moment they had left with Kara, whom I told to rejoin us at the door leading from the great courtyard on to the stairway as soon as he had made fast behind the girls. Thither, too, Umslopogaas and I made our way, followed by the Queen and her women. As we went we tore off mouthfuls of food, and between them I told her what I knew of the danger which encompassed her, and how we found Kara, and how all the guards and men-servants were gone, and she was alone with her women in that great place; and she told me, too, that a rumour had spread through the town that our army had been utterly destroyed, and that Sorais was marching in triumph on Milosis, and how in consequence thereof all men had fallen away from her.

Though all this takes some time to tell, we had not been but six or seven minutes in the palace; and notwithstanding that the golden roof of the temple being very lofty was ablaze with the rays of the rising sun, it was not yet dawn, nor would be for another ten minutes. We were in the courtyard now, and here my wound pained me so that I had to take Nyleptha's arm, while Umslopogaas rolled along after us, eating as he went.

Now we were across it, and had reached the narrow doorway through the palace wall that opened on to the mighty stair.

I looked through and stood aghast, as well I might. The door was gone, and so were the outer gates of bronze—entirely gone. They had been taken from their hinges, and as we afterwards found, hurled from the stairway to the ground two hundred feet beneath. There in front of us was the semicircular standing-space, about twice the size of a large oval dining-table, and the ten curved black marble steps leading on to the main stair—and that was all.

XXII

How Umslopogaas Held the Stair

We looked at one another.

'Thou seest,' I said, 'they have taken away the door. Is there aught with which we may fill the place? Speak quickly for they will be on us ere the daylight.' I spoke thus, because I knew that we must hold this place or none, as there were no inner doors in the palace, the rooms being separated one from another by curtains. I also knew that if we could by any means defend this doorway the murderers could get in nowhere else; for the palace is absolutely impregnable, that is, since the secret door by which Sorais had entered on that memorable night of attempted murder had, by Nyleptha's order, been closed up with masonry.

'I have it,' said Nyleptha, who, as usual with her, rose to the emergency in a wonderful way. 'On the farther side of the courtyard are blocks of cut marble—the workmen brought them there for the bed of the new statue of Incubu, my lord; let us block the door with them.'

I jumped at the idea; and having despatched one of the remaining maidens down the great stair to see if she could obtain assistance from the docks below, where her father, who was a great merchant employing many men, had his dwelling-place, and set another to watch through the doorway, we made our way back across the courtyard to where the hewn marble lay; and here we met Kara returning from despatching the first two messengers. There were the marble blocks, sure enough, broad, massive lumps, some six inches thick, and weighing about eighty pounds each, and there, too, were a couple of implements like small stretchers, that the workmen used to carry them on. Without delay we got some of the blocks on to the stretchers, and four of the girls carried them to the doorway.

'Listen, Macumazahn,' said Umslopogaas, 'if those low fellows come, it is I who will hold the stair against them till the door is built up. Nay, nay, it will be a man's death: gainsay me not, old friend. It has been a good day, let it now be good night. See, I throw myself down to rest on the marble there; when their footsteps are nigh, wake thou me, not before, for I need my strength,' and without a word he went outside and flung himself down on the marble, and was instantly asleep.

At this time, I too was overcome, and was forced to sit down by the doorway, and content myself with directing operations. The girls brought the block, while Kara and Nyleptha built them up across the six-foot-wide doorway, a triple row of them, for less would be useless. But the marble had to be brought forty yards and then there were forty yards to run back, and though the girls laboured gloriously, even staggering along alone, each with a block in her arms, it was slow work, dreadfully slow.

The light was growing now, and presently, in the silence, we heard a commotion at the far-bottom of the stair, and the faint clinking of armed men. As yet the wall was only two feet high, and we had been eight minutes at the building of it. So they had come. Alphonse had heard aright.

The clanking sound came nearer, and in the ghostly grey of the dawning we could make out long files of men, some fifty or so in all, slowly creeping up the stair. They were now at the half-way standing place that rested on the great flying arch; and here, perceiving that something was going on above, they, to our great gain, halted for three or four minutes and consulted, then slowly and cautiously advanced again.

We had been nearly a quarter of an hour at the work now, and it was almost three feet high.

Then I woke Umslopogaas. The great man rose, stretched himself, and swung Inkosi-kaas round his head.

'It is well,' he said. 'I feel as a young man once more. My strength has come back to me, ay, even as a lamp flares up before it dies. Fear not, I shall fight a good fight; the wine and the sleep have put a new heart into me.

'Macumazahn, I have dreamed a dream. I dreamed that thou and I stood together on a star, and looked down on the world, and thou wast as a spirit, Macumazahn, for light flamed through thy flesh, but I could not see what was the fashion of mine own face. The hour has come for us, old hunter. So be it: we have had our time, but I would that in it I had seen some more such fights as yesterday's.

'Let them bury me after the fashion of my people, Macumazahn, and set my eyes towards Zululand;' and he took my hand and shook it, and then turned to face the advancing foe.

Just then, to my astonishment, the Zu-Vendi officer Kara clambered over our improvised wall in his quiet, determined sort of way, and took his stand by the Zulu, unsheathing his sword as he did so.

'What, comest thou too?' laughed out the old warrior. 'Welcome—a welcome to thee, brave heart! Ow! for the man who can die like a man; ow! for the death grip and the ringing of steel. Ow! we are ready. We wet our beaks like eagles, our spears flash in the sun; we shake our assegais, and are hungry to fight. Who comes to give greeting to the Chieftainess (Inkosi-kaas)? Who would taste her kiss, whereof the fruit is death? I, the Woodpecker, I, the Slaughterer, I the Swiftfooted! I, Umslopogaas, of the tribe of the Maquilisini, of the people of Amazulu, a captain of the regiment of the Nkomabakosi: I, Umslopogaas, the son of Indabazimbi, the son of Arpi the son of Mosilikaatze, I of the royal blood of T'Chaka, I of the King's House, I the Ringed Man, I the Induna, I call to them as a buck calls, I challenge them, I await them. Ow! it is thou, it is thou!'

As he spake, or rather chanted, his wild war-song, the armed men, among whom in the growing light I recognized both Nasta and Agon, came streaming up the stair with a rush, and one big fellow, armed with a heavy spear, dashed up the ten semicircular steps ahead of his comrades and struck at the great Zulu with the spear. Umslopogaas moved his body but not his legs, so that the blow missed him, and next instant Inkosi-kaas crashed through headpiece, hair and skull, and the man's corpse was rattling down the steps. As he dropped, his round hippopotamus-hide shield fell from his hand on to the marble, and the Zulu stooped down and seized it, still chanting as he did so.

In another second the sturdy Kara had also slain a man, and then began a scene the like of which has not been known to me.

Up rushed the assailants, one, two, three at a time, and as fast as they came, the axe crashed and the sword swung, and down they rolled again, dead or dying. And ever as the fight thickened, the old Zulu's eye seemed to get quicker and his arm stronger. He shouted out his war-cries and the names of chiefs whom he had slain, and the blows of his awful axe rained straight and true, shearing through everything they fell on. There was none of the scientific method he was so fond of about this last immortal fight of his; he had no time for it, but struck with his full strength, and at every stroke a man sank in his tracks, and went rattling down the marble steps.

They hacked and hewed at him with swords and spears, wounding him in a dozen places till he streamed red with blood; but the shield protected his head and the chain-shirt his vitals, and for minute after minute, aided by the gallant Zu-Vendi, he still held the stair.

At last Kara's sword broke, and he grappled with a foe, and they rolled down together, and he was cut to pieces, dying like the brave man that he was.

Umslopogaas was alone now, but he never blenched or turned. Shouting out some wild Zulu battle-cry, he beat down a foe, ay, and another, and another, till at last they drew back from the slippery blood-stained steps, and stared at him with amazement, thinking that he was no mortal man.

The wall of marble block was four feet six high now, and hope rose in my teeth as I leaned there against it a miserable helpless log, and ground my teeth, and watched that glorious struggle. I could do no more for I had lost my revolver in the battle.

And old Umslopogaas, he leaned too on his good axe, and, faint as he was with wounds, he mocked them, he called them 'women'— the grand old warrior, standing there one against so many! And for a breathing space none would come against him, notwithstanding Nasta's exhortations, till at last old Agon, who, to do him justice, was a brave man, mad with baffled rage, and seeing that the wall would soon be built and his plans defeated, shook the great spear he held, and rushed up the dripping steps.

'Ah, ah!' shouted the Zulu, as he recognized the priest's flowing white beard, 'it is thou, old "witch-finder"! Come on! I await thee, white "medicine man"; come on! come on! I have sworn to slay thee, and I ever keep my faith.'

On he came, taking him at his word, and drave the big spear with such force at Umslopogaas that it sunk right through the tough shield and pierced him in the neck. The Zulu cast down the transfixed shield, and that moment was Agon's last, for before he could free his spear and strike again, with a shout of '*There's for thee, Rain-maker!*' Umslopogaas gripped Inkosi-kaas with both hands and whirled on high and drave her right on to his venerable head, so that Agon rolled down dead among the corpses of his fellow-murderers, and there was an end to him and his plots altogether. And even as he fell, a great cry rose from the foot of the stair, and looking out through the portion of the doorway that was yet unclosed, we saw armed men rushing up to the rescue, and called an answer to their shouts. Then the would-be murderers who yet remained on the stairway, and amongst whom I saw several priests, turned to fly, but, having nowhere to go, were butchered as they fled. Only one man stayed, and he was the great lord

Nasta, Nyleptha's suitor, and the father of the plot. For a moment the black-bearded Nasta stood with bowed face leaning on his long sword as though in despair, and then, with a dreadful shout, he too rushed up at the Zulu, and, swinging the glittering sword around his head, dealt him such a mighty blow beneath his guard, that the keen steel of the heavy blade bit right through the chain armour and deep into Umslopogaas' side, for a moment paralysing him and causing him to drop his axe.

Raising the sword again, Nasta sprang forward to make an end of him, but little he knew his foe. With a shake and a yell of fury, the Zulu gathered himself together and sprang straight at Nasta's throat, as I have sometimes seen a wounded lion spring. He struck him full as his foot was on the topmost stair, and his long arms closing round him like iron bands, down they rolled together struggling furiously. Nasta was a strong man and a desperate, but he could not match the strongest man in Zululand, sore wounded though he was, whose strength was as the strength of a bull. In a minute the end came. I saw old Umslopogaas stagger to his feet—ay, and saw him by a single gigantic effort swing up the struggling Nasta and with a shout of triumph hurl him straight over the parapet of the bridge, to be crushed to powder on the rocks two hundred feet below.

The succour which had been summoned by the girl who had passed down the stair before the assassins passed up was at hand, and the loud shouts which reached us from the outer gates told us that the town was also aroused, and the men awakened by the women were calling to be admitted. Some of Nyleptha's brave ladies, who in their night-shifts and with their long hair streaming down their backs, just as they had been aroused from rest, went off to admit them at the side entrance, whilst others, assisted by the rescuing party outside, pushed and pulled down the marble blocks they had placed there with so much labour.

Soon the wall was down again, and through the doorway, followed by a crowd of rescuers, staggered old Umslopogaas, an awful and, in a way, a glorious figure. The man was a mass of wounds, and a glance at his wild eye told me that he was dying. The 'keshla' gum-ring upon his head was severed in two places by sword-cuts, one just over the curious hole in his skull, and the blood poured down his face from the gashes. Also on the right side of his neck was a stab from a spear, inflicted by Agon; there was a deep cut on his left arm just below where the mail shirt-sleeve stopped, and on the right side of his body the armour was severed by a gash six inches long, where Nasta's mighty sword had bitten through it and deep into its wearer's vitals.

On, axe in hand, he staggered, that dreadful-looking, splendid savage, and the ladies forgot to turn faint at the scene of blood, and cheered him, as well they might, but he never stayed or heeded. With outstretched arms and tottering gait he pursued his way, followed by us all along the broad shell-strewn walk that ran through the courtyard, past the spot where the blocks of marble lay, through the round arched doorway and the thick curtains that hung within it, down the short passage and into the great hall, which was now filling with hastily-armed men, who poured through the side entrance. Straight up the hall he went, leaving behind him a track of blood on the marble pavement, till at last he reached the sacred stone, which stood in the centre of it, and here his strength seemed to fail him, for he stopped and leaned upon his axe. Then suddenly he lifted up his voice and cried aloud—

'I die, I die—but it was a kingly fray. Where are they who came up the great stair? I see them not. Art thou there, Macumazahn, or art thou gone before to wait for me in the dark whither I go? The blood blinds me—the place turns round—I hear the voice of waters.'

Next, as though a new thought had struck him, he lifted the red axe and kissed the blade.

'Farewell, Inkosi-kaas,' he cried. 'Nay, nay, we will go together; we cannot part, thou and I. We have lived too long one with another, thou and I.

'One more stroke, only one! A good stroke! a straight stroke! a strong stroke!' and, drawing himself to his full height, with a wild heart-shaking shout, he with both hands began to whirl the axe round his head till it looked like a circle of flaming steel. Then, suddenly, with awful force he brought it down straight on to the crown of the mass of sacred stone. A shower of sparks flew up, and such was the almost superhuman strength of the blow, that the massive marble split with a rending sound into a score of pieces, whilst of Inkosi-kaas there remained but some fragments of steel and a fibrous rope of shattered horn that had been the handle. Down with a crash on to the pavement fell the fragments of the holy stone, and down with a crash on to them, still grasping the knob of Inkosi-kaas, fell the brave old Zulu—*dead*.

And thus the hero died.

A gasp of wonder and astonishment rose from all those who witnessed the extraordinary sight, and then somebody cried, '*The prophecy! the prophecy!* He has shattered the sacred stone!' and at once a murmuring arose.

'Ay,' said Nyleptha, with that quick wit which distinguishes her. 'Ay, my people, he has shattered the stone, and behold the prophecy is fulfilled, for a stranger king rules in Zu-Vendis. Incubu, my lord, hath beat Sorais back, and I fear her no more, and to him who hath saved the Crown it shall surely be. And this man,' she said, turning to me and laying her hand upon my shoulder, 'wot ye that, though wounded in the fight of yesterday, he rode with that old warrior who lies there, one hundred miles 'twixt sun set and rise to save me from the plots of cruel men. Ay, and he has saved me, by a very little, and therefore because of the deeds that they have done—deeds of glory such as our history cannot show the like—therefore I say that the name of Macumazahn and the name of dead Umslopogaas, ay, and the name of Kara, my servant, who aided him to hold the stair, shall be blazoned in letters of gold above my throne, and shall be glorious for ever while the land endures. I, the Queen, have said it.'

This spirited speech was met with loud cheering, and I said that after all we had only done our duty, as it is the fashion of both Englishmen and Zulus to do, and there was nothing to make an outcry about; at which they cheered still more, and then I was supported across the outer courtyard to my old quarters, in order that I might be put to bed. As I went, my eyes lit upon the brave horse Daylight that lay there, his white head outstretched on the pavement, exactly as he had fallen on entering the yard; and I bade those who supported me take me near him, that I might look on the good beast once more before he was dragged away. And as I looked, to my astonishment he opened his eyes and, lifting his head a little, whinnied faintly. I could have shouted for joy to find that he was not dead, only unfortunately I had not a shout left in me; but as it was, grooms were sent for and he was lifted up and wine poured down his throat, and in a fortnight he was as well and strong as ever, and is the pride and joy of all the people of Milosis, who, whenever they see him, point him out to the little children as the 'horse which saved the White Queen's life'.

Then I went on and got off to bed, and was washed and had my mail shirt removed. They hurt me a great deal in getting it off, and no wonder, for on my left breast and side was a black bruise the size of a saucer.

The next thing that I remember was the tramp of horsemen outside the palace wall, some ten hours later. I raised myself and asked what was the news, and they told me that a large body of cavalry sent by Curtis to assist the Queen had arrived from the scene of the battle, which they had left two hours after sundown. When they left, the wreck of Sorais' army was in full retreat upon M'Arstuna, followed by all our effective cavalry. Sir Henry was encamping the remains of his worn-out forces on the site (such is the fortune of war) that Sorais had occupied the night before, and proposed marching to M'Arstuna on the morrow. Having heard this, I felt that I could die with a light heart, and then everything became a blank.

When next I awoke the first thing I saw was the round disc of a sympathetic eyeglass, behind which was Good.

'How are you getting on, old chap?' said a voice from the neighbourhood of the eyeglass.

'What are you doing here?' I asked faintly. 'You ought to be at M'Arstuna—have you run away, or what?'

'M'Arstuna,' he replied cheerfully. 'Ah, M'Arstuna fell last week—you've been unconscious for a fortnight, you see—with all the honours of war, you know—trumpets blowing, flags flying, just as though they had had the best of it; but for all that, weren't they glad to go. Israel made for his tents, I can tell you—never saw such a sight in my life.'

'And Sorais?' I asked.

'Sorais—oh, Sorais is a prisoner; they gave her up, the scoundrels,' he added, with a change of tone—'sacrificed the Queen to save their skins, you see. She is being brought up here, and I don't know what will happen to her, poor soul!' and he sighed.

'Where is Curtis?' I asked.

'He is with Nyleptha. She rode out to meet us today, and there was a grand to-do, I can tell you. He is coming to see you tomorrow; the doctors (for there is a medical "faculty" in Zu-Vendis as elsewhere) thought that he had better not come today.'

I said nothing, but somehow I thought to myself that notwithstanding the doctors he might have given me a look; but there, when a man is newly married and has just gained a great victory, he is apt to listen to the advice of doctors, and quite right too.

Just then I heard a familiar voice informing me that 'Monsieur must now couch himself,' and looking up perceived Alphonse's enormous black mustachios curling away in the distance.

'So you are here?' I said.

'Mais oui, Monsieur; the war is now finished, my military instincts are satisfied, and I return to nurse Monsieur.'

I laughed, or rather tried to; but whatever may have been Alphonse's failings as a warrior (and I fear that he did not come up to the level of his heroic grandfather in this particular, showing thereby how true is the saying that it is a bad thing to be overshadowed by some great ancestral name), a better or kinder nurse never lived. Poor Alphonse! I hope he will always think of me as kindly as I think of him.

On the morrow I saw Curtis and Nyleptha with him, and he told me the whole history of what had happened since Umslopogaas and I galloped wildly away from the battle to save the life of the Queen. It seemed to me that he had managed the thing exceedingly well, and showed great ability as a general. Of course, however, our loss had been dreadfully heavy—indeed, I am afraid to say how many perished in the desperate battle I have described, but I know that the slaughter has appreciably affected the male population of the country. He was very pleased to see me, dear fellow that he is, and thanked me with tears in his eyes for the little that I had been able to do. I saw him, however, start violently when his eyes fell upon my face.

As for Nyleptha, she was positively radiant now that 'her dear lord' had come back with no other injury than an ugly scar on his forehead. I do not believe that she allowed all the fearful slaughter that had taken place to weigh ever so little in the balance against this one fact, or even to greatly diminish her joy; and I cannot blame her for it, seeing that it is the nature of loving woman to look at all things through the spectacles of her love, and little does she reck of the misery of the many if the happiness of the *one* be assured. That is human nature, which the Positivists tell us is just perfection; so no doubt it is all right.

'And what art thou going to do with Sorais?' I asked her.

Instantly her bright brow darkened to a frown.

'Sorais,' she said, with a little stamp of the foot; 'ah, but Sorais!'

Sir Henry hastened to turn the subject.

'You will soon be about and all right again now, old fellow,' he said.

I shook my head and laughed.

'Don't deceive yourselves,' I said. 'I may be about for a little, but I shall never be all right again. I am a dying man, Curtis. I may die slow, but die I must. Do you know I have been spitting blood all the morning? I tell you there is something working away into my lung; I

H. RIDER HAGGARD

can feel it. There, don't look distressed; I have had my day, and am ready to go. Give me the mirror, will you? I want to look at myself.'

He made some excuse, but I saw through it and insisted, and at last he handed me one of the discs of polished silver set in a wooden frame like a hand-screen, which serve as looking-glasses in Zu-Vendis. I looked and put it down.

'Ah,' I said quietly, 'I thought so; and you talk of my getting all right!' I did not like to let them see how shocked I really was at my own appearance. My grizzled stubby hair was turned snow-white, and my yellow face was shrunk like an aged woman's and had two deep purple rings painted beneath the eyes.

Here Nyleptha began to cry, and Sir Henry again turned the subject, telling me that the artists had taken a cast of the dead body of old Umslopogaas, and that a great statue in black marble was to be erected of him in the act of splitting the sacred stone, which was to be matched by another statue in white marble of myself and the horse Daylight as he appeared when, at the termination of that wild ride, he sank beneath me in the courtyard of the palace. I have since seen these statues, which at the time of writing this, six months after the battle, are nearly finished; and very beautiful they are, especially that of Umslopogaas, which is exactly like him. As for that of myself, it is good, but they have idealized my ugly face a little, which is perhaps as well, seeing that thousands of people will probably look at it in the centuries to come, and it is not pleasant to look at ugly things.

Then they told me that Umslopogaas' last wish had been carried out, and that, instead of being cremated, as I shall be, after the usual custom here, he had been tied up, Zulu fashion, with his knees beneath his chin, and, having been wrapped in a thin sheet of beaten gold, entombed in a hole hollowed out of the masonry of the semicircular space at the top of the stair he defended so splendidly, which faces, as far as we can judge, almost exactly towards Zululand. There he sits, and will sit for ever, for they embalmed him with spices, and put him in an air-tight stone coffer, keeping his grim watch beneath the spot he held alone against a multitude; and the people say that at night his ghost rises and stands shaking the phantom of Inkosi-kaas at phantom foes. Certainly they fear during the dark hours to pass the place where the hero is buried.

Oddly enough, too, a new legend or prophecy has arisen in the land in that unaccountable way in which such things to arise among barbarous and semi-civilized people, blowing, like the wind, no man knows whence. According to this saying, so long as the old Zulu sits there, looking down the stairway he defended when alive, so long will the New House of the Stairway, springing from the union of the Englishman and Nyleptha, endure and flourish; but when he is taken from thence, or when, ages after, his bones at last crumble into dust, the House will fall, and the Stairway shall fall, and the Nation of the Zu-Vendi shall cease to be a Nation.

XXIII

I Have Spoken

It was a week after Nyleptha's visit, when I had begun to get about a little in the middle of the day, that a message came to me from Sir Henry to say that Sorais would be brought before them in the Queen's first antechamber at midday, and requesting my attendance if possible. Accordingly, greatly drawn by curiosity to see this unhappy woman once more, I made shift, with the help of that kind little fellow Alphonse, who is a perfect treasure to me, and that of another waiting-man, to reach the antechamber. I got there, indeed, before anybody else, except a few of the great Court officials who had been bidden to be present, but I had scarcely seated myself before Sorais was brought in by a party of guards, looking as beautiful and defiant as ever, but with a worn expression on her proud face. She was, as usual, dressed in her royal 'kaf', emblazoned with the emblem of the Sun, and in her right hand she still held the toy spear of silver. A pang of admiration and pity went through me as I looked at her, and struggling to my feet I bowed deeply, at the same time expressing my sorrow that I was not able, owing to my condition, to remain standing before her.

She coloured a little and then laughed bitterly. 'Thou dost forget, Macumazahn,' she said, 'I am no more a Queen, save in blood; I am an outcast and a prisoner, one whom all men should scorn, and none show deference to.'

'At least,' I replied, 'thou art still a lady, and therefore one to whom deference is due. Also, thou art in an evil case, and therefore it is doubly due.'

'Ah!' she answered, with a little laugh, 'thou dost forget that I would have wrapped thee in a sheet of gold and hung thee to the angel's trumpet at the topmost pinnacle of the Temple.'

'No,' I answered, 'I assure thee that I forgot it not; indeed, I often thought of it when it seemed to me that the battle of the Pass was turning against us; but the trumpet is there, and I am still here, though perchance not for long, so why talk of it now?'

'Ah!' she went on, 'the battle! the battle! Oh, would that I were once more a Queen, if only for one little hour, and I would take such a vengeance on those accursed jackals who deserted me in my need; that it should only be spoken of in whispers; those woman, those pigeon-hearted half-breeds who suffered themselves to be overcome!' and she choked in her wrath.

'Ay, and that little coward beside thee,' she went on, pointing at Alphonse with the silver spear, whereat he looked very uncomfortable; 'he escaped and betrayed my plans. I tried to make a general of him, telling the soldiers it was Bougwan, and to scourge valour into him' (here Alphonse shivered at some unhappy recollection), 'but it was of no avail. He hid beneath a banner in my tent and thus overheard my plans. I would that I had slain him, but, alas! I held my hand.

'And thou, Macumazahn, I have heard of what thou didst; thou art brave, and hast a loyal heart. And the black one too, ah, he was a *man*. I would fain have seen him hurl Nasta from the stairway.'

'Thou art a strange woman, Sorais,' I said; 'I pray thee now plead with the Queen Nyleptha, that perchance she may show mercy unto thee.'

She laughed out loud. 'I plead for mercy!' she said and at that moment the Queen entered, accompanied by Sir Henry and Good, and took her seat with an impassive face. As for poor Good, he looked intensely ill at ease.

'Greeting, Sorais!' said Nyleptha, after a short pause. 'Thou hast rent the kingdom like a rag, thou hast put thousands of my people to the sword, thou hast twice basely plotted to destroy my life by murder, thou hast sworn to slay my lord and his companions and to hurl me from the Stairway. What hast thou to say why thou shouldst not die? Speak, O Sorais!'

'Methinks my sister the Queen hath forgotten the chief count of the indictment,' answered Sorais in her slow musical tones. 'It runs thus: "Thou didst strive to win the love of my lord Incubu." It is for this crime that my sister will slay me, not because I levied war. It is perchance happy for thee, Nyleptha, that I fixed my mind upon his love too late.

'Listen,' she went on, raising her voice. 'I have nought to say save that I would I had won instead of lost. Do thou with me even as thou wilt, O Queen, and let my lord the King there' (pointing to Sir Henry)—'for now will he be King—carry out the sentence, as it is meet he should, for as he is the beginning of the evil, let him also be the end.' And she drew herself up and shot one angry glance at him from her deep fringed eyes, and then began to toy with her spear.

H. RIDER HAGGARD

Sir Henry bent towards Nyleptha and whispered something that I could not catch, and then the Queen spoke.

'Sorais, ever have I been a good sister to thee. When our father died, and there was much talk in the land as to whether thou shouldst sit upon the throne with me, I being the elder, I gave my voice for thee and said, "Nay, let her sit. She is twin with me; we were born at a birth; wherefore should the one be preferred before the other?" And so has it ever been 'twixt thee and me, my sister. But now thou knowest in what sort thou hast repaid me, but I have prevailed, and thy life is forfeit, Sorais. And yet art thou my sister, born at a birth with me, and we played together when we were little and loved each other much, and at night we slept in the same cot with our arms each around the other's neck, and therefore even now does my heart go out to thee, Sorais.

'But not for that would I spare thy life, for thy offence has been too heavy; it doth drag down the wide wings of my mercy even to the ground. Also, while thou dost live the land will never be at peace.

'Yet shalt thou not die, Sorais, because my dear lord here hath begged thy life of me as a boon; therefore as a boon and as a marriage gift give I it to him, to do with even as he wills, knowing that, though thou dost love him, he loves thee not, Sorais, for all thy beauty. Nay, though thou art lovely as the night in all her stars, O Lady of the Night, yet it is me his wife whom he loves, and not thee, and therefore do I give thy life to him.'

Sorais flushed up to her eyes and said nothing, and I do not think that I ever saw a man look more miserable than did Sir Henry at that moment. Somehow, Nyleptha's way of putting the thing, though true and forcible enough, was not altogether pleasant.

'I understand,' stammered Curtis, looking at Good, 'I understood that he were attached—eh—attached to—to the Queen Sorais. I am—eh—not aware what the—in short, the state of your feelings may be just now; but if they happened to be that way inclined, it has struck me that—in short, it might put a satisfactory end to an unpleasant business. The lady also has ample private estates, where I am sure she would be at liberty to live unmolested as far as we are concerned, eh, Nyleptha? Of course, I only suggest.'

'So far as I am concerned,' said Good, colouring up, 'I am quite willing to forget the past; and if the Lady of the Night thinks me worth the taking I will marry her tomorrow, or when she likes, and try to make her a good husband.'

All eyes were now turned to Sorais, who stood with that same slow smile upon her beautiful face which I had noticed the first time that I ever saw her. She paused a little while, and cleared her throat, and then thrice she curtseyed low, once to Nyleptha, once to Curtis, and once to Good, and began to speak in measured tones.

'I thank thee, most gracious Queen and royal sister, for the loving-kindness thou hast shown me from my youth up, and especially in that thou hast been pleased to give my person and my fate as a gift to the Lord Incubu—the King that is to be. May prosperity, peace and plenty deck the life-path of one so merciful and so tender, even as flowers do. Long mayst thou reign, O great and glorious Queen, and hold thy husband's love in both thy hands, and many be the sons and daughters of thy beauty. And I thank thee, my Lord Incubu—the King that is to be—I thank thee a thousand times in that thou hast been pleased to accept that gracious gift, and to pass it on to thy comrade in arms and in adventure, the Lord Bougwan. Surely the act is worthy of thy greatness, my Lord Incubu. And now, lastly, I thank thee also, my Lord Bougwan, who in thy turn hast deigned to accept me and my poor beauty. I thank thee a thousand times, and I will add that thou art a good and honest man, and I put my hand upon my heart and swear that I would that I could say thee "yea". And now that I have rendered thanks to all in turn'—and again she smiled—'I will add one short word.

'Little can you understand of me, Queen Nyleptha and my lords, if ye know not that for me there is no middle path; that I scorn your pity and hate you for it; that I cast off your forgiveness as though it were a serpent's sting; and that standing here, betrayed, deserted, insulted, and alone, I yet triumph over you, mock you, and defy you, one and all, and *thus* I answer you.' And then, of a sudden, before anybody guessed what she intended to do, she drove the little silver spear she carried in her hand into her side with such a strong and steady aim that the keen point projected through her back, and she fell prone upon the pavement.

Nyleptha shrieked, and poor Good almost fainted at the sight, while the rest of us rushed towards her. But Sorais of the Night lifted herself upon her hand, and for a moment fixed her glorious eyes intently on Curtis' face, as though there were some message in the glance, then dropped her head and sighed, and with a sob her dark but splendid spirit passed.

Well, they gave her a royal funeral, and there was an end of her.

H. RIDER HAGGARD

It was a month after the last act of the Sorais tragedy that a great ceremony was held in the Flower Temple, and Curtis was formally declared King-Consort of Zu-Vendis. I was too ill to go myself; and indeed, I hate all that sort of thing, with the crowds and the trumpet-blowing and banner-waving; but Good, who was there (in his full-dress uniform), came back much impressed, and told me that Nyleptha had looked lovely, and Curtis had borne himself in a right royal fashion, and had been received with acclamations that left no doubt as to his popularity. Also he told me that when the horse Daylight was led along in the procession, the populace had shouted '*Macumazahn, Macumazahn!*' till they were hoarse, and would only be appeased when he, Good, rose in his chariot and told them that I was too ill to be present.

Afterwards, too, Sir Henry, or rather the King, came to see me, looking very tired, and vowing that he had never been so bored in his life; but I dare say that that was a slight exaggeration. It is not in human nature that a man should be altogether bored on such an extraordinary occasion; and, indeed, as I pointed out to him, it was a marvellous thing that a man, who but little more than one short year before had entered a great country as an unknown wanderer, should today be married to its beautiful and beloved Queen, and lifted, amidst public rejoicings, to its throne. I even went the length to exhort him in the future not to be carried away by the pride and pomp of absolute power, but always to strive to remember that he was first a Christian gentleman, and next a public servant, called by Providence to a great and almost unprecedented trust. These remarks, which he might fairly have resented, he was so good as to receive with patience, and even to thank me for making them.

It was immediately after this ceremony that I caused myself to be moved to the house where I am now writing. It is a very pleasant country seat, situated about two miles from the Frowning City, on to which it looks. That was five months ago, during the whole of which time I have, being confined to a kind of couch, employed my leisure in compiling this history of our wanderings from my journal and from our joint memories. It is probable that it will never be read, but it does not much matter whether it is or not; at any rate, it has served to while away many hours of suffering, for I have suffered a deal of pain lately. Thank God, however, there will not be much more of it.

It is a week since I wrote the above, and now I take up my pen for the last time, for I know that the end is at hand. My brain is still clear and I can manage to write, though with difficulty. The pain in my lung, which has been very bad during the last week, has suddenly quite left me, and been succeeded by a feeling of numbness of which I cannot mistake the meaning. And just as the pain has gone, so with it all fear of that end has departed, and I feel only as though I were going to sink into the arms of an unutterable rest. Happily, contentedly, and with the same sense of security with which an infant lays itself to sleep in its mother's arms, do I lay myself down in the arms of the Angel Death. All the tremors, all the heart-shaking fears which have haunted me through a life that seems long as I looked back upon it, have left me now; the storms have passed, and the Star of our Eternal Hope shines clear and steady on the horizon that seems so far from man, and yet is so very near to me tonight.

And so this is the end of it—a brief space of troubling, a few restless, fevered, anguished years, and then the arms of that great Angel Death. Many times have I been near to them, and now it is my turn at last, and it is well. Twenty-four hours more and the world will be gone from me, and with it all its hopes and all its fears. The air will close in over the space that my form filled and my place know me no more; for the dull breath of the world's forgetfulness will first dim the brightness of my memory, and then blot it out for ever, and of a truth I shall be dead. So is it with us all. How many millions have lain as I lie, and thought these thoughts and been forgotten!—thousands upon thousands of years ago they thought them, those dying men of the dim past; and thousands on thousands of years hence will their descendants think them and be in their turn forgotten. 'As the breath of the oxen in winter, as the quick star that runs along the sky, as a little shadow that loses itself at sunset,' as I once heard a Zulu called Ignosi put it, such is the order of our life, the order that passeth away.

Well, it is not a good world—nobody can say that it is, save those who wilfully blind themselves to facts. How can a world be good in which Money is the moving power, and Self-interest the guiding star? The wonder is not that it is so bad, but that there should be any good left in it.

Still, now that my life is over, I am glad to have lived, glad to have known the dear breath of woman's love, and that true friendship which can even surpass the love of woman, glad to have heard the laughter of

H. RIDER HAGGARD

little children, to have seen the sun and the moon and the stars, to have felt the kiss of the salt sea on my face, and watched the wild game trek down to the water in the moonlight. But I should not wish to live again!

Everything is changing to me. The darkness draws near, and the light departs. And yet it seems to me that through that darkness I can already see the shining welcome of many a long-lost face. Harry is there, and others; one above all, to my mind the sweetest and most perfect woman that ever gladdened this grey earth. But of her I have already written elsewhere, and at length, so why speak of her now? Why speak of her after this long silence, now that she is again so near to me, now that I go where she has gone?

The sinking sun is turning the golden roof of the great Temple to a fiery flame, and my fingers tire.

So to all who have known me, or known of me, to all who can think one kindly thought of the old hunter, I stretch out my hand from the far-off shore and bid a long farewell.

And now into the hands of Almighty God, who sent it, do I commit my spirit.

'*I have spoken,*' as the Zulus say.

A Note About the Author

Sir Henry Rider Haggard, (1856–1925) commonly known as H. Rider Haggard was an English author active during the Victorian era. Considered a pioneer of the lost world genre, Haggard was known for his adventure fiction. His work often depicted African settings inspired by the seven years he lived in South Africa with his family. In 1880, Haggard married Marianna Louisa Margitson and together they had four children, one of which followed her father's footsteps and became an author. Haggard is still widely read today, and is celebrated for his imaginative wit and impact on 19th century adventure literature.

A Note from the Publisher

Spanning many genres, from non-fiction essays to literature classics to children's books and lyric poetry, Mint Edition books showcase the master works of our time in a modern new package. The text is freshly typeset, is clean and easy to read, and features a new note about the author in each volume. Many books also include exclusive new introductory material. Every book boasts a striking new cover, which makes it as appropriate for collecting as it is for gift giving. Mint Edition books are only printed when a reader orders them, so natural resources are not wasted. We're proud that our books are never manufactured in excess and exist only in the exact quantity they need to be read and enjoyed. To learn more and view our library, go to minteditionbooks.com

bookfinity & MINT EDITIONS

Enjoy more of your favorite classics with Bookfinity,
a new search and discovery experience for readers.
With Bookfinity, you can discover more vintage
literature for your collection, find your Reader Type,
track books you've read or want to read,
and add reviews to your favorite books.
Visit www.bookfinity.com, and click on
Take the Quiz to get started.

Don't forget to follow us
@bookfinityofficial and @mint_editions